Praise for
Clean

"Really well done." —*USA Today*

"A fun blend of *Chinatown* and *Blade Runner*."
—James Knapp, author of *State of Decay*

"[A] tightly written futuristic detective story set in an alternate Atlanta. . . . This crisp debut marks Hughes as a writer to watch." —*Publishers Weekly*

"Reminds me very much (and very fondly) of Jim Butcher's Dresden Files." —SF Signal

"An excellent start on a series . . . so many twists, turns, and double-crossings . . . I'm going to be first in line for the next novel in this Mindspace Investigations series."
—Night Owl Reviews

"I am addicted to this world, this character, and this writer. Alex Hughes spins stories like wizards spin spells . . . a stellar debut!"
—James R. Tuck, author of the Deacon Chalk series

"Fans will want more by Alex Hughes." —SFRevu

D1373728

SHARP

A MINDSPACE INVESTIGATIONS NOVEL

Alex Hughes

A ROC BOOK

ROC
Published by the Penguin Group
Penguin Group (USA) Inc., 375 Hudson Street,
New York, New York 10014, USA

USA I Canada I UK I Ireland I Australia I New Zealand I India I South Africa I China

Penguin Books Ltd., Registered Offices: 80 Strand, London WC2R 0RL, England
For more information about the Penguin Group visit penguin.com.

First published by Roc, an imprint of New American Library,
a division of Penguin Group (USA) Inc.

First Printing, April 2013

 REGISTERED TRADEMARK—MARCA REGISTRADA

ISBN 978-0-451-46504-7

Printed in the United States of America
10 9 8 7 6 5 4 3 2 1

To my parents and to my grandparents,
who believed first.

CHAPTER 1

I stood in the observation room smoking, long sinuous trails of gray smoke drifting up into the ceiling. The recording technician coughed and turned the filter setting up even higher, the whirr of the motor the loudest sound in the place, the popping of ionizing energy removing the pollutants from the air. Even with the police department's recent budget cuts, the filter was a solid, midrange-quality one, good enough to handle the smoke without blinking. With the air so bad out, we needed every advantage we could get.

With the higher setting, the tech stopped caring about the smoke, and I could focus on the pleasant little buzz of the cigarette without worrying about her discomfort.

On the other side of the one-way glass, in the interview room sitting alone, was a sweating overweight man in an old-style trucker hat and a shirt full of holes, decorated with the silhouette of a naked woman. His hat had a large fishhook clipped on the brim. A company uniform shirt, blue with white stitching, lay wadded on the table.

A knock on the door behind me made me look up.

"Put that out, would you?" the woman said with an odd pushy cheer. A plain blonde, she was hefty, tall, and focused. She must be new; we didn't have many women in the department.

I tried to read her telepathically, and came up largely

blank; since a case six weeks ago when I'd burned out my mind, I was struggling to recover, my telepathy coming back only in fits and starts. I'd seen enough old students go through the process, heck, helped them through the process, that I knew what to expect. I had rested like I was supposed to, done the exercises like I was supposed to, over and over again, and tried to be patient. I had some of the telepathy back—in the mornings, before two or three o'clock, before I was too tired and it got spotty again. Now was the hard part, when I had to keep from pushing, when I had to keep from setting myself back.

I could read a lot of people at surface level now, if the waves of their minds transmitted through Mindspace strongly enough, if they had Ability even the barest touch above the normal population. The new detective had to be as normal as they came, her mind not "speaking up" enough for me to hear, even though it was early in the day. Either that or we had poor valence, the waves of our minds syncing up badly. Either way it was disturbing, like meeting someone blindfolded with cotton balls in your ears.

I put the cigarette out, reluctantly, since she'd asked.

"Who are you again?" she asked. "I don't think we've met yet. I'm Lisa Morris."

"I'm Adam, the telepath consultant." I was a Level Eight, or had been; incredibly strong, and trained very well by the Telepath's Guild, who'd kicked me out years ago. But I wouldn't tell her; normals were nervous enough around weaker telepaths. And neither she nor the rest of the department could know I'd hurt my brain. I needed this job.

She stuck out a hand, but I didn't take it. "Sorry. Telepath rules, right?"

I nodded, tried a sheepish smile.

"I'm the new detective," she said to cover the awkwardness. "New transfer from South DeKalb. Working under Bransen's detective division. Primarily Robbery, though I pick up the occasional armed assault."

"Nice to meet you. So, what's the situation?" I clarified: "With the guy on the other side of that glass."

"Ah. Thomas Hunter. He drives a truck for a company on Lawrenceville Highway. Seems an upstanding guy, salt of the earth, or at least as much as you'd care about. His record's clean. But his truck was hijacked by armed robbers this morning, and his supervisor says it's the second time." She shrugged. "Plus he's lying." A good cop has an instinct for liars.

"You want to know what's going on."

"Sure. I want to know what's going on. I also want to fill out the paperwork to the TCO on time and get a day off this week. Right now none of that looks likely, but they say you're the best."

I shifted my shoulders. "No pressure or anything."

The technician stifled a laugh. Morris shrugged.

"Why Tech Control Organization forms?" I asked. Since the Tech Wars sixty years ago, since a madman had taken control of the semisentient computers and destroyed a good third of the world, since people had died, rotting in their houses and cars, their implants turned into computer-virus transmission platforms, since people had died in the millions in horrible ways, well, the world was afraid of Tech. Even now, with the smaller stuff—the oven timers and basic chips of the world—let out, cautiously, on a leash. Even now the stronger, more powerful stuff was forbidden, tracked, and shut down.

"The company Hunter works for manufactures capacitors, resistors, basic glucose and carbon-based circuits for use in artificial organs, and copper wire." At my blank look, she added, "Components for electronics. Add in the biologic support systems . . ."

"And you get Tech," I said. "Basic Tech, with the potential for more. A lot more."

"Yeah, the scary stuff. The components themselves aren't illegal, but . . ."

"Yeah." I swallowed. "Like shipments of fertilizer, you watch them. And when they disappear, you react. Let me go get my files."

A hijacking victim wasn't my usual shtick. Usually I got the difficult cases, suspects who wouldn't talk and witnesses who wouldn't talk about anything useful—anyone who'd gone through another interrogator and survived unscathed. But I was open to new challenges, and with any luck I wouldn't need the telepathy too much.

I carried the stack of files under one arm and a couple of bad coffees in the other. Bellury was today's babysitter, a semiretired cop who didn't mind me in his head and cheerfully gave me advice as to the best way to legally threaten suspects. A good guy, steady, hard to rattle, hard to surprise.

I'd sent Bellury ahead to talk to the trucker a few minutes ago, to act as friendly as he could, and to offer him a sandwich and a cup of coffee. The sandwich wouldn't ever appear; neither Bellury nor I was giving up our lunch today. But the coffee was doable, and we'd at least get him thinking the moment wasn't as hostile as it looked.

The files were props, cases solved when my grandparents were in diapers, full of pictures of various shock levels and lightly printed notes you couldn't quite read upside down. I probably wouldn't need them this time around, but I'd be lying if I said they didn't make me feel better.

I paused at the door, put down the files and coffee on the floor, and messed up my hair. Unbuttoned the top button of the shirt, set the collar crooked. In an ideal world, I'd grab a set of old-fashioned glasses too, since they'd announce like a highway board that I didn't have the money for the corrective procedure. But I didn't want to spend the time. We had a full interview docket today and I couldn't afford to get too behind.

I took a breath. Thomas Hunter. Considering the hat . . .

"Tommy," I said in bright tones as I entered the interview room. Bellury looked up, found himself a chair in the corner with an amused look.

"Tom," the trucker said firmly. He backed up from the table, clearly preparing to move if a fight should come up.

"Sorry about that," I said, jovially. Or at least, as jovially as I could pull off; cheerfulness wasn't a specialty. Bellury stifled a laugh, but I don't think the suspect noticed.

Tom was too busy moving his weight forward, watching me carefully to see what violence I'd bring on. This was a man who'd been in more than a few bar fights, I thought. The question was, how'd the hijackers take him down without at least a few bruises? I couldn't feel any pain coming off him, just wariness and a tinge of guilt not inappropriate for his situation. He'd lost a shipment, after all. For the second time.

"Mind if I sit?"

"It's your table."

"You know, you're right." I settled into the chair like I didn't have a care in the world. This was the clean interview room, the table in good repair, the walls spotless and empty except for a small mirror on the wall.

I fanned out the files on the table and made a show of looking for a pen. Bellury behind me had one, but, as requested, he waited a good forty seconds before offering. I wanted to look as bumbling as possible.

Finally he held out that pen.

"Thanks," I said, and took it with an uncomfortable laugh. Might have overshot; the trucker was looking at me oddly. I opened the file—the one without the pictures—and made a show of reading it. Just when the trucker seemed to be getting uncomfortable, I looked up. "Says here your truck was hijacked by robbers." I added a questioning lilt to the end of the sentence, the kind of raised tone most people heard as indecisive.

"That's right," Tom said gruffly.

"Armed? They had guns?"

"That's right. I already told the other guy all of this."

I made a show of blinking in surprise and went back to pretend-reading the file. "Oh, gotcha. You were transporting electronics components."

"Yeah? So?"

"Things that could be made into illegal Tech." The raised lilt again, like a question.

"I suppose."

"Well, there's special procedures for these situations. Paperwork stuff. If you'll work with me, we'll get you out of here as quickly as possible."

Up close, Tom looked less stereotypical. His shirt, while worn, was scrupulously clean. The fishhook on his cap looked usable. He was completely without a sunburn. And there was a light in his eyes, an awareness of his surroundings, that made me size him up differently. There was muscle under that fat.

"How long am I going to have to be here?" His voice was firm, and while the accent was slow and Southern, the firmness wasn't anyone's fool.

Ah, a stress point. I shifted in the chair, body language more alert. "It's up to you. We just need you to tell the truth about what happened."

He winced like I'd socked him in the jaw. Interesting. I reached out in Mindspace—and suppressed a sigh. This job was a lot harder when you couldn't read the suspect clearly. At least I was getting a little low-grade emotion, had no headache, and I only had two visual light flashes this morning, symptoms of my brain rewiring. I still wished I could read him, though. It was frustrating.

Well, we'd do this out loud, where the recorders could see us and Bellury could testify to their accuracy. It was what Tom said that mattered, anyway. Or, well, if Tommy bothered him . . .

"Tommy," I said.

"Tom," he corrected. "And who are you?"

Ah, lovely. I wouldn't even have to offer a prompt this time. I leaned forward, a cheerful shark nibbling on the prey. "I'm a Level Eight telepath," I said. "If you ask, I'm legally required to tell you. I'm also required to warn you that touching a telepath can be hazardous to your health and mental well-being." It was true—or was when the telepathy was working—and it always made the normals nervous. The Guild—and the end of the Tech Wars—had made sure of that.

He pushed back from the table, eyes wide. "It wasn't like that, really. You don't have to make a—"

"Ah, but I do," I said. When in doubt, push where they're uncomfortable. There's always something there. "I do, Tommy, really I do. If you hadn't lied to the nice detective lady, well, then maybe—"

"I told her, I didn't see anything."

"But you were lying," I pushed, with the ring of truth in my voice. The certainty that came with being a telepath. Bluff in this case, but . . .

We balanced on a knife's edge for a long moment, then he broke.

"They took my driver's license," he burst out with in a rush. "You have to understand, they took my license. They told me they knew where I lived. They knew where my family lived. And then they . . ."

Success. "And then they what? They told you if you didn't help them, what, Tommy?"

He leaned forward, over his hands, on the table, hands clenched around the blue uniform shirt wadded on the table. I could feel him thinking, shapes changing like a lava lamp inside his brain—but not the content. Finally he spoke. "My daughter is four. She's a good kid. She's smart. She deserves . . ."

My tone got quiet. Soft. "They said they'd kill her if you talked to anyone."

He nodded.

"I know anyway," I said. Pure bull in this case, but you were allowed to lie to suspects. Even to witnesses. I gentled my voice. "You might as well tell me what happened. Help us get these guys off the street. Keep them from coming back."

He hesitated.

"Tell me, and work with the sketch artist. It's the best chance you have now of keeping your daughter safe. Of keeping yourself safe."

He hesitated again. "They said . . ."

"You've been at the station a long time now," I said gently. "They might take it badly anyway. They probably will. But if you help us catch these guys, Tom. If you help us get them off the streets, they can't hurt you—they can't hurt your daughter. It's your best bet out of this, I promise you. Tell me what happened."

He swallowed, his eyes on his hands. I let him think, my body language sympathetic. I let the wheels turn.

Finally he reached out and grabbed the shirt in front of him. "You won't tell the company?" A faint, out-of-focus thought came from him, barely strong enough for me to pick up. It must be important; it must be a strong thought for me to hear it. He'd lose his job if the truth got out. He'd helped them. . . . He'd had no choice, but he'd helped them.

"I'll do everything in my power to keep this confidential," I promised, my voice pitched to be trustworthy. "I'll do everything I can. We'll even try to send out a unit to watch your family. We'll help you figure out how to get them out of town if you want. But you have to help us."

I gave him a moment to process it as his forehead creased.

"Tell me what happened," I prompted. "Tell me the truth."

Like a levee cracking under overwhelming pressure, the words flowed out of him in a long, full rush. Behind me, Bellury was smiling.

When my precognition decided to work, my rating was 78P, which meant my predictions of the future were accurate three times out of four or better. It didn't work often, though, and when it did it was nearly always regarding my personal safety.

So when the sense flashed danger at me on the way out of the interview room, I moved. Fast. I threw myself down, on the dirty floor, without any regard for dignity, pulling myself into the closest corner, pencil in hand ready as a weapon.

Two point three seconds later, a man came barreling out of another interview room, literally foaming at the mouth. He was carrying an industrial-weight hole punch, held like an unwieldy club in his hands. He tripped, fell directly into where I would have been standing, and hit his head. Hard. On the hole punch and then the floor with a sickening *crack*. His head started to bleed.

And on the back of it, I saw the round metallic gleam of an implant. The skin around it red and swollen, small black stitches pulling the inflamed tissue so that it ran long lines of pus.

Suddenly the man started seizing, limbs jerking hard in every direction. I stared at him, helpless from two feet away. You weren't supposed to touch someone seizing.

He suddenly went still, far, far too still. Quarantine. We'd need quarantine.

"EMT!" I screamed and—damn it—tried to find his pulse. "EMT now!" I couldn't feel a mental signature, even with touch, but with my telepathy that didn't mean anything. He wasn't dead yet, I told myself.

I turned him over, frantically rehearsing my CPR training as part of the department job. Was it five breaths? Was it six? Two compressions or three? The hell with it; I angled his head up and gave him that first breath. I'd do the best I could until the EMTs—

I fell back on my butt on the hard concrete floor as Clark pushed me aside. Clark, who hated me and was doing his best to get the other cops to hate me too.

"How can I help?" I asked him.

"Go . . . Away . . . ," he said in between compressions. "You've already done enough."

I stared at him. Even with his distrust of telepaths, he couldn't think I'd caused this. "This wasn't my fault. That's an illegal Tech implant. There's any number of viruses his brain could have caught—"

"Get the fuck away from me," Clark spat, and suddenly the narrow corridor was full of rushing feet. Full of EMTs.

I stood back, in that corner, until I was sure they had it under control. Then I went upstairs and brushed my teeth three times, with antimicrobial toothpaste. There hadn't been time to get the damn mouth shield, and who knows what that guy was carrying? You had to be stone-cold stupid to get an implant these days, and a black-market one was even worse. If you didn't get a wetware virus from the Tech itself, you were signing up for whatever bug the three guys before you had had.

I brushed my teeth again, and gargled with heavy-salted vinegar. It tasted nasty—really, really nasty—but it cut infection rates in half.

I spat.

"Please, come in," Lieutenant Paulsen said without looking up from her desk. "Close the door."

I pulled the door closed, suddenly wary, and took a seat in her battered guest chair. The seat squeaked as I sat down. A feeling of oppression filled the room, but I couldn't tell if it was Mindspace or my own panicky mind. With the increased stress of the morning, I was starting to see floating lines of light go in and out of my vision. I took a deep breath and tried to calm, to slow my heart rate. Whatever was going on with Paulsen, I'd need to be at my best to handle it, not struggling to keep my attention.

Paulsen pushed some papers into a folder and set it aside. Pulled another folder toward her. Then she looked up. I expected her to speak, but she only cleared her throat. For the first time ever, I could see every year of her sixty-mumble age written on her face, wrinkles cutting deep, her warm brown skin ashen.

"Are you okay?" I said.

"I'm fine," she said firmly, the phrase imbued with all the weight of decades as a cop trained to show no weakness. Then she paused again.

Paulsen was a decisive woman, a strong woman. A cop who got things done and constantly held me to her high standards. If she was pausing, this would be bad.

Had she found out my telepathy wasn't working? It was better now, healing slowly in dribs and drabs more or less at the pace I was expecting, but I'd been keeping it a secret. Cops didn't like secrets.

"Am I being fired?" I asked, and tried with everything in me to stay calm.

"No," she said, then amended: "It's possible." She cleared her throat. "DeKalb County and the city of Decatur have decided to cut police funding again. By millions. Every department is being hit, across the board. Not just equipment budgets. Not just training this time. We're being forced to let people go. And the damn politicians are going after what they call wasteful practices. Things like vacation time, recovery time from injuries, and most of all and especially . . ." She paused here again and met my eyes. "Especially contractors. Unlicensed contractors are at the top of the list of cuts."

I sat back, the chair squeaking again. I was numb. Wait, this wasn't about my secret? That almost made it worse.

"How long?" I asked. I liked this job. I needed this job.

"Not yet," she said firmly. "Not quite yet. We have a couple of months before things go into full effect. I'd suggest—in strong terms—you go out and find yourself a license. A certification. Something on paper, in the next six weeks."

I took a breath. "Six weeks? Wait, my Guild certification doesn't count?" That was half a million ROCs in training, more, even if the Guild had gotten far more out of me in labor afterward. Before they kicked me out for the drug problem that had landed me on the streets, years ago.

"It's suspended, has been for a decade according to the information you gave us." She put her hand on the folder in front of her, what had to be my file.

"I have the training! I thought you guys liked that I was an independent. There aren't that many people outside the Guild, much less at my level. Even they say my training's still good. It's not like I can't do the job." And with the normals hating the Guild and fearing telepaths, well, I'd thought my lack of certification (of affiliation) was a plus. Apparently not.

"I know," she said, and sighed. "I know. But the commissioner's under pressure to make cuts. A lot of pressure. And politically, well, it doesn't look good for you. Don't be an easy target."

"This isn't fair." I tried to reach out, to peek into her head, but all I got was a sense of mourning, and determination. No matter how I tried to push, that was all the information I could get, and even that moved away like sand through my fingers. Paulsen was familiar, which helped, but we were right after lunch, approaching my afternoon cutoff for reliable telepathy, and my heart was beating a hundred miles an hour.

I pulled back and focused on what she was saying in the here and now: "—work in the interview room will be critical. Cherabino's cases too. Give them a reason to keep you. Give me ammunition."

I took a breath. "Right before Christmas. You're telling me I could be laid off right before Christmas." I felt like I was in free fall, like I was standing at the top of a cliff looking down at my life on the streets again. And to make it over Christmas—Christmas still made me think of my mom before she died. Did we have to add another heartbreak on top of that one?

She paused. "This is the worst-case scenario for everyone. I'm sorry."

"I know," I said, and stood. I clenched my hands together so she wouldn't see them shaking. So I wouldn't be tempted to lash out. So I wouldn't burn whatever bridges I had left. But I wanted to. The adrenaline was coursing through my system all too hard, and I wanted to lash out.

Three years clean, and none of it mattered in that moment. I wanted my drug, I wanted to fall off the earth and run away. But I couldn't. I wouldn't. I'd come too far, I'd built too much to give up now. No matter how much I wanted to.

So instead of being stupid, I did what any sane Narcotics

Anonymous member did—I called my sponsor. And then I went outside to the smoking porch and I chain-smoked six cigarettes in a row while outside the awning it rained, a nasty hard rain that suited my mood perfectly.

And if Mindspace got jumpy, going in and out like a badly tuned radio, I ignored it and tried to get my heart to stop leaping out of my chest.

I needed this job. They'd hired me back after I'd fallen off the wagon in front of them. And if I couldn't handle money as a result, well, that was proof enough I was untrustworthy. Who else in their right mind was going to hire me now?

I had to keep this job. Whatever it took, whatever I had to pay—I'd pay in blood, if I had to. I couldn't fall back down that cliff to the streets. I just didn't have it in me, not a second time.

CHAPTER 2

On the way out of the bathroom, I felt Cherabino's mind bobbing down the hall in this general direction. I hardened my heart, expecting another near miss in the hallway.

But she kept walking in my direction, like she was looking for me. Her new lackey Michael Hwang was with her.

Homicide detective Isabella Cherabino was beautiful as hell, with dark hair, piercing eyes, large breasts, a mind that wouldn't stop, and a black belt in something Asian and deadly. She was prone to migraines, she liked her coffee with a liquid creamer, half of one of those blue not-sugar packets, and a little water. She'd give her right arm for her job. We'd been working on and off together for years, but six weeks ago she'd had her tongue in my mouth in one of the hottest kisses I'd ever experienced. After the Link and the serial killer case, well, I'd been an ass. Briefly. And now she was avoiding me.

It was my fault we were Linked. My fault, and the fault of my feelings for her. I'd used her as an anchor to the real world during investigations just too often, leaned too hard on her while dropping into Mindspace, spent too much time warming myself in the edges of her strong and steady mind. I found her, well, calming. For all she bitched and complained. I found her beautiful. So the edges of our minds had gotten a little fuzzy, a little sticky, and the beginnings of a Link had formed by accident.

Guild ethics said I couldn't keep a Link, no matter how light and accidental, to myself. But I had. And the information had come out at the worst possible time, in the middle of a serial killer case where the killer was targeting her because of me. Worse, I'd had to presume on that Link, make it deeper and stronger and more permanent, to save her life. To save mine. And it couldn't be undone. It would fade over time, slowly, and there was nothing to do to speed it up, no matter how much it bothered her.

In the beginning, for the first few weeks after I'd burned out my telepathy, the Link had been all I had left. All I could feel of the world outside me, no matter how much I pushed. And while the rest of Mindspace disappeared as my brain healed, disappeared completely until I felt like I was stumbling around in the dark, the Link was still there. Our brains were connected in Mindspace in a way no one fully understood, like two particles in quantum entanglement. The state of one affected the other, no matter what you did to them, and only time would loosen the holds between them. If she was angry, my mood turned angry, and if she slept, I got overwhelmingly tired. I could listen to her emotions, to her thoughts, unless she specifically stood in my way with the technique I'd taught her to shield. Distance helped that insulation shielding, as the noise of the universe added up in the distance between us, and so, after a few weeks—and a fight—she'd started keeping her distance.

The one thing she'd ever asked of me was to keep my hands and my mind to myself. I understood. Since her husband had died six years ago, she was terrified of anyone getting too close. I understood. I did. The longer this

went on, the worse it got for her. And it was my fault the
Link had settled in, my fault despite everything.

But I'd been paying for the Link for weeks. Weeks.
And I'd saved her life, and it didn't matter. She'd gotten
herself a new lackey, and was running every chance she'd
get. It was starting to grate.

I wasn't going to take it personally, damn it. I wasn't.

"Hi, Michael," I said pointedly.

"Hello." Michael was a slight Asian guy, mid-twenties,
and today his normally cheerful demeanor was starting
to wilt around the edges. I wondered if it was me or the
caseload; Homicide wasn't exactly the most cheerful
place to be, and working full-time under Cherabino had
to be tough. She was a workaholic, and had been stressed
lately—which meant she was working harder. Still, he
got to follow her around, got to see her forehead wrinkle
when she got an idea, got to be there for all the good stuff.

Cherabino, hanging back, finally got even with me.

"I need your help," she said, no transition. Her I could
read without effort unless I was specifically trying not to,
like a wire connecting our brains. No interference, no
noise in the way. No matter how tired I was, unless she or
I blocked—and sometimes even then—I could read her.
Right now she was feeling self-conscious, picking up on
me listening to her thoughts. She blocked—hard. A flash
of light passed over my field of vision as the difference in
mental pressure set my damn brain off again.

"How can I help?" I asked.

Michael looked back and forth between us.

"Housewife turned up dead at the dinner table in
Avondale Estates. I'd like you to look at the scene."

She'd been avoiding me for weeks. I had to know.
"Why this case?" And why now? I'd been trying to avoid
crime scenes for weeks while my mind healed, and when

all else failed I went early in the mornings when the telepathy worked better. It was well after noon already.

"Why not?" Cherabino said. She was hiding something, something I could pull from her through the Link if I wanted. But I left it alone; I was hiding things too.

"I'd love to see you work," Michael said. "I've never worked with a telepath before."

Okay, now I hated him. He was far too cheerful, and far too *there*. "You realize I'm a Level Eight telepath? Aren't you scared I'll read your secrets?"

"I don't have many secrets," was his immediate response.

"Look, people," Cherabino put in. "They're waiting for us at the crime scene. Are you going to help or not?"

"Tell me why," I said, trying to buy more time. Maybe I could pick a fight and get out of having to go see the scene. "Tell me why."

Her shoulders tensed. "It's an olive branch, okay?"

I was silent. She knew the telepathy wasn't working.

"I owe Freeman a favor. And he wants to go on vacation next week. My caseload's full already. I was hoping you'd give me a lead to get this one done quickly."

Agreeing to look at a scene when I was in this state was pathetic and stupid. Doing it in the afternoon was worse, risky as hell. But the truth was, when it came to Cherabino, well, I'd do anything for her. Anything.

I sighed. "Let me get an umbrella."

One tense car ride over, with Cherabino blocking heavily against my mind, we turned into Avondale Estates. Less than a handful of miles from the department, the small house sat on a small lot, in the middle of ancient twisted trees. The neighborhood was cramped, with small streets and close houses full of old Southern porches, tall facades, and tiny strips of barely tended yards. Like the others on the street, this house was far deeper than it was wide. Two stories with a basement, original brick and fresh paint, it had doubtlessly been remodeled a dozen times. The quiet street, full of trees, looked like an oasis in the middle of the bustling city, an oasis of calm and old-style Southern charm.

Well, except for the two police cars with flashing lights and the crime scene van, the latter of which was currently settling down onto street level, its anti-grav engines whining under the strain.

Cherabino parked the car, and, taking my courage in hand, I got out.

Like a two-by-four to the head, Mindspace hit me with a firestorm of emotion, a force like a hurricane. I fell back against the car, struggling.

I finally got the blocks up. This had to be a hot spot, a place where Mindspace grabbed onto emotion and stewed on it for a long time. Most places Mindspace forgot things, slowly, as the memory of them faded over time.

But here the residue was strong, too strong. It screamed from the house with intense emotion I could feel even through my shields—screamed of pain and twisted love, layer upon layer of abuse and pain. The pain was wavering, but I could feel it; no chance I'd duck out of this nastiness. I didn't know how much detail I'd get, but the Mindspace and its tortured emotional baggage would push itself into my brain whether I liked it or not. I would be able to read the scene.

"Beautiful home," Michael said, admiring the wide wraparound porch, the pretty painted flowers.

"No." I straightened. "No, it's not."

Cherabino gave me a funny look but declined to comment. Probably she felt the edge of this through the Link; I was shielding as much as I could, but this was intense. Michael was obviously mind-deaf, it seemed; he was perfectly at ease, while Mindspace all around him screamed at beatings, nasty barbed words . . . and worse. I didn't want to go into this house.

"Are you coming?" Cherabino asked flatly.

"Yeah." I swallowed my discomfort, that lingering sense of self-preservation, and followed Cherabino up the old porch stairs. They, like the rest of the house, had a bright fresh yellow coat of paint. The front door was beveled glass, with the green tinge of the extraordinarily bulletproof alloys. We were only a few blocks from a bad area of town, after all. But that glass must have cost a thousand ROCs—a thousand Re-Oriented Currency units or more—to get in a decorative pattern.

An emotion ghost, a child blinking through various ages, sat collapsed in the porch swing, despair wafting from her like incense. I stared at her in shock. For me to see her, without going down into Mindspace and with my present troubles—well, the girl had to have some significant Ability and some very strong emotions. I could feel the child's fear and despair faintly, even through the shields.

Cherabino was holding the door open for me. I shivered, and left the child ghost and walked, one foot in front of the other, through the door. I made my shields as tough, as hard, as impenetrable as I could make them. And still I squinted against the onslaught of deep emotion, emotion like a hundred sharp razors dragging slowly through skin. I'd never felt a section of Mindspace this strong, this cloying. It was like the metaphysical equivalent of quicksand.

"About time you showed up," a deep baritone came from in front of me. I looked up. Detective Freeman, a grouchy man with a dark complexion and scarring on the right side of his face. He was one of Cherabino's counterparts in the homicide department, and always seemed tired when we ran into him. Today was no exception.

"Sorry about that," Michael said.

We met Freeman's partner, a fragile-looking man in his forties. They'd arrived twenty minutes ago. And Forensics had just gotten started.

Still struggling against the emotions surrounding me, I looked around the house. We were standing in what looked like a front living room, a television on one end across from a bulky sofa covered in frilly flowers. Judging from the rooster wall hangings, the old wooden floor, and the paper books laid out like props—and covered in a thin coat of dust—the owner liked the appearance of a country style. Oddly, a glass-and-chrome model of a skyscraper sat in the middle of the coffee table, looking out of place and aggressive.

Farther on, a narrow opening led to an eating area and what I assumed was a kitchen. The edge of a woman's back showed, slumped into the table, a dark bloodstain the size of a pizza pan sunk into the floor below her chair. A crime scene photographer moved in front of my view, and the flash of a picture made me blink. To the left was a large wooden staircase and a large oil painting of a family, a powerful-looking man, a mousy woman who looked very familiar somehow, and a preteen girl.

Techs were everywhere, here in the living room, on the staircase, and, from the sound of it, farther on in the kitchen. The ones I could see were armed with Luminol, looking for hidden blood spatters. By the emotions hitting me now, they'd likely find a lot of them.

"What do we have?" Cherabino prompted Freeman.

"Victim is Emily Hamilton, owner of the house along with her husband—currently absent—Dan. She's late thirties, apparent bleed out from a throat injury, seems to have more than her fair share of old cuts and bruises. The ME will have to tell you for certain, but none of them look around the time of death to me. Neighbor's dog ran into the yard and the neighbor saw the scene through the window. He's already been interviewed, seems clear." He paused. "Thanks for doing this."

Cherabino shrugged. "Not a problem."

"Has anyone talked to the husband yet?" I asked.

"Not yet. He's AWOL." Freeman's face took on a gesture of hostility, what seemed to me far out of proportion to speaking up. I wasn't making any effort to read him—even if my telepathy was up to snuff, this house would be a nightmare—but according to his facial cues he resented me. I wondered if other personnel were being laid off, real cops this time. If so, I could be in trouble with more folks than just Clark.

Cherabino glanced at me. "Well, even serious injuries aren't uncommon in domestic abuse cases, and it doesn't take much to go too far. Where is the husband?"

Freeman turned away from me like a dismissal. "Didn't come into work today, according to his supervisor. Architects' office, though I'm told he's a civil engineer. I've gone ahead and flagged the car with the local patrol. Something will pop."

"Thanks. Where's the daughter?" She gestured to the painting.

"Still in school. We have an officer going down to meet her when it's over. Supposedly there's a sister close by. Hell of a way to lose your parents."

"Assuming the husband doesn't turn up," Michael said.

"You a rookie?"

"That's right." Michael's voice was even, too even, like the question bothered him.

"Well, Hwang, trust me, if the spouse don't turn up in

a day or two, either he's dead or he killed her. Either way, that little girl has lost both her parents."

Michael talked to the detective a little longer. I tried to keep up with all the new information, my attention feeling far too short for the situation. Cherabino paced through the opening into the kitchen, and, after as long of a break as I could get away with, I followed. This was going to be hellish.

I was still shielded up to my gills, the steady barrage of sensation unsettling after so much quiet from the telepathy over the last few weeks. My tolerance was down, and the constant waves of sensation felt like sandpaper on my mind.

"You're looking green," one of the forensics techs commented in my general direction, not in a friendly way. That was Jamal, a smart guy with an attitude who hated telepaths in general and me in specific. The irony was, he was getting twitchy enough here I thought he might have a trace of telepathy himself.

"Thank you," I said, instead of barking at him.

He looked at me funny, but didn't say anything. Score one for me.

Cherabino was already circling the dark wooden table, frowning as she looked for a good angle to see the body. The crime scene photographer was kneeling at an angle, and took another flashbulb. I crouched, careful of where I put my shoes on the dull antique tile.

A woman. A blond woman in gray-patterned pajamas with little clouds on them. The same woman as in the oil painting, I assumed, though from this angle it was hard to tell. She was slumped forward, her forehead resting in a cereal bowl full of Cheerios. Spilled, sour protein-plus milk had flowed out of the bowl in thick trails, off the side of the table, and hit the floor, Cheerios and all. The milk and cereal were congealing, and on the edges, mixing with the blood, until it made an odd pink Jell-O tide. Small dots of blood, and milk, and occasional Cheerios sat on the floor and wall to her right, only one line like she'd thrown her arm up and then stopped suddenly.

The victim was collapsed in on herself, arms dangling, blood covering the entire front of her body, legs, and the chair seat. Her neck was folded down on itself; all I could see was the bloody line. There was clearly some large damage to the neck, with all this blood—not only down her front and along the floor and wall in that line, but puddled under her chair, soaked into the tile in a stain maybe two feet across. Maybe less; I was eyeballing it from a funny angle. Her back was covered in multicolored healing bruises, and one long half-healed scrape; like Freeman had said, far too old to have been done around the time of the murder.

I crouched down, to see around the table, and looked back at the body. She didn't have a bra on; the light gray shirt soaked with blood covered her like an obscene wet-T-shirt contest. It made me want to throw up, suddenly, intensely, and I swallowed, looking down.

Cherabino asked Freeman, "Have we found the blade he used yet?"

Freeman shook his head. "All the kitchen knives in the block are clean. If there's something else, we haven't found it. Maybe he took it with him."

"Hmm. Any way we can get a better look at the neck?"

"Jim, you done?" Freeman asked the crime scene photographer from the doorway. "I don't guess the coroner's going to care one way or the other."

"I care," I said.

"What?" Freeman responded. "Why is that?"

I forced myself not to respond to the hostility; the constant barrage of emotion was already giving me a headache, but I couldn't afford to antagonize yet another detective. "Look, if you want me to take a look at the Mindspace signatures around the body, we need to keep the immediate area as pristine as possible." I was not looking forward to this, not at all, even assuming I could read something deeper than the ambient emotion.

Cherabino frowned. "Fine, we'll back up a bit." She pulled Freeman aside. "How do you want to work the case transfer?"

I stopped paying attention; the steady sound of talking wouldn't bother me, not if no one was upset.

"Could you back up maybe four feet?" I asked Jim, the crime scene photographer, largely to get another moment to catch my breath. Cherabino was paying just enough attention, the cops were paying just enough attention that I couldn't walk away for a break.

I crouched there and pretended to be studying the victim while I got myself together. Telepathy and Mindspace sometimes were about faith. You got what you believed you'd get. So here, now, I had to convince myself I wasn't going to fail. But the sidelong glances from the cops around me just kept chipping away at that belief—they wanted me to fail. As the crime scene photographer finished packing up his kit and moved out, I stood, wishing for a cigarette or a vial or anything.

"Ahem," Cherabino said. Through the Link she was already ready to brace me, to provide me with an anchor back to the real world. She was holding out that careful mental hand, ready if I didn't grab too much, if I was polite and distant. She knew I needed this at a scene, and she liked the results enough to put up with it.

I lowered my shields, slowly. Like a frog in a pot of increasingly hot water, I could adjust—to a point. Mindspace screamed of misery, of desperation, humiliation, control, and pain, and waves of it washed over me over and over, the water coming to a quick boil, blistering my mind. And over it all, a high-pitched plea of disbelieving, choking death.

I felt a line, around my throat, pulling, pulling, until something in my throat broke, cutting, cutting, until panic set in and my fast-beating heart threw blood out of my body, spurt after spurt until I knew I would die, until my mind screamed what my voice could not. Screamed over and over again.

The sharp *pain* of him calling me worthless, ugly, nasty, worthless whore, over and over again, until I could hear his voice in my head . . .

A fist, hard, across my cheek, a hand ripping off my skirt . . .

Despair like poison, overwhelming, sinking into my bones . . .

The little bit of me that was still *Adam* grabbed for Cherabino with all I had. I was floundering. I was melting. She was still holding out a mental hand and I grabbed.

She almost dropped me, almost kicked me out in panic, feeling the edge of the sharp pleading pain. But she held on. Stilling the pain, stilling the response, like it was a migraine and she, under it. And her stillness—her rock-like stillness—brought me back into stillness too.

The fear, the pain, the choking death still lingered, along with years and years of abuse—but it didn't control me anymore. I paused, able to think again. Able to be surprised. I didn't know Cherabino could do that.

I breathed. Breathed over and over again, reestablishing me. I was not that woman. I was not what she had become. I was not. I was Adam, a telepath, and a guy. A single guy with battle training, not a victim, not a victim ever. Not ever anymore.

Go, Cherabino said, in that forceful, strained stillness.

In the distance, we heard Freeman say something to her, repeating something she still didn't understand. *Go, damn it. I can't do this forever—it hurts.*

Mind aching but with no choice, I obeyed. I sank into Mindspace, into the depths, until it was all I could perceive. A place where distance, location, emotion, were felt rather than seen, like the echolocation of a bat, the waves of the world focused back in the deeps. It was a place utterly without color—except for the yellow cord, yellow where no yellow should be, a cord that led back to Cherabino. The shallows wavered, strongly, as my battered, injured brain struggled to focus. I tried to push through—I tried—

In front of me, where the woman's body would be in real space, was a hole, the space left by a death when a mind went . . . wherever minds went when they died. It was fading fast, a smudge, nearly gone, but I would still avoid it. Falling In didn't happen often, but you didn't want to chance it, not ever.

Mindspace started to waver, in and out, in violent ways I knew were all about me—my injury, my inability. I swallowed it down and forced myself to focus past the pain, pushing no matter what it took—

The screaming here was so loud, the images, the despair so pressing I could feel water leak from my eyes, sheer pressure of emotions pressing, pressing, the fabric of the space tearing, tearing at my mind until it rang. But I held, and held, and learned—mind shaking—to see, slowly, in flashes, beyond it.

And, like a lid snapping into place, the world steadied. There was the hole, there was her death—I moved carefully, spiraling slowly in tiny degrees to look at different angles. Through the pain, I tried to think. Tried. In little bits.

From the neck wound direction (back and up) and the

fact that she'd fallen forward, he'd attacked her from the back. I looked there, specifically, over the ambient screams, and breathed in the space, studying every smell, every trace left behind. My head pounded, the edges of the world streaking like watercolors, but I was almost done.

There. Calm. Calm, with a faint dark undercurrent. Sharp focus, sharp pull, sharp satisfaction, and above all calm. Dark, beautiful, deep calm with a sharp edge that made me feel . . . accomplished somehow. Subtle, dangerous accomplishment, one less problem to solve, one more success to report.

Report? Report. He . . . he? Yes, a man, a man who had done this before, many times before. A man with someone to report it to.

And the woman—that twisted-up mind—I knew that mind. Or I knew what it had once been.

The emotions of the scene swelled again, the woman's silent screams drilling into my skull. And the pain was overwhelming, tearing, and the world was streaking apart until there was nothing left.

You okay? came Cherabino's thought again, frustrated. Tap, tap, her mind against mine, tap, tap, as if she could somehow feel my distress and reacted with impatience instead of care. Tap, tap, along the long yellow line back to the real world.

I followed that line, hand over hand, inch by painful blind inch, laboriously surfacing, one overwhelming moment at a time. She kept tapping. She kept pushing. It was the only thing that got me all the way there.

I woke to the clear view of the floor and my knees, twelve inches from the bloodstain, my nose overcome with bad smells. I hadn't thrown up. I could say that much. And—mind shaking, aching, shivering in reaction pain—I realized I was back to mind-deaf. My head rang with pain, pain—but no emotion. I was deaf and blind again.

"You okay?" Cherabino asked.

I shook my head—and immediately thought better of it; the movement made the world spin.

My eyes caught the victim's foot, her bare foot on the tile, and I saw a small tattoo, a circle of wavy lines, neurons, encircling a stylized S and Q. I sat down hard, on the tile. I knew that tattoo.

I knew that tattoo, and in combination with it the female mind, or who she'd once been. Her name hadn't been Hamilton when I'd known her, but she hadn't been married. Emily, her name had been. Even through the overwhelming pain in my head, I couldn't let go of the thought. Emily had been one of my best advanced students, years ago. Before it all fell apart. Before her mind twisted into a knot—into something not an Abled mind anymore. Before I'd done the unthinkable. A miracle I could feel her at all, here, but great pain—well, great pain had been known to blast through incredible barriers.

"Are you okay?" Cherabino repeated.

I fought the guilt and the disorientation of seeing Emily again, seeing her dead. I fought the exposure sickness, the injury. I sat on them, hard, and built a barrier between us with bleeding fingers. Cherabino couldn't know. She knew too many of my failures as it was.

One small knee shuffle at a time, I moved back, away from Emily. It wasn't her fault she smelled of urine, dried blood, and darker things, but it wasn't mine either.

"Well, did the husband do it?" Freeman asked.

"Are you okay?" Cherabino repeated.

I pulled myself to my feet and fished out my sunglasses over my now-light-sensitive eyes. "Unless the husband's an ex-SEAL or something," I said in a rasp, "somebody

else did it. And now, unless there's some kind of emergency, I'll be in the car."

Uncaring of reactions, I stumbled out of the devil
house, away from the seat of every failure I'd ever had,
down the stupid steep stairs, and climbed into the back-
seat of the cop car. I needed to be horizontal. Now.

CHAPTER 3

My mind threatened to pass out, once, twice, then finally stabilized as I held on to consciousness through sheer will and training. My guilt helped there, the guilt of what I'd done, guilt that burned like volcanic ash in my belly. The guilt that would never, never leave me. I would have walked over red-hot coals to fight that guilt, to do something productive. To fight for Emily.

At the Guild, I'd been a professor of Deconstruction, a lucrative specialty, the folks who could put you in a coma or take you out of one, change the structure of your mind so you saw in color for the first time or could recognize your wife's face for the first time in years. That was the stuff you'd pay the sun and the moon for, and that was the stuff routinely making Deconstructionists and the Guild millions. I taught that stuff, the advanced Structure lessons like the final years of neurosurgery training, the capstone courses before you went out into the world. By the time they'd gotten to my classes, the students had jobs lined up, and were well on their way—assuming hard work and discipline—to a career that would buy them anything they wanted.

Well, until that day. I'd been teaching Emily, Tamika, and Charles, three students at once, the ability that had gotten me the professorship in the first place. It was a routine day. But I was high as a kite and I hadn't realized Satin—for all I'd been trying to hide it—had an effect on the mind.

Before I knew it, in the space between one heartbeat and the next, the world had tilted and I'd lost control. Three students, three million ROC students, burned out like cinders in an instant. Gone, gone beyond any redemption, from an accident. From a slip—from a side effect—from something I hadn't controlled. Couldn't control. Because I couldn't let go of the drug I wasn't supposed to have.

Charles was found dead—by his own hand—in a pool of blood in his suite three days later. His future was gone, gone in an instant; what did he have to live for? The other two—well, they hadn't killed themselves. But their minds were shredded beyond repair because of my mistake. At the hearing . . . Emily's mind had curled in on itself like a sodden, wooden knot. Tamika was too traumatized to even show up.

How do you go from being an elite telepath to a normal in a day? How do you adjust to everything you'd ever loved being taken away from you in an instant? My head pounded like a fleet of ice picks to the brain.

I'd found out. My fiancée at the time, Kara, had been the first to find us, the first to see what had happened. The first to report me, testify against me, and see me thrown out of the Guild. As much as her betrayal still burned like fire, it paled in comparison to what I'd done. What I'd done to innocents, to students.

Now, here in the car, I gave up fighting the guilt, the telepathy, the inconceivable reaction pain and rocking world, and I let myself pass out.

I was aware of distant speech for a long time before I decided to wake up. Slowly the sounds made words, and the words made sense, like a sharpening image finally clicking into place, far away but understandable.

"We're not going anywhere until he wakes up on his own," Cherabino's voice insisted on the other side of my head, through the cracked car window. "I'm not a telepath, and I'm not messing with the normal course of events. For all I know we wake him up early and he scrambles our brains like in the movies. You want to be responsible for that?"

Freeman's voice made a frustrated sound. "I've been up twenty-two hours already and regs say I can't leave anyone at the scene."

I realized, slowly, my headache had dimmed to a dull roar, something I could actually manage.

"I thought this was our case now," Michael's voice put in.

"Not until the paperwork goes through, not really," Freeman said. "Right now it's courtesy. If somebody screws something up, it's still my watch. It's still my beating to take."

I winced, the word "beating" conjuring up far too many images and emotions.

"We're the last on the scene already," Cherabino said. "I won't tell if you won't."

"What will a few more minutes harm?" Michael said.

"Clearly you haven't been listening, *Officer*. I haven't slept in . . . well, far too long. And you're the last item on my to-do list before a nice warm bed calls my name. I don't cut corners. You have five minutes or I'll move the car myself. He can sleep at the station."

My head was pounding dully, my stomach still entirely unsettled, but neither was overwhelming and both no reason to get Cherabino in trouble.

"I told you, I'm not—" Her head came up to look in the car.

I pulled myself to a seated position. "I'm okay," I said, echoed it through the Link with as little pain as possible. *I didn't mean to scare you.*

"Then we're ready to go." Cherabino shot a dose of annoyance straight at me. *Stop the pain thing. Now.* Then to Freeman: "You'll have the paperwork on your desk before your shift starts." She paused. "Want me to tell Branson you'll be late?"

Freeman and Cherabino locked gazes for a long, long moment. Then Freeman nodded. "A couple hours only."

"I'll tell him."

Then Cherabino gestured for Michael to get in the car, and opened her own door. I took the moment to put on a seat belt. Only then did I realize I still had the sunglasses on. One of the arms was pasted to my head; I loosened it and felt a dissipation of some of the headache.

"Are you all right?" Michael asked. "The scene wasn't that bad, I didn't think. No kids or anything." He looked to Cherabino, who was turned all the way around in her seat preparing to back the car down the twisty driveway around the trees. She made it all the way to the street before she turned on the anti-grav generators and made a highly illegal jump to airspace. Over a neighborhood no-fly zone. With a floating marker above us.

I slammed my eyes closed. We'd die or we wouldn't, and either way I'd rather not see it coming.

She avoided the marker and we survived, at least for another day.

"I'm okay," I said, when I finally felt safe opening my eyes. "Shell-shocked, a bit. Nasty reaction headache, but nothing critical."

"Why didn't you answer me about time of death?" Cherabino asked, her voice too biting. Maybe I had scared her. Maybe . . .

Shut up, came across the Link and she slammed up the

blunt-edged shield I'd taught her, which made the headache worse. I gritted my teeth.

"You asked me about time of death?" I asked. "When
was this exactly?" My attention wasn't all that great these
days.

"Shouldn't we be asking questions right now?" Michael
asked. "You dashed out without a word and now you're
not talking. Is this a telepath thing?"

"No," I gritted out. "It's a cranky partner thing. What
was it you wanted to know?"

"Time of death," Cherabino said. "And who did it."

"Not in the last few hours, not several days ago. The
coroner can tell you a hell of a lot more. As for who?" I
paused. "Not the husband. He's killed this way before. It's
a . . . sharp mind. A practiced one."

Michael asked, "Why isn't he here, then?"

"Maybe he cut him up into pieces and stuffed him
down the drainpipes," I said testily.

Cherabino met my eyes through the rearview mirror,
and a question sense leaked over the Link. I noticed her
forehead was creased like she had a migraine; maybe
some of my headache was leaking over.

I upped my barriers between us and accepted the result-
ing fireworks in my skull as the necessary price. I took a
breath. Tried to remember what the question was.

"Well, did he?" Cherabino asked. "Stuff the pieces
down the drainpipes?"

"I don't think so. If he did, though, he didn't kill the
man there, or anywhere close. I only felt the one death,
though in that house there could be a herd of tap-dancing
psychic monkeys and I wouldn't know the difference."

"What's wrong with the house?" Cherabino asked.

"Monkeys get psychic?" Michael put in.

"I told you. He beat her—and worse. And he did it a
lot. Every board of that house was covered with a crazy

level of emotion. And I don't know. Maybe not; I've never seen testing on monkeys, and the Guild tests everything."

"So you couldn't see anything." Cherabino paused. "Why not?"

Why was she pushing this in front of Michael? "It's complicated," I said, stalling.

"Say it with the fish tank." She merged into air traffic without so much as checking her blind spot, and I swallowed a yelp. Michael was hanging on for dear life.

"Okay," I said, for his benefit, once it was apparent we were going to live. "Imagine the world is a fish tank, one of those big tanks you see in doctors' offices."

"It has sand, a ceiling, maybe some coral, and lots of goldfish," Cherabino said in a continuous stream. "Bottom-feeders and the like. Me and Michael and half the world are shiny orange goldfish, the Guild and you, maybe, are huge Japanese koi. We get it."

I sighed. "Are you going to let me tell it or not?"

"Do you have to be difficult?"

"Boy, someone's testy today," I said. When she swerved to avoid an airbus, I swallowed my words. "I take it back, you're the soul of sweetness and light."

"Goldfish. Fish tank. Talk."

I tried to find some kind of explanation that didn't depend on either my injury or me doing something wrong. Finally I settled on, "It's like there was algae in the water, okay? Or thousands of slow piranhas the size of a fingernail coming after me. I fell into the tank and spent most of my time fighting them off."

She got quiet then.

"That's why you dashed out?" Michael said. "To get away from the piranhas?"

"More or less." I looked down, ignored the latest swerve as Cherabino decided to get in the ground exit at the last possible second. She screeched into the parking lot of a Thai restaurant, stopping hard enough to throw me against the seat belt. Great. Since last summer with the crime scene behind a Thai restaurant in East Atlanta, I couldn't smell peanut sauce without gagging.

"Can't we do Mexican?" I asked.

"Was that really necessary?" Michael asked her, testy.

"No and no." Cherabino opened her car door, turned back around to look at me. "You're eating." Then at Michael: "Don't criticize the driving. It's bad for your health."

I sighed and unbuckled my seat belt. Probably good to get fuel in me; I'd passed out, after all, and was still feeling weak. Plus the whole head-pounding-and-possible-major-reinjury thing. "You realize I'm nauseated already?" I asked her.

"You can have plain rice, fine. But you're eating." She paused as I unbuckled my seat belt. "What else aren't you telling me about the scene?"

"Nothing, really."

Silence came from her as Michael stopped, uncomfortably, outside the car.

"The killer feels familiar," I said, just realizing it. "I've seen him—or at least his mental signature—before."

"Guild?" she asked quietly.

"I don't know."

Swartz arrived early, and I was already waiting on the curb, my headache low and ignorable. Swartz was always early; he was one of those old men who never slept, and as my Narcotics Anonymous sponsor, well, he was even older. He'd been clean when I was in diapers.

It was raining again, long drizzly streams, which suited my mood. But the good news was, it had been raining for days; probably all the nasty pollution was long gone, pulled out of the air days ago. This would just be dirty water and cloud spit. I pulled up the collar of my coat and stubbed out the cigarette. My umbrella sat beside me, unused.

Swartz's aircar grounded with a lurch. The anti-grav system must be on the fritz—Swartz worked for DeKalb County schools on the southern section as a teacher, working with some of the poorest kids in the area. He didn't get paid much.

Swartz opened the door from the inside; the lock must be stuck now too.

"How are you?" I asked, by rote, as I slid into the seat. My head protested the sudden movement, but it settled.

Swartz nodded hello and pulled off into traffic, caution and precision guiding his movements. He drove like an old man, checking his blind spot five times before a vertical lane change, keeping a careful eye on all the other cars in all directions. Easier to head the problem off before you got to it, he often said.

"Today?" His slate gray hair, heavy wrinkles, and weathered features argued with the strength still in his shoulders and arms. Swartz was no weakling, age or none. He could still kick my ass any time he wanted.

"Today what?" After all day trying to force work past my limitations, my attention span now rivaled a gnat's. If the gnat was feeling peckish. "Could you repeat that please?"

"What are you grateful for today?" he prompted.

"Oh. Grateful."

Every week at our usual morning coffee, he made me list three things I was grateful for, and had for the last six years. Even the question made me taste the strong licorice coffee all over again. But we'd missed this week—parent-teacher conference for one of his kids that morning—and I hadn't rescheduled. He wasn't saying anything about it, but I knew he was watching.

"That's a morning thing."

"Good to have a reminder of what you've got."

I took a breath. "My job's on the line now."

"You say that every few months," Swartz returned, turning up the speed of the windshield wipers with equanimity. "They're no more going to get rid of you than the school's going to start teaching gun classes."

I shifted and thought. "Well, maybe they should teach classes. The kids certainly have enough of them. This time they're serious, though. Paulsen says I've got to get a certification or some such to keep my job—those are the rules, the politicians say. There's a budget crisis." I took a breath, waited for the thoughts to settle again. "Oh, and Cherabino's still pissed at me and I ran into an old student today—dead, at a crime scene."

Swartz whistled. "Big day."

"Yeah."

"Can you renew your thing at the Guild?"

"I don't know." I slumped down in the seat.

Swartz only let me sulk for so long. "Three things," he prompted. "Gratefulness."

I sighed, breathed. "Okay. Three. Telepathy's getting more reliable. With the exception of me overdoing it today, it's been coming back more or less like I expected. It looks like I don't need to go see the Guild doctor after all."

"Good to hear." He nodded, slowed down to stop at a floating air light turning yellow. "What did you do to yourself today?"

"Something stupid. Cherabino asked me for a favor and I couldn't not do it for her."

Swartz was oddly silent.

I added, "Like I said, I've coached a lot of students through recovery, nothing this bad, but it seems to be on the same pace. I know the exercises to do. I know what's going on. There's no reason to give the Guild—or the department, for that matter—any ammunition to use against me."

"You're being bullheaded, son."

"Even so."

He nodded and shifted tactics. "You been praying about it? About what to do if it doesn't come back on its own?"

I took a breath. Swartz was a lot more comfortable about the God part of the Twelve Steps than I was. "Sometimes," I admitted quietly, like it was a shameful secret. "I need a miracle. This is my life, Swartz. This is who I am. I'm a telepath, a damn strong, ethical telepath. A good one. I need this. So, yeah, I'm praying, okay? I'm praying."

"Sometimes God works quietly. We'll both pray a little harder. He'll listen. Sometimes you've got to ask for help."

I took a breath, the moment, the longing too intense.

"Now tell me about the student," Swartz said.

I was silent.

"The dead student at the crime scene."

"I heard you."

He waited, as we drove closer and closer to our regular meeting.

I sighed. "It's Emily, okay? Emily."

"You know I told you to find her and the other one to make restitution."

I looked down at my feet. "I sent letters."

"They were very short letters. Making amends is about more than a half-assed letter, son. I've said this before."

And what sat like a fog in the car between us was the certain knowledge I couldn't apologize to Emily in person now. Death had a way of making things too final, too quick. "I can solve the case at least. I can find Emily's killer. Won't that make amends?"

"It's a start. You need to find the other one and apologize in person. You've let this go too long."

"I could do that, I guess." But I knew I wouldn't, not if I could help it. "Solving this case will make amends."

Swartz was quiet as he parked. I knew the subject wasn't done, even if it was shelved for a while. He turned to me, taking off the seat belt. "You know there's more than one certification in the world."

"I know. It's just . . ."

"You're worried about the felonies."

I nodded.

"They're all drug related. Since the Second Chance Act, if you can pass the tests they don't matter. If you did the rehab. And you did. We've got all the paperwork; it'll be fine. You'll find something. How much time do you have to figure it out?"

"A few weeks at least." I felt distant, like there was some overwhelming shock that hadn't quite registered yet. That's right, I was going to lose my job. My job and my support system and everything else. In a time when my telepathy—the only thing I did that mattered—was on the fritz. I was inches from that cliff, inches, even if I chose not to think about it.

"We'll figure it out." His certainty put a cap on the end of the conversation.

It was the last week of September, I thought, as I stepped out of the car into an inch of dirty water, my gray umbrella fighting with the wind. September. We'd be looking at Step Nine one more time, making restitution for the harm we'd done. Again.

I limped along after Swartz, who as usual had brought out his own ugly striped umbrella. I hated September.

That night I stared at my ceiling, barely visible blockish shapes attesting to the Tech still hidden in the walls—Tech I'd converted to shield me from Mindspace while I slept, a therapy, a failed attempt at normalcy. That kind of Tech was illegal, against the spirit if not the letter of the laws, but I'd tuned it to cancel out my brain waves in Mindspace so I could actually rest, so I could actually think. It was worth the trouble for my sanity, if nothing else, and the components had been here when I'd moved in, the old office building badly converted. As long as I never got caught it wasn't a big deal.

Besides, since I'd tuned the thing to the shape of my mind before the injury, it was slow encouragement to heal the right way. Better encouragement than the drugs the Guild gave out like candy, drugs I shouldn't take.

But the exercises, well, those I did. In the mornings, I stretched my mind, flexing muscles and holding painful poses like the world's worst mental yoga session. At night, when I was as exhausted as this, I did crossword puzzles and word searches, even physical pasteboard picture puzzles, anything to make my brain rewire faster. Tonight, though, the letters in front of me were dancing off the page, wavering so badly I couldn't read a single line, no matter how I tried. My head hurt still, a low, thin pound of pain.

I stuck the pencil in the center of the book and tossed the book down onto the dirty floor. I punched the pillow a few times to give it some shape, and turned over to put my face in it.

Like this, I faced the compartment in the walls. A hinged, hidden spot where I used to keep my emergency stash. I stared at the spot in the wall that hid the compartment. I didn't have any vials. No Satin-filled glass vials behind me; I hadn't restocked them. Three years and change clean, but at moments like this all I was thinking about was where to get my poison. Whether the bus down to south Fulton County would still get me what I wanted, or whether they would have talked to the dealers in

Decatur, and refuse me. They were idle thoughts. Mostly. But I was exhausted, my willpower and mind nearly gone.

My mind spiraled around and around the events of the day, like a dog chewing at a bone. Emily, dead. Charles, dead. Cherabino, hating me. Me probably losing my job in the middle of the holiday season. Me sitting here without even a single vial, without one even for me to hold. I got more and more anxious until my heart beat like a drum.

Finally I couldn't stand it anymore. I got up, I put on clothes, and I stood, in front of the door outside, as the war inside me raged.

Sometime later, through some miracle, I managed to let go of the doorknob. I sat on my crappy couch, got out a blue-wrapped cigarette pack and a lighter. The pack of solitaire cards was already on the table. I played through half a pack, I played until my eyes grew heavy, I played until I stubbed out the end of the latest burning cigarette, and finally, finally slept.

CHAPTER 4

The elevator stopped at the second floor, and I braced myself. It had been several weeks since I'd walked this gantlet. And, in a delightful twist of fate, my telepathy had decided to wake up unexpectedly this morning and participate in the mental exercises, even giving me a few glimpses of the shape of Mindspace without pain. I'd gotten lucky, crazy, unreasonably lucky yesterday; I'd pushed far enough to make me sick, but apparently, not enough to reinjure, a minor miracle all by itself. Maybe this prayer thing was working.

Here, now, I held my cooperating mind closely, wrapped in cotton; for all I was cautiously optimistic, there were times when telepathy wasn't pleasant.

The cubicles all around me were filled with cops, mostly detectives with a smattering of other specialties like accountants and other noncop investigators. The cubicles started with Robbery, Vice, then Homicide and Electronic Crimes at the end, data crunchers and active duty intermingled, all the senior and important cops who weren't—quite—supervisory yet. The forest of cubicles had two major downsides: one, there was one major walkway in the place, and two, my destination was all the way at the end of that walkway.

I took my courage in my hands and starting walking. Pace after pace down the central walkway, as every head in the place turned to me and thoughts started flying like water balloons. Observations hit me from every side, everything from the set of my shoulders to the shape of my ass, the contents of the bag in my hand to the smell of the cigarette clinging to me. Just for fun, the cops' minds added rumors of Cherabino's displeasure, political shortcuts, and nasty things other cops had said about me. And the hostility—the general low-level fear and hostility that had peaked yesterday at the announcement of layoffs. It might not be my fault, maybe, but as an outsider I was sure I was easy to blame.

I shielded harder, while the waves of negative energy splashed on the shields from every side, the impacts stinging. My mind was still sensitive from yesterday, for all the pain had mostly gone, and I was feeling less patient than ever—so I met the eyes of the people staring at me. Most turned back to their work—a few, Clark's buddies, kept my gaze.

Finally I'd reached the end of the gantlet and could turn into the more secure cubicles, this area shielded for sound. Below, the secretaries' minds were quiet and secure in their gossip; above, the senior brass worried quietly; the gauntlet was over.

Cherabino's cubicle neighbor, Andrew, waved hello to me as I passed. Andrew was an accountant, his mind habitually filled with numbers, coffee, and calm. The only labels he put on things were numbers.

Michael was sitting in my spot. Mine. The little chair at the back of Cherabino's cubicle, the little chair I'd been using for years. I mean, yeah, I'd moved downstairs to an empty desk because Cherabino had jumped like I'd stung her with a bee every time I'd moved into her cubicle—I'd had to do something. To give her space. So I could be trusted again. But this?

Michael had covered my little corner of the cubicle with pictures, personal pictures of his wife and him, a framed document with some kind of Asian characters, even a pile of reference books on the small counter that had been my workspace. Titles like *Homicide Investigator's Guide to Optimal Practices* and *Blood Spatter and You* filled the space that should have been mine. I hated it. I hated him, cozied up to Cherabino at her desk, leaning over some doubtlessly important work document. I hated him.

"Adam," Cherabino greeted me before I could leave. She frowned, like she was getting the edge of my jealousy. I erected a firm brick wall between us, hard, and tried to pull my anger in.

"I brought you coffee with real chocolate syrup."

That made her eyes lighten, and she took the drink carrier from me, diving into both so fast I barely had a chance to save my own coffee.

Michael stood awkwardly to the side.

"I didn't get enough for you too," I said insincerely. "Sorry."

He frowned, and part of me rejoiced.

"We're about to go over to the lab," Cherabino said. She added, almost as an afterthought, "You should come along."

So I did.

I followed Cherabino across the street, down West Trinity Avenue, to the big, square concrete court system offices. She and Michael huddled under a single umbrella, and I carried my own umbrella above me, the plop of the rain like soft bullets on its skin.

The forensics offices were huge, since they handled a lot of overflow from every detective group in the county. Things like blood analysis, photography analysis, blood

spatter, DNA, hairs, nonhuman traces (think dogs, para-
keets, and helper monkeys), and everything else you could
think of. The *everything else* would be investigated in
Trace Evidence, the catch-all group for the county forensics department, where you went when you had something that didn't fit the rest. Carpet fibers, for example, or
paint from a car, or even better, an odd white powder you
couldn't identify or the speck of something that might be
important.

I'd been told we were going to see some kind of trace
evidence from the body, and hopefully get more information Michael could use to track its source down. Not that
he was overachieving or anything.

But I'd made it down to the trace evidence rooms of
the forensics offices several times before, usually to run
small errands for Cherabino. They knew me there, and as
I was known to bring treats and bribery when something
was running behind, I was hoping they wouldn't be hostile to me no matter what was going on with layoffs.

Michael held the door open for her, of course, juggling
umbrella and heavy metal door with alacrity. I nodded
and walked through whether he'd intended to let me
through or not. My own umbrella went in the shedding
pile beside the door, the water from the pile making the
marble floor slick. Why he bothered me so much I didn't
know. But I couldn't read him at all, which made it worse.

A few turns and we were at the trace evidence rooms,
a few small specialty rooms splitting off from a large,
central open space filled with every kind of scientific
mechanical you could think of, including at least five
microscopes of various strengths and a minicentrifuge.
Two forgettable techs in lab coats worked at the back of
the room, another tech with pink hair disappearing
through the door to the dark lab on the right as we entered.
I recognized her from meetings a few weeks back; she'd

had some useful things to say about dish soap and latex gloves.

A tired woman in hospital-type scrubs perched on a tall stool near the front of the room, pulled up to the long machine-laden counter filled with small glass slides. In her mid-fifties, Dotty had skin so fair you could see the veins in her neck, her hair was light blond turning to gray, and her hands were rough, like they'd been used hard for years. Today there were also dark circles under her eyes and she had her right knee propped up like it was hurting again.

"What?" she asked grumpily, without getting up. Then her eyes fell on me. "Adam! Did you bring me more of those faux-macadamia cookies?"

"Not this time." I assumed a dejected expression as I wandered in her direction. "You told me you were going on a diet. I was trying to be nice."

She reached out and swatted me on the shoulder. As her hand touched, even through the shirt, I could feel a small wave of pain off her knee. Dotty wasn't the type to complain—holding the pain in so close it hardly registered in Mindspace even when I was at full strength—but she'd been struggling with the joint for years. Apparently she was allergic to the artificial type-1 collagen that would form the frame for whatever new joint they'd grow for her; not worth it, and there were no guarantees the older metal-and-plastic models would get rid of the pain. So she'd been sticking it out. I respected her for that, and for her unwillingness to take any pain meds stronger than aspirin.

Dotty had greeted Cherabino while I was distracted. Now she asked, "And who is this handsome young thing?" There was a lilt in her voice; Michael sidled away.

"He's Officer Hwang," Cherabino said. "He's shy."

"Well, that's a shame, then."

"Thanks for putting our stuff on rush."

"Well, I owed you that favor anyway. Let's see what we have." She stood up—with difficulty—pulling her knee down from the prop with her hands. She hobbled gracefully through the small door to the left and into the next room. The rest of us followed.

We entered a smaller room, maybe five feet by seven, most of the room taken up by a mammoth table on which sat a beat-up gray machine with two huge circular extensions over a lighted plate the size of my hand. On the plate was a clear tube-thing, less than a quarter of an inch long, covered in spots of vaguely translucent reddish brown blood. At head height on the machine was a bright monitor the size of my head, on which a much larger version of the thing was displayed.

"What did you find?" Michael asked.

"Based on where it was found in her neck, it's likely a piece of a ligature."

Cherabino held up a hand. "Wait, ligature? There was blood everywhere. I'm pretty sure this was a bladed weapon."

Dotty shrugged. "I'm not the ME, but I can tell you what I have in front of me. This is a new material, unusual, not a smooth surface, and according to the file it was found lodged against her spine—the ME marked it as ligature with a question mark. Take a look." Dotty pushed a few buttons, and the circular thing whirred and moved closer to the plate. On the screen, the image got larger—much larger, until it was as big as my thumb around, and I could suddenly see what she meant—the center section was long and skinny, like a piece of a long cord, the sides shearing off like they'd torn. But the closer we got, the less the cord seemed smooth; the edges suddenly looked rough, the cord almost . . . striped. In the corner of the monitor, a brown spot fizzled, colored distortions around it, as if the monitor was dying in that spot. I tried not to look at the spot and focus on the image, but it pulled my attention to it like a flytrap.

She pointed to the screen. "If you look—the cross section of this sucker is a twelve-pointed star. If you apply pressure, there's twelve lovely edges to cut someone with. Nasty thing, it is."

I was frowning, trying to figure out exactly what Dotty was talking about.

Michael leaned forward to look at the end she was holding up.

But Cherabino was thinking, thoughts like bees buzzing around her head. Suddenly they all flew in a single direction—clarity. "So it's not a length of fishing line, or anything like that, pulled too hard. Nothing like that would go through the skin with a clean cut, not that deep."

"No, my dear. It looks to me like it was specialty made, or at least adapted from a specific project. Whatever this thing is, it was meant to cut. Designed for it." She put the end down and rotated a few knobs, zooming way, way in until I blinked. "As you can see from the striations and the regular imperfections, the material is a part-biological superfibroid distillation. I can't tell you which one; we don't have the chemistry set here to tease out the components without making them interact or get toxic. And I don't have that kind of training. But I can say the major molecule is carbon—"

"Like diamond?" Michael asked.

"More or less," Dotty replied, in the tone of voice of a pleased teacher at a good student question. "It's tough stuff. I wouldn't normally have said something like this would break off. It clearly was designed to be flexible; maybe there was an issue with the chemical binding for this particular length, something that made it more brittle than intended. Good news for us. The bad news? Well, to put it simply, it's from the same kind of technology that makes biological computer components. Plus that nasty starred edge."

"Tech." Cherabino's voice was quiet, but it seemed to echo in the small room. She was disturbed; that much I could feel echoing down the Link.

"Is it illegal?" I asked Dotty. "This material?"

"I wouldn't guess it's common. It would set off the same sniffers and alarms the biological Tech would, and get you in a hell of a lot of trouble explaining your way out to some government agent with a big gun and a small sense of humor. It'd be more trouble than it's worth, just for that."

"So it's not illegal." Michael poked at the plate, and Dotty slapped his hand away.

"I didn't say that. I called you in early so you could take a look, but I'm passing this one up to the Georgia Bureau, just in case. It's a more advanced material than anything I've seen."

Cherabino's thoughts were buzzing again. "What would we call this? How would we track it down?"

"I'd call it a specialty cutting cord, or a supermaterial, or some such. But you may have to call around to find the industry terms. Like I said, a bit above my expertise."

"Okay . . ."

"There's one more thing." Dotty added a tinted cover to the lighted plate and zoomed the machine even farther in, pressing a few buttons that made the monitor light up with neon colors in a long tube. I assumed the slightly striped tube was the center part, the cord, blown up.

She pressed another button, and suddenly a shape emerged from the darkness, a shape in quiet black against a sea of neon. I could see a crooked C, then maybe a half circle torn away . . .

"There's letters on that thing?" Cherabino's voice rang out.

"Whatever it is, it's labeled," Dotty said. "I'll see if I can't get you more information once we cross-check the databases. We'll need computer time. . . ."

"You'll get it. Again, I appreciate you prioritizing this one. I assume you'll send over the rest of your findings as you have them?"

Dotty nodded. "I'll run a few more tests on this thing and give a look at the trace you sent over. I don't have much hope of anything better, but you never know."

"What trace?" Michael asked.

"Why, the swabs and fibers the detective here sent over yesterday. Like I said, I owe you a favor and I'm happy to pay up when I can. We get a priority homicide through here, though . . ."

"I understand," Cherabino said. "Thank you."

Dotty leaned over and rubbed her knee, nodding an acknowledgment as the cops turned to leave.

On an impulse, and to see if I could actually do it, I reached over and touched her on the shoulder, right at the neckline where my fingers could sit on her skin without issue. "I appreciate it," I said, to give the action some socially acceptable context. But her mind opened up like a door; she wasn't guarded at all. Pain blossomed between us like a flower.

It was still morning, and this was one of the more simple Structure procedures. All knowledge and practice, no precision, no raw power. I found my way to the pain center of the mind and put in a simple, fuzzy, fragile shunt. Not a block; she'd do real damage to the knee without a warning system in place. When I backed away, both mentally and physically, I checked my work. I smiled, big, when it held. The pain coming off her was noticeably less.

For the next day or two—as long as she didn't think too hard about it—the pain would be less, with a lot less distress about it. The debilitating part about chronic pain isn't always the pain; it's the wear and tear of the pain on the brain and the personality. The shunt was temporary, but it would give her a break. Ten seconds later, I was out the door trying to catch up to Cherabino and Michael. I gritted my teeth and told my right knee it didn't really hurt, not quite controlling the limp despite my best efforts. Looked like I hadn't gotten it quite right after all.

It took two hours for the damn limp to wear off, two hours of me kicking myself for a stupid unfocused mistake. By then I had a headache and didn't give two shits what else hurt.

Next time, Dotty was getting the damn cookies.

CHAPTER 5

I'd taken over an empty desk downstairs, in the secretaries' pool, to do paperwork, to give Cherabino her damn space. I was there now, killing time with forms. Trying not to think about anything at all.

The phone rang. I stared at it for a long moment. This wasn't even technically my desk. I mean, yeah, I'd been here a lot, but . . . I sighed and picked up the phone.

The scheduling officer's voice came on the line. "This Adam?"

"Yes. Does Cherabino need me on another scene?"

"I have no idea," she said. "There's a fed guy on the other line for you."

"Okay . . ." I trailed off as the sound of the department's public safety recording filled the earpiece. What the hell was a fed doing calling me? Probably got confused with Cherabino's cases, read the wrong line on a file I gave an opinion on or something.

As the recording suddenly went silent, I ventured, "If you're looking for Cherabino, I can—"

"No." A man's voice cut me off. "No, I'm looking for you. This is Adam?"

"That's right." I paused suspiciously.

"Well, I work for the Federal Bureau of Investigation. I assume you've heard of us?"

"Is that a serious question?"

"I'm Special Agent Louis Jarrod. I'm calling to let you know we'll be monitoring you for the next few weeks for an administrative matter."

I backed up, looked at the phone, put it back to my ear. "Hold on. What?"

"I'm afraid I can't give you details, but we'll be calling a few of your coworkers and friends."

My stomach went into free fall. "Okay, seriously. What's going on? Am I in trouble?"

"It's a routine inquiry, given your background and current opportunities. This call is a matter of respect, since it's possible one of your associates will tell you we called, and I'd rather inform you myself."

"My background? Why the hell would the FBI care about my background? I've been working here . . . Did Clark call you?"

"Watch your language, please. Let's just say there aren't many independent telepaths anymore, and leave it at that. I didn't have to call you." And he hung up.

I stared at the phone currently giving me the dial tone. What the crap? If someone had called to complain about me to the FBI, I was going to be really pissed. I mean, I didn't have anything I could get in trouble for—assuming nobody searched my apartment with a voltage meter—but it was the principle of the thing.

I debated pulling Clark aside and starting a fistfight or worse, but with my luck it would just start more trouble. And Paulsen wasn't going to like me complaining to her about somebody else being underhanded; she'd made that more than clear. And I didn't want to lose my job for bringing it up—the FBI monitoring me made me look guilty as hell.

I wished I could believe this was just about the layoffs. I really did. But since the Guild stepped up at the end of the Tech Wars—and got really scary to do it, in public—the normals didn't trust telepaths. Paulsen had four guys a month in her office wanting me gone. And I couldn't do a damn thing about it. I wasn't Guild, not anymore, but to certain people, I was still a telepath—still tarred and feathered with the same brush.

Hell, I'd just have to ride it out. I grabbed my pack of cigarettes and the lighter and went back out to the smoking porch in the drizzly rain, while my hands shook and I promised myself it would be okay.

It wouldn't. Not if I couldn't keep this job. And Emily—well, this was just one more reason for me to find the guy who'd killed her. I owed her for it. And maybe now my job—and whatever the hell the FBI was looking into—depended on me solving this case. Depended on me proving myself. But no pressure or anything.

I looked at my watch and realized I was late—very late—to the interview rooms.

Bellury was sitting in the interview room, half sandwich in hand, while across the table from him a pretty woman held the other half and laughed. A handful of magazines were spread out over the table, another empty chair pulled up to it, a neon sign that I should have been there. Probably that was my sandwich, my lunch.

The woman looked up as I came into the room, the sandwich half in her hands, a small pad of paper and a pencil in front of her. I curved my back, my body language small and unassuming, and did my best to look apologetic.

She looked up, and all the cheer drained out of her face like I'd pulled the drain from a tub. Her scowl was specific, directed at me, and the hostility I could feel coming off her in Mindspace was tangible. It was early afternoon, my lunch hour, and apparently not late enough yet for the telepathy to leave the building.

"I've been waiting. For. Two hours," she enunciated, syllables precise and full of anger.

"Apologies for that," I responded out of rote. I was so late I hadn't even looked at the file, and I felt off my game.

The woman shifted in her chair.

Time to regain control of the room. I straightened my spine and sat down in the chair, hand on the table, legs spread as if I hadn't a care in the world. "I need to ask you a few questions and then you can be on your way."

"Did you not have the *time* in your busy day to see me *on time*?"

The words hit me like a yellow jacket sting, and only practice kept me from saying something nasty. Instead, I opened the folder and glanced through things. Crap. This was Emily's sister, a Linda something, and I'd already made a bad impression. If she shared genes with her sister—genes for Ability—it also explained why I could read her so late in the day.

"We're investigating a murder. Your sister, in fact. Do you want to sit here and argue about timing or do you want to help me catch whoever did this?" I modulated my tone at the end to try to soften it. I couldn't screw this up. I just couldn't.

She thought for a minute, furious flies stirring around her brain. "I don't like you."

"I can see that."

Bellury stood up and gave me a look. "Let me take your sandwich wrapper," he told Linda with a small calm smile. He bundled the leftovers into his cheap paper sack and crinkled it up loudly into a little ball. By the time he was done, she had been distracted. And I was down a sandwich for lunch.

Bellury settled quietly into the observer's chair at the corner of the room. "I just have a few questions for you," I told the woman across from me.

She leaned forward, and said something about her daughter and a friend's house. "The friend isn't good with supervision."

"Okay." I pushed the pad of paper to the side. They'd be recording all of this anyway, and I was having a hard time concentrating with split attention. I opened up my telepathic senses wider. And suppressed a wince as I pushed too hard; finally I could tell it was getting later in the day.

"Your name, for the record."

"Linda Powell. Since we're both married now, we have different last names."

I didn't know why she felt like she had to say something about it; it was a relatively common thing. I finally decided I hadn't met her before; I would have remembered this prissy forcefulness. The realization didn't decrease my guilt.

"Well?" she prompted.

"Where were you Monday evening between the hours of five and nine?" First question, since close relatives were often the perpetrators.

"At my daughter's ballet recital," she replied evenly.

"All four hours?"

"She had to be there early to have another parent do the buns. The recital has eighteen classes performing, including the seniors, who have a miniballet. Trust me, the thing was endless."

"Can anyone verify you were there the whole time?"

"Other than my husband?" She gave me a list of other mothers who'd been there. She looked up and to the right, usually a sign of truthfulness in right-handers. More importantly, I could feel the edge of her mind echoing the information before she gave it, along with images I didn't quite catch. She was certain. Not to say that couldn't be a false positive if she was a very good liar, telepathic signals and all; the good liars lied to themselves first. But I believed her.

"Thank you," I said. Politeness would get you everywhere, and I had a lot of ground to make up. "Do you know where your sister was during that time period?"

Sadness leaked from her. "Laney had the same recital, so I took her and she stayed over at our house. Dan was supposed to be out with friends, so Emily was planning to stay home with a bottle of wine, a bubble bath, and a season of soap operas. She deserved the break," she added pointedly. "She was a good mom."

"Did you know Dan beat her?" I let the question sit like a rotten fruit on the table.

She looked down. "I . . . I guess I suspected. Emily wouldn't . . . she wouldn't hear of talking about it. But she always had bruises. I . . . Once I went to the trouble of looking up women's shelters. I left the information in her sewing bag. But the next day her bruises were worse and she wouldn't talk to me. I thought maybe I'd done the wrong thing." She looked up. "Did he kill her?"

That was the question, wasn't it? "We're still trying to determine how and by whose hand she died," I said, a variant on the standard no-information line we gave so many witnesses and suspects. This time it felt wrong, like she deserved more information. But I didn't know the husband and the sharp man weren't the same guy, and I didn't know she wasn't talking to him. Not for sure. "Did you have any reason to think he would kill her?"

"Other than the fact that he hit her?" She let the question play out, the word "hit" like a curse word. Her mind opened up then and I read her as clearly as a large-print book. She regretted that information, regretted it badly, and part of the regret was the fact that she'd honestly rather not have known. Would rather not have known about her own sister. "No. No reason. He was stressed, that was all. Bill—my husband—didn't like him, especially not when he was near the end of a project."

I kept pressing for information. "What kind of project?"

"I don't know, something big. Dan was one of those high-stakes engineering/architect types. He'd brag he didn't hardly work for weeks—but he'd get close to the deadline and he'd work like a madman. I never understood it; that kind of stress would drive me crazy. Especially on the kind of multimillion-ROC projects he was always bragging about. But he got . . . different . . . at the end of a project. Harsh. Cruel, sometimes. I worried about Emily. She always seemed to end up with more bruises then."

"Did she work outside the home?" I asked, expecting the answer to be no since the neighbor had found her and no one at a job had reported her missing.

"Um, yes. She had the week off, though. She'd just hit her big sales quota."

"Sales quota?" I asked, starting to feel like a parrot. But when in doubt, keep them talking.

"She had a sales job for this transport company, um, I think it's called Dymani. Most of the money is commission based, so it's rough sometimes, peaks and valleys, you know. But she's good at it. Was." She looked very small then, her voice quiet. "I can't get used to this."

"You're doing just fine. What did she sell for them?"

"Contracts, mostly, to move materials. They specialized in big, hard-to-move items—you know, components for shuttles to the space station, huge panels and supports and such. It's a lot of money, when it's working. She'd just come off a real tough patch; she told me if she didn't meet her quota soon there'd be hell to pay. Dan was yelling at her about money. She thought she might lose her job. But this was months ago. Lately, everything seemed okay."

"You said the husband was under stress right now, though?"

"Well, I assumed, what with her bruises . . ."

"Just give me the information you have, Ms. Powell, and we'll put it together with other people's information to make a complete picture. Try not to assume anything, please."

She sat up, back ramrod straight. "As if I'd lie to you. Seriously, it's been over twenty-four hours. What have you people been doing to catch my sister's killer other than talking to innocent people about trivial things?" She glanced at Bellury, as if for support. Sadly, I was telepath enough to know most of the anger was for effect. Inside, she was frustrated yes, but mostly tired, and sad. I knew how she felt.

"Was your sister involved in anything . . . shall we say, in the gray area of the law?" I asked. "Did she have any enemies? Any powerful friends?"

Ms. Powell sighed and looked down at the table. After a pause, she answered slowly, "Not that I know of, but lately she wasn't really talking to me. She'd come and get Laney and kind of wave. She used to stop and talk. She used to care. But the last couple of months . . . well, it's like we were strangers."

She was so overwhelmingly sad in that moment. I tried to get more—and got a stab of pain. Flashes of light started drifting across the right side of my vision, and I rode it out.

After a second, I forced a smile, careful not to move my head. "Thank you for your help, Ms. Powell."

She stood as well, glanced at Bellury, who was settled and calm in the corner. "You sure that's all you needed? All you kept me waiting for so long?"

"I may have another few questions for you as the case develops, but most of the time we can do that over the phone or I can drive to you," I said on autopilot. "I appreciate you coming down to the station." I was gripping the pad of paper in front of me, the tactile sensation grounding.

"Catch this guy, okay? No screwups."

"We'll do our absolute best."

"Do better."

She got her umbrella from the corner of the room and left. Bellury pulled himself out of the chair and hurried after her.

I sat, and waited for the world to steady.

CHAPTER 6

"**Let's go over** what we know about the Hamiltons," Cherabino said. We were sitting in her cubicle near the end of the workday, going over the case, and I was doing my best to keep up, my attention—and the telepathy—long gone. Cherabino said something about the husband, Dan.

Michael nodded. "He works for a large architecture firm. He's disliked by his coworkers, based on our interviews, and more than one of them suspected he'd stolen money—or slacked off—or done something similarly dishonest. None had proof."

"He beat his wife," I put in pointedly. "Likely his daughter too. He was an all-around asshole."

Cherabino said something about him being missing from work. Then, "He hasn't been seen at any bank or pawnshop in the area, so, assuming there's no holds or checks on the bank accounts, he's working under limited resources."

Michael said something I didn't catch.

She responded, "I want to find this guy. I want to know why we can't find this guy."

"Maybe he went farther out than our net would cover," Michael added. "Too much outside DeKalb County or the metro counties, we have little we can do to track him. He gets outside Georgia . . ."

"And basically he disappears from our radar." Cherabino nodded.

"Hold on," I said, trying to follow all the new information. "Why are we assuming the accounts are clean? Don't we know?"

"The credit union's being difficult."

Michael added, "They've turned over the recordings of the lobby, as they're legally required to do under the loophole that lets them record in the first place. But they're not letting us touch the accounts. All they'll say is they can confirm that Daniel Hamilton and his wife, Emily, have accounts there. They're lawyering up over the Privacy Accords and we're likely to be stuck in a runaround for a while."

I thought about that for a minute. "Maybe we can ask Andrew for help," I suggested.

"Who's Andrew?"

Cherabino sat up. "Good idea. Andrew is the forensics accountant assigned to our department. At least, the only one who has time for the normal rank and file. We'll have to get approval for the time, but it's a great idea. That man seems to pull out miracles. Maybe he can get at them from taxes or something."

"Dan is still MIA," Michael put in, almost too quickly. He continued. "None of the morgues in metro Atlanta have a John Doe matching that description, same for the hospitals and publically available housing. Major hotels say they don't have a room under that name—"

"But they could be lying, be privacy advocates, or he could simply have checked in with cash and a different name. And it's not like we can call all the smaller hotels and B and Bs. Let's face it, if he really wants to disappear, he can."

"I did finally find the car," Michael said.

"The car?" I asked. I felt like I was a step behind, maybe more.

"Where was it?" Cherabino asked, perking up.

"Parked in the lot of a major discount store, in the supermall in North DeKalb," Michael said. "Four cars were reported stolen from that same lot that weekend, but that's a normal number for that mall."

"Track them down anyway," Cherabino said, and then something about finding them abandoned. "If you can find them abandoned, maybe we can trace his movements."

The two of them went off on a tangent I couldn't follow. After a few moments, I interrupted. "Shouldn't we be focusing on the crime scene we do have? I mean, for all we know he's dead and we just haven't found the body."

Cherabino sighed, and nodded. A few thoughts of hers drifted in my direction, but I couldn't catch any of them. "You still determined to leave at five?" she asked Michael out loud.

"Please," Michael said, and smiled. "The wife and I have a dinner planned."

"You want to work here, you have to put in the hours," I said, because I was exhausted and wanted to go home myself. "Cherabino told you that in the beginning. We work late here." As much as I wished we didn't.

Cherabino looked at me, and I got a flash through the Link that she was irritated at me. "I'm tired myself, and one early night isn't going to hurt anybody. We'll go over the victimology tomorrow, track down that clear cord material, and plan our next steps."

Suddenly my brain tried to throw up how I knew Emily—my guilt over keeping the secret. Worse, Cherabino turned her head all the way around as if she was trying to listen. I had to distract her.

"You're a damn rookie," I told Michael, knowing it was too much, but desperate. "You can't twist Cherabino around your little finger like you're something special."

Michael frowned, uncertain. "All I said was—"

"If you need to go home, go home, then. Rookie."

"You want some coffee?" Cherabino abruptly asked Michael.

"Um, no."

"Let me put this another way. You're getting yourself some coffee. Or some fresh air. Or you're going home. But whatever it is, you're doing it now."

He blinked at her. "Did I—"

"No."

I gritted my teeth. "Scram."

"I'll see you tomorrow, then." He picked up his jacket and walked out. Cherabino waited until he was past the secure cubicles, past the noise shield, before she turned back to me.

"What in *hell* do you think you're doing?"

"What in hell do you think I think I'm doing?" I asked, just to buy time while I tried to sort out the images coming through the Link. Why were we doing this now? I needed time, damn it! I needed to figure out what the hell was going on and to get my brain to focus.

She barreled full steam ahead. "What in hell cause do you have to speak that way to Michael?"

"He's expecting special treatment," I said, the first thing popping into my head.

"How?"

He'd taken over my chair. He'd taken over my place at Cherabino's side. He'd taken over . . . Well . . . My mind filled with all the things I couldn't say. All the angry, nasty things I couldn't even think, for fear she'd overhear me, and honestly none of them were justified anyway. I stood up. "He's an annoying cheerful bastard."

"The hell." Cherabino stood too, her body language going into a fighter's pose. "He's the nicest guy I know."

I flinched like she'd hit me.

I sat there, looking at Cherabino, beautiful, pissed-off, strong, crazy, amazing Cherabino, the woman who'd kissed me like she was drowning. I looked at her, and it was like the weight of the world, the distance to the sun, was between us.

"This isn't about Michael, is it?"

I turned. "I'll try to be nicer to him," I told the cubicle wall, and took a few steps toward it. But she was quiet, so very quiet behind me. I turned back.

"I didn't establish the Link on purpose," I said, too tired not to say it. "I didn't mean to do it. And I saved your life. Don't I get any credit for saving your life?"

"Back in the beginning, I asked for two things. Only two."

"Keep my hands and mind to myself. I know. I didn't do this on purpose."

"It doesn't matter!" she almost screamed. She looked away, but not before I could see the pain, the fear in her eyes. She hated this thing in her head; she hated it enough she'd have cut it out of her if she could, whatever damage it cost. And now she was tired, was irritated just as much as I was. That was how the Link worked. "You told me it would fade. You promised—" And her voice broke. She took a shuddery breath. "You promised it would fade." *Too close, too close,* her brain echoed, echoed. *Too close and he'll hurt me.*

I felt like a hundred tons of rock were crushing me. Broken promises. Failures. Mistakes. And the terrible, terrible certainty it would all fall apart. I had to fix this, to keep this job, to keep her. I had to. But her adrenaline was waking her up now; her fear was waking me up. I could think again. "It will fade, Cherabino. It will. It's taking longer than it should, but I promise you it will fade eventually." We hadn't slept together; it had to fade. A month, a year, two, no Link I'd ever heard of that didn't involve a physical component . . . well. It would fade. The knowledge was like a double-edged sword; it cut me on both sides.

In telepath circles a Link was a rare and precious thing, an intimacy, a source of strength and grounding like nothing else you'd ever seen. Like fire, you treated it cautiously. You didn't just play around. But on its best day, used correctly, a Link was the most beautiful thing in the world. There were telepaths who would kill for what we had. And she was treating it—and me—like garbage. "I'm not a bad guy, Cherabino. I used to be good at this. You can ask Kara. A Link isn't anything to be afraid of. I promise you. I'm not going to hurt you. I'm not going to die and leave you like Peter did. I can do this. This I can do."

"Don't talk about Peter. You don't have the right."

"It's sitting in the air between us."

She shut down like someone turning a light switch. The death of her husband had scarred her too badly; she was terrified, honestly, irrationally terrified of letting anyone—most of all me—too close. "Your shield is slipping again," I said, out of obligation, respect, and the twist of the knife of shame and failure.

And in that moment, I saw two things at the depth of certainty: she didn't trust me, she wouldn't trust me completely; I'd proven untrustworthy. That hurt—it hurt like the edge of a razor—but it was true—at least about the drug. And she was afraid.

"I'm not going to take advantage of you," I said, one more try, even though it hurt. "I've proven you can trust me not to take advantage of you, proven twice over." Hell, I'd turned her down when she literally had thrown herself at me. "Isn't that good enough? What is it going to take, Cherabino?"

She was quiet, utterly quiet. But inside she was angry

now and afraid, emotions that were now echoing in me despite my best efforts to fight them.

If it wasn't for her nephew, she thought . . .

"Your nephew?"

Her gaze focused past me. "It's time we went home." Then, like the coward she was, she left. She ran away like she'd been doing for weeks.

Her fear haunted me the rest of the night, like a smell that clung to me and wouldn't let me go, and I didn't have the control to block it out.

CHAPTER 7

I have no idea why I agreed to a second shift, but halfway through, the interviews ran out and I had to try paperwork. Paperwork, where the letters jumped and wavered, the words refusing to make sense. This time of night, the sea of desks downstairs was basically empty, the secretaries gone for the night and the night cops mostly out on the streets working. But even with the—reluctant—introduction of computer databases into the department, Paulsen and the other diehards still remembered the aftermath of the Tech Wars. Still remembered decades of history wiped out in a day, history gone because it was stored in computers. I understood why we did paperwork. I did. Hard copy first, hard copy last, and you printed in small block caps to keep it legible for the next cop to pull it out, in a hundred years or so. I got it. But this time of day, with my bone-deep weariness and my uncooperative brain, it might as well be written in Greek.

I woke up an hour later, my brain in a fog, a small pile of drool on the back of my hand. I blinked, and looked up at the clock. This was not how to keep my job, was all I could think. And Bellury wouldn't drive me home for two hours yet.

Was this how Emily had felt, locked away from her telepathy because of me? Emily had been a fighter, when I'd known her, and in the memories I'd seen of her in the house, even through the abuse she'd been a fighter. So far in the investigation we'd learned she'd been saving up money—a lot of money—at a separate bank her husband didn't know about, and applying for jobs out of state. She'd been on her way to get out of the situation, and she'd always protected her daughter. Emily was still a fighter, even in that situation. She'd been a fighter. But losing your telepathy, losing the thing that made you special, made you *you* . . . Charles had killed himself, Tamika had checked herself into a non-Guild mental treatment facility, and Emily . . . well, she'd ended up with an abuser. For a while, at least, she'd given up. Let somebody else's fists punish her for the thing she'd lost.

All of them—all three terrible fates—were my responsibility. It didn't help that to this day I didn't know what I did wrong. The damage was done, that terrible, terrible damage—an accident, and one I couldn't reverse. Maybe Swartz was right. Maybe I needed to go to Tamika, the only one left alive, and try to apologize. Try to make it right to whatever degree I could.

To get away from the guilt and fear as best I could, I walked. I wandered upstairs, through the more sedate minds of the second-shift cops in their cubicles, and went through the paperwork Cherabino had left from the case. I knew the key code to her filing cabinet; she thought it loudly and often. And something was nagging at me. Something maybe deeper than the guilt, deeper even than my increasing exhaustion.

I found the right murder book. Then the medical examiner's report for Emily, in its sterile rows of transcribed notes on the body, all she left behind. It had pictures, and text in small bits. Even shielding the rest of the page so I could only see the small bits didn't help much. I turned on a brighter light, rubbed my eyes, and tried. This was Emily. And she'd gone through worse because of me.

Old bruises, cuts, wounds, and breaks, more than some soldiers from war zones. A pin in her arm from a compound fracture years ago—that one was a picture. I puzzled out a note about having a baby, which I knew. A concussion, a few weeks old. And a small, cramped note it took me far too long to figure out—and when I did I winced. Brain scarring, scarring from years ago—it cut at something inside me, to see what I'd done have a physical effect. It had been an accident, but it had cost Emily everything, and I'd never brought myself to face her again, not even to apologize. I made myself keep trying, keep trying to puzzle it out despite my exhaustion, despite the pain from concentrating so hard, so long.

The major wound, expected, part ligature strangulation, part deep cut into her throat, evidence of that odd sharp cord we'd seen earlier. The hyoid bone was broken, consistent with strangulation, but the blood—there was so much blood, such deep damage. No evidence of cord slippage, no fresh bruise lines on the throat. No recent bruising on the hands or arms, no fresh slices or bruises to indicate defensive wounds around the time of the murder; all of her wounds seemed too old, days and weeks old. He'd beat her, but she hadn't seemed to struggle nearly as much as you'd expect during the murder itself.

I closed the folder. Emily had died Monday, I thought, slowly, closing my eyes so I could think clearer. It was Thursday now, Thursday night. How we'd gotten an autopsy on such short notice I didn't know, but Cherabino routinely worked miracles.

There had been that one line of milk and blood at the scene, one line like an arm throwing itself up. On the report, there had been a circle around her right hand. Even if I couldn't read it right now, it had to be a simple defensive wound. Why just one? Stranglings usually had crazy defensive wounds, more than you'd expect. Why hadn't she shrugged as much as that?

That thing nagging at me poked harder. An unknown drug? I'd check tomorrow, when I could read tox screens, but I had a fuzzy memory of Cherabino saying she'd been clean except for a little alcohol. No struggle . . . it made me think. Telepathy? Was I stretching?

I opened my eyes and blinked at the clock until I could read it. Nine fifty, I think. I needed to talk to Kara. Hell, I needed to talk to Kara anyway. Swartz said I should try to get my old certification back, and I could just—just—handle the phone right now.

I sat down at Cherabino's incredibly messy desk, moving piles away from where I needed, setting them down on the floor so they didn't interact with other piles. She claimed she had a method, a system, and from the few glimpses I'd gotten through the Link, I knew she thought she did.

Then I picked up the phone. Kara Chenoa, current Guild attaché to the metro Atlanta area. A lithe blond teleporter, a Guild woman to the core—and once, long ago, my fiancée. She was married now, to a guy I'd never met. A Guild guy.

I found my fingers hitting the worn buttons after all, punching in a number I hadn't realized I'd memorized. It rang and rang, and I mentally prepared a message to leave for her for the morning.

"Hello?" a tired women's voice came over the line.

"Kara?"

"Yes?"

"It's me. Um, isn't it a little late for you to be at the office?"

"Guild attaché is more than a full-time job." She sighed. "What is it now?"

I rubbed at the back of my neck. Thought. Finally went for it. "Could you meet me for breakfast?"

The line went silent. "Are you all right?"

"I just have a favor to ask, okay?"

She sighed. "What do you need?"

"Can I ask in person?" I was not nearly coherent enough to do anything right now.

"When and where?"

I named the place and set the time even earlier than my usual meeting with Swartz. "My morning interviews start really early tomorrow."

"This had better be important."

"It is."

We said our good-byes and she hung up. All our history, our engagement, our Link, her betraying me, all gone to the sound of the dial tone.

Exhausted, I stumbled over to the crash room to put my head down for just a second.

It was the first time I'd slept without my wave-cancellation machine in a long time, and of course, I dreamed.

The dream wasn't a dream; it smelled of truth before it began, truth of what could be, or would be, a vision of the future from the stupid stubborn precognition.

I was somewhere else. Somewhere dark, with heavy concrete overhead and the smell of mold and wet below. I had a needle in my hand. A needle, and my arm was encircled by a rubber tube to make the vein pop out. I felt my hands pull off the tube, set the needle down, my head lolling back as I waited.

A few breaths and the familiar rush of Satin flowed into my brain, turning the dirt and mold and polluted rain into a kaleidoscoping symphony of smells, the visual of my surroundings rippling and flowing in odd ways as it settled into my brain and said hello.

The world was bigger, and smaller, and infinitely more perfect. I looked at my dirt-caked hands, the ratty torn clothes around me, and the rain falling down through the cracks in the concrete, and they all were joy, and they all were sorrow, ice-crystal, sharp-edged sorrow and strong, furry joy like a small animal meant to be petted.

That brought me back to myself, and I looked around, fighting the drug—what was this vision trying to tell me? I was still in my apartment in reality, still here . . .

A small, dirty canvas backpack sat next to me, just out of the polluted rain falling in streams around the concrete beams. A dirty backpack and a small bedroll, stained, torn with holes from some kind of animal gnawing at it. I lived here, I realized. Or at least I lived in this kind of place, moving on from day to day. A sense of despair stuck to the bedroll and the backpack, a sense of despair like an unwelcome relative who would not leave.

A long, beat-up knife lay on the ground in front of me as I sat, back against the concrete, ready to defend my perch from all comers. I couldn't depend on the telepathy to work reliably under the influence. And there was no one else who would care if I died.

A roach skittering past my leg, heading for its own shelter; I lifted my bag out of its way with sad resignation, hands shaking, missing the clasp twice before I got it. The roach was well on its way, but the bag went in my lap and I hugged it close.

I was alone in my own head, completely alone; no Cherabino, no Link, no minds around me that I could feel; Mindspace appeared and disappeared in stages, like beautiful, perfect bubbles floating in my head.

I shifted and the top of the bag fell open, and I looked. Two syringes, and a sheet of heavy paper over wadded-up clothes and a little soap—I opened the paper, which thanked me for my service to the DeKalb County Police

Department and gave instructions on how to claim my
funds. Which were about twenty currency units; the last
metal coins rattled at the bottom of the bag.

I felt tears run down my face in a steady stream, one
after the other, like the rain around me. No one was coming. No one would care if I died. And soon, two syringes
soon, I'd have to lie or cheat or steal or worse to get the
money for more. I had no one and nothing holding me—
but I was less free than I had ever been in my life.

The tears ran as the bubbles in my head flexed through
their beautiful dance as the world fell away, and my foot
settled on top of the knife, just in case. Just in case.

I fell back into myself, devastation echoing through
my brain, staring at a ceiling in the dim light of night.

The department. The empty crash room. Alone.

I tossed and turned the rest of the night, despair riding
me like a tick the size of a boulder, sucking me dry of
hope. No one was there. No one, not even Swartz.

I was up and on the bus before dawn. There was nowhere
else to go.

CHAPTER 8

Right before the seven a.m. opening, there was a line of patrons already lined up for the Flattened Biscuit. Grungy students and overdressed yuppies rubbed shoulders with gay couples, artists, and more than a few dogs in little jackets, more primped than their owners. Midtown was an amalgamation of groups, with a bright energy and take-no-prisoners attitude that mixed in interesting ways, always fun for a telepath, even if I couldn't really read it now. I hadn't gotten enough sleep, not nearly. But I was here.

The new owner of the Biscuit was a twenty-year NA veteran, a friend of Swartz, was always happy to see us when we stopped in, and lately he'd been kind enough to start up a tab for me so I could come in without Swartz. It was one of two places outside of Decatur where I could actually take Kara and pay for her meal.

Food was always an issue for me. Since my last fall off the wagon at the department, a condition of my reemployment was that I couldn't handle money directly. I couldn't own anything (that they knew of) I could trade for drugs. But Bellury took me shopping for shoes and shirts and such, there were basic groceries delivered, and it was tolerable. Well, until I wanted to do anything on my own. Swartz kept telling me depending on other people was good for me, but lately it was starting to rub me the wrong way.

The Flattened Biscuit had a cult following; before the war it had had another name, and when a bomb had landed directly on the building it was housed in, the then owner had, in typical Midtown fashion, shaken his head, flicked out the finger, and rebuilt better than before. The boxy postwar building was three stories high, concrete, rebar, and heavy Georgia brick, with a concrete-and-insulation-layered roof that was like a dare to try again. The apartments on the top floors would feel claustrophobic, I'm sure, but the Biscuit on the bottom floor had a crazy, worn, cramped feel with medieval arrow slit windows that only added to the postwar appeal. The contrast with the smoky gray crystalline two-floor structure next door, a law firm by the looks of it, couldn't be more striking. Its single-material delicacy, a product of modern engineering and supermaterials, in contrast just seemed to be trying too hard.

Just then Kara arrived, and greeted me with a small, polite smile. She was all dolled up in a flowy pantsuit of some kind, a long powder blue trench coat keeping her warm in the morning chill. The streetlight behind her flickered.

She joined me in my place in line, now nearly in front of the door.

Next to us, a small crane on wheels had moved next to the streetlight, the crane extending up over the roof of the crystalline building next door. A man in the crane basket adjusted his hard hat and brought out a loudspeaker.

"People on the street!" he said. "We will be measuring the structural integrity of this building for approximately ten seconds. Please maintain silence during this time!"

A low rumble came from the crowd, and then, quietly, with a shrug, silence fell.

The man brought out a pipette and dropped a stream of water onto the crystalline roof, a woman at street level with a dish-shaped sound collector pointing it carefully. After a moment, the water stopped, and a tone came from the collector. "A pass," the woman said.

"Thank you!" The man projected through the loud-speaker. "We're done!"

"Two?" someone said.

"What?" I turned.

Four feet away, right inside the open restaurant door, the hostess smiled. "Table for two?"

We moved forward, quickly, into the restaurant.

The hostess was a pretty blond college student with a huge bar pierced through the skin of her forehead. I stared; it looked painful.

"Yes, please." Kara frowned at me. We'd been engaged, years ago, and for all everything had changed since—for all she'd betrayed me to the Guild after I had burned out those students—sometimes I could still see her, I could still understand her, without the need for telepathy, or words. "Could we get a table in the corner please?"

"You're in luck. There's one available." The hostess walked across the room like there was something stuck in her shoe. The shoe in question had large spikes coming out of it on several sides. Admittedly, I did not understand fashion at all; Kara's quieter flowy thing made sense, but this . . . ?

We sat, Kara setting her coat over a hook on the wall, and we ordered fresh real coffee, fancy omelets, and biscuits from the waitress. This place made the best biscuits and gravy in the city, and they could do things with cheap meal-replacement pellets you had to taste to believe. Pellet omelet? You'd better believe it. With spinach and soy feta and smoked habanero, it was exactly what I needed this morning.

"Why am I here?" Kara asked me, once the waitress had left. With us being in a concrete-reinforced corner of the room, behind a life-sized movie replica character, the low rumble of conversation around us would cover anything we said.

I took a breath. Surrounded by normal things, here, the vision didn't seem as overwhelming as it had last night, but it was a vision all the same. And my accuracy was unfortunately high, especially when it came to my personal safety. I had to believe what I'd been shown. "I need to ask for a favor," I said.

"You told me. What's the favor?" Kara was wary, and perhaps she had some right to be. As the liaison between the Guild and the Atlanta public and government, she got a lot of requests, I was sure.

"I need a certification to keep my job, and I'd like to renew my telepath certification at the Guild. I realize it's unusual, but I have the skills." This was the worst possible time, with my mind still healing, with my telepathy still on the fritz, but if last night's vision had said anything to me, it was that I no longer had the luxury of waiting. "I can pass the lower-level tests today, if you'll give me the standard three attempts. We can work out a schedule for—"

The waitress arrived with our coffee and I got quiet.

Kara stirred sugar into her coffee. "Why do you need a schedule?" she asked. Then, almost with compassion: "Are the leftover chemicals in your system messing with your reliability?"

"No!" I took a breath, and leaned forward. "No, I just had a run-in with a really horrible hot spot in Mindspace and pushed too hard." It wasn't quite a lie. Not quite. If I hadn't still been healing from the thing with Bradley, that probably wouldn't have fazed me.

"You were out of commission at the Guild inquiry too. You haven't initiated a mind-to-mind conversation in several months, according to my notes."

"I don't owe you answers. I can pass a low-level test. I just need a certification. Kara, I need this job. I need it. And politics are—"

"Politics are what they are." She nodded. Our food arrived.

I dug into the omelet to end all omelets as she thought. Finally she put her fork down. "Well. Here's the reality of my politics. Since the Bradley inquiry, the higher-ups have been asking more questions about you—a lot more questions, especially recently." She held up a hand to cut off my protest. "That doesn't mean, well, anything right now. But it means until they figure out what they want and how to deal with you—you have to realize you're an unusual situation."

I nodded. Most people who left the Guild joined another Guild somewhere else, lived quietly without using their gifts, or died quietly—some even from natural causes. The others, well, usually they'd done something overt to cause trouble. Usually.

"Until they figure out policy, they're not likely to let anything through casually. I'll have to fight for it. Which, for a lower-level certification—a Level Five, maybe—shouldn't be hard. Especially if you're willing to keep coming in and paying the fees for the test. The Guild likes money. But honestly, Adam, do you really want to show them you're not up to snuff?"

"I may not have a choice. How much money?" I asked, but my heart sank. The accountants did have some money saved up for me in an account somewhere, but I didn't know how much. And the Guild was notoriously expensive for nonmembers.

"I'll see what I can do to get you a discount if that's what you want." Kara took another bite of her "kitchen sink" omelet, more fillings even than egg.

"Thank you."

She swallowed. "Now, why did you really ask me to breakfast?"

"What?"

Kara met my eyes. "That was a phone call. Now, what's the real reason I'm here?"

I swallowed. She still knew me, apparently. After a decade or more, maybe she still knew me. The thought was both comforting and disturbing. "Can I ask you a sensitive question?"

She sat back in her chair, wary. "You can ask."

"Are there any rogue Abilities in the area? Nonstandards?"

She blinked. "There's always nonstandards here, Adam. It's the US Headquarters."

"Um, I'm wondering, well, I'm trying to figure out a murder scene. The woman was killed by strangulation— but she didn't fight back, not nearly like she should have. I'm wondering, well, I'm wondering if there's a rogue Ability that would let you sit there and let yourself be strangled. Because I can't think of anything else this could be."

"You realize normals kill each other? A lot? I assume there's special circumstances?"

I took a breath. Braced. "The murder victim is Emily Hamilton. Used to be Emily Grant, back when she worked for the Guild."

Kara put down her fork.

"Did you keep up with her?" I asked quietly. "Did you keep up with what happened to her at all?" I hoped to God she had. Otherwise she'd betrayed me for nothing.

"Emily's dead?" She looked like I'd sucker punched her. "Um, yes. I did. I did for several years. I promise you,

I tried. When Charles . . . well, a lot of us tried. But she didn't want it after a while. She just didn't . . . A few months before her baby was born she told me to stop calling. I tried to respect her wishes." She took a shaky breath. "How did it happen?"

"I don't know details yet. But a strangling . . . I think Emily would have fought back, at least enough to make defensive wounds. More than she had. I just want to know if there's anything on the Guild end that could have done this."

"She wasn't exactly a standard mind anymore, not after that. And she was married to that guy . . ."

"What happened to her? How did she end up with an abuser?"

Kara shook her head, determinedly cut the last of her omelet up into smaller pieces. "I don't know. He never seemed quite right to me, but she was determined. It was like she wanted the family thing, badly. She wanted a baby. She wanted what she called a normal life. If she couldn't have the Guild, I guess she wanted the next best thing. We offered her a job here, her and Tamika both . . ."

"But she didn't take it."

"No. She was too proud. She went out and found herself a job and got that family she wanted. She was pregnant within a year, Adam."

I didn't know what to say. Kara and I . . . well, we'd never really wanted kids. Never talked about it for more than a minute or two, laughed it off for future selves and other people. But the wistfulness in her voice now . . .

"She called me," Kara said. "A few days ago. I was in meetings all day and the message only said to call her back. I did, but I never got ahold of her."

"It's not your fault." I reached over and put my hand over hers.

A small, sad smile.

"I—just, could you keep an eye out please? We'll find whoever did this. It's just odd enough, and after Bradley . . ."

"Yeah, I get it. We're all running scared after Bradley started killing normals. I'll help however I can," Kara said. "If I haven't said so before, thank you for your help. I'm glad we caught him."

"Me too," I said, and glanced at my watch. I'd have to hurry to finish the omelet so I could get permission to put this on my tab and still catch the bus.

"Adam?"

I looked up.

"If I can get you a certification, I will. At least the chance to try."

"I appreciate it." I took another, mammoth bite of the omelet. Swartz always said I owed Kara one of my biggest apologies. Maybe, for the first time, I was starting to see why. I swallowed. "I really do."

I knocked on Paulsen's door. It was open. She held up a finger, a clear message to wait. She'd asked me to meet her first thing, despite the double shift the night before.

Paulsen's office was even messier than usual, piles of paper everywhere, colored file folders, tabs in every shade of the rainbow, notes stuck on the wall behind her with sticky tape and pins, her careful handwriting covering miles of paper all around her.

Finally Paulsen finished writing something, dropped her pen, and pushed the stack of papers aside. "Come in."

I inched in and perched uncomfortably on the guest chair—straight posture might keep me awake. I'd thought about closing the door, but no, that would make things seem a much bigger deal than they were. Paulsen had threatened my job, yes, but she'd tried hard not to make it personal.

"You feeling better?" she asked me.

I nodded. "Is the plant new? It's kinda cool."

It was a very plump, hourglass-shaped cactus with tiny quills and three peculiarly large black-and-white-striped flowers in a very ugly pot. On closer examination, the cactus skin shone faintly in the light.

Paulsen's nose wrinkled. "It's a birthday gift from Bransen."

"Happy birthday," I said. Had I known it was her birthday?

"Thanks. He says it's supposed to keep you from getting headaches. With as many headaches as this department gives me, the idea was a good one anyway. Something about a chemical it releases in the air. The hell of the thing is, though, it seems to be working. At least so far."

The air did smell faintly clean, but that could have been my imagination. "Bioengineered?"

"I assume so." She settled back in her chair. "Just for my information, what happened to make you pass out?"

"I was tired," I said. "I won't ask to be paid for last night. I only worked half the shift."

"Nothing critical came up, and according to Bellury you were in the crash room in case somebody needed you. You should have reported it, but I assume that's what you're doing here. I'm talking about Wednesday."

I shifted. Wednesday's crime scene seemed forever ago. And I'd have to be careful not to lie to her, but also not to let her know I wasn't up to par. "Well. It won't happen again."

She waited.

"It's . . . it's complicated."

"So explain it."

I finally settled on an explanation. "I made a stupid mistake. You know the frog-in-the-pot thing? Where the water gets hotter and hotter without him noticing? I thought I could take more heat than I really could."

"And you passed out." Her tone of voice was skeptical.

I took a breath. She didn't know, she couldn't know, why this situation was shameful to a telepath, even with an injury. "Long story short, I overloaded my system and it knocked me out while my brain waves reset themselves. It shouldn't have taken that long, though. Usually the reset takes no more than twenty minutes." Now that I had a little perspective, I was thinking I was lucky as hell to have gotten off as lightly as I had—I could have ended up with real damage if something else had happened. Real damage, especially with my brain already in trouble. I could have done something permanent.

Paulsen leaned on the desk. I heard her considering whether to tell me something. I realized it was early and she was familiar, but it was still heaven to hear her without straining. Without trying. Maybe I was on the mend.

"What's going on?" I asked. "You can tell me."

"The trucker you interviewed a few days ago?" Sadness came from her, and anger.

Okay, now I was wary. "What about him?"

"He was found dead this morning." She held up a hand. "It's not your fault. Morris is on the case. She was just one day too slow requisitioning the uniforms to watch the house—she's taking the death personally. But you may need to help out there, if something else happens. This is the third hijacking—but the only death. We're putting major weight behind it now."

Had I promised Tom too much to get his help? Had I . . . lied in a way that had gotten him killed? Was it my fault?

"It's not your fault," Paulsen said, heading off the thought as well as any telepath. "This might have happened with any of the interrogators. It's an unfortunate side effect of dealing with criminals, but Bransen says he's putting real weight behind this one. They'll find the killer, Morris will get the notch on her belt, and everyone will have learned something. But I did want to tell you."

"There's a requisitioning process for uniforms?"

"I'll get someone to show you. Morris is already getting instruction."

"Thank you."

Paulsen nodded, her hand on the desk. "Cherabino tells me she's borrowing you for another case."

I took a breath. "That's right. Supposedly domestic abuse, but there's something about this one bothering me. I think we've run into him before."

"If you have, you'll do the department a big favor if you catch him. Make sure you keep Bransen in the loop." Bransen was the head of the homicide department, a boss on Paulsen's level, and Cherabino's boss. When I worked with Cherabino I effectively worked for Bransen. But Paulsen was still my boss.

"It could be a lot of time out of the interview rooms," I began.

She waved a hand. "I know you need to prove yourself. You know you need to prove yourself to keep the job. Do what you need to do. Just write your reports on time this time around. And make sure Clark knows when you're gone."

"If it's all the same to you, I'd rather go through you," I said quickly.

"I'm getting tired of playing kindergarten teacher with you two."

I waited.

"Keep me in the loop. I don't want to be caught off guard if you're gone."

"Fine." I leaned forward. The thing with Tom bothered me. A lot. I'd promised him, damn it. Promised him we'd keep him safe.

"Are you okay?" Paulsen asked, an odd question from a cop. "You haven't been . . ."

"I'm fine," I said automatically. Surrounded by this many cops, I'd say it lit on fire and covered in supercancer. I wasn't, of course; my world was tilting on its axis lately, and I was gripping on with the edges of my fingernails. But I was gripping. And maybe, today, the telepathy could work. Maybe I could prove myself. Maybe I could keep this job.

Her posture straightened all at once. "Make sure you stay that way, okay? Talk to me before something major happens." She paused, like she was waiting for me to say something else. Finally, when I didn't, she said, "Close the door on your way out."

It occurred to me suddenly that I hadn't put Cherabino's cubicle back in its dubious order when I'd left it last night. Not a good move when I was trying to get back in her good graces. I checked the time—I had an hour before the big group of interviews started this morning. Maybe I could go fix this, and show I was trying.

I arrived at the cubicle, coffee peace offering in hand, but she wasn't there. The mess, however, was. So I straightened up as best I could, restoring her piles where I thought I'd left them. The casebook with Emily's autopsy was out in the center of the desk, where I'd left it, and she'd left it in the cabinet.

I put the file back, my hands running over the smooth rows of binders, a visceral representation of order. Or disorder; this was Cherabino's Unsolved Cabinet, and just this drawer was stuffed to the brim with maybe twenty-five cases. Rows of binders, of folders, small and large—new ones to the front, carefully labeled in Cherabino's messy scrawl, colored tags sticking up from cases that had gone cold or were waiting on something. I think the yellow flags were court appearances. I went back and read the labels carefully, trying to see if they sparked anything.

I recognized a lot of the names. A beheading, a stab victim, one shooting precise and tidy in a new school, one with the brains splattered in the old bathroom in the south side. That strangler in the car with the female cop. The guy trampled to death behind a horse barn.

Wait—strangler? I went back, pulling Officer Peeler's murder book out—the book had a blue flag, whatever that meant. I spread out the book's gory pictures, the crime scene in all its glory.

The woman in the car, strangled with a clear cord. A clear cord with an edge that cut into her neck, opening it like an eerie red smile. Blood splattered everywhere. Everywhere but the passenger seat—a space for the child, the child who got away, the child who wouldn't hardly talk afterward.

And at the center of the scene in the car, in the center of Mindspace, a calm, sharp mind. A mind I'd felt before. A mind I'd felt at the house a few days ago. The mind of our killer.

I shut the file drawer hard, the sound echoing, as Cherabino arrived.

"What are you doing in my files?" she asked.

"I know who Emily's killer is," I returned. "Or at least a starting place." I caught her up with what I'd found. "We never caught the hit man, remember? The guy who actually killed Peeler. It's the same mind, I'd swear it. And the cord he abandoned—that clear cord. It's just like the fragment of cord Dotty was talking about. Did we ever get analysis back on that?"

"We did," Cherabino said. "Let me see." She came over and stood too close to me, looking at the pictures spread out over her desk.

"Where's Michael?" I asked.

"System flush," she said absently. "He picked up a little lung cancer while out in the field, and the doctor says they might as well go ahead and take care of it. He should be back this afternoon. I've got a session myself next week." She looked up. "Isn't it time for your checkup again? You are a smoker."

"I know, I know." I had no intention of going to the doctor, though. At least not until the telepathy healed up; I didn't want the chance of the Guild getting any information on me I couldn't control.

Cherabino reached out and touched one of the pictures on the desk in front of her. "How sure are you it's the same mind?"

Not very, my mind echoed immediately. I think she got the edge of it. "As sure as I can be right now," I added. "You don't find killers that calm in the middle of things, you just don't. And the feel of that mind . . ." I struggled to describe a sense she'd never had and never seen, grasping at something . . . "Smell. If it was smell, he's sharp like the smell of ammonia. Distinctive. I'd know it again, I swear. And I was there at the first scene. He got interrupted and he left that cord."

"In the bottom drawer of the Unsolved files, there's a red binder. It's the one with Strangler Number Four written on it. Pull that out for me."

"Sure," I said, and did.

We waited while she went over the files. "That cord should have been a tip-off. Damn it. He's a cop killer, for crying out loud. I had flags all over the place. I don't know why I didn't catch this before."

"You mean other than the hundreds of cases that have been across your desk since?"

She fingered the blue flag on the side of the binder, and another, bent-over green flag. "I had it marked to look at

over the holiday at least. And sent out a notice. Most of the
county and the GBI knows to flag me if they find a murder
fitting the description. I would have picked it up again over
Christmas with new information." Most of the department
took a lot of time off in December, so nonessential work
was pushed to January, frequently. Cherabino worked
straight through, and used the time to catch up on out-
standing cases. Last year I had stayed too, to keep up.

She paged through and made small "hmmph" sounds.
"Ah, okay. This guy doesn't usually leave the bodies out
like this. He's much more methodical than that. You add
in the domestic violence thing and you've got my brain
going in a whole other direction. I mean, they're under
money pressure as it is. Why add the expense of a killer
for hire when you can just do it yourself?"

"Maybe he knows Emily, or something."

"You keep calling her Emily. It's not good to get too
close to the victim, you know."

I purposefully ignored that. "It's weird, I'll give you,
considering the circumstances. But it was definitely that
guy at the scene. The cop killer."

"The scene where you passed out? That one?"

"Doesn't mean I was blind to what mattered. It's him.
You want a rabbit out of the hat, this is what I have."

She blew out a line of air. "I asked for help, I'll take
the help. But I want you to understand, if this is the same
guy I've been trying to find, there's something else going
on. Something we need to find."

I felt the information about Emily almost on the tip of
my tongue, almost ready to blurt out—but something, like
a deepwater fish, darted across Cherabino's mind. I got a
picture of an intense sexual moment—and she turned
bright red. Her embarrassment covered any details.

I reached for something, anything, to cover the moment.
"What are the other cases?" I asked.

She took a breath and latched onto the change in subject like a lifeline. "There was another sighting in Stone Mountain. No cord, though. And a case that might have had something to do with it, maybe not. It's been a long few months."

"Why not a cord?"

"He doesn't usually leave them behind. The scene in the car was interrupted, remember?"

That's right, because of the kid in the car. "Wait, what did Dotty's report on the cord say?"

"She and Michael have traced the cord material to three major companies in the area—the only companies in a hundred miles that even could have produced that kind of material, especially with the black-light lettering; apparently that takes some kind of specialized industrial process or something. In any case, Michael's pretty sure he knows which—one of them uses Dymani Systems for their shipping."

"Where—" I hurriedly corrected myself. "Where our victim worked."

"You've got it. No guarantee it's a real link, by the way, but suspicious. We'll have Andrew going over their books with a fine-tooth comb. Going to have to wait a day or two—there's a priority he's working on right now."

"In the meantime, we're going to interview the other companies and Dymani Systems, maybe Emily's boss?" I asked.

Cherabino looked at me, smiled, and then winced from her headache. "That's on the agenda, yes." She gathered up the pictures. "This is a good lead. I'm glad you found it."

The moment was suddenly thick and perfect. I wanted—I wanted things I couldn't have. And I wouldn't scare her, I wouldn't push her, I wouldn't.

I pulled for the first change of subject I could think of.

Work. "Did they ever identify the body in Stone Mountain?"

A pang rang through me as she looked away.

"No. No, there was too much gone. Artificial organs, biological implants, nothing was in good enough shape to be any help. And DNA and Missing Persons didn't find any matches." She paused. "He pulled out the teeth, all of them, so nothing was left for dental. And he buried him. This guy can clean up his tracks when he wants to. Assuming it's him."

"He didn't clean up at the house."

"No." She straightened her shoulders. "No, he didn't. At the car scene, we surprised him. He didn't have an option. But here he did—he had all the time he wanted. And he left her out for us to find, staged just like that."

"And you think that's significant."

"Yeah. It has to be. He killed a cop, Adam. Officer Peeler. One of us. And that wasn't his first, or his fifth, kill. I swore to myself I'd find this guy. I swore, and then I let it get pushed aside."

"You'll find him," I said, with full assurance.

"Maybe. I'm not going to give up, I can tell you that much. You can't just kill a cop and walk away. But he's smart, he's well connected. Since we still haven't been able to find him, despite all the money trails, all the stakeouts and hard work, means he's a professional. Until he makes a mistake or I get lucky . . ."

"What if the house is a mistake?" I asked. "The messy scene. Could we find him that way?"

"I sure as hell am going to try."

The morning and most of the afternoon passed in a blur of difficult interviews, which became more difficult as the afternoon wore on and my telepathy started to have issues again. Finally I tapped out and settled down at a desk to do paperwork. At least the letters weren't swimming today; I had to really focus, but I could read them.

"Good news," Michael said. I looked up from my desk. Yes, that was really him, and he was talking to me. Directly. Without Cherabino. He looked run-down today, with a slight green tinge to his skin left over from the flush.

I thought about asking about it to be polite, and then decided I didn't really want the rundown. "Good news about what?"

He had a stack of paper files, computer printouts, and legal-pad notes in hand. A heavy stack. "The records search came up with information on the strangler you guys are looking for. A lot of it, actually. I finished it up just now."

"Cherabino told you about that?"

"Yes. She asked me to try to see where else he's struck over the last few years, see if we can find a pattern."

I cleared space on the desk and pulled a chair over. "Why aren't you telling this to Cherabino?"

"She's in court." He set down the stack of files on the desk and opened one of them. "Here, Gwinnett County. They have six hits on stranglers in the last five years, most of them just as messy as our case, one a more conventional ligature. There was also a hanging—looked like a kill rather than self-induced, but it didn't sound important." He pulled out a handwritten list with Cobb County listed at the top. "Marietta City Police said—"

"Hold up." I put my hands in the time-out position.

"What?"

"How many counties did you call?"

"All of them?"

"In Georgia?"

"In metro, why?"

I took a breath. "That's way more work than anybody would expect you to do. Holy cow, that's a lot of legwork. Did anybody give you any trouble with the data?"

"I talked to the records clerks. It was pretty straight-forward."

I sat back and looked at Michael with fresh eyes. Yeah, he was generally happy. Yeah, he'd stolen my spot next to Cherabino—but he just might be brilliant. He just might be an asset, a help. And maybe I needed to get over myself and listen to the guy.

"Is that bad?" he asked.

"No, not at all. Just unexpected. Every other cop in the place tends not to talk to me." Oops, too honest there.

"You're on the team."

"Well, yes."

"Well, there you go, then." He looked at me like I was being an idiot. Maybe I was.

"What do we have in DeKalb?" I asked, to change the subject. "I assume about the same?" DeKalb might be a bit more densely populated, but it was smaller. It had to be similar population numbers.

"Well, no. At least thirty."

"Thirty? In comparison to four?"

"According to the records. It's a trend in the South DeKalb zone, at least according to the numbers. Domestic abuse with bruises all the way up to serious brain damage and death. Sometimes in the same couple over the span of a few months. What's interesting to me is we don't have any police reports of this couple in particular. . . ."

"He beat her," I said.

"Yes. You said that. But did he strangle her?"

I flashed through a whole bunch of strong emotions I'd had foisted on me at the scene. He'd abused her in a hun-dred ways, including rape, but . . . "No," it hurt me to admit, "no strangulation. Where are you going with this line of reasoning?"

He pulled out another folder, this one in a brighter color—likely one he'd bought himself rather than a department purchase. "See, *Homicide* magazine says hired killers generally have a preferred method, something they go back to again and again. They'll get paid to make something look like an accident, say, and most will probably do it, but the next job, they'll go back to their comfort zone. So I put together a report like Cherabino said and sent it over to her federal contact to see if they have cases in other states, if somebody else is trying to catch this guy."

"Federal contact?" I asked, nervous, reminded of that phone call from the FBI. I wasn't talking about that unless someone brought it up, I told myself. And Kara was getting me a certification.

"Have you sent over a description of the crimes to the GBI?" I remembered the state profiler who'd helped us on the last case with Bradley, a woman by the name of Piccanonni. Ordered woman—she thought in rows and boxes. "Dotty said she was sending the information on the cord, but they'll have a lot of access to information we just don't on the local level. Might be worth checking in to see if they'll share."

"Is that antijurisdictional?"

"If the federal thing is okay, the state wouldn't be? Don't look at me. That would be a question for Cherabino." I took a second to skim into his head deep enough to figure out what in the heck he was talking about. Oh, sharing information bad? Huh. Paulsen always seemed pretty open to such things, but maybe she was a rebel. Wait, I'd been able to read him. Mind-deaf Michael. In the afternoon. And my head hadn't hurt, not at all. Holy crap, this was awesome! Maybe the universe was finally smiling on me. Maybe I could make this happen.

I leaned forward and started to page through the folders. His careful handwriting was everywhere—this must have taken him hours. It would have taken me days.

Fulton County had a bright green sticky note on it—
City Hall? Space Port? Then another sticker on Fayette
County, one on Paulding, Jackson . . .

"How many victims did you find?" I looked up at
Michael. "By your standards. If you're looking for the hit
man. How many do you think he's killed in the last five
years?"

"Thirty-six."

Seemed like a lot of people. "Thirty-six?"

"Well, if you consider maybe a hit a month over five
years, just the ones we've caught. If you really think he's
a killer for hire, the number's not all that unreasonable."

I whistled. Still. "The metro area has six million people. I guess it's a big enough population to support a business like that."

"There has to be a way to trace him through the money
or through the victims," Michael said. "Cherabino says
there's always a common thread."

Money. "We have to get on Andrew's list ASAP. Hired
killers need to be paid. Let me teach you how to get
through the priority system—it's called gifts. Good gifts.
Do you have a short list?"

"A short list?"

"Victims you think for certain for certain are the same
killer's handiwork. We need to have all our ducks in a
row—and the right present—if there's any chance we can
get Andrew's boss to push us higher in the priority list."

He went blank for a second. "I can make one."

"You do that. I'll have to figure out what Brown needs
these days and if we can afford it. In the meantime,
maybe we can start tracing back commonalities and give
us a head start on finding the guy." I stood up and grabbed
a beaten-up chair from the empty desk next to me. I
brought it back, setting it down on the side of the open
space. "Here, sit down, we'll go through what you've

got. When's Cherabino getting back?" I asked him, regretfully—I should know these things.

But maybe I should also have a pile of research like the one in front of me. Maybe—maybe I could find a way to live with this, if I was still on the case. If she was finally starting to talk to me. And I'd take whatever I could get that would keep me here, in this job, proving myself. The vision had to not happen, I told myself. I had to catch Emily's killer. Everything was riding on this case—but maybe, actually, it was solvable.

"She's back at three o'clock. Did I tell you about Fulton?"

I pulled out a pad of paper and a writing utensil and focused. "No, tell me about Fulton."

CHAPTER 9

I was sitting at my borrowed desk midafternoon, focusing on the paperwork hurting my brain, trying to get everything in order before I asked for Andrew's time. The interview rooms were empty at the moment and my good mood was starting to wear off, my brain circling around the case, my job on the line, the phone call from the FBI agent . . .—I told myself it was time to focus. To stop circling around the drain and get it done, to solve the case and put Emily's killer behind bars . . . and figure out who the hell hired him. Now.

Bellury knocked on the desk in front of me.

I looked up.

"There's somebody from the Guild to see you," he said disapprovingly.

Bellury didn't usually disapprove of anything. Wait, the Guild?

"Kara?" I asked. "Tall blonde, she's been here before?" Why would she be here to see me? We had just had breakfast this morning.

"No, this one's male, forties, looks like trouble." He added, "I talked to the FBI today. I told him you weren't working with the Guild. Are you making me a liar?"

"No. Seriously, no. Male, forties?" That description didn't sound like anyone I knew off the top of my head. I hadn't seen most of the Guild in years anyway. "I have no idea what's going on. Is there a conference room free?" I didn't want the conversation to be public gossip. "Did he have a badge on of any kind?"

Bellury was staring at me. "You have a couple hundred cops in this building who are barely okay with one telepath. Adding in a second is asking for trouble. You're not going to lie to me, boy, are you?"

"I told you. If it's not Kara I have no idea what's going on. I am a telepath. The Guild has jurisdiction over me, over some things, and neither you nor me nor anybody else can change that without an act of Congress. Let's go figure out what the hell is going on, okay?"

After a moment, he backed down. "Holmes is free." The smaller conference room, the nicer one.

"Thanks."

He followed me as I walked down to the official front door, to the pseudo waiting area made up of two beat-up dirty chairs and a dusty fake plant. I was upset and my mind going in circles. This could be related to the FBI call, couldn't it? To my job being on the line? Kara hadn't mentioned anything this morning, but there was a hell of a lot of coincidences going on this week.

The man stood as he felt me coming. I shielded reflexively; this guy was no slouch in the telepath department—from the feel of him, almost as strong as me. And from his looks—six foot or more, with the solid, lean muscle you didn't get from the gym—he wasn't used to relying solely on his telepathy. He'd be a dangerous one, all the way around. Why was he here?

"Edgar Stone," he said, with the significant nod the Guild used instead of handshakes. I nodded back, with the same weighted movement.

I introduced myself in turn. "Why are you here exactly, if I may ask?"

Bellury beside me was standing on the balls of his

feet, tense like a small dog faced with a larger one in his territory. Determined to defend, determined to fight if necessary, teeth bared in warning, but cautious. Not entirely sure he'd win in a fight. For that matter, neither was I. My mind was in no shape for a fight.

"I'm with Guild Enforcement. I've been assigned to look into your case."

Shit. Double shit. Enforcement was my worst nightmare—my worst. There was no innocent until proven guilty, not in Guild practice, not here. At best this guy would be neutral, neither for nor against me, and all too willing to tip the scales whichever way they went.

Stone was staring at me, trying to judge my expression. I had to say something, and quick. Silence was suspicious; I knew that as an interviewer. Normally at this point in the conversation, politeness dictated you'd say something like "Nice to meet you." The trouble is, it wasn't, and he'd probably smell the lie. So I settled on "Nice of you to come to the station." And I sat on my panic and anger, stuffed it into a box and sat down hard; there was no way in hell I was going to telegraph anything to this guy. Not to Enforcement.

"Not a problem," Stone replied gravely. A small lie in that one, hardly noticeable in the stream of expected conversation. I didn't pursue it.

Enforcement was the bogeyman under the bed for every professional telepath—judge, jury, and executioner in one. Terrifying. He could legally kill me in broad daylight in the middle of the street and the Guild would have nothing worse than a PR crisis—Koshna meant, for people like me, one word from Enforcement was all it took.

"There's a conference room open," I said, still controlling my emotions hard, shielding up to my gills. Bellury looked back and forth between us, increasingly uncomfortable, while a crowd of cops started to gather around to stare hostilely.

Stone glanced around at the cops around him, coming up on the balls of his own feet. "A conference room sounds like a good idea."

What in the hell was he doing here? There was nothing in the whole world that would spark suspicion against me faster than a Guild visit—unannounced—at my workplace. They knew the normals didn't trust them and then they go and pull a stunt like this, something that looks like conspiracy and worse.

But maybe that was the point. Maybe they were trying to get me fired.

On that fun thought, I walked him to the conference room.

Bellury wanted to sit in on the meeting—well, of course he did. He was my babysitter, and if there was ever a time for babysitting, this would be it.

It looked awfully suspicious, I got that.

"Go on," I told Stone, and stood closer to Bellury. I glanced around the open hallway, just to be sure no one was overhearing.

"You told me you weren't working for the Guild." Bellury frowned at me.

I unclenched my fists by sheer willpower. Yeah, this looked bad. And yeah, with Clark probably starting rumors and calling the FBI on me, it looked worse. That didn't mean I had to like it. "We've been through this. The Guild kicked me out. With extreme prejudice. And I'm not going back. That was a lifetime ago and honestly I don't like them very much for it. But. No matter what the movies say—no matter what Clark says—the Guild isn't on some big crusade to take over the world. Furthermore, if they were, I wouldn't help them. I'm not stealing secrets for the mother ship. I'm not reporting back on your every mood, or Paulsen's, or anyone else's. I'm exactly the guy you already know about. The one you give the drug test to every week, and the one who interviews suspects for a living. That's it. Yeah, I can read minds, but so what? I've read your mind and you're still you and your secrets are still secret. I don't know what's going on, but whatever it is doesn't change crap. In fact, they're probably doing this to stir up drama and get me fired in the first place. That would be like them."

"Fine," Bellury said. "I still have to be there. It's my job."

I took a breath, closed my hand. Tried to be reasonable. "He's a Guild heavy hitter. Enforcement doesn't have the same sense of ethics the rest of us have. It's not a good idea. Likely he'd just wipe your memory anyway."

Bellury's eyebrows came down, and a huffy betrayal emanated. "And you'd just stand back?"

I tried to figure out how to explain it without lying or admitting I was at less than full strength. While still making my loyalties absolutely clear. "If I tried to stop him, there would be a mind-fight in the middle of the department. He's certainly better trained in offensive stuff, has fewer ethical limitations, and he's way more in practice. I don't really want to go to that fight and I don't want to put the department in danger." Even at full strength I wouldn't want that fight without a lot of warning, planning, and the advantage of surprise.

The first glimmer of an idea was brewing in my brain. I knew if I'd just give it a moment . . .

The small muscles in Bellury's face were tense, every one. "I'm going to Paulsen."

"I understand." Good. I'd have backup in ten minutes, fifteen if she was in the middle of things. "You do that," I said significantly.

His eyes narrowed and he started thinking. "I think I will."

Somewhere in my gut, one small tension relaxed. Stone couldn't kill me, not today, not without a fuss going all the way back to the Guild upper echelons. Paulsen wouldn't let him.

As long as I had this job anyway.

I shut the door to the empty conference room with a *click*. Stone was standing in front of a murder board somebody hadn't bothered to clean up, the book the things belonged in sitting next to it on the table. The board was covered in cruel, disturbing pictures, what someone who called himself human had done to a child—a child who was now dead, her intestines leaking out into the blood-soaked dirt. I looked away, by now knowing other people's cases would haunt me too much if I didn't. I got enough flashes and photos in my head by accident without going looking for more, and a telepath's mind was never truly private. But Stone kept looking.

"Have they caught the guy?" he asked finally.

"It's not my case. It's not Cherabino's case either. I wouldn't know. Probably it wouldn't be on the board if they had."

I racked my brain, trying to figure out why he was here, who'd sent him. Damn it, if Kara had known about this . . . A sinking feeling hit me and I wondered if my phone call to her was what had started this whole damn thing. Why hadn't she said something?

Stone stood there for another long moment, shielded to the hilt—but I could see his hand clenched, knuckles white. "At the Guild, he would already be dead."

"I know," I said, and oddly, I felt a little less afraid, like I was suddenly dealing with another cop. A cop with a lot of power, a cop with tools and procedures the guys here would envy—or hate—but a kind of cop nonetheless.

"Let's talk." I found a seat at the table and relaxed my body language.

He sat too, looking disturbed. If the pictures distracted him, well, I hadn't planned it, but it was more than welcome.

"I'm guessing the Guild doesn't like how I handled the Bradley situation," I said. Cops usually liked it when you cut through the bullshit so they didn't have to. "That's stupid. No matter how it looked in the papers, the Guild got one of its bad apples exposed to the light—and stopped. Without any secrets being exposed, no matter how close it got. I've fulfilled my obligations, more than fulfilled my promises, and I'm not sure why anyone has a problem."

Stone blinked, surprise floating off him. "That's not exactly why I'm here."

"Why are you here?"

He was shielding so hard he was a shiny mirror in Mindspace, reflecting the surroundings. But I was an interrogator, and he didn't guard his face nearly as well. He was rethinking his approach, and probably considering whether to lie to me. It's not like I hadn't seen that face a hundred times from suspects.

He cleared his throat. "Well, you've attracted the wrong kind of attention. When the Guild kicked you out, it was assumed you would eventually die. Or at least serve as a good example of what happens when you fall from grace at the Guild."

"Thanks a lot."

"Or the thought was, if you did manage to pull yourself together, you'd come back. With the situation with Bradley, especially when he wasn't able to be revived. . . . Well, the case attracted the attention of certain high-ranking members of the Guild."

"Well, I'm not dead." Though I had no illusions: nine out of ten guys with the kind of scars on their arms I had ended up dead. From dirty needles, ODs, fights, or worse. I'd been lucky, and I knew it. But it was still awfully cynical to assume I'd die in a gutter. "And honestly, why would I come back? The Guild kicked me out, literally stripped me of all of my credentials, and told me I was an embarrassment to everyone who'd ever trained me. I'd be an idiot to go back. And I'm not an idiot, Stone."

"You're a Level Eight telepath." He leaned forward. Suddenly I felt the threat of him, in my hindbrain where the survivor-creature lived. It said, *Back up, back up slowly.*

I barreled in anyway. "I'm also a damn ethical telepath." I was now anyway. The years on the street had nothing to do with anything. "I've kept the Guild's secrets. All of them."

"You didn't keep Bradley a secret." Stone raised a hand to fend off objections. "Bradley was a low-down, stupid, destructive, crazy son of a bitch who deserved whatever came to him. But you got the normals involved to do our job for us."

"I thought this wasn't about Bradley."

"It's about you."

I paused, and when he didn't speak: "What do you want from me?"

"We want you to come back to the Guild."

I thought about it, teetering on the edge of consideration. If I lost my job here, I might not have another choice. "I'd get a teaching job again?" I probably couldn't teach the advanced courses anymore; I'd burned out an essential part of my mind, was still recovering, and hell, I was out of practice. But the basic stuff . . . Well, if the choices were that or a mind-wipe, maybe teaching wouldn't be so bad. Kara was still there, after all. There had to still be some good there.

"No," Stone said. "No. We'll find you something more suited to your position." The clear, half-projected subtext on the sentence was that neither one of us thought I was a good influence on children, now did we? I should be grateful for whatever low-status job they'd hand out.

The cynicism—and the pain—returned to my soul like a barreling train. "Yeah, how it's going to be, isn't it? I suppose you're holding my freedom—and my life—hostage until I do whatever it is you want." Like everyone else was these days, damn it. If the vision hadn't put the stamp on it, I'd walk away.

"You're not interested in returning to the Guild?"

"Is that seriously why you're here?"

He pursed his lips. "Well, no. My supervisors had hoped—"

"Your supervisors are delusional." I was being reckless, tugging at the tail of the tiger, but I now expected Paulsen at any moment.

Stone blinked. "Well, they can be sometimes, I suppose." He cleared his throat. "I'll cut to the chase. I'm supposed to determine if you're a threat to the Guild and our way of life. There aren't many independents out there, and you, unlike most of the others, have decided to make a spectacle of yourself."

"So I was supposed to let Bradley murder at will?"

"You were supposed to let the professionals handle it, or, at worst, fade quietly into the background. It's traditional, when someone leaves the Guild, for them to stay quietly in the background. You're not doing that."

Screw traditional. I was a Level Eight, and no one's plaything. "Bradley was weeks ago. Why come now?" Had they waited deliberately for me to be understrength? If so, why not earlier, when the telepathy was out completely?

"It's really not my problem when the higher-ups decide to do things."

I waited.

"If you'll consent to a tag on your mind and occasional monitoring, I'll walk away."

"No. Hell no. I've done nothing wrong, and I'm not consenting to a tag." There was no way in hell I was going to let him stick a piece of his mind to mine so he could find me anywhere and read me any time he felt like it. I wasn't a prisoner.

"It's in your best interests to cooperate with Enforcement," Stone said.

Just then Paulsen showed up, the conference room door kicking open with such force it smashed against the wall with a *bang*.

"You are not invited into my station," Paulsen said, cutting off any further conversation.

Stone didn't seem impressed. He left, but I got the impression it was more out of courtesy than any real need.

"This isn't over," he said.

"Who was that?" Paulsen asked me. "And why the hell is the Guild traipsing into police territory without even a phone call? What the hell are you up to?"

I turned, burning with anger and resentment at this whole situation—and Kara for not telling me. "The damn Guild is trying to intimidate me into going back. Or tag me like a damn animal to be checked up on whenever you want. I'm not going, and I'm not doing it. I've been straight with you—had no warning of this, I swear. But he's not going to settle. He's going to go up the chain of command and try to put the pressure on until he gets what he wants. At least that's what I think he'll do next," I said. "Given you'll notice if I end up missing or dead. That is, I assume you'll care if I turn up missing or dead."

Paulsen frowned. "You told me when you signed on that the Guild didn't care what you did anymore."

"Well, apparently they do now." I waited for her to fire

me, to tell me this was just too damn much trouble for someone already on the edge.

Bellury and Paulsen exchanged a look, and then she met my eyes. "As long as you work here, I'm not putting up with anyone coming in off the street trying to intimidate my people. But you should be aware. The Guild has a lot of power, I have only so much coin to spend on this kind of nonsense, and you're nearly on the chopping block as it is. I'm going to be watching you. And Bellury is going to be haunting practically your every step and checking up on you regularly. You will not be getting anything over on me, am I clear? If I find your loyalties have shifted, you can and will be out on the street faster than you can read the thought. Understood?"

"Yes, ma'am."

"Good." She stalked out.

I spent the next hour trying not to explain who and what Enforcement was to Bellury—and why a visit from them had made my knees shake. By the end, I still think he was convinced I wasn't telling the whole truth.

Normals didn't trust telepaths. It was a fact of life. And any credit I had ever earned in trust, day after day, was disappearing like a fleck of sand in the tide.

CHAPTER 10

The weekend passed all too quickly, as Swartz had me in meeting after meeting, service project after service project. For once, I was happy to go along and not think. With my world falling apart—and me unable to do anything about it at that moment—I needed all the distraction I could get.

Monday morning, I came out of the coffee closet with donut in hand.

"Why aren't you dressed?" Cherabino's voice came at me, stern and unforgiving.

I looked down. Yes, I had pants. A shirt. Even shoes. I turned. "What the hell are you talking about?"

She had on a plain black knee-length dress and pointy shoes. Panty hose and makeup even, makeup almost heavy enough to cover the circles under her eyes. "The funeral. The Hamilton funeral. I told you twice. We're going to be late if you don't get something decent on soon."

"We never talked about this, I swear to you." I blew out a breath. I had thought the memory lapses and the attention problems were going away, but apparently not. "How much time do I have?" Funerals supposedly were great for clues; a lot of people showed up you wouldn't ordinarily see. It would be worth going, if I could make it.

"Two minutes. Literally. If you miss that you can drive down with Michael—I need to be there for enough of the visitation I can tell if anyone sneaks out."

I sighed, trying desperately to figure out if I had clothes for a funeral. Probably Bellury would have them and let me borrow; Bellury kept a lot of clothes at the station. "There's no way I can make two minutes. If Michael can drive me, let's do that. You need to tell me these things, though."

"I've told you twice. For a damn mind reader, you sure don't pay attention."

She turned on her heel and stalked down the length of the hall, her butt moving in interesting ways with those heeled shoes on.

Stop that, I heard through the Link, *and get dressed, damn it!*

Michael waited patiently for me, even donating a tie to the cause to get me on the road faster. He borrowed an unmarked car from the pool; apparently his old black-and-white had been reassigned to somebody from his old unit and he hadn't gotten another yet. I knew this because he told me. Twice. Michael didn't like silence.

In direct contradiction to every other cop I'd ever seen, Michael drove safely, like a normal person, putting on blinkers before he changed lanes, checking all mirrors every few moments, but hitting reasonable speeds and reacting in reasonable time to the usual homicidal rush that was Atlanta traffic. He also made conversation while he drove. A lot of conversation, some of which I kept up with and some of which I let pass me by. Finally, apparently I let something go too long and the dreaded silence filled the inside of the car.

He broke it suddenly. "What's your story?"

"What?"

"Your story. Cherabino says you're the best, but you mostly seem to sulk and be rude. My wife says I should ask you what your story is."

"You're talking to your wife about me?"

"Nothing confidential. But anything else—well, there's not much we keep from each other. Like I said, I don't have many secrets."

I wondered what that would be like. Even at the Guild, there were some things I kept back. It was hard to live in a community of telepaths and keep secrets, but if you were careful and had good shields, if you paid attention to where you were and who was around, it was actually, barely, possible. You could also bury things so deep you never thought about them, never dealt with them. . . . I shied away.

"What's your story?" I asked.

"I'm a cop."

Okay. "Well, what part of the city did you patrol before you moved to Homicide?"

"West South DeKalb and the eastern part of East Atlanta."

Suddenly I looked at him with a little more respect; that was a tough area, not as tough as the gang-ridden center of Fulton County, but full of poor, desperate people. The drug trade was a big deal there; I knew because that's where I found my suppliers the last time off the wagon, before I'd climbed back on and helped to shut them down. Decatur I'd shut down years before that—the drug dealers weren't exactly excited to see me coming now, which was why I had to take the bus all the way out to Fulton County.

The radio sputtered then, and Michael answered it, exchanging numbers and location information. The dispatcher took his explanation of what he was doing—on the way to a victim funeral—with an acknowledgment and a reminder not to be too long with the borrowed car. Michael acknowledged and hung up, like he'd done this every day for years. He probably had.

"You don't want to talk about yourself much, do you?" Michael asked.

"Not really."

The late morning sun bathed the graveside in an odd brightness, and the changing leaves rustled in the breeze like they were mocking me. We found seats near the back, where we could see everyone, and suddenly it hit me: this wasn't just another victim's funeral. This was the end of Emily's funeral, the woman whose life I destroyed— and the woman whose killer we weren't much closer to catching than we were a few days ago. The woman I owed.

Her sister was there, in a smart black cocktail dress and pearls, her husband looming uncomfortably in a dark suit beside her. Beside them, two girls, one of whom would be the girl from the painting, the girl whose mother had just died and whose father was still missing. There were reasons I stood well back, and few of those reasons had anything to do with the coffin at the front. Emily's empty shell held no fear for me, not at this point; no ghosts would cling to it, and the expanse of the cemetery away from the mourners was quiet and still in Mindspace. If this had been a hospital or a hospice, on the other hand, I wouldn't be able to tolerate the lingering death for long.

I made myself focus as Michael nodded to Cherabino a few rows ahead of us. She gestured, forcefully, for us to come up there. I ignored her, and Michael looked back and forth before settling more firmly beside me. He was, in fact, deaf as a doornail in Mindspace, and in these surroundings not a problem, even as I tried to scope out the surroundings in Mindspace.

Apparently the sister's family were atheists. The man giving the ceremony at the graveside didn't have the look of any religion I could name, and the platitudes he mouthed seemed short and unsatisfying. The whole moment above the coffin seemed too short, inadequate for anyone's life, much less the life of a woman who'd battled back from losing everything—and made a life.

The trees, leaves changing, looked on as I scanned the crowd. The family, as expected, and a group of solemn-faced folks in very nice clothes who had the look of sales-people. Work friends of Emily's, maybe. A smattering of women her age, some rich-looking, some in more modest clothes, friends, maybe. And last, quietly, sitting by her-self, the elegant microbraids falling around her down-looking face, Tamika.

Tamika—the woman I'd destroyed when I'd destroyed Emily and Charles. The only one still alive. In the back of my head, I heard Swartz's voice tell me now would be a good time to approach her and apologize. The guilt twisted and I ignored that voice.

And last, across the row, were two women I knew. One was Kara, and if she'd known about Stone and hadn't warned me, there would be hell to pay. And the other . . .

Jamie Skelton, my old mentor at the Guild. My old teacher, and one of the strongest—and most controlled—telepaths in the world. Back in my time she'd been head of the research division for a while before becoming much more involved in the advanced school. She'd come to visit me, once, the first time I did rehab. She was the only one from the Guild who'd ever bothered. If I hadn't been so distracted today, I would have known her immediately; despite her control, that strength made a hell of an effect in Mindspace.

The interment ceremony was over quickly, as the man in charge threw a ceremonial clod of dirt on the coffin and said his last platitude. People began to get up, to file past the coffin or talk or whatever their temperaments called for. At the first moment I felt I could, I made a bee-line for Jamie, to try to say hi—only to come up short. A tall redhead dressed to the nines barred my way. "Are you with the police?" she asked me, grabbing my arm with no regard to her mental health.

Even through the fabric of the long sleeves, I was thrown into her mind. A whirling maelstrom of conniving intelligence, she was plotting desperately how to keep the police from suspecting her. From knowing Emily had reported her for sexual harassment of an intern—and nearly cost her her job.

Michael literally stepped between us, and the contact was broken—just in time. I stepped back, panting and scared; I hadn't been expecting that kind of contact. If she'd been skin to skin, bad things would have happened. As it was, as I panted and pulled myself together through sheer nerve and training, I thought, There was a reason for the damn Guild patches. So people didn't do that. So I didn't end up crazy—or killing her by accident.

"I'm Officer Hwang." Michael flashed his badge. "What can I help you with?"

"She was murdered, right? They say she was murdered."

"That's right, ma'am. We're in the process of investigating what happened. May I ask how you knew the victim?"

The redhead pulled herself up to her full height, a few inches shorter than Michael, the tight bun she had pulling her face taut. "I'm Theodora Wilcox, Emily's direct superior. You know her husband was a horse's ass. I wouldn't be surprised if he beat her to death."

I was starting to regain my center, and couldn't help jumping on the statement, my interrogator's instincts firing. "You seem awfully intent on driving our attention away from you. Is there a reason?"

"That's . . . Well, that's ridiculous. Emily and I were close as sisters. Why, just last week I gave her an extraordinary bonus for contracts sold. There would be no reason I'd . . . Why, that's ridiculous. Frankly, I'm insulted you'd even suggest such a thing."

"We know about the sexual harassment complaint," I said, pushing. "With an intern, no less. That could cost you everything. To have one of your own people report it and get the intern to speak out, why, that had to hurt. She'd gone behind your back. People just don't do that to people."

I almost had it—I almost had it; I saw the angry justifications welling up behind her eyes. But Cherabino chose that moment to come over, reacting to my focus in Mindspace.

"What's going on?" she asked. And Ms. Wilcox, Emily's "direct superior," clammed up. I saw the truth waft away on the wind.

"Your timing stinks," I told her tightly. And Ms. Wilcox found another person to talk to. Worse, Jamie and Kara had already left. So I told Cherabino exactly how much I appreciated her interrupting an interrogation.

Which was why I was walking back to the car, guilt, frustration, and anger, mine and Cherabino's both, stirring up in my mind.

"What are you doing here?" Tamika asked. She stood stiff, a purse held out in front of her like a shield. As I'd feared, her mind was like a sodden knot, twisted on itself and unbreakable, too collapsed to allow her to interact with Mindspace at all. Too twisted to let Mindspace interact with her either; nothing I could do could touch that mind.

She was right, maybe. I was quick to justify my presence. "I'm part of the team investigating Emily's murder."

Something flashed over Tamika's face then, something like scorn—and then it disappeared in the face of surprise. "Isn't that the Guild's job now?"

"She's still being classified as a normal for these purposes. She paid taxes to the county. Now the county is doing its job by her."

"Probably just as well," Tamika said. "Guild doesn't care anymore what happens to the rest of us."

Swartz's admonishments echoed in my head, and I squirmed under them. I didn't want to apologize. I didn't. "Kara says you're working for the Guild now. You still in the research department?" For a while there, she'd been working for my friend Dane, before he died. He'd said she was good at the technology part of Structure. I could see that would be a worthwhile job even without the Ability.

"No," her voice spat, like a bullet burst. A wavery breath, then she met my eyes like she was daring me to make something of it. "No, they kicked me out of Research about a year ago. Kara shoehorned me into a job with the courier logistics department."

I didn't know what to say. "It's good they're giving you a job."

"I hate courier. It's a glorified postal service. But the Guild says they won't release my employment records, and I don't have any *other* skills," she said, bitter.

I made an apologetic sound, the most I could get myself to do.

"I got your letter, from rehab," Tamika said. "You

sounded like your life was over. And now here you are, working for the police."

"I'm just an interrogator."

"It doesn't matter."

We stood there a long moment, under the shade of the huge, spotted oak tree, a small pollution-monitoring vine trailing up its side, in the process of turning red. The soil apparently was toxic in this cemetery—hopefully most of it was the embalming fluid.

"I think you should go now. I think you should leave."

So I left, huddling in the back of the police car, until Michael came to find me.

Oddly, on the way back Michael let the silence sit in the car while I stewed. He turned on some quiet pop music.

"You asked me what my story was," I finally said, half-way back to the station, at least ten minutes later. Mostly because he hadn't asked again. Cherabino's anger was still poking at me. And the guilt over Tamika. The guilt, like burning coals.

"That's right."

I took a breath. "Well. I'm an ex-addict. I got hooked on a drug that should have been a short-term deal. The Guild was doing a study. But I couldn't—I wouldn't—let it go. And I made a mistake. A big, expensive, horrible mistake, as a result. The Guild finally kicked me out for it, and it took me two years to get gone enough to find real life again."

I let that sit for a long moment, but Michael said nothing. "About the time I was looking for it, Cherabino shows up in the bad part of town, not far from where I was squatting, looking for a dealer who she was pretty sure had killed a college girl. Harry did kill her, of course; he'd killed more than one person who'd gotten in his way in the past, and I knew enough to keep my mouth shut and my head low and let it go by. He was bad news, was Harry. But he *was* the streets in that area. You dealt with him or you didn't deal."

I felt the words slide out of me like they were coated in butter, and I didn't feel like stopping them. "Anyway, Cherabino wanted some help and I needed somebody to vouch for me at the sliding scale rehab place before they'd let me in. I ended up helping—and saving her life about twice—and she got me into the rehab center I wanted. She also got Harry, cold, and took out most of the organization involved in the sales. What got me, though, was she looked me up six months later, just to say hello. Like she cared or something. She offered me a job, if I could keep my nose clean, and it took me another round of rehab and a lot of Swartz, my NA sponsor, knocking my head against reality, but I did. When I showed up at the station, I was shaking in my boots, but she met me at the door with that matter-of-fact thing she has, and that was that. That was more than five years ago. Now it turns out the same things that made me a good telepath make me a good interrogator too, a damn good interrogator, and Cherabino, well . . ."

Michael's brow creased as he negotiated an odd vertical merge in the only skylane over a curvy road. "You like her, don't you? More than just the job?"

I was silent. Apparently I'd given away more than I intended, but I couldn't take it back now. "She's afraid of me right now. Of the telepathy."

"I'm sorry." Michael made another turn; we were getting close to the station. I could feel a decision crystallize in his head. "I don't know anything about telepathy, but I've been married awhile now and I know something about women. Let me give you some free advice."

"Okay." Did I really just say okay?

He glanced over at me. "All the words in the world don't matter as much as what you do. You show up and you don't mess it up, and if you do that often enough, it matters. Your actions show what you really mean."

I nodded, a kind of numb sadness hitting me. He was kinda right; I hadn't been acting like I'd acted before. Letting her go, letting her avoid me, on reflection, well, it was cowardly. Worse, it wasn't working. She'd dealt with the telepathy before, but I'd saved her life and gotten cases closed, and it had worked.

"I'll add one more thing, and then I'll leave it alone. I'm the new guy, I get that. I don't expect the clouds to open up and friendliness shine down. But the hostility, well, I don't think it's helping your case with the girl. It's not an observation about anything except Cherabino."

I sighed. "I'll try to lighten up."

"I'd appreciate it."

Cherabino showed up at my borrowed desk downstairs with food. Two large cardboard containers of delicious-smelling Mexican food. Through the Link, I could feel her determination—and small, quiet fear. It was the best, the simplest, the most understandable thing I'd felt all day.

"Break room?" she asked.

"Sure."

She didn't like Mexican food, my all-time favorite kind of meal. For her to bring it to me was a big deal, especially with what had happened at the funeral. "What's going on?" I asked. It was too early for dinner, and too late for lunch. But I hadn't eaten and neither had she.

Cherabino led the way, and settled down, handing out napkins and silverware with studied concentration.

"I thought you were pissed," I said.

She blew out a breath. "We'll get Emily's boss back in

the station if we can; if not, we'll go there. You were out of line to yell at me, but I was out of line to interrupt you in the middle of your thing. You're good at the interrogations, and if you say you were getting somewhere—"

"Apology accepted."

She shot me a look, and annoyance leaked out over the Link. That's right, when she was apologizing, she wanted to apologize.

I pulled out my heaping pile of tofu enchiladas and chimichangas—the latter with real meat, it looked like—and waited for Cherabino to cut up her plain cheese quesadillas. I might have eaten several heaping forkfuls while I waited.

"I have to work a double for Electronics Crimes tonight," she said, like an excuse. "I need the calories. And if I was ordering anyway . . ."

"You said you weren't helping them out anymore," I said, taking the bait. I'd talk about air; hell, I'd talk about shoes if it would make her more comfortable.

She finished chewing with a determined look. Then: "Manuel quit. It's just for a month or so while they hire somebody to replace him."

I nodded companionably, like I actually believed her. "And your close rate's still higher than most of Homicide, am I right? Just how many hours did you work last week, anyway?"

She swallowed. "None of your business."

Ah, eighty-plus, then. Some things didn't change. I took another bite of the chimichanga, deciding it was a really, really well-seasoned faux beef. Delicious, though, with just enough jalapeno to be interesting. Yum.

"People deserve justice," Cherabino said, still avoiding the subject she'd come for. "There's widows and families out there who deserve answers. People left behind."

Like she'd been left behind, once. She shied away from the thought of her dead husband, as she always did; it was too painful. But I'd seen the grave site now. I knew what it was she wouldn't think about.

"What did you come here to ask me?" I prompted. I could steal it from her mind—assuming the Link and my rusty telepathy would let me—but she had made a big deal of politeness and I was trying to do the same.

She took a breath, put her fork down. "I hate this Link. I hate it. But you're right, you didn't mean to do it, and it's going to fade." Determination punctuated her words. "It will fade. And it's . . . there's some things I . . ."

"Yes?"

"I need your help, okay? Not just the case stuff. I'm trying to apologize, okay? For being unreasonable about the Link thing. I'm trying."

"I know." I gently rebuilt the shields on my side. I don't think she realized the panic that was coming through them. But if she was going to sit here and talk, and try, well, I'd be an idiot not to listen. Maybe this would help. Maybe my screwup could be patched over; I'd stuck in there, hoping, praying, for weeks, for just this moment. "Look, this Link doesn't have to be a bad thing. It—"

"No," she said. "No," and rebuilt the brick wall that sat between us. "No. It will fade."

I sighed, disappointment cutting at me like a dull blade. If this was anyone but Cherabino, well, this wouldn't be going on like it was. "What is it you want my help about?"

"You're . . ." She paused, looked down. "Well. Um."

I let her have her space to think. Finally she spoke.

"Okay. My nephew, my sister's child, he's—he's amazing, okay? Smart, and thoughtful, and a great kid. But he's sick a lot of the time, and lately he's been starting to show signs."

"Signs of what?"

"Well, my sister says sometimes he knows when she's sad even when she's hiding it."

I waited. Since I'd offended her grandmother weeks ago, I was surprised she was even talking to me about this. I'd be careful. I'd be helpful. I had to.

"And he seems to know what I'm thinking. He asked me about a case the other day, one I know I didn't even talk to Nicole about. I told him the age-appropriate parts, but the questions he asked—it was like he was filling in holes in information he already had." She frowned, looking disturbed. "But the next day I went in with the brick thing you showed me and it didn't seem to happen. He kept asking me what I was feeling, though. Too much."

My heart sped up just a little, and I reined in the emotion. "How old is he?"

"Nine and a half."

I nodded. That was about right for the brain to have developed enough for the Ability to be consistent. I said, cautiously, "I take it there's a history of telepathy in your family."

"No." Her voice rang out like a shot. "No. Nothing like that. But Jacob, well, he's a special kid. Nicole called me today."

I sat there for a moment, waiting. "You know the Guild tests in the fourth grade. In the spring, usually."

"I know. Trust me, I know." She looked down at her food, which was getting cold. "I need you to help me decide what to do. Nicole says she'll listen to me. She says I know way more about this than she does." She had to swallow. It was like the weight of the world, of someone she loved, was sitting squarely on her, and I hurt to see it. This was *Cherabino*, for all our differences. This was the woman who'd given me a chance, and a new life. I'd do anything for her. Anything.

"You want me to tell you whether to let him join the Guild or not."

"Yes. You were there, but you left. You've seen both sides. With the Bradley thing . . . Well, I don't quite trust them."

There was good reason for that; I didn't trust them either. But to go it on your own—it was tough. And worse for a kid. "Getting him training will be important. Either way. If he's weak enough, you can hire yourself a Guild tutor, somebody low-level who's really there for him, to make him more comfortable and train him in ethics. That's probably the way to go, if his numbers are low. You'd still have him in the family. He wouldn't have to join the Guild. The cost—well, the cost will be worth it. If his numbers are low, the Guild will largely leave him alone."

She looked up. "If his numbers are low?"

Okay. I took a breath. "I can't tell you his rating without meeting him."

"You need to meet him?" She was thinking of the debacle with her grandmother. "Is that really necessary?"

"I'm afraid so."

She took a moment, absorbed that. Then asked, "What if his numbers are high?"

Guild membership—and full-time training at a Guild center—was mandatory at a certain strength. "Let's not borrow trouble," I said. "Statistically, with no family history of telepathy, he'll be relatively weak on the scale and be able to live whatever life he chooses."

"Statistically?"

"I'll need to meet him."

"I'll see what I can set up." Her tone was frustrated, but her body language—and the dribs and drabs of emotion flowing through the blocked Link—was over-whelmingly relieved. We ate in companionable silence for the rest of the meal and she even stole food off my plate. Even better, I settled down on the edges of her mind, for calm and for the joy of it, and she let me.

CHAPTER 11

Tuesday morning I was wakened from a sound sleep by my phone ringing, a high, shrill sound that pierced my brain like a needle.

"Hello?"

Paulsen's voice echoed out over the line. "Remember Morris? You interviewed a trucker for her last week? The trucker who was killed?"

"Mmph?" I said eloquently, sleep catching in my throat.

"Well, she's got a scene she wants help on, and I don't have anybody else to send. Forensics is going to be another hour or more. I want you to take a look—Bellury will pick you up in a few minutes."

I sat up, bleary-eyed. "Ma'am?" I wanted to protest that this wasn't my job—but if she was wanting me to work, I needed to work. Whatever I could do to keep this job I'd do. Anything to keep that vision from coming true. "Where am I going?"

She told me. "Don't keep Morris waiting."

Even in the thin dawn light I saw the skid mark long before I saw the truck. Then came the tire pieces, shredded like they'd hit the ground hard, from a significant height. Then, finally, long pieces of warped steel, which told me the impact had shredded more than the tires. I saw the glass on the road, blocked off by traffic cones, about the time we rounded the corner to see our destination. The other traffic on the road had slowed down to look, and getting there was surprisingly difficult.

Unfortunately, the stop-and-go cars gave me a lot of time to observe, and to feel Bellury's frustration. He'd agreed to drive me this morning after a significant bribe.

It was a wreck of epic proportions. The huge anti-grav tractor-trailer lay on its side like a beached whale, its torpid body blocking two lanes of the ground-level Interstate 285. The round silver cones of the huge anti-gravity engines, what should have been the bottom of the truck, were instead facing us—and pieces of them sat on the interstate like cast stones. Worse, an ambulance sat on the opposite side of the wreck, and I could see small figures floating a stretcher—without any great hurry—into the back of it. When the ambulance crew was standing around talking, there clearly wasn't anything anybody could do for the poor souls actually involved in the accident.

Bellury maneuvered past the other cars, then hit the anti-grav to coast carefully around the cones and the wreck, before coming to a rest on the other side of the truck next to the other police cars.

Detective Morris, the blond Valkyrie I'd met in the interview rooms with the other trucker, stood with her arms crossed, hair blowing in the light wind while fury came from her in long waves in Mindspace, waves I could feel from ten feet away.

Bellury and I sat in the car, until he said, "Aren't you getting out?"

"Aren't you?"

"I'm the babysitter, not the detective."

"Technically, I'm not a detective either." I braced myself, and opened the car door. Bellury settled down with a crossword puzzle.

Outside, Morris scowled at me. "You're my backup? Really?"

I straightened and gave my best impression of a competent cop. Cherabino—or any of the other cops—would ignore the dig, so that's what I did, even if it stung. I needed this job, I told myself. "What's the situation?" I asked. I had no idea why Paulsen had sent me and only me—but Paulsen, like God, moved in mysterious ways and, through luck of lucks, had sent me out first thing in the morning when my brain was at its best.

Morris huffed at me.

Screw it. "I'm what you got. You going to talk to me or not?"

"Fine. From witness reports—the one, count them, one witness we've managed to locate, a vagrant trying to hitchhike to Alabama—from his report, which I might add he'd only give in exchange for food and a pack of cigarettes, a white van of indeterminate make and model, no license plate, pulled up with a flasher that looked like police lights and signaled for the truck to pull over. The truck apparently wasn't having any, and two men in masks came out of the van on illegal disc floaters and pursued. There was a dramatic chase, one I'm sure he'd be happy to describe to you in detail. Anyway, the chase ended when the truck miscalculated over an overpass and his anti-gravity engines slipped and stalled in third gear too close to a mass. Momentum sent the truck over the side"—she pointed back three hundred feet or so to the overpass—"and we have what's in front of me. Driver hit his head on impact and started to bleed out. The assailants landed as soon as the truck came to a stop, and the witness heard a gunshot and crawled into a small recess underneath the overpass to hide. Truck was directly under the lights."

"Who was shot?" I asked, still digesting details.

"The driver, evidently; he's dead, solid in the chest. But there's a shotgun rack in the truck, and blood on the ground not too far outside what's left of the cab. He winged somebody good on the way out of the world, at least there's that."

"Shotgun?"

"Gone, along with most of the cargo."

"There's some left? Can I see it?"

"What the hell?" Morris said. "Forensics won't be here for a while. As long as you don't contaminate the scene, I don't see the harm."

"Thanks for the vote of confidence."

"You're an interviewer, not a scene guy. No offense."

"I'm a little of both, but that's fine." It wasn't, but she was mad already, and I didn't see any point in poking at the pit bull. "This is a departure for these guys, isn't it?"

"Assuming it's the same crew. There's a lot of white vans in the world."

"Driving around without plates?"

"Well, would you go to a major crime with plates on your van? It seems awfully basic to take the things off and hope nobody notices."

"Personally, I wouldn't want the cop attention from not having them," I said. "Same reason as keeping to the speed limit. If you want to get the cargo home, you don't attract attention."

"Hell, maybe they stop at the first service station they see and switch them out."

"We could stop at all the service stations and ask if anyone saw anything."

"That would take an army of uniforms, and probably find nothing."

"Just trying to help."

She breathed out, her frustration building. "They've never killed anyone before this week. Now it's not just the guy who talked, it's the driver. Two shots to the chest, and illegal disc floaters besides. They're getting more equipment. They're getting more committed. They're getting more dangerous."

"They're escalating. Or they're after something specific. Or both." The statement sat in the air for a long moment. "Can you show me the cargo?"

"Yeah, whatever." She stomped back to the rounded rear end of the sideways-lying truck, the flat tailgate sticking off to the right. Both corners currently on the ground were worn away by friction with the Sigmacrete-floored interstate in this section, deep grooves in the white material to the right holding pieces of the metal. You could see the floor of the interstate a good halfway up the body of the truck.

She was right, though: most of the flat cardboard and wooden boxes and crates were gone; a few were burst open, strewn about the floor. One was stuck to the upper right-hand corner, what was the ceiling now but had once been the floor, some kind of clear tubing falling out of it.

"What was the cargo?" I asked.

Morris huffed again, frustrated. She was wondering about my competency and regretting the lack of other backup—and partner—intensely. This was her newbie initiation, wasn't it? To be stuck with a stupid telepath instead of a proper backup team. And so on in that vein.

A few years ago, when I'd first started working with the cops, I would have interrupted her. I would have politely said I can hear you, and please don't slander me where I can hear you; it's uncomfortable for both of us. It was the polite thing to do in a society where telepaths were regular occurrences. In a group of cops, though, that kind of talk made you enemies. A lot of enemies; I was still feeling the fallout from those conversations.

I wanted a cigarette, desperately. But I had to prove myself every chance I got. I had to keep this job.

"What was the cargo?" I repeated.

"Manifest says more electrical parts. I haven't gone through everything. I don't have the manpower."

I stepped into the back of the truck carefully, keeping my feet mostly on the Sigmacrete where I could to avoid contaminating anything in the truck itself. But I had to step onto what had been the side of the truck, the semi-rounded, now torn-up side of the truck now acting as the floor. The truck shifted with my weight with a screeching sound, and I braced. Nothing changed.

"Don't touch anything!" Morris yelled at me. But I was already inside, most of the way down, and her voice echoed off me and the walls like an empty mountain.

I dared to take another step, and another, the light getting progressively less strong down here. It felt . . . strange . . . here, like being inside the belly of the whale. The floor shifted again, and my hands went out instinctually, one to the wall. Crap. I'd have to give handprints again to avoid a false positive.

I took a breath and, carefully, opened myself up to the Mindspace around me. I couldn't go all the way under, or, well, I wouldn't go all the way under, not without an anchor to help me find my way out. Morris wasn't an option, and Bellury . . . well, Bellury was comfortably ensconced in the police car with a crossword puzzle. I wouldn't be getting any help from him.

I looked ahead, a strange, almost double vision in front of me as the back of my head dealt with the physicality of Mindspace laid upon the real world. The left side of the back wall was a vertical window cracked open, blood spatter coating the pieces left in the frame, sunlight seeping through from the door above. The inside of the cab I could see was also covered in spurts of blood, now drying, and a forgotten jacket, well worn, hung on the passenger-side seat. Death was hole in the room, a deep black hole centered on the driver's side.

And directly in front of me, a pile of broken boards, left over from a large crate maybe, and what looked like another broken crate, hip-high. I looked back, slowly; a truck this size had to have had dozens of the crates in it, from the pattern on the right wall for tie-downs, some pieces bigger than these, most a lot smaller. How in the world had they managed to transport so much in a single white van?

"Hurry up," Morris yelled at me. "I'm getting cold in this wind."

"Do my best."

Something odd then—from the boards behind me. Like a blip, almost. There and gone.

I turned. Nothing. If it had been anything but first thing in the morning, when I was sure my telepathy was stable, I would have doubted myself. But here, now—there was something going on.

"Yell at me again!"

"Stupid damn consultant wants me to yell at him," I barely heard. Then, much louder, "How's this?"

The blip again, harder, this time—

My own frustration, in a rainbow-pressed kaleidoscope burn through Mindspace, like a pulse from a quasar, like the signal light on a hill, on and then off again. A pulse of energy, twisted, sudden, then gone.

What the hell?

This time I projected on purpose—curiosity. Strong picture of where I was.

A pulse again, the same twisted kaleidoscope pulse. A reflection, a ping back.

I was moving the boards like a madman, uncovering the box underneath. It was small, half the size of the crate. My fingernails broke on the hard wood of the lid, but I kept going, heedless of the pain. Finally I forced it open.

"What the hell?" came from behind me, then fast footsteps.

Didn't matter. I sent a picture again—and there it was, like a shining pulse of light, there, then gone. The light all in Mindspace. It was pretty, but it was pretty like the skin of a cobra; you stared at it too long and you died.

As the lid came off, warm steam lifted into the cold truck. I tore off three layers of air-filled protective packaging in a rush. Picked up the contents, at least the top package, a hard board covered in softer wrapping, and unpeeled.

I had to take it into the light to understand what I was seeing. There, in the sunbeam from the cab, was a network of leads, small flexible medical-type tubes in a nest, and in the center, connected to all the leads, a thin round piece the size of my hand, thin blue veins covering its surface, deeper splotches of green within, sickly green like bile or infant feces. The things looked like one of the neuron cells you saw under a microscope, the main body fat and translucent, the long tube connections like dendrites coming out on all ends. It reacted to the air by pulling in, its tubular extensions shrinking quickly away from the leads and starting to shake. The hard board I was holding had been my body temperature but was now cooling quickly.

"What the hell is that?" Morris's voice came from behind me; I'd felt her approach and shielded partially already. She was quiet, curious now.

"I'm not an expert. Hell, I'm not supposed to get within a hundred feet of these, but I think it's a biological."

Behind me, she opened her mouth to ask—

But I'd already read the question. "It's Tech. Real Tech. The stuff no one's had the guts to make since the wars. The stuff that, networked together with synthetics and other biologicals, used to run the world. The stuff that made the computer viruses go blood-borne."

I wrapped up the thing hurriedly and put it back in the box, the lid back on top of it all. Part of me wanted to get out a blowtorch and burn the whole thing, burn it with fire so hot the residue would steam an hour later.

Part of me was suddenly very afraid.

But Morris took the lid back off, pulled stuff away. Opened the next. And the next. Like a fool, pulled apart the broken crate, pulled until every piece was flat on the wall of the trailer.

"A heater," she said. "A heater and two more. High-end electronic components. Glucose and minerals and a hell of a lot of stuff I have no idea what it is, labeled in packages I'll bet anything are for keeping these damn things alive."

She looked up at me. "How do you know what this is?"

I took a step back. "It fluoresces. It pinged back in Mindspace. Like two things do in the whole world. Two. They teach us what to look for, to know what you're looking at—to know when to run."

Morris shook her head, hair shifting. "They teach you how to recognize biological illegal Tech. Why would the Guild teach you to recognize *illegal biological Tech*?"

I swallowed, took another step back. "For the same reason they taught us to avoid sharks, snipers, and a hell of a lot of other dangers. There are stories . . ."

"Stories of what?" She stood up. "Of the Guild doing bad, bad things? Of the normals coming after you with pitchforks?"

"No. Stories of men going into a data center, good tele-paths, and leaving in body bags. Screaming. These little babies will shred a telepath's mind like a forest of razor blades. The fields don't play well with mental fields, not in aggregate, but worse . . . Worse, they do exactly what this one does, echoing back strong thoughts, twisting them—twisting them and echoing them and amplify-ing them until your own thoughts pull your mind apart."

I swallowed. "Would you mind very much if I killed them?"

Her eyes flashed. "It's evidence. You don't destroy evi-dence, no matter what it is. Not until the trial is over. And especially not if some of this will finally get the Guild to answer to the law."

So she was one of those, was she? The anti-Guild radi-cals, who thought the Guild should answer to the normals. As scary as the Guild could be, as much as Enforcement scared me like the monster under the bed, all of that existed because of people like her. The people who hated and feared telepaths, who wanted to control and mitigate them. I hadn't realized Morris was one of them.

She dusted off her hands. "Now get out of the crime scene before you ruin whatever evidence we might actu-ally have left."

I opened my mouth to protest that she'd done worse than me—then closed it at the anger still in her mind.

"We need to call the feds," I said. "The Tech Control Organization."

As we waited for the local TCO officer to show, I watched the Sigmacrete heal itself. The nanoid cells moved too slowly for the eye to pick up, but you looked away for a moment and came back, and a piece of the interstate's long skid damage had filled in. A tiny piece, sure, less than the width of a thumbnail, but over time, the deep grooves were getting narrower and narrower, less and less deep. It was fun to watch, or try to.

Occasionally, transportation officials came on the news and told us the nanoids' cells had reached their projected life span, and nobody could make more without forbidden Tech and a great deal of micromanufacturing power besides. They kept warning that the interstates would dry up one day soon, and start blowing away like sand on the wind. But thus far the nanoids seemed as stable as they'd been for more than a century.

Besides, worse come to worst, we'd repave the interstate with concrete or asphalt like a normal road and go back to regular maintenance. The Transportation guys were making too much out of nothing, or so Swartz said. I was inclined to agree, but the newspeople had to fill airtime, I supposed.

Finally a nondescript black aircar settled down on the Sigmacrete on the other side of where the ambulance had been, before they'd pulled away, and a guy in a black conservative suit came out. I stood up from my perch leaning against the car and walked over to stand next to Morris.

As the TCO officer got close, he put his hand over the back of his left wrist and frowned.

"You're not wearing a patch," he told me, frowning at me hard like I'd broken some sacred rule.

How in the heck did he know I was a telepath to begin with? "I'm not Guild. They don't have a police telepath patch." Probably for the simple reason that I was the only one.

"Well, I'd suggest you make one," the guy told me. Then he stuck out a hand to Morris, who shook it.

"Detective Morris," she introduced herself. "And you are?"

"Agent Ruffins. The rest of my guys will be here in a

moment." He turned back to me, his hand returning to his left wrist, scratching. "I'm afraid I'm going to have to ask you to leave the scene. You're too strong—even the lower-level guys might pick up the electromagnetic bleed-over, and we need our senses sharp."

"I'm sorry, what?" I moved a little closer.

"Stay there." He pulled his left sleeve up. "You're setting off my tattoo." Under red scratch marks, there was a long tattoo, like the top half of a bracelet with multicolored stripes. "It vibrates when it's around EM frequencies higher than the standard background level. And you're setting it off. I'm going to have to ask you to leave." He scratched it again, harder, and pulled his sleeve back down.

I got a funny feeling from him, but his mind seemed normal; maybe it was the tattoo, somehow. He was thinking the vibration was too strong. He'd just gotten the telepath stripe on the tattoo when he'd gotten promoted two months ago, and it was going off like crazy. It had never done this before; either I was crazy strong, far stronger than you'd expect, or the material they'd implanted in his skin was doing something weird, reacting far too strongly to the stimulus. Either way, he didn't care.

"I'm not kidding. I have the full power of the US government behind me and I'm going to have to ask you to leave," he said. Then he relented and pulled out a card. "Call me so I can get a statement."

The feds had a telepathy tattoo now? I mean, I'd known about the Tech one in theory for a while, and had always been a little creeped out. But telepathy? Why in hell would they need to know who had telepathy and who didn't? If the government was starting to side with the radical anti-Guild faction, that was not good for me. In fact, it was downright disturbing.

So, because it bothered him, I dragged my feet and

offered useless advice, even pulling Bellury into it to make the moment go as slowly as possible.

In the end, when Ruffins was seriously thinking about bodily carrying me out of the scene—with protective gloves on—I left. Morris would probably help him, and if I got Bellury bruised, his wife would yell at me.

There was something wrong with the world where, in a scene full of Tech that could endanger the world, instead they spent time harassing me.

I took the card with me; I'd give a statement. I already had the damn FBI on my back; for all Ruffins was a boorish idiot, I didn't need the TCO causing me trouble too. Especially if they had those new disturbing tattoos.

Hours later, I was back at the station and preparing for the next round of interviews at the borrowed desk downstairs. The phone on my little desk rang with an ear-shattering, vibrating off-kilter literal ring. I nearly jumped out of my skin. Then I picked it up and answered with my name.

Bellury's voice grumbled. "Your girlfriend's calling you from the Guild. Want me to patch her through?"

"You talking about Kara?"

"That would be the one."

"She's not my girlfriend. We used to be engaged, like ten years ago. She's married and everything."

A pause from Bellury. "My mistake. You realize I'm going to listen to this, right? Paulsen's watching you, you know."

"Knock yourself out." I swallowed, and tried to figure out what Kara could possibly be calling me about. With any luck, it was good news on the certification. I could use some good news right now. Or an apology. She owed me that, and more, for not telling me.

"Did you know about Stone?" I asked when the phone went silent.

"Hi to you too. Don't you have a direct number? I just got yelled at by three different people. You're lucky I didn't just hang up."

"I asked you a question, Kara."

She blew out a long line of air.

"I couldn't tell you. I'm sorry, Adam. They made me promise. And I only found out that morning." Which would explain why she had been so odd over breakfast. But still.

"Tell me at least I'm going to get my certification."

"I'll keep pushing, Adam, but right now it doesn't look good. And me asking has set off a whole bunch of—"

I interrupted her. "Why are they doing this, Kara? Why send Enforcement on me? I haven't done anything."

"I swear I don't know. I walked in on a meeting halfway through—and I hadn't even been invited. There's crap going on in the Guild right now, a lot of crap. The higher-ups want to cover their asses. They're worried you're a threat. Thus Stone, and the trouble with the certification. They want reassurance."

"I just want to do my damn job here and have people leave me alone. I called you on the Bradley thing," I grumbled, frustrated beyond words. "Really, Kara, I can't believe you'd do this to me. Or maybe I can." It wasn't the first time she'd betrayed me for the Guild. "I saved lives, damn it. I took out a bad apple. This is beyond the pale. At least tell me they're done now. A little posturing and a little pressure and this is it. I'm surrounded by cops. How much trouble can I really get into?"

"You know they could have done this at any time," Kara said quietly. "There aren't many free agents out in the world, and you attracted a lot of attention. You did the right thing, and you've made something of yourself. But they can't make an example out of you anymore, and they're not listening to me. I've done everything I can for you. I swear, Adam."

They'd all thought I'd die in the gutter when I left. When they threw me out. Well, screw the Guild, I wasn't going to roll over for them or anyone else.

But Kara kept talking. "I've begged, borrowed, and strong-armed. At least I can tell you they've assigned somebody honest. Stone came and talked to me today, after he got confirmed as watcher and—"

"Wait, he got a watcher assignment? For me?" I swallowed. Crap. This wasn't going to end. This wasn't going to end until they got their way. "Why in hell didn't you call me? What did you tell him?"

"I told him the truth. You kept your head and helped us handle an explosive situation with minimal fuss. I told him if it was up to me I'd reinstate your numbers and leave you alone. I promise you, I fought. It's an investigation. No force justified. I fought like hell to get that put in place. But you're a Level Eight, Adam. They're not comfortable with that kind of strength suddenly showing up and challenging their interests."

"Challenging their interests? I caught a fucking serial killer *without* making the Guild look bad! How is this a problem, Kara? How?"

"I can't stop this, Adam. I'm sorry."

"Yeah, me too." And then I hung up on her.

I waited patiently for Bellury to show up at the desk, and when he did, I stood.

"Let's go talk to Paulsen," I preempted him.

"Why don't we," he said, a statement. From the feel of his mind, that was happening today with or without me anyway. He hadn't understood everything he'd heard—but he was damn suspicious.

We waited, uncomfortably, outside Paulsen's office while she finished up a phone call with the county's budgetary committee. My hearing was working overtime today, so I got snips and portions of what she was saying even through the closed door. Paulsen was arguing for more money for the department, with a list of reasons and statistics that impressed me even in pieces.

Several cops walked by, getting hostile as they saw me. I got flashes of officers getting termination papers and their general anger that I was still here, still getting attention from Paulsen, while they took pay cuts and watched their friends leave. I didn't hunch over, and I didn't look away. I needed this job, damn it. I needed it worse than they did.

At least my brain was cooperating enough to pick up the anger, if that's indeed what I was picking up, and not a reflection of my own crappy mood.

No; it was the telepathy. Bellury began to think about his conversation with the FBI guy who'd called him yesterday, and my heart sank. Bellury was too honest not to give both the good and the bad, and he'd seen enough to at least suspect I was having trouble with the telepathy—and worse, suspect I was doing something with the Guild. However this worked out with the watcher—assuming he didn't convict and kill me—I had the FBI on my tail right after.

It was almost a relief when Paulsen hung up the phone, took a deep breath, and then gestured for us to open the door and come in.

She had only the one chair today, so I stayed standing, next to Bellury, right in front of the large battered desk dominating most of the room. Paulsen's wrinkles seemed deeper and she seemed more tired than ever. Her new cactus was sitting on the edge of the desk, looking a little battered. My slight headache did ease up when I got close enough to smell it.

"What's going on?" she said in a clipped tone. "I have a full day today and I don't have time for nonsense."

"Kara just called me. The Guild contact we worked with on the Bradley case—you met her, I believe. She teleported me out to save Cherabino's life, and she did it without charging the department and without complaining. She's a good guy, for all she works for the Guild, and she's demonstrated that to you personally."

"Where is this going?" Paulsen asked me.

"The guy who came down to the station," Bellury said. "They said he's been assigned as some kind of watcher and he's under suspicion."

"Unjustified suspicion," I put in quickly. "Because of the way the Bradley case went down. It's like an internal affairs investigation." I barreled right through. "I don't work for the Guild anymore, but with the Koshna Accords they still have jurisdiction. They have an investment in my training, and because I'm a telepath there's a liability if I cause trouble. I knew this could happen if I contacted them about the Bradley case, but I didn't think it would be this bad. I didn't think I'd get a watcher, and no way in hell did I think they would come to the station and make a stink in front of you guys. But they still have the right to do the internal affairs investigation on me, and they still have the right to enforce the decision if they make a bad one." I paused. "You should also know I got a phone call from the FBI last week, and they're also doing an inquiry. I swear to you there is no information about me you don't have. I have no idea why people are doing this to me." But then my mind flashed: my telepathy. I was hiding the recovery. And the Tech in my walls at the apartment. But those didn't count.

Paulsen sat back. "I called the FBI. I thought they could use your talents, and as you might be in the wind before too long, it seemed to make sense. It's an inquiry as part of a job application process."

"What—um, thank—" She had called the FBI? Was that a good thing? Did it mean she thought I had talent? Or was it that I was going to lose my job and she knew I couldn't get another one?

"But if you've got the Guild on your case—whether or not I believe you on why—you're running out of options, Adam. Neither they nor I am going to look kindly on an all-out war with the Guild."

"I've done everything you've asked. I went to the crime scene this morning, I found that Tech, and we have a significant suspect in Cherabino's case that Andrew's tracking down on the money side. Plus I got three confessions this week. Three. I've been straight with you about the Guild. I came to you. What more do you want from me?" I felt my voice crack, and forced down shame. I needed this job. I needed it, and if begging would let me keep it a little longer, I'd even beg. I would.

Paulsen sighed. "You need more than this. You need that certification, and you need to get me some big ammunition to fight for you with. This is not that ammunition—this is ammunition for the politicians on the other side of the table, and, Adam, I can't protect you if you won't help me."

I stammered, trying to figure out what to say.

"You need to leave now. Bellury, hang back. We need to talk."

I left with my tail between my legs. I locked myself in the coffee closet, ate two stale donuts, and called Swartz. Then I smoked. A lot.

Clark was staring at me from the booking officer's desk. My MO would be to duck into the coffee closet, the back smoking porch, or sneak upstairs until it all blew over. Clark was one of those out-of-sight, out-of-mind folks and if it went a few hours without my presence there—and without him having to clean up my messes—it generally went away. The trouble was, this time he'd clearly seen me first.

I'm watching you, he mouthed.

I nodded as cheerfully as I could manage. Of course he was. Why not? Half the damn universe was watching me already. What was one more? But I went down to the interview rooms early, at least twenty minutes early, so he'd see me do it. He still gave me half his workload, in a bitter fit, and called me names. It hurt. It did; my armadillo-armored soul was wearing thin today, so even a grouchy bastard like Clark was getting to me.

Bellury drove me home, very late, after I'd effectively worked a whole extra shift. A whole extra shift, with no pay, while Clark went home early feeling smug. I could have applied for overtime after the fact—but the department was running short of funds and I didn't get to see the money anyway. Instead, Bellury and I went out for a halfway decent steak dinner at an all-night diner (his wife was visiting a relative; he was glad for the company), me promising to pay him back for the whole amount via the accountants, and him dropping me off with equanimity on the doorstop of my building. I was tired, bone tired.

I exited the stairs and limped all the way down the narrow apartment hallway, noting two of the overhead lightbulbs were burned out again. There were odd shadows along the doors. I reached the end of the hallway and my own plain door marked 42, the last lightbulb in the row flickering like it was about to die.

My keys were in my hand, the real steak sitting heavy in my gut, when I tripped over the squishy shadow on my doorstop. I hit the doorframe hard with my forehead.

What . . . ?

I looked down. Crouched to get a better look. My eyes wouldn't focus in the flickering light, wouldn't make sense of it.

Fur. Two lumps of fur covered in tacky reddish brown, covered from top to bottom. I swallowed. Animals? Dead animals?

But no smell, the logical, crime scene part of my brain said. And I took another breath. Paint. The smell of drying paint.

I opened myself up to Mindspace, slowly, cautiously, with shields ready to cascade at the least provocation. Empty. The closest minds were my neighbors, quiet and miserable in their small apartments around me, and Mrs. Doberman above, actually awake and conscious for once. No one in the hall. And when I went deeper, only a cold, small whiff of what might have been anger. Whoever had left whatever that was had been here only a few minutes, and the object hadn't been handled enough or with enough emotion to matter.

I got back up and opened the door of my apartment, turning on the light.

The plain blue welcome mat had a smear of drying red on it, red that extended onto the furry thing, the furry brown thing with a round body and red-spattered arms and legs. A teddy bear head lay on its side a few inches away, stuffing coming out of it like cotton snow.

There was a decapitated teddy bear on my doorstop. A teddy bear covered in red paint like blood, blood that dripped from the severed neck down the round, plush body and onto my welcome mat.

A teddy bear, a dead teddy bear, with no explanation, with no note, with no more than a lingering angry whiff of Mindspace left on it. Blank. Blank and dead, its one remaining eye staring up at me.

My back was suddenly against the wall of the hallway, without any memory of how I'd gotten there. My heart beat a hundred miles an hour.

Don't be stupid, I told myself. *It's a stuffed toy. A macabre joke. A stupid prank by somebody's kid in the building.* Teddy bears were not the Guild's style, and I couldn't imagine a world in which the FBI did this to job candidates they were about to reject. I told myself it was a prank, just a prank.

But it took me ten minutes to stop looking around in Mindspace, ten minutes to calm down enough to go back in the apartment, ten minutes before my hands would even hold a cigarette, they were shaking so badly.

I smoked and told myself this was a stupid prank and probably not even specifically against me. For all I knew, everybody in the building had had a teddy bear on their doorstop this morning, and I was just the last one home. But I couldn't shake the thought the strangler, the man we were chasing, had seen us poking around in his financials and decided to send me a message. But why me? It didn't make any sense. Andrew, or Cherabino, was a far better target.

I got two heavy trash bags and folded the thing up in them, fingers protected by plastic, and took it out to the dumpster behind the apartment. The moon was out, the pollution thick, as I threw the dead bear into the garbage. The moon was out, like a sentinel over a fallen battlefield.

It took me fifteen minutes to scrub the paint out of my mat with a bristled brush, to erase the thing like it had never existed. Fifteen minutes crouched over the mat while my mind patrolled the hall in Mindspace and I tried to lose the feeling that somebody was watching me.

I locked the door, all three locks, and pulled the ratty

couch over in front of it. Then I stared at a forensics text-book for at least an hour before I could sleep, my head going up at every small, normal noise, every fluctuation in Mindspace.

I hardly slept.

CHAPTER 12

By the next morning I'd decided I couldn't report it. I looked bad enough as it was, and a teddy bear and paint weren't going to impress anyone else with my competence. So I sat on the thought and tried to get calm.

I was kidding myself; with as little sleep as I'd gotten, with my brain still limping along, with my roiling upset and legitimate fear about the future, the telepathy was falling apart. I was seeing the light flashes on the edge of my vision again, hearing whispers across the room, and watching Mindspace fade in and out in a constant movement threatening to give me seasickness.

I was better, my brain healing on schedule. I'd even gotten stray thoughts from the cops yesterday. But I couldn't not sleep, clearly. My system wouldn't take it. So, like a stupid kindergartener, I caught a nap in the crash room over lunch, and woke up feeling considerably better.

That early afternoon, like that morning, was spent taking out my anger on suspects. I even got a confession.

At three o'clock, though, Cherabino drove me to meet her nephew.

She was very quiet, and she drove sedately down Clairmont, but her mind crawled with worry and anxious thoughts, their stingers pushing into her like angry wasps.

"I'll be on my best behavior, I promise." I was dealing with my own angry wasps, but it wasn't a lie. The nap had done me good; I'd be able to keep it together. "I won't offend anyone this time."

"It's not that," she said, but I could feel the lie. She blew out a long line of air. "It's just . . ."

"What?"

"Jacob is medically fragile, okay? You didn't lie to me earlier when you said you didn't have a cold, did you?"

I frowned, trying to work that one out. "I'm not sick."

"You sneezed before we got in the car." Her voice was accusatory.

"I'm allergic to pollution." And God knew there was plenty of pollution in the police parking lot, open to the regular air, off a major road in the center of Decatur. Even here, with more trees around, replants and twisted survivors of the Tech Wars, even here the pollution was bad.

"Is your snot clear?"

"What?"

"When you blow your nose, is your snot clear or colored, like white or yellow? Answer the damn question. It's the most reliable way to know if you have a cold."

"Um, what if I didn't look?"

"Damn it, Adam." She took a breath.

"You're seriously angry with me because I didn't look at my snot? You have to give me warning for this sort of thing, Cherabino." If she wanted reports on my bodily fluids, well . . . my mind promptly told me the rest of the universe already got reports on my urine on a regular basis. Oddly, I was amused. "Calm down, okay? It will be okay. I took a shower and everything. We sprayed me down with disinfectant. It's fine."

She blew out a breath, and made an irritated sound.

The closer we got—down North Decatur Road with huge twisted trees on every side, trees centuries old and still standing, road thick and pitted from their roots underneath—oddly, the closer we got, the more Cherabino tensed up.

And the more I did too.

Cherabino's sister's house wasn't far from Emory University, in one of the most beautiful areas of metro Atlanta, trees and low stone buildings on every side, old stately houses that cost millions. Despite appearances and prices, though, this area was innately more dangerous than Decatur proper, from the closeness of the CDC. No less than three plagues had gotten away from them during the Tech Wars, when even their technology turned against them. The Black Plague had fizzled; most of the rich houses surrounding held well-fed individuals with good immune systems. But cholera, and Ebola . . . well, it wasn't just the Tech that had killed the world in the Tech Wars.

Cherabino pulled into a long driveway, turning off the car. Through the window I could see a manicured lawn of short purple-tinged grass, and huge bushes with purple flowers standing against a huge three-story monstrosity of old brick and Southern-style columns, the small porch in the front more for decoration than use. As she parked the car, I wondered how the flowers survived this late in the season, especially in the high levels of pollution.

A housefly flying around settled on one of the flowers and I had my answer. The flower snapped shut like a Venus flytrap, and the fly's frantic struggles moved the flower less and less until it was still. At least three other flowers in the long line of bushes were shut, and another was slowly opening as I watched, getting ready for its next round of prey. I noticed then the centers of the flowers were almost black, and shiny.

I swallowed, and got out of the car.

Cherabino picked up a vacuum-sealed robot toy from the back of her car, visibly braced herself, and started walking up the brick walkway to the door. She batted away one of the flowers without comment, but her disquiet let me know she wasn't any happier with them than I was.

A woman opened the door seconds after Cherabino's knock. The woman was tall and pleasantly plump, with a red-cheeked healthiness and a ready smile that put you at ease at once. This made me distrust her.

But she hugged Cherabino, a full-on hug, like she was glad to see her. She even turned to me with the same intention.

"Ah, no." I stepped back.

She frowned.

"Telepath," I said as sheepishly as I could manage. "Remember, that's why you wanted me to come visit."

"Oh, that's right," the sister said, seeming to settle down with an explanation. "I'm Nicole. I've got a ham on to cook. You do eat pork?" She paused, as if the answer to this question was far more important than the hug.

"Yes, ma'am."

She smiled and held open the door for me. Clearly now I was in. Southern families, got to love them.

Jacob was in the living room, sitting on a small chair just his size. He was small for his age, and very thin, with big eyes and a smile that lit up when he saw us coming. His thick dark hair was the exact shade of Cherabino's, and the smile was all his mother's.

He also had a presence, a slight but real presence in Mindspace, a childlike mind with some definite Ability. The question was, what was that Ability? I'd done my research before I'd come and thought it through. I'd try to find out what he could do without hurting either one of us. I walled away my own worries and anger and fear. With the nap, I had the control to do what I needed to do—if I was careful.

Jacob stood up, still behind the low, padded coffee table, and Nicole went over to sit down on the floor where she could be right next to him.

"Hello," he said.

"Hello. My name is Adam." I thought better of his mother, seeing her join him on the floor. When she looked up, she thought loudly, hoping I would hear, that she wouldn't interfere. Whatever I needed to do to help Jacob, I should go ahead and do. She wasn't going to get offended like her grandmother had.

I nodded at her, acknowledging the thought. Cherabino sat down on the sofa and put her hand on her sister's shoulder in support.

"Do you know who I am?" I asked Jacob. I kept my mind calm, still, and dropped my shields slowly so he'd see I was sincere. That is, if he was equipped to read me. Odds were he was an empath at best.

I waited for him to answer the question on his own.

"You're Aunt Isa's partner, sort of," Jacob said seriously. "You can read minds. What's an empath?"

I took a breath. Okay. I kept my mind open, deliberately open, and ruthlessly eliminated stray thoughts. "An empath is a person who can feel other people's emotions. Usually the closer he is to the person or the more he touches skin—say, holding the person's hand—the stronger he can feel the emotions. Sometimes, if the empath is strong, he has a hard time telling which emotions are his and which are the other person's." I paused. "Do you ever have trouble telling which feelings are yours and which are other people's?"

"Sometimes." Jacob turned to look at his mom, who was suddenly worried. "Don't be sad, Mom. Adam is going to help me."

He moved around the coffee table and looked up at me—way up. He was a little over four feet tall, and I was a few inches shy of six feet. I saw myself through his eyes—short hair, long, friendly face, as tall as his mom but not his dad, and calm. Very calm, where most people in his life had thoughts like bees, constantly buzzing around.

I sat down on the carpeted floor, ignoring the sofa, because that was what he wanted. He sat down too.

Well, we already knew he could do a passive read, so I'd skip that part.

"I'm going to ask you some things. And get you to try to do some things. Sometimes I'll ask you in your mind." *In here,* I said.

He blinked, startled. "Okay . . ." His voice trailed off, not sure what to think of this, but he wasn't afraid.

"And sometimes I'll ask you out loud. If you can't do something, it's fine. I can't do everything either, but when I ask I want you to try. Honest try. Not showing off or pushing anything that hurts."

"Okay," Jacob said. His legs crossed in what looked like a meditation yoga pose, with the boneless comfort of a child.

I looked around the room, posh designer-chosen furniture in muted colors, expensive real paintings on the wall, an upright piano on the opposite end of the room. And a small desk, antique looking, in the corner. The only thing that didn't match was the smaller chair, a chair that had a specialty-shaped pillow and a row of buttons on the side. That chair, I was betting, was newer than the rest, specifically for Jacob.

What do I have in my pocket? I kept my shields down and put the information out on the front of my mind, waiting. I felt him poke around and finally grasp it.

"A candle."

"Good. What color?"

"White." He smiled like this was a great game. "Am I right?"

I fished in my pocket for a small votive candle I'd brought with me, pulling it out along with a couple of quarters. I set the quarters down on the plush tan carpet, and handed the candle to Jacob.

It was a perfectly normal votive candle, small, with a preburned black wick and mass-produced plain white soy wax in a shallow metal round cup. "You were right."

He smiled.

I calmed my mind and focused on confidence. "Tell the candle to light."

Jacob looked at me, then the candle.

"Honest try."

"Okay. . . ." He frowned at the thing. *Light,* I heard with intensity.

Of course, the candle just sat there.

I forced down a laugh. "That's how I'd do it. No, the little atoms in the wick there. Tell them to move faster, to get hot, really hot. So hot they burst into flame."

He looked at me with skepticism.

"I shouldn't have laughed. Honest try. It's not something I can do, but if you can, it should come easily." The candle was already set to burn, the wick lit once already. It should light when Jacob told it to, I said in my mind. I reached back for confidence and found it through will and necessity.

Jacob frowned at the candle for at least a minute, his brow pulling down.

Right before he got a headache, I stopped him. "Good." I held out my hand as if to get the candle back from him. *Put the candle on the floor,* I thought, with a small push to take the thought out into Mindspace but not fully in his head. I went back to confidence.

He put the votive on the floor and shifted to his knees.

"Very good. Now, can you ask your aunt to hand you that pillow?"

Next to Cherabino on the sofa was one of those silly pillows that only existed for decoration, round and embroidered with goldish thread, with a ridiculous pale blue bow.

He turned, and started to ask.

"Wait just a second." I looked Cherabino directly in the eye.

You'll need to lower your shields, I told her through the Link, which wouldn't be overheard. *Think of the bricks you build falling down and disappearing. Be as calm and accepting of him as possible, okay? He might be clumsy.*

She swallowed, and with visible bravery took the bricks down. I waited, patiently, projecting confidence for Jacob.

"Okay. We're ready. Ask her with your mind, like this."

I reached out over Mindspace—not the Link—and said, clearly and distinctly, as publicly as possible, *Don't give him the pillow until you hear it in your head.*

Cherabino nodded, braced and ready.

A long minute passed.

Jacob turned back to me. "I asked her, honest."

"No big deal," I said, trying for confidence rather than the relief I felt. He was weak enough to get out of the Guild if he wanted. Strong enough for parlor tricks, but weak enough for freedom. It was the best-case scenario for us. "It's a fact, normal people are harder to read. Their waves in Mindspace are smaller and harder to see. And projecting loud enough so they can hear you is really tough." I held out my hand, and Cherabino gave me the pillow. I put it on the plush tan carpet between us. "Now." *Can you lift the pillow without using your hands? Up in the air. If it's too heavy, you can move just the quarters next to it.*

"Up in the air?"

"Let's say six inches off the floor. Floating. You'll have to keep it there against gravity, which will take some concentration."

"Okay . . ." Jacob frowned again at it for a long time.

I held on to quiet confidence through sheer will. No matter how rare the Ability, it was important at this moment that I believed he could do this. And I did, I told myself. "Good try. Can you move the pillow back to the couch? This time try moving it through Mindspace." When he looked at me like I was crazy, I explained: *The same way you talked to me in your head. See if you can move the pillow like you moved your words.*

"I can't do that. That's just silly."

"Honest try." I could feel how tired he was getting, so I added, *This is the last thing, I promise.*

Okay. . . .

I could feel his mind trying to get a grip, then . . .

A *whoomp* of air and a *crack* as he suddenly appeared over on the couch, still cross-legged. Cherabino was up and back, reaching for a gun she hadn't brought in.

It's your nephew. Calm down and put your shield up, damn it. You're scaring him, I told her, fighting down my own startlement. I hadn't expected . . . but, hey. My ex-fiancée was a teleporter. It wasn't like I hadn't been around it. A sinking feeling hit me, though. His freedom had just disappeared in a *crack* of displaced air.

After Cherabino stood down and calmed, Jacob had a chance to process.

"Cool!" he finally said, with a huge smile, and Jumped back. He appeared next to me on the floor with a *crack*. This time I just shook my head in amusement.

He Jumped three more times, from the feel of it, upstairs and back, before he ran out of steam.

Suddenly he was next to me again, and very, very pale.

"I don't feel so good, Mom," he said, in a mumble, and fell.

I caught him—barely. He was completely limp in my hands and light like a bird. Suddenly I was nervous. "What's his medical condition again?"

Cherabino blew out a long line of air. "Brallac's disease. It's an autoimmune digestive disorder, a really bad one. His version is drug-resistant too, which is worse. Here, put him in the chair."

His mom was terrified, her hands wringing in her distress. As soon as I settled the boy in the chair, she was pulling out a clear bag attached to a tube, sliding up the boy's sleeve, attaching the tube to a port in his arm, hanging the bag on a hook on the back of the chair. A low whirring sound came from the chair as its feet slowly rose and a blood pressure cuff settled in around the boy's arm.

Cherabino's mind was open, and I saw if the nutrient drip didn't work, they'd have to take him to the doctor—preferably his physician, but the hospital if they couldn't get him on the phone—and run tests.

"It's time for you to leave," Nicole, the boy's mother, said.

I complied without a word, and waited by the car for a long time. I waited and watched the carnivorous bushes eat insects, while inside Cherabino waited, heart racing, to see if the drip would take.

The minutes wore on, and my energy deserted me. I sat down on the ground behind the car, head leaning against the bumper, eyes closed. That much focus, and my night last night . . . I couldn't teach Jacob, at least not now, not even in telepathy. That much was clear. Less than an hour and I was wiped. I'd be upset with myself if I wasn't so tired.

I opened my eyes and pulled myself up, bones aching,

as Cherabino opened the door to come out. Tears were running down her face—tears of relief. She wiped at them surreptitiously, I tried not to fall over as I stood, and we both pretended we hadn't seen.

Cherabino parked outside a chicken and waffles restaurant a few miles away and turned off the car. It was lunchtime—well past it, actually—but she was violently not hungry and I could wait on food if it would help. I did have dehydrated food in the apartment. Maybe I could do that and go to sleep early. I could put the cheap couch in front of the door so the teddy bear guy didn't come back.

I waited for her to speak first.

She blew out a breath and finally, unexpectedly, laughed. She laughed until her chest hurt with the force of it, until tears ran down her eyes. She laughed with the heavy irony of something horrible, and I stared, taken completely aback.

Finally she wiped the tears from her eyes. "Of course. Of course. The only thing in the world to make it harder for Nicole to take care of him. The only thing worse than telepathy and the Guild and the whole nine yards. Oh, Jacob is going to be such a handful." She settled her head back on the seat's headrest and made a breathy sound. "Of course he can teleport." She considered being angry at me for teaching him a new trick, but she couldn't build up the energy.

I rubbed the back of my aching neck. "If it helps, he would have figured it out on his own sometime in the next few years. Maybe at an inconvenient moment—or a dangerous one."

She didn't move from the headrest, her eyes closed.

"That doesn't help, does it?"

"Not really." She took a breath that made her chest expand and drew attention to her very nice breasts, currently separated by the seat belt. "No checking out my boobs," she said tiredly.

"Sorry." I looked away. I hadn't actually meant to admire them where she could overhear through the Link. I should at least pick a time when she was distracted—or shield better. But all that focus with Jacob had eroded my focus in the real world, clearly.

We sat, her thinking, me trying not to fall asleep, for a minute.

"So," she said, in the tone of voice of someone deliberately changing the subject, "Jacob. I take it he's probably going to show up on the Guild tests."

"That's right." I paused, not sure how much detail she wanted.

"How strong is he? They homeschool him, but he'll have to go in for standardized testing eventually and I'm told the Guild gets a register."

"He's at least a four on the telepathy scale, and very reliable and controlled for the age. It wouldn't surprise me if he ends up at least a light five, which is strong. The control is the bigger deal, though, especially at that age. You have a big family, right?"

"Twenty or more when we all get together. Just adults. He has two sisters, but they go to regular school when they can and live in a different part of the house. He's not at the big groups often, but . . ."

I felt like I wasn't focusing. "Does he seem distressed in the big groups?"

She thought about it. "He did when he was younger. Now he's quiet, but he just kind of sits back and takes it all in. He always seems to know the gossip, but with the way my sisters talk . . ." She gave a mental shrug.

"Maybe that's where the control comes from. That's a big group for a telepath, especially in a family setting where everyone is feeling open." I thought for a second, trying to make the ideas crystallize. "He doesn't go to normal school?"

She frowned, as if the edge of my exhaustion was coming through despite the barrier she'd built. "No. Not for years. They just don't want him in the same pool as all those germs. They've mostly got the digestive issues under control, but you put him in a group of normal kids, normal exposure to germs, and he's going to get a lot worse, quickly. He hasn't had one of those attacks in months. I think you scared my sister."

"I didn't mean to. I was watching him. . . ."

She sighed. "He's okay, at least for now. If he goes popping all over the house like that again, I don't know what my sister's going to do."

"With a normal kid, he'll build up endurance. The mind learns to be more efficient with the energy it uses. But the teleporters particularly eat like crazy their first few years." I paused, trying to make it make sense for her. "Um, they lose weight, most of them, and a lot, if they don't work at it." Kara had been known to eat a jar of peanut butter a night, back when she was doing courier work. On top of normal food and healthy portions. Even so, she'd lose five pounds or more in a heavy weekend, and start getting dizzy, even with all her training. Once she'd even fainted, coming down hard on a concrete floor, narrowly missing a concussion. I couldn't even remember the number of times I'd made her an extra protein shake and pleaded with her to eat it. Or the number of times she'd gotten so excited about gaining weight that she'd danced all over the apartment, and me too. I wondered if she danced now, on desk duty. I wondered if she ever remembered those days.

"You're thinking about Kara." Cherabino sat straight, actually looking at me with a sad expression.

I tried to piece together some decent shields. "That shouldn't have happened. I'm just really tired."

"It's all right."

We sat.

She still had that edge of sadness to her, but now she was thinking. "He's double trouble, isn't he? What you called Bradley?"

"I'm afraid so." It was vanishingly rare to have both telepathic skills and teleportation. Rare and valuable.

"And the speech you gave me about how the Guild should be watching his every move, how the Guild should have killed him long before he got to us . . ."

"Yeah. They're not going to want him to go anywhere except directly into the Guild system. Even with his health problems. If the Guild-trained medics can't fix his illness, they'll hire the best doctors in the world, and spend the next ten years figuring out what his practical limits are."

"They'll get him treatment at least?" she asked quietly.

"The Guild uses its assets, Cherabino."

"He's not an asset. He's a little boy."

"He's an asset to them. A rating and a skill level. That's what we all are."

She stared me straight in the eye. "That's why you and I are going to figure this out. We are going to . . ."

"Going to what?"

"Going to save him. We have to."

"Sure," I agreed, but deep inside, deep behind my own set of blocks and exhaustion, I knew it might not be possible. Jacob would need training, and a lot of it, soon.

The buses were running behind Wednesday morning, so I was about ten minutes late to my coffee shop meeting with Swartz. With all the parent-teacher conferences he was doing, we were off our usual day, but that was okay.

When I walked in the door, as expected, he was already seated at the worn faux-leather and old-wood booth, the ugly pot of steaming licorice coffee in front of him, one cup poured, one cup empty and waiting for me.

The owner, a large grizzled man with a faded navy tattoo, nodded to me from the bar as I came in and turned to brew another pot of coffee. Swartz and I had been meeting here once a week for years, at what once had been a pub before this guy's grandfather had gone into AA. The old bar now held old ladies with newspapers and cups of tea, long booths with ancient sports memorabilia and young patrons, and likely half the city's Narcotics and Alcoholics Anonymous groups at battered tables near the back. The owner knew most of us by name—and the rest by face and preference.

"Cherabino has a nephew," I told Swartz as I slid into the booth.

"Good morning." He nodded solemnly.

"This nephew has Ability. And she wants me to help her figure out what to do." I thought about telling him more about the Ability and why it was an issue, but my warning from before still echoed in my ears. The fewer people who knew, the better, and it wasn't my secret to spill. "Bottom line is it's a lot of pressure. And I'm still not sure how to solve the problem."

"Why is it a problem?" Swartz's voice brought me back to him. "More to the point, why is it your problem?"

"It's Cherabino," I said, like that explained everything.

"And?" Swartz put another spoonful of sugar in his licorice coffee.

I blew on my own cup, letting the strong smell of licorice and coffee beans warm my nose up. "And . . . and, well, she's finally being nice to me again. Bringing me on the team. I think it's in exchange for this thing—not that she's not really letting the rest of it go—but it's like a test.

If I come through, I'm on the good list and maybe she stops freaking out about me being in her head. If I fail . . ."

Swartz took a sip. "If you fail, what?"

"Well, maybe she doesn't put me on the good list."

He put the cup down. "I don't think your partner is Santa Claus. I don't think there's a good list and bad list."

"She's not technically my partner."

"Even so. Have a little faith in human nature, son. You've given her the space she asked for. You've kept what secrets of hers have wandered over into your head. And you've proven trustworthy. Keep doing that, you'll be okay. Now. Three things."

I took a deep breath and thought. "My job. Cherabino. And the way the air smells after it rains."

"You've already said Cherabino."

"Have I?"

"But you're on the right track, kid. I'll let you use her name again. Listen, I have something I've been meaning to talk to you about."

Swartz pulled out his battered copy of the Big Book, but instead of turning to the tenth step, the normal October reading, he turned to Step Nine. Making amends to those whom you have wronged.

"You've been getting lazy about restitution," Swartz said. He held up a hand to forestall objections. "I've been letting you do it. I know you've had some trouble. But today—today it's time for us to tackle it head-on. Finding your student's killer is a start, but I've been thinking, you need to make a more solid effort with the last one, Tequila, was it?"

I took a breath. This was the last thing in the whole world I wanted to talk about. But Swartz was implacable, and, well, when Swartz said dance I did a jig. "Her name is Tamika. I saw her at the funeral."

He waited, patiently, as I took another sip of the coffee. "And?" he prompted.

I looked at the table. "I apologized again. She wasn't happy."

"She doesn't have to be happy. What, exactly, did this apology look like?"

Reluctantly, haltingly, I ran him through the conversation as it had happened.

He sat back, the tinge of disappointment in the air. "Ah, Adam. That wasn't an apology. Not for a wrong as big as you made against her."

"I sent her the letter you made me send. Her and Emily both."

"I saw those. I asked you to rewrite them." He looked sad, almost.

"What do you want me to do, Swartz? She doesn't want to hear from me. I said I was sorry." I hated saying I was sorry. It stung like the fires of hell every time.

"I need you to apologize, and mean it. To do your best to make restitution, as best you can, so you can make a start on forgiving yourself."

"I don't deserve forgiveness." The words popped out of my mouth before I could call them back. I flushed, embarrassed even to say the words, words I knew Swartz would hate.

But he didn't yell. Instead, looking grave, he put a hand on the table. "Let's talk about that today."

It was a brutally hard day in the interview rooms, and I returned home to find Stone in my apartment.

"What the hell are you doing?" I asked, from the open door. I'd left the damn thing locked. "You can't just barge into my apartment."

Stone looked up from a pile of my belongings, what

few I owned, now all concentrated in a pile on the couch. His hands had the characteristic shininess of high-grade skin sealant. "Technically, I can. You're still a telepath, still under Guild jurisdiction. Your apartment is under the same rules as your personal living quarters at the Guild complex. I can search whatever I wish."

"Give me that." I yanked the jacket out of his hands, the jacket whose seams he'd been fondling—like I'd hide something there. Please. "These are my things. Mine. And there's already an army of people who make sure I'm on the up-and-up. I don't need you too."

Stone pulled out a small bottle of Dissolve and a rag from a pocket. He soaked the rag and rubbed the sealant off his hands; the Dissolve had a painfully sharp smell, like oranges on steroids, oranges with bad attitudes and big guns. My head swam from the pungent smell, but I didn't step back. That's what he wanted me to do.

"You need to leave. Now."

He threw the rag in the trash can next to the tiny counter where the sink and stove fought for space with the microwave, and washed his hands. He shut off the water and looked for a towel. At finding none, he held his hands up and shook them over the sink three times, with precision. He turned. "I've already gone through your apartment. There's traces of an illegal substance in a hiding place in the wall over your bed." The implication—clearly sent through Mindspace strong enough for me to catch even when tired—was that he could use this information against me with the cops.

Now I was pissed. "Cherabino already knows about that. Swartz told the whole crew, okay? It's old news." I was grateful I'd never made it down to Fulton County to restock. There was literally nothing he'd be able to find here to use against me. "Whatever you're going to do, do it. I'm not going back to work for the Guild. It's just not going to happen, and you going through my things isn't helping your case."

He leaned against the counter, weight still on the tips of his toes so he could move. "You realize you have Level Two Restricted Technology in the walls of your room? A proprietary Guild design at that."

I stopped. Okay, maybe that one was an issue. "It's Dane's design. He gave it to me. It helps me sleep without Mindspace and precog dreams. In the normal world, you need crap like that just to get by. Nobody has Guild-level shields out here, and even if they did, I couldn't afford them. It's none of your business."

"I doubt the normals would see it quite that way. I doubt your girlfriend would see it quite that way."

"What?" It took me a second. "You mean Cherabino? What is it with you people and girlfriends? What are you going to do, tell her I stole illegal Guild technology?"

"I wouldn't have to. The normals see the Tech and that's it. You'll be up on charges by the end of the day."

"And the Guild would fulfill the sentence under Koshna. Clever. But you can't risk me telling where I got the design. I don't have to keep Guild secrets, you know."

Now he pushed up from the counter. "Make no mistake, Adam, I am willing to play this game awhile. But if I think you'll become a real threat to the Guild . . ." A vivid image of my death came across the room, with notations and illustrations of where in the brain he'd hobble me before he did it. I was somewhat impressed by the strength and detail of the sending, again more than loud enough for my addled mind to pick up. The threats, however, weren't nearly up to the level of creativity of my usual interviewee.

The difference was, he was in a position to follow through with them. "You've made your point."

"You're in a valuable position, a trusted position, working for the normals. If you won't go back to the Guild, we're happy to work with you. Your help on certain situations in exchange for your independence."

"I already have my independence, no thanks to the Guild." I took a step forward. "Listen, you shoot me if you're going to shoot me. I'm not going along with this." I waited a long moment, tensed for a full-out mind battle. Waiting, to defend myself with rusty skills and what little power I had to command this time of night. I couldn't beat him, not now, not in my present state, but I could at least make him work for it.

"I need your cooperation for the mind tag," Stone said quietly. "You're trained enough that if I try to do something to you surreptitiously, either it won't work or you'll undo it. And this is not the kind of monitoring that responds well to force. I need to know the truth, not whatever you think I want to hear. So I'm willing to be patient. But your so-called friends at the department are blocking my search, with financial records, with employment files. Mark my words, I will find out everything. Everything. And I will make my ruling. You will agree to the mind tag. You will cooperate."

"Or what?"

"Or I'll reveal to your employers exactly what you've been hiding from them. Not just the Tech, but the healing period you've been hiding from them, the unreliable telepathy. How long do you think you'll keep that job then?"

"I'm already losing it, damn it!" I lashed out at him in anger—only to have my mental fist locked in a grip as hard as concrete. I tried to pull away—

And there he was, taking from me the information sitting on the top of my mind. The job offer from the FBI, my guilt over Emily's death and my determination to catch the hit man who murdered her, and my Link with Cherabino. My accidental, unethical Link with Cherabino.

He slid down to try to find it—and I pulled free.

By instinct I hit him with the pain of a crushed nerve, with the deep, unthinkable nerve pain radiating from his whole body. I gritted my teeth, enduring the same pain and more, and hurt him, hurt him badly. But I was out of practice, exhausted and weak; I had to let it go almost immediately.

Both of us breathed hard, aftermath of the pain. He was slumped, lines deep on his face from the strain. A group of light flashes, almost like fireworks, settled in to my right field of vision. And the mother of all headaches came to visit me inside my skull.

But I had done it. I had done something I had not been able to do in weeks, not since before the injury.

"I'm not a lightweight," I said. "Furthermore, I hold a grudge. If you screw with me, I will find you, and I will take you down. You have your job to do. But trust me. One iota out of line, and you will regret it. I am not a good person when I have nothing left to lose." I grabbed his shirt and frog-marched him out of the apartment, through that still-open door.

Stone simply reached out and cut my motor functions—I slumped to the floor. My control came back halfway through, just in time for me to keep my head from hitting the floor. My heart beat a million miles an hour. I hadn't fallen like that in years, not at someone else's call. Not without being able to fight back.

He stared down at me, shield impressive, like mirrored glass. "You are in no condition to fight me, and we both know it. I will be back, and you'd better be ready to talk. Or I will do far worse than you imagine."

I pulled myself to a sitting position, the headache

settling in with terrible nausea, and watched as he walked away. Anger was like a coal in my belly. But there beside it, like an unwelcome houseguest, a bloom of fear that wouldn't go away no matter how much I pushed at it.

At least he hadn't seen Jacob.

CHAPTER 13

Thursday morning, bright and early, I was relieved to be back at work. Back to where, for now at least, Stone couldn't ambush me, and I could do some good, even with a reaction-headache the size of Texas from last night's occurrences and this morning's too-difficult exercises. Mindspace was steady, though, if painful; I was getting stronger over time. If I'd stop pushing it, if I'd let it be, I'd probably be healed up in a few weeks.

I needed to stick to crosswords and stretching for a while.

I reported to the conference room. Cherabino had told Michael to send all the information about the case to Piccanonni, the state-level Georgia Bureau of Investigation profiler who'd helped us out previously. Now it was time for the woman to call us back.

Michael was there when I arrived. I sat a respectable distance from him, still within arm's reach of Cherabino, but I gestured to the coffee I'd brought him. Olive branch bringer, that was me.

"Am I early?"

"She's running late, apparently." Cherabino was blocking me, visualizing a brick wall between us so starkly I could actually see the bricks. "Are you okay?" she asked, in a tone designed not to travel the length of the table to Michael.

I ignored the overture. "Did she get any information for us?"

She looked down at the table, then back at me. She wanted to push it. I could feel how much she wanted to push it, but she was a cop. A cop who was surrounded with guys in the middle of some really horrible emotional stuff. She knew the code.

"Did Michael's research help?"

"This is the first I've heard from her in days. You know what I know." She paused. "The GBI is doing us a favor. We'll wait as long as it takes."

I pulled a few sheets from the stack of recycled fiber paper in the small supply hutch in the corner. We were in the smaller of the two conference rooms, this one called Dupin after some fictional detective I'd never heard of. Other than the hutch and the ridiculously large table and chairs, there wasn't room for anything else in the room but walls. The walls themselves were dotted with hundreds of tiny holes, the occasional pushpin still sticking to a scrap of paper. This wasn't the conference room for guests.

The phone in the center of the table started ringing right when I sat down. I creased the paper as Cherabino answered, on speaker.

"Cherabino. Nice to hear from you," the phone said in a precise soprano. "Thank you for waiting. You've stumbled across one of the big question marks in our department, and I had to go up the chain of command to get clearance for the details." What I remembered about Piccanonni from our one in-person meeting was her overly ordered mind, every thought organized, every idea tagged and arranged in precise cubbies. As for physical appearance, she wasn't young, she didn't wear a lot of makeup, and she wasn't abnormally thin or fat or tall or short. Other details got lost in the precision of that mind.

"How so?" Michael asked.

"Who is this?"

"Officer Michael Hwang. I'm new to Homicide."

"A pleasure to meet you, Hwang. To answer your question, in my experience there are two categories of criminals. The messy, splashy ones who operate out of emotion, and the quieter, thinking kind who plan things. What I think you have on your hands is a criminal who looks like the former but in actuality seems to be of the second kind."

I finished folding a paper crane and perched it on top of a pen. Then I went to work on the next figure, folding the piece of paper in half, finger putting pressure down the crease in a long, solid line.

Cherabino frowned at the phone. "You'll have to be more specific. What exactly are we dealing with?"

A long sigh came through. "A professional. A good professional, because he's been operating in the state for several years, we believe, without getting caught. We believe he's the hand behind a number of the political killings in Fulton County—you remember the rash of deaths attached to the retail contract awards for the Hartsfield-Jackson Air and Space Port—and also some private work, meaning rich men's enemies who appeared dead at convenient times. We believe, based on some of the evidence at the splashier scenes, that he has some kind of advanced military training. That, and his propensity to strangle a statistically interesting percentage of victims, led our office to tag him the Python. It's a fanciful name, but it's the only one we have. Thus far, he's covered his tracks."

Cherabino leaned forward. "How likely do you think this guy is to have done our killing? We still have a missing husband of the victim we're having trouble tracking, a viable suspect." From her direction came the vague knowledge that there's a bias in consults toward the splashier answer. Still, Piccanonni had info she didn't. . . .

Wait, where did the bricks go? A rush of surprise passed between us, and then suddenly she put up the wall again.

I went back to folding paper.

Piccanonni continued, oblivious. "Obviously you'll need to track down all the viable leads. But in my opinion, this one has the mark of this particular professional. The lack of struggle, in particular, without any drugs or restraints, is an odd detail—and one that has been popping up only in the last few months. The partial response from your last victim is indicative of a partial success from his method, in my estimation. We have yet to determine cause of the trend. We can, however, confirm fifteen killings in the area that match the pattern of strangulation with a sharper-than-expected cord, from behind. I've identified these killings as his handiwork."

"Fifteen?" I murmured, and then had to introduce myself when she heard the new voice. "Where are these fifteen killings?" I finished up the second crane and settled it next to the first.

"Many of them are associated with Fiske's empire and his dealings with rival criminal organizations," Piccanonni returned. "While Fiske of course is likely to employ multiple professionals of this nature, the Python for some reason is his preferred one. It's odd that he left the woman in the house and you were able to recover a portion of the cord. Unless there's an interruption or a specific order from Fiske, the Python normally hides his tracks better than this. If this was a higher-profile victim, I'd venture to say the body was left as a message. But you say she has no connection to large-scale criminal activities."

"Um," I started, then dived in before I could change my mind. "What's his pattern? Would he be likely to taunt his victims before he kills them?"

"What kind of message, would you say?" Michael asked, and then looked over at me and mouthed, *Sorry*.

"How certain are you that this guy is connected to Fiske?" Cherabino asked. "I've been assisting with that case for eighteen months now, and no one is connecting him to any Python."

"One question at a time please. The Python's typical pattern is to strike unannounced, in a situation in which the victim is not expecting attack. The message in this case, I believe, is to potential investigators, a statement of power over the victim. As for Fiske, it's a loose association at best—but it's there."

Cherabino was silent for a long moment. "Can we go after him?"

"He killed a woman. Of course we go after him. He's just a killer like any other."

"And the Net is a collection of bits and bytes," Piccanonni replied. "Nothing to do with superviruses, Tech that kills you, or death by computer."

Everyone went silent at that. The world hadn't lost millions in the Tech Wars sixty years ago just to make the same mistakes again. That's why we had Quarantine. That's why computers were kept under lock and key and even Cherabino had to go through a quarterly deep-background check just to have one.

"It's a good question. Assuming we are correct and he's tied to Fiske's operation closely, taking him down might flag Fiske's attention before the larger task force is ready to move. That would be dangerous, for everyone concerned."

"So we should proceed with caution and a lot of questions. You've been coordinating with the whole group. How likely do you think this is a professional hit from Fiske himself?" Cherabino was frowning, mind streaming possibilities and odds. *Fiske isn't Nice People,* her mind flashed. And her sensei said not-nice people should be watched, closely, so you'd see their moves in advance.

I started folding a frog.

Michael shifted. "We sent you over all that information. . . ."

"It's odd, if it's him. We know a great deal about Fiske and a lot about how he operates, both within and outside his organization. If you get in the way, he'll order a hit. He'll eliminate the family too, to make a point, if he needs to, but it's not his standard operating procedure. Fiske is more direct. The death of a woman, messy and left for anyone to find, plus the disappearance of the husband . . . it's odd. It doesn't line up with how he has done business in the past."

"If you have so much proof of this guy's murder tactics," I said, "why haven't you arrested him yet?"

Cherabino's mind was suddenly, overwhelmingly full of information, and there was a silence on the end of the phone.

"If I may make the observation, you're a telepath, not a policeman," Piccanonni said.

"So?"

"Detective Cherabino, will you explain it to him, please?"

Cherabino sighed. "Fine. Here's what every cop in the city knows. Fiske is pure evil. He teaches the devil how to cheat at poker and they bond over tortured souls. But he's a powerful guy. His guys get out on bail before you're finished locking them in. His lawyers cheat and the judges let them do it with a smile and a nod to next Sunday's pay-check. But every witness who'll stand against him gets killed before they can testify. Every one. And our legal system won't weigh a transcript like it will a witness testimony. It just won't. Convicting his guys—much less him—under those kinds of odds is playing Russian roulette with taxpayer money and, worse, the detectives' lives."

"Thank you, Detective. To put it simply, when we move against Fiske—*when* we move, I repeat, *when*—the case will be so ironclad, so unbreakable, that no one—I repeat, no one, his hellish minions and for-hire judges and all the rest—will be able to lift a finger in his defense. We'll build a case landing him on death row with his lawyers' best efforts all for naught. That's the kind of case we must build. *That's* the kind of stakes Cherabino is concerned about, if you are to go after the Python."

"I see." I stared at the two frogs between my cranes, and sighed. "And Cherabino's been helping you with the case against Fiske."

Cherabino turned around to frown at me. That's right, I'd overheard information about Fiske from her head weeks ago.

"But if he's really that powerful, isn't it dangerous?" I asked her.

"It is," the phone said. "Which is why it's critical you don't mention it to anyone who doesn't have an active need to know."

"Oh."

"I'm afraid I have to emphasize this. No one, are we understood?"

"I'm a telepath. No one has stoned me yet. Obviously I can keep a secret."

"Good, then."

While Cherabino asked a few questions, I worried

about us—her danger, my danger, both. If I hadn't been so absolutely sure what would happen if I lost this job, I might be thinking about leaving.

Cherabino hung up the phone, her brick wall stronger than I'd seen it in a long time.

"Are we really going to let this guy walk because he might—might—be attached to this Fiske guy?" I asked. For all the danger, this was Emily. Emily, dead because of me.

She looked up. "Don't be stupid. Justice has to happen. We just need to be careful. We're playing in the big leagues, and we need to cover our asses."

I took the phone into the coffee closet and called Swartz. I already knew what he was going to say.

"Today is the day," Swartz said.

"Does it have to be in person?" I wheedled. "Can't I just call her?"

"Did you make the donation I told you to?"

"Yes. It was a pain in the butt to get the accountants to do it, but it's done."

"Good. And you found her contact information. You know when she'll be getting out of work? You made an appointment?"

"No. Can't I just call her?"

He sighed, a long, disappointed sigh. "If calling her means you do it, then call her. But do it now. You have to face the things you're afraid of, son."

I swallowed. My heart was beating entirely too fast. "Can I call you back after it's over?"

"Sure. I'm on planning period for another forty minutes. If you do it promptly, you'll have plenty of time."

"Okay."

I hung up and looked at the phone, at my scrawled note with her number on it. My chest felt tight.

I had to do this, I told myself. I reached out with a shaking hand and picked up the receiver. I dialed the number, and it rang.

I hung up. Breathed again. Swartz's lecture from our morning meeting played through my head.

I picked up the phone again. This time, when it rang, I let it go through. But no one picked up. I called three more times, and no one picked up.

Swartz was not going to be happy with that answer. But what could I do?

"You're brooding," Bellury said in a disapproving tone.

I sat up straight. We were in the interview rooms, waiting for one last interviewee who probably wasn't going to show up now. I'd gotten so in my own head I'd almost forgotten he was there. I must trust him, at least in the parts of me looking for telepathic threats. "What do you care?"

He folded up the crossword book and set it in his lap. "Thus far the checks are coming up clean. You seem to be telling the truth. And maybe I like watching the waves you make when you're bothering to use that brain of yours. Like now, for example. You've got at least two cases I can count and you're not doing anything on either one."

I straightened, trying to focus. "Is there an obvious answer I'm missing?"

He shrugged. "Above my pay grade. I'm just saying, with your job at stake, you probably don't want to sit around pouting. You only get one chance with most lieutenants, you know. Paulsen's given you at least three. You might want to give back."

"I'm *trying*."

"No, you're not. You're sitting there and brooding." He

sighed and fished a sheaf of papers out of the bag next to
him, on the floor. He plopped the papers over on the table
in front of me, and I caught them, barely, from escaping
my lap.

"What is this?" I asked, papers erupting from my
hands like cotton candy from a machine.

"I'd hoped you'd come up with something useful on
your own, but here you go. The driver's paperwork." He
pulled out a slim leather book. "And the manifest with all
his travels in the last year."

I stared at the book. "Where'd you get that?"

"The cab of the truck from that big wreck on 285.
I kept waiting for Morris—or better, you—to ask.
Nobody did."

A long silence while Bellury waited and I processed.

"Thank you," I said finally.

"No problem." He set the book on the hutch between
the seats and pulled his crosswords back out.

"Did you look at this stuff?"

He looked up from his crossword. "Above my pay
grade."

I fanned out the papers in front of me, on the full length
of the table. Then I started reading. Morris and the rest
were hip-deep in the physical evidence—and the feds—
for the hijackings, and Michael and Cherabino were doing
research and on-site interviews on Emily's case while I
was stuck in the interview rooms making up hours. But
the next guy was late, and this at least I could do. A bor-
ing, stupid job, but I could do it. It was early enough in the
day that I could even do it well.

Endless figures and long lines of the driver's cramped
handwriting blew past my eyes. Alabama. Florida. South
Carolina, Tennessee, even Texas and Long Island. This

guy got around. He was an independent—some of the papers were his records of truck ownership, indemnity, etc., for his own personal business, his own personal piece of the American way. He was ten thousand ROCs in debt for the truck, down from almost two hundred thousand. He'd paid it off, a couple of hundred, a few thousand at a time over years. Next April was his big day to make the final payment and finally, finally own the truck outright.

That day in April had three exclamation marks by it—three. From a grown man. Now I was glad I hadn't seen his body in the truck, in the shattered remnants of what he'd worked so hard to build, all ruined in a single day. For Tech parts he might not even have known he was carrying.

I paused. Was there any way he really couldn't have known he was carrying something sensitive? Especially since he ran so hard from the hijackers? The fee . . . well, it was high, but not out of the ordinary.

Part of me felt like I knew him from this information; the further I got in, the clearer picture I got of this guy, this normal guy trying to prove himself and pay off debt. I could understand this guy. But he was running illegal shipments.

"You're brooding again," Bellury said.

"You sure you're not a telepath?"

"If that's your poker face, you should play poker with me. A lot," he said, from the crosswords.

I shrugged, and tried to focus again on the papers. Something about the routes was nagging at me. Charleston to Augusta to here, Montgomery to Columbus to here, but the cargo was different. Chattanooga to Savannah. St. Louis to Charlotte, over and over. And back to Charleston to Augusta to Atlanta, Montgomery to Columbus and the same.

Guild routes. Guild courier routes. The Guild had way stations for teleporter couriers in Charleston and Augusta on the way to Atlanta, same with Montgomery. A place to take a rest stop inside the two-hundred-mile Jump window, get your breath and some food before you had to Jump again. This trucker had hopped, skipped, and followed both the Guild's short- and the long-haul courier routes, over and over again. This had to be coincidence.

I went back through the last few papers and found a requisition order with a small, imprinted seal on the bottom. An IOU, effectively, guaranteeing payment with the hard-to-duplicate raised stamp in the shape of a stylized bird. I knew that symbol. Guild courier department, not the public face dealing with the public, but the private, Guild-only stuff. I guess it could have been planted there, forged, or gotten mixed in by accident. But what would be the point? What use would a trucker (a businessman paying off his truck, an American dreamer, my mind echoed)—what use would a trucker have with that symbol unless it was legitimate?

I went back to the scheduling. Some of the routes were all the way back to Canada, back to the less strict border crossings and lighter Tech laws. I knew for a fact that the Guild was still experimenting with machines and Tech—I'd been friends with Dane, the man who'd been doing the research, the man who'd designed the gadget in my apartment, before he died.

But if this was the Guild's Tech . . . Especially that load of biologicals, that had to be the Guild's. That wasn't something that you'd be able to get just anywhere. No hijacker would have found it by accident. And we had a strangled ex-Guild woman found, in her house, working for a shipping company. This couldn't all be coincidence—could it?

Even if it was, this Tech shouldn't be. It was another round of nasty Guild secrets. Part of me felt like I should cover it up, like I should paper over the cracks of their failure or dangerous habits and move on. I'd grown up in the Guild, I'd been so close with Dane, who'd done research on this kind of thing despite all illegalities. But Swartz said, when it came to people, you didn't cover things up. And moreover, the Guild's way measurably wasn't working. For Emily. For the Bradleys and abusers of the world. For whatever system had gotten ahold of the truck routes for the Guild's Tech experiments and decided to take them. For the other trucker, the one to whom I'd promised safety—and who'd ended up dead.

I decided then and there I'd do whatever it took to get the truth out, come hell or high water, with the Guild or against them.

A sudden movement caught my eye—like a fading shadow in Mindspace, a shadow that had moved. A shadow that tasted like Stone, like the watcher who'd sworn to see everything.

And who had just seen me decide to side with the normals, with the Tech laws. Against the Guild.

Cherabino had asked me to show up to the last-minute "team huddle" over the case late that afternoon.

"I said I would catch this cop-killer strangler, and I meant it. But we've got a stack of new cases hitting my desk every other day, and I can't afford to neglect them forever. We need results now. Let's assume for a second that the strangler is our guy. He doesn't work for free— we saw that in the other case. Andrew's doing his best to work the money, but the real question we need to ask is, who hired him to kill Mrs. Hamilton?"

"What about the boss?" Michael said. "Her job

was really on the line after the sexual harassment complaint."

"She banks at the same credit union our victim does," Cherabino said. "If the money's there, unless Andrew pulls out a miracle, we'll never find it. We also need to consider Fiske. He's the usual employer."

I thought about suggesting the shipping angle, with the Guild Tech. But this was a major deal and I didn't have any proof. . . . And this was Emily we were talking about. Emily, who'd been as straight as a board, as unflinching about right and wrong as any human being in the world. Seeing her involved with illegal Tech . . . I literally couldn't see it. But she had been abused—maybe she was doing something to help her get out of this. Maybe she needed the money to get away. That sounded like the Emily I knew.

Michael jumped in while I was dithering. "We've interviewed three of Dan's friends. They're heavy gamblers and none will talk about the poker game that night. Maybe the stakes were higher that night. Maybe Dan owes bigger money. Maybe this is a warning shot, to the other guys. They seem scared."

"With Dan likely dead at this point?" Cherabino asked.

"He could just be really good at hiding. With a loan shark on his tail, he'd have every reason to get good, and quick."

"Hell," I said. "For all we know, this is a Guild hit. It's not their style, but if . . ."

They both were staring at me.

"What?"

Cherabino read it right off the top of my mind. "Our victim used to be Guild and you know her?" Shock radiated down the Link, shock and anger.

"It was a long time ago," I said, realizing I hadn't told her. Crap. For all my work . . . the Link went both ways. "We haven't talked in over a decade."

"You need to tell me these things, damn it!"

"It was a long time ago!" But guilt ate at me like a hairy caterpillar eating on a leaf, implacable, determined, and steady.

"Stop," Michael's voice cracked like a whip. "Stop. We're on limited time here, right? Let's figure this out."

"What about Fiske?" I asked, in desperation. "He's holding our strangler's reins, supposedly."

"Maybe he told Dan to do something to pay off the debt and he didn't do it."

"Not his style," Cherabino said, her mind leaking contempt and mistrust. She was also picturing hitting me clean across the face, knocking me over, and tap-dancing on my kidneys.

I winced and added a suit of chain mail to the picture. "Who knows? Maybe he has a new style."

"Maybe it was Emily. She has connections to both the DeKalb-Peachtree Airport—her father owns a major share—and works in a shipping company. A major shipping company. Maybe there was something there that Fiske wanted," Michael put in.

Both of us turned to look at him, me uncomfortable that his thoughts were so close to mine.

"You're thinking smuggling?" Cherabino asked. "Or hijacking? There's been a rush of odd items on the black market lately, according to scuttlebutt, and there's all those hijackings . . ."

I went for it. "I have reason to believe the last shipment, with those illegal biologicals they found, was the Guild's."

Michael gasped.

I met Cherabino's eyes. "This is not to be included in a

report. Neither you nor I nor the whole department can take on the Guild, not with something this flimsy, not with them after me anyway. No one here will survive it. And I don't have proof, not proof that rides on anything but my word." Which, with my felonies, we all knew was useless. "For all we know, it was a shipment from Canada to Mexico, or something destined for bioengineering or medical healing. My life is on the line if something gets out. Maybe even if it doesn't. But—I thought you should know. If Emily was involved in a transport operation, they could have killed her to shut her up. To cover their tracks. Hell, this wouldn't be the first—or the last—time the Guild took somebody out." I kept the same intensity to my voice. "Legally, she's still Koshna, damage to her brain or not. Once you're inducted on the rolls of the Guild—after sixty days of you not fighting it—legally, you belong to them. Forever, or close enough. I've had Kara look it up. She's still on the rolls. She's still the Guild's. Which means if they killed her it's not a crime."

This is why Jacob can't join the Guild, Cherabino thought.

Michael shuttered. "They can't be everywhere. And why leave her body out?"

"I don't know."

"Fiske can't have his fingers in every pie. I say it's an independent player. Somebody who knew the victim. It's always somebody who knows the victim, and adding a killer-for-hire to the mix doesn't change that."

Cherabino frowned. "Fiske is involved in a hell of a lot, and a lot of his enemies have ended up dead in the last few years. If there's a major operation going on, you can be sure he at least knows about it and is taking his cut. But you're right. Just because he or the Guild is connected doesn't mean a minor player didn't do this. There's something funny going on with that boss of hers, and her dodging our calls isn't helping. Tell me about the company again."

Michael looked down at his notes, but there was a leashed tension to him. "Fine. Dymani Systems. Emily worked for their sales division, one of the top earners. They did ten million in sales last year, mostly awkward loads and large cargo, and she sold almost two million of that directly, some through deals with her father's airport. But the company is barely breaking even, at least in this office in the US; the parent office in India seems to be giving them a lot of grief as the lowest profit margins worldwide. As of yet, they haven't figured out why."

"Maybe somebody's skimming," I said.

"They're based out of India?" Cherabino sat up, shock reverberating down the Link. "Are their Tech inspections up to date? Do we know they're legit?"

Michael put down his notebook and leaned forward. "They're a registered business here in Atlanta and have been for thirty years. All their taxes are current. All their permits are filed on time—early, even. Just because they're foreigners—"

"They're from India," Cherabino interrupted. "India."

"Just because they're from India doesn't make them Tech smugglers," Michael said. "Frankly, it's insulting that you'd make that jump so quickly. And me? Because my grandparents are from Korea, that makes me a Communist? This kind of cruel prejudice is what puts a gun in the hand of a black kid and makes him shoot the white one, and both of them turn and shoot the innocent Asian one." He stood up, looked at her with this disappointment and anger, and I saw suddenly the strong emotional memory this was coming from.

Michael's little brother had been shot, in front of him, when they were both kids, a stray bullet in a gang fight. It never left him. It never would. Now, after seeing his brother's lifeblood seeping out onto the street, it would never leave me either. There was tragedy, real, earth-shattering tragedy, under Michael's cheerful exterior.

He paused, like he'd caught me reading him. Then he looked away. "I'm getting myself some coffee."

I stared at him walking away, shock and sorrow blooming inside me.

CHAPTER 14

The Thursday night NA meeting was at a church, but the basement was flooded. They sent us up to the huge sanctuary instead. Our circle of chairs was set up in the back of the huge room, curled around the last pew, some solid wooden thing with a seat arched to fit the curve of your butt. Its seat was worn enough from the pressure of a hundred thousand butts to make me think it was actually used. A lot. Well, Swartz said God gave a lot of people comfort, especially in hard times. And for all the God-talk in this group, I suppose the church wasn't going to make or break anything.

Someone had set up a folding table in the back of the room for snacks. Raquel had brought two pans of her carob chip loaf, slices of lumpy carob heaven. I took two. And, of course, a cup of coffee. Plus Norman had figured out some kind of thick barbecue sauce for bacterial-protein cubes that made them taste like chewy old-fashioned cocktail weenies. I took a double spoonful and a pile of toothpicks to eat them with.

"You outdid yourself, Norman," I said.

"Thanks."

Swartz came behind me at the table to get his own snacks. He was still quiet, his mind . . . Off. Likely he was worried about one of his kids. At least, I hoped that was what it was. He wasn't talking, and I respected him too much to go rummaging around in his head for the answer, but I was still worried a little.

I handed him the soy-powder canister without being told to. He opened and closed his hand once with a frown on his face before he took it and doctored his coffee.

He picked up the cup and took a few steps toward the waiting pew. "Why don't you . . ." He stopped talking then, and got a strange look on his face. A strange feeling from him in Mindspace.

Suddenly the coffee cup was on the floor, liquid splashing everywhere. Swartz was on his knees, gasping.

Pain, sudden pain, was in the air, my pain, his pain, shock, dismay, as he clutched his chest and I stared, unable to move.

Raquel was on the floor next to him. *Heart attack,* she mouthed. "Call the ambulance."

And behind me, a tall, skinny guy, a new guy, turned and started to blubber. My legs felt like concrete blocks; I couldn't move. I couldn't move! Swartz was on the floor, while all around me people rushed in and out. Colors blurred, lights and sound turning into whispering nothingness, as on the floor Swartz gasped like a fish in air and panicked.

My heart beat, far too fast, fast like a bongo drum hit with someone's hard hand over and over, as Swartz stopped breathing. I couldn't move. I still couldn't move as the ambulance crew arrived and swarmed over him with cold efficiency and hard plastic tubes.

We pulled up to the hospital. A huge red-and-blue sign proclaimed EMERGENCY ENTRANCE; a central sliding door opened and shut, feeding into the hospital from the circular drive we were on.

Raquel put the car in park. "Go on, go. I'll take care of the car and meet you in there."

"Do they know he smokes?" Smoked, I guess, but he'd only quit a few months ago. My brain kept grabbing onto details—him smoking, the ashen gray color he was turning on the floor, Raquel's faux-blond hair against her chestnut skin.

"We told the ambulance crew, but you'd better make sure they have the information. Better go now."

I pulled off my seat belt with numb fingers and fumbled with the latch of the door. She reached over past me and unlocked it, pushing my arm to encourage me to go.

I wasn't expecting the skin-to-skin contact; her brain hit me like a tidal wave, all force—and then gone. I sat, blinking.

"They're flagging me to move. Now would be a good time."

I staggered out of the car. Everywhere around me were screaming people, crying people, people terrified about injury and sickness and emergencies of all kinds. Police waved at Raquel's car again, and she pulled out with a lurch to be replaced by another car.

Three women piled out of the car, screaming at the tops of their lungs, while one of them clutched a bloody limb wrapped with gauze; her pain hit me like a club in Mindspace and I staggered back—Only to run into a woman literally foaming at the mouth, her mind spitting blocks of razor blades through my brain. I screamed, and ran—straight into the mouth of the waiting doors, a burst of air pressure hitting me as I passed the threshold.

A full room of worried patients filled the air with the strong scent of despair, long rows of antiseptic chairs in faded patterns filled with people of every kind, blood seeping from various wounds into gauze, a child crying softly in the corner. A male nurse in blue scrubs and ugly white shoes stood to one side, giving court in front of a massive array of air filters, the whole right side of which was color-coded as antimicrobial. A steady stream of air pushed out from them into the waiting room; another, smaller set of fans pushed used air out through the doors to make the air pressure I'd felt.

He gave me a tired glance. "If you're here for psychiatric admittance, it's two doors down."

"No, my friend—"

He looked up then. "Is he—"

"The ambulance should be here already. I need to see him. . . ."

"Hold on, buddy. Hold on." The nurse grabbed a board from an open window to one side of the room. "Okay, who is he and what was his complaint?"

"He collapsed," I said, suddenly everything rushing in all at once. "He couldn't breathe. He was holding his chest. The ambulance . . ." It was like my throat closed up, and I couldn't move again.

The nurse grabbed my arm, and another mind was jabbed forcibly onto mine. I pulled away, raw and aching. Something about triage, overloaded staff, who would die and who would not.

And the information I needed, including a detailed mental map of the hospital and my next steps: "He'll be in Cardiology, next wing, first floor. Check in with the nurses' station in Intake at the front of the hospital, six doors on the left, one turn past the probiotic aerators. Anything else I need to know? Any place I can't go?"

He backed up like he'd been stung. "What . . ."

"Telepath. Sorry, no badge today. Yeah. I'll find it." I'd hardly noticed the telepathy actually working on time, perfectly, the first time. In the evening, no less.

His mouth twisted. "Leave the patients alone."

I ignored his fear, though it tried to grip me like my own panic, the panic of Swartz on the floor like a fish. I walked, ignoring the commotion to my right as more nurses and doctors struggled to save someone dying. The soul was already Falling In, making a ripple in the fabric of Mindspace I could feel from here. I held on to my sanity with white-knuckled hands, wanting my drug with every fiber of my being, knowing I needed to find Swartz. Now. No matter what this damn hospital cost me, or how much damage I did to myself just by being here.

In the waiting room, my numb panic merging with the exhausted despair of everyone else waiting for loved ones, everyone else waiting for someone to pass between life and death—or make it back out, somehow, to come back to them. Waves of distress hit me from all sides, and I sat, struggling to breathe, to think, to do anything but endure. It was like my final test before I'd gotten my certification, my final control test as a telepath, all over again.

I'd called Selah, Swartz's wife, who would be here in a few moments. Cherabino was in the hallway, on the phone, taking care of department business. The emotion ghosts across the way sat in chairs too, generations of people sitting, waiting for surgeons, waiting for news. The air was bitter, the strong taste of neutral bacteria aerated in the air to crowd out anything that would possibly make us sick. I coughed; they claimed the stuff wouldn't affect you, but I could almost feel it coating the inside of my lungs.

Cherabino walked into the room like a pool of crisp water in the middle of a muddy maelstrom. I latched onto her, the anchor I needed. Instead of blocking me out with bricks upon bricks of defenses, she held out a mental hand.

I grabbed onto it, gentling, and she sat. We waited a long, long time.

The surgeon was a short, fat man with sweat-drenched hair flattened in the shape of a headband. He was standing like his back hurt, slumped like he was exhausted. I was shielding too hard here in the hospital to know for sure, but I was betting he'd just been through the fight of his life. He did, however, meet Selah's eyes squarely and without apology.

"I'm Dr. Carver." He held out a hand utterly without apology for the name. "You must be Mrs. Swartz."

"That's right," Selah said in a small voice, and took his hand. "Is my husband okay?"

"Your husband had a myocardial infarction," the surgeon said gently. "A heart attack. A very serious heart attack. Even with surgery, there are complications."

"Will he live?" I demanded.

"There was some real damage. His brain seems okay, and the patch we put on the artery seems to be holding. He's stable for now, and I'm having him moved down to Intensive Care; he should be reasonably stable for the next day or so. But after that . . . You have to understand, Mrs. Swartz, that the damage was extremely extensive. I can't just put in an artificial heart; the tissue in that area is just too fragile."

"What does that mean?" Selah asked in a terrified voice.

"We got him through the immediate danger. He'll likely wake up in the next day or two. You'll have some time with him. But unless something dramatic changes, I'm sorry, Mrs. Swartz, but this is almost certainly fatal.

I've bought you some time with him. I'm sorry, but that's all I can do."

My insides felt . . . empty, like someone had scooped me out with a spoon. This was Swartz. Swartz—the man who'd stood by me no matter what, who'd cared enough to show up with cookies to rehab after a major fall off the wagon, who believed I could do something, that I could still make it despite the huge crushing weight of failure that dogged my every step. Who took my calls no matter what. Who dropped everything to drive me to a meeting, or to show up at my apartment and just sit. Who would yell at me or praise me, make me work and make me think. This was Swartz.

"How long?" Selah asked.

He stood up straighter, and yet somehow seemed more exhausted. "A week. Maybe less. I'm sorry, Mrs. Swartz. I genuinely am."

Selah nodded mutely, and the doctor bid her good-bye. I just stood there, literally unable to think, unable to process. Despair was crashing in on me, and the emotion ghosts around me felt like attacking bees, constant stinging, constant despair.

"Would you wait with me?" Selah asked.

Hospitals were horrible, horrible things to telepaths. But I heard myself saying, "Yes, of course."

Hours later, I was feeling as mind-sick as I ever had felt in my life, almost burned completely out from the relentless pressure of the minds and death around me. Death, attacking me like a tangible force.

But another thought was pulling at me, and I couldn't let it go. With all the people around me—with the FBI and the Guild and a known killer targeting me—had I caused this? Had something happened to Swartz because I had pissed somebody off?

I went to find the nurse, hands shaking so hard she asked what I was on.

"Nothing. I'm a telepath."

She replaced a panel on the aerator, the white-dotted sludge inside a stronger-smelling version of the bitter taste to the air. Engineered microbes; they seemed ominous somehow, for all they were used in every hospital in the country.

"What do you need?" the nurse asked me, looking sympathetic.

I explained my suspicions. She, God bless her, went to find the doctor immediately, sitting me down in a chair in the middle of the hall.

When the doctor arrived, I asked him the same terrible question.

"No, no, that I can say for sure," Dr. Carver said. "It was obvious during the surgery. This has been building for years. With his medical history—well, there's a lot of damage."

I took a breath. A long, cleansing breath. "The drugs? It was all the drugs he took and the cigarettes."

His eyes were kind. "That would be my guess as to cause. There's no family history. I'm sorry. This is a bad situation. But you had nothing—nothing—to do with it."

I went back to sit in the waiting room, Mindspace crowding in on me in terrible pressure, relief there too.

But an hour later while Selah tried to hide her tears and Cherabino and I pretended we didn't notice, it occurred to me. Had I done to my body what Swartz had done to his?

Would I die in a hospital, surrounded by dying memories in Mindspace? The Guild facility wouldn't take me, not anymore. Was I going to die like this?

As my brain started to overload from all the pressure,

my vision started to tunnel in, slowly, blackness curling in around the edges of my vision.

"What's wrong?" Cherabino asked me, her face screwed up like she had a migraine. "Adam, tell me what's wrong."

At four a.m. Cherabino bodily pulled me out of the hospital. I was nearly seizuring, and barely able to walk, even with support.

She pushed me in her car and it was too much.

I threw up. In Cherabino's car. Shame drenched me like the vomit.

She breathed, outside. "Well, that was attractive." But that was it. She got towels from the trunk and handed them to me, and didn't say another word.

"I need to go be with Selah," I kept repeating. I couldn't think. I held the towel in front of me. "I need to sit with Selah. Is she okay?"

Cherabino got in the car, grabbed the towel, and started patting me down. "I called the NA chapter. I called her son," Cherabino said again and again until I believed her. "I called her neighbors. I even woke up Bellury. I'm a cop. We can do this. People will be there. Someone will be there, Adam. I promise you someone will be there."

It was then and only then that I let her shut the car door. Only then did I let her take me back to the apartment and push me into the shower. She waited outside while the warm water rushed over me, more water dripping from my eyes as my insides screamed and screamed like they would never stop.

Cherabino stayed that night, on my couch. She didn't leave. She didn't leave even when I asked her to, when I begged her to, when the water came streaming down from my eyes again. And in the morning, right before dawn, when the phone rang to call her in to a murder scene, I had somehow fallen asleep with my head in her lap, her arms around me.

She kissed me, lightly, before she left, and only then built back brick by brick the shield between us.

CHAPTER 15

After the door closed behind her, I couldn't get the doctor's words out of my head. Swartz might die today.

I caught the first bus of the day, the early Friday special. The commuters in the morning shied away from me, perhaps reading my mood. Swartz's life hung in the balance, and I could no more go back to that hospital today than I could fly; trying either one would have painful—and deadly—consequences. But this was Swartz.

Two bus changes, and I found myself in north Fulton County, the Buckhead business district. Then three blocks on foot to get to where I needed to go. I kept moving, urgency like a ticking time bomb in my head.

The Guild campus towered above, four fragile-looking glass-and-chrome boxes, one a tall skyscraper, like an impossibly heavy trophy set in concrete. Most of the other skyscrapers in the area had the aggressive boxy defensive postwar look of anti-gravity supports, reinforced steel, and antimissile turrets; this area had been flattened by the Tech Wars sixty years ago, after all. The Guild was the only one dumb enough—or arrogant enough—to build back with the old glass and chrome, the only one willing to be so open to the sunlight and so vulnerable to attack. But then again the Guild didn't need walls to defend them.

Inside, through the huge glass-paneled doors, was the small guard's desk, done in chrome. The foyer itself was a huge circular room topped by an impressive glass dome; weighty marble columns ringed the room above a flawless marble floor polished until you could see the blue of the sky. Small statues of Guild founders and heroes looked down from alcoves along the paneled walls. I'd been impressed, back when I'd walked through the doors as a kid. I'd been proud, working here, teaching here as a professor. Now it just seemed like a waste of space—a waste without even the dignity of a few chairs to wait in.

I told the guard what I wanted.

"Is she expecting you?" the guard asked. He was a short man, skinny and pale, with the too-bright follicles of artificial hair implants. He looked harmless, but he was security for the Guild; whatever it was he could do, he wasn't harmless.

"No," I said. "Page her anyway." My emotions got away from me and desperation, despair, and Swartz's crisis leaked out into the air between us.

He shook his head, but he dialed.

And I tried to put my world in a box and sit on it, sit hard on everything that meant anything, so I'd be acceptable in the public space of telepaths.

In response to some cue I couldn't see, the guard cleared his throat. He held out a lapel clip, a plain white square.

"What is that?"

"New recorder." The guard held out the square again. "Standard procedure."

"I'm not wearing that," I said. The little square seemed suddenly dangerous, like a cobra in a plain box. No way was I going to consent to brain wave recording. No way. Not on a good day, and today . . .

"It's all right, Tristan," a woman's voice said from behind me. "A plain locator should accomplish the goal here. I'll vouch for him."

I turned. Walking down the marble floor in quiet shoes was a woman, late fifties, small and unassuming with white, white hair pulled back in a chignon. Yes, a chignon; she insisted on the term. Despite her small size, delicate features, and obvious age, she carried herself with confidence. Well, maybe "confidence" wasn't the right word. The attitude of a woman carrying a big, crass, brightly painted grenade launcher, with an antiaircraft laser attachment for good measure? That. With a string of pearls. Let's just say she got what she wanted more often than she didn't, one way or the other.

Jamie wasn't flashy; she didn't go out of her way to weigh Mindspace, to loom over the minds around her. In fact, she did the opposite, holding herself back, still, quiet. But the wake her mind made even so . . . The ripples altered the feel of the room in subtle ways, no matter how still she stood. Jamie was a Level Ten telepath, one of two in the world, and the strongest telepath I'd ever met. Strong enough to crush me like a soap bubble, if she caught me unaware. She was also—or had been—my mentor, the one who'd taught me what it meant to be a telepath, what it meant to be a responsible, ethical professional in a sea of pretenders. Other than the short moment at the funeral, I hadn't seen her since rehab.

"If you're sure, Ms. Skelton," the guard said.

She nodded to him. "I assume you're here to see Kara?"

I nodded, most of my energy spent on not broadcasting my turmoil. . . .

Apparently some of it leaked out anyway, because she looked sad. "Her office is at the end of the new wing. I'll take you there."

"Thanks." I held myself as tightly as I could, like a tuning fork against a chair. Finally: *It's good to see you too. I—*

I'm glad you came back, she returned, with a wave of warmth and cautious affection. Her mental voice, as always, felt like lemonade on a hot day, blowing grass under a blazing sun. *I always . . . well, I'd hoped you would find your way back.* Back to the Guild, she meant. But more, back to real life. I felt her decide not to mention the current state of my mind. I was clean, she could tell that much, and that was enough.

"This is just a visit," I clarified. "I'm not coming back to the Guild."

A small dot of concern and curiosity; then she pulled them back from the air. "Well, even so," she said out loud. *It's good to see you.*

"It's good to see you too."

She held out a hand, wordlessly offering a little strength, free of charge. She could see how empty I was running.

I looked at her for a long moment, and I then I took her hand, and the strength, a small stream of raw mental power scented with her sunshine-and-ozone self. It was over nearly before it began.

She lowered the hand and kept walking, without comment. She hadn't taken anything—even information—from me in return.

I realized all at once there were things I missed about the Guild.

Thank you.

I knocked on the doorframe as Jamie's mind moved away behind me.

Kara was seated behind a curved white glass desk, a small pencil cup and a picture frame the only things on the surface besides the papers she was working on. She looked good today, with a recent haircut, precise makeup, and a poufy ivory blouse.

She looked up. "Adam. Look, I'm sorry, your certification will definitely not be renewed, not even if the watcher certifies you as trustworthy. I don't know what you heard—"

I cut her off, my desperation making none of that important. "Swartz is dying. My sponsor. Swartz. He's dying, and I need you to arrange for a medic. A microkinesis Guild-trained medic." I put my hands behind my head. "I need you to come through for me, Kara. You owe me this."

She stood, gestured to the chair in front of her. "Sit down, okay?"

"I don't want to sit down, I want you to get me a medic."

"*Sit down.*"

I stood there, staring at her.

"What kind of medic?" she asked quietly.

"Cardiac. Heart attack, with some kind of additional damage that means he can't have an artificial heart. Some kind of complications from his drug use years ago."

She closed her eyes, just for a second. "It had to be cardiac. Adam, the Guild is short on cardiac medics. There are three in the country, and two are traveling in high-profile areas right now. The third is working on the president's uncle, who is also dying. There's no way I can do it."

I moved forward until my thighs hit the front of her desk. "You *have to*. This is Swartz. Kara, I have never treated you badly for betraying me. For getting me kicked out of the Guild. For ruining my life. I have never—but you owe me this. You owe me more than this."

It was like her face opened, her heart ripping out as I saw her sorrow and deep, deep regret like crimson lines painted in Mindspace between us. "You should not have been kicked out," she said, eyes glistening with half-shed tears. "I swear to you, I never thought it would be like that. You should have been cleaned up and given help. But even so. It was the right thing to do. The right thing to do, and you would have done the same." She took a breath.

"I'm sorry," I said. I didn't say sorry lightly; every time was like rehab. Maybe she was right, but: "Swartz is dying."

She turned away, looked out the window, let the silence sit as the wheels turned in her head. Finally she turned back. "I can't do the impossible, Adam. I wish with all my heart I could. If I tried—if I tried, it would be my career and your head both."

"I don't care." I was no lightweight, and for Swartz, for Swartz I'd fight all comers. "You want to do the right thing, Kara? This is the right damn thing!" I was almost yelling, emotions radiating out. I had no control left. The hospital, the damn hospital and Swartz's illness, had stolen my control and now my eyes were watering again.

Kara met my gaze, her eyes watering too. "Even if I tried, odds are your mentor will still not get the help he needs."

Now I sat down in the chair, staring at my hands. "I—"

"There is one thing I could try. But you won't like the consequences."

"Do it."

Stone entered the room with an angry gait. He was holding a length of sticky cord, a restraint, down at his side. His body language was wary.

"Thank you for coming." Kara sat on the side of her desk, hands resting on its edge. "I have a proposition that gets you the tag you wanted."

What? I yelled at her mentally. We still had a faint Link left over from years ago; Stone wouldn't be able to overhear a Link. *I'm not getting any—*

Shut up and let me work.

"I'm listening," Stone said, his eyes darting back and forth between us. I sat, Kara stood, but our body language and relative positions had to look like a united front against him.

"Adam will consent to a voluntary—temporary—tag." Kara's diction was extremely precise. "For the length of this particular inquiry, and will consent to periodic mental checks and the release of his private information and current employment files to Enforcement for the purposes of your investigation, provided all tags and checks end when your determination is made. You'll get full access to my records and Adam's private record from the Guild training facility, and one—count it, one—interview with me about our past. *In return*, you will provide your private Enforcement medic to treat . . . " She paused here and looked at me.

"Jonathon Swartz," I offered, nerves stretched almost to the breaking point.

"Jonathon Swartz, Adam's mentor, who is currently dying of cardiac issues. Within the next forty-eight hours. Said treatment to be the best available. Your Enforcement medic is cross-trained in trauma of all kinds, I am fully aware, and according to my information he is also currently in town and unassigned. The terms of this deal are contingent on timely care."

Stone thought about it for a second, looked at me.

"If you'll save Swartz I'll do anything you want and gladly."

"The medic is available," he said cautiously.

Relief hit like a long, cold drink of water. Maybe, maybe this was going to work. Maybe I could save Swartz. "Thank you, Kara. I . . ."

She looked me straight in the eye. "For the record, I don't owe you anything."

I nodded. "This is more than—"

"No. I don't owe you anything because it was the right thing to do. And this—this was the right thing too." She looked at the clock and stood up, suddenly exhausted. "I'm sorry, but I'm going to have to ask you to leave my office. I have an urgent meeting in ten minutes I have to be ready for."

"Thank you," I told her.

She nodded, and suddenly was hugging me. I got a glimpse of her mind, her satisfaction at a deal well made and sadness—quiet sadness. "I'm sorry about Swartz. I really am. He's been sending me updates on you every month for years. He's a good man." Then she glanced toward the door, concerned about time.

"I'm going," I said. "I'm going right now."

Swartz had sent her updates?

Stone and I walked down the hall, to a small alcove under a window at the end. A statue of the Guild founder, Cooper, sat on top of the small table there. I reached out and straightened the statue; his code of ethics still meant a lot to me.

"You realize it's not going to be that easy," Stone told me.

"What?" Suddenly my stomach was bad in free fall. "Why the *hell* not?"

His body language seemed aggressive suddenly, and I was on full alert, ready to fight. I would be hard-pressed not to lose, and even if through some miracle I survived, in the middle of the Guild building . . . well, I wouldn't get far afterward.

But he only fidgeted with the sticky cord where I could see it, a threat, but a veiled one. "A cardiac medic is the most expensive commodity in the Guild stable right now. And you're getting someone with similar skills, better skills maybe, as he's versed in trauma and recovery. What you're offering in return is not nearly worth what you're getting."

He was bargaining with a life. A normal life. A sudden, horrible thought occurred to me. "If the Guild had *anything, anything* to do with—"

"No," Stone said at once, looking discomfited. "No, we wouldn't—I wouldn't. Not randomly and not without cause. And not, on first choice, to a noncombatant. I have some ethics."

"You'd say that even if it was you." I didn't bother to hide my cynicism. "And I've already blocked your investigation at least once and promised you I'd do it again. This plays right into your hands."

"I swear on the Guild founders that this was neither me nor anyone else acting on behalf of the Guild. Demand any proof you like. This was not me."

Every interrogator instinct in me said he was telling the truth. And even if he wasn't I still needed what he offered. "You swear it?"

"I do, on any oath you name."

"What do you need to make up the difference?"

He straightened a bit. "It's a large difference. I don't know what will make that debt work."

He was fleecing me. I could see him setting me up like a mark on the street. But the trouble was, I needed what he was offering and according to Kara—whom I believed—there was no way else to get it. "Fine, we'll call it a debt. But I need the medic, and I need it now."

"We do the tag first."

"Temporary," I stipulated. My stomach roiled. To have somebody able to check on me at any moment of any day . . . I already had Swartz, I told myself, Swartz and Bellury checking up on me. But if I wanted to keep Swartz, it had to be done. "A fully removable tag. You know I'm strong enough—and trained enough—to check."

He nodded.

I swallowed.

"It's standard procedure. And I will check at random. But this isn't my first case, or my thirtieth, and I'm fair. After the first few seconds you'll know I'm there. I'm not cruel and I'm not invasive. If I don't understand something or it looks suspicious, I will look for more information before I make a determination."

I nodded, the fear still there, but tempered.

If it was anybody but Swartz . . . Swartz, who'd picked me up when I was a punk and convinced me I could be better. That I could have a chance at a real life again. Swartz, who'd dragging me kicking and screaming into a place where self-respect was possible, and happened. Swartz, who kicked me in the ass when I thought about going sideways. "Swartz needs the medic now. Now, or it's useless to him and me both."

I let him put the tag on me, squirming and jittery the whole time. And there it was, a square patch of his mind sitting on the right side of mine. A square patch of not-me, something a shield couldn't stop. Like a boil sitting on the top of my mental skin, painful and swollen and all too firmly attached.

"Try to block me," Stone said.

So I did, hard.

But, out of my control, there he was. *It's working,* the stranger said, inside all my defenses. I tried to throw him out, I tried to expel him like food poisoning, like vomit, but— *Calm down. Calm. It's okay.*

I took a breath, then another, tolerating him like a bit in my mouth.

And then he was gone.

"I'll be checking in on you in random intervals for at least a week, likely longer, considering your history."

Then he opened the door and let me go. I kept looking

over my shoulder as I walked out the door and down to the elevators. Kept looking, and waiting for the other shoe to drop.

Swartz was going to get the help he needed, right?

On the way out of the building, when I thought it couldn't possibly get any worse, it did.

I was walking through the middle of the huge open glass-and-steel atrium in the center of the main sky-scraper, the central glass elevator tubes extending like the spine of some huge animal above me, tiered floors all around. And there, not far from the elevator, in a crowd of folks dressed in office clothes, was Tamika. She was star-ing at me with accusing eyes.

And I turned around and left, in the fastest walk I could manage. Acid burned in my gut, a sharp pain like a fillet knife dragging my gut, so I left. Like the coward I was.

CHAPTER 16

Back at the department, I snuck past Cherabino's cubicle and went farther back into the secure area, the really secure area, past the new plastic sheeting separating their airflow from ours. Something about wanting to contain contagions. Honestly, computer viruses had only morphed to infect non-Tech-implanted humans once, and we had vaccines now; separate air for four cubicles was overkill. I mean, if we were all going to die, we would have died by now. But there was no telling the head of Electronic Crimes that.

I was carrying a piece of paper with all the information we knew about the strangler, written in nice, clear, large block letters, arranged logically by type and logic. I was out of time, out of patience, with a vision riding on my back and a tag in my head. If I wanted to save Swartz, to save my job and find Emily's killer, I had to act. I had to make this happen—me, no waiting for anyone else.

The cubicle I needed was the second on the right, currently full of the large bulk of a man.

"Hey, Bob," I said.

"What now?" Bob turned. He was a balding caricature of an aging cop, the kind who went four steps after a suspect, then collapsed into a panting mess. Bob didn't have to chase suspects on foot, though; and he was as stubborn

as a bulldog about getting the answers you were looking
for in a much, much more dangerous space than just the
street. Bob dealt with the Net, the tiny, dangerous, cracked
remains of the data-soaked superhighway that had once
ruled the world. In that space, he was a cowboy, a cowboy
with an Uzi and an attitude, and the power he held sat
badly on that pudgy body, disturbing as hell and twice as
dangerous.

Bob had an implant—a real, honest-to-God computer
implant—in the back of his neck that tapped directly into
his brain, and he was one of the youngest people I'd ever
seen with a legal one. When untold thousands of people
had died in a rash of wetware viruses and electrical burn-
outs during the Tech Wars, well, implants weren't so pop-
ular anymore.

"Something you needed, genius?" Bob asked with a
scowl.

"I have a new problem for you."

His eyes lit up, and he grabbed the paper out of my
hand. Twenty-eight seconds while he processed the text,
implant-aided sight making short work of the information. The computer screen behind him flashed strings of
numbers, images of snakes and trees, and a few disturb-
ingly vivid crime scene photos. It stayed on the last, the
brown-red pool of blood by a woman's bare feet, a picture
from the scene I'd seen a few days ago.

Bob looked up, the living personification of a computer prompt.

"I strongly suspect this guy is in the databases of several federal agencies, since he's associated with Fiske,
which is a federal case. I also know he's been tied to
maybe a dozen murders here in the metro area. But I don't
know what the agencies have to say about him, and I
don't know which murders."

"That's an open-ended query. Not a walk in the park. Plus the feds are off-limits."

"As are you, supposedly. But here we are."

"It'll cost you."

"I saw these dulce de leche donuts with a side of Bavarian crème on the way into work," I said. The donut shop would take my stupid cardboard food voucher from the department; I wasn't allowed to handle money, but they got more than half of their business from the cops anyway and didn't mind paperwork. "How about a dozen?"

"Every day for a week."

Inside, I winced. His prices were getting higher. "You used to do this for me for free."

"You used to ask easier questions."

"Fine. You want the donuts first thing in the morning?"

"Afternoons."

"Fine."

Bob turned all the way around in the chair and faced the computer. The screen started flashing pictures too fast for me to follow, the occasional polygon, a federal seal, and then it hurt my eyes to even try—I looked at the side of the cubicle and watched the flashing light, the shadow of Bob's hands conducting like an orchestra.

This is why I went to Bob even though I wasn't supposed to. This was why I paid whatever the greedy idiot wanted. Because this search capability—well, the computer, a secure computer like Cherabino's, could do that in a few seconds. No, what took so long is sorting through the data, knocking out the important bits from the dross of the thing. And that—that—is what Bob's brain on an implant could do in thirty seconds or less.

Only right now it was taking longer. A lot longer. Maybe this federal database thing hadn't been a good idea after all. Maybe I'd get a call and a visit from scary men in black suits . . . And, well, prison was starting to sound all too possible. The prison or the Guild. At least neither was that horrible vision, I told myself.

The screen went bright red, and the phone rang.

Bob tapped his temple, and the ringing abruptly stopped. "No, it's me. We're pulling a file. Literally one file. Calm down. Yes, I know that's classified. Do you want plausible deniability or not?" He glanced over at me, a nasty look. "No, it's for the homicide division. They're looking into this guy. There's been some murders in the area. How the hell do I know why they don't want to go through channels? You want to loosen up the sphincter or what? Yeah, yeah, I'll decrypt it so they can't look at your codes. Like I wouldn't do that anyway. Yeah, you can delete the military mission crap. We don't care about that stuff anyways." He tapped his temple again. "Cranky bastards."

Then he turned all the way around in the chair, and I could almost see the data swimming behind his eyes. Suddenly, abruptly, it was gone and he looked tired. He waved in my general direction. "You now owe me two weeks of donuts. And coffee. The file will be printing on the computer by the time you get there; they just need a minute to redact stuff."

I turned to go, but his voice stopped me before I left the cubicle.

"You have two days before I tell Zahir; it'll show up then anyway, and I'm not taking the fall for it." He paused. "Why not just read it off somebody's hard drive?" He meant their minds, I was sure. Typically we called that wetware, but Bob was jacked in.

I looked back at him. "Telepathy is local. Twenty feet or so, unless there's something that breaks the rules. This guy's in Washington or somewhere else with the other spooks. Much, much farther than twenty feet."

"Oh." He turned back around, giving me the cold shoulder. As if the thought of such limitations was dumb, and unbelievable.

Bob's phone rang, and he answered, "Yeah, he's still here."

He handed the phone off to me without explanation.

"You're lucky I have a flag on your record," a man's voice said without introduction. "I just intercepted a major search-and-contain order against you. Why exactly do you need classified information?"

"Who is this?" I asked warily.

"Special Agent Jarrod, FBI. I called you a few days ago. I'll repeat myself. Why do you need this information?"

I swallowed. Great, now I was in trouble with the FBI. "We have a murder case we've traced back to this guy. I've read the signatures myself, and we've traced his methods back to at least fifty other for-hire kills in the area. But I don't have a name and I don't have a way to get to him, other than his association with somebody I've been told we cannot touch. I need more information; I knew the victim and I am *not*, I repeat, *not* going to let her killer get away scot-free because I didn't get all the information. No matter what Cherabino says. No matter what the rules say."

There was a short silence over the phone, and my emphatic words started cooling into fear.

Finally he spoke. "That would be a good reason to hack a classified file. And the records say you only took one, and one for a guy in your territory and likely connected to the investigation you're discussing. Don't make a habit of this, am I clear? But I'll handle the issue on our end."

I swallowed.

"Adam?"

"Yes?"

After a short pause: "You might call me next time, you know. The FBI has a history of cooperation with local police departments."

I didn't know what to say to that. Had he really been looking at me for a job? Had I failed to screw it up yet somehow? This seemed surreal.

"Okay. Well, as it happens, I've seen that file before. The name of the guy you're tracking is Sibley. Blair Sibley. A British expat with specialized military training who was dismissed from service under circumstances the British government won't talk about. He has a . . . tendency toward ligature strangulation and knife work, and has employed that tendency in situations well outside his job description, even in the special ops circumstances he was operating in. My guess is he finally killed someone innocent or political enough they had to get rid of him. He was in Los Angeles for about ten years, and recently settled in Atlanta somewhere, we believe as the result of a direct call from Fiske. The association between them is there, but as near as I can tell, loose. Sibley still takes a number of jobs separate from their association, and Fiske gets the group rate for most of his jobs. A symbiotic relationship if ever there was one, but in my opinion, if you continue in the vein you've been tracing, you have the wiggle room to take down Sibley without tipping the department's hand. It'll have to be done carefully. I'd appreciate updates and coordination before you make a move."

"That's fine. Wait, what's your number?"

"I'll have a card sent over by courier so you can't lose it in the walk between Bob's desk and yours."

"Wait. Again, sorry, how did you know it was me? Bob never said . . ."

"That is the question, isn't it? Keep me updated, please."

I stood staring at the telephone handset, the sound of the dial tone echoing from it. He'd hung up on me.

I walked to the secure printer in a sort of daze, and forced myself to read through the information.

My eyes flew over the pages with increasing disbelief. He'd given me the highlights, pretty much everything I needed to know. But there—at the end of the file—labeled with Jarrod's compliments, was a list of the cases Sibley was attached to—a long, long list that spanned several states. And a note: *If you take down this guy, I'll buy you a beer.*

Swartz was still at the hospital, still out of reach of any visit I could safely make for days yet. Worse, the nurses wouldn't let me talk to him, or Selah, or anyone. They did say a medic was there, but they couldn't—or wouldn't—tell me anything more.

It was driving me nuts, not seeing him. It was like a gaping hole in my chest, this itchy queasy feeling . . . and my mind kept playing Cherabino, Cherabino's discomfort at me in her head, that kiss, Paulsen's anger and near promise I would lose my job, and Swartz, Swartz sick, Swartz dying with me not able to do anything.

The day passed in a blur and Bellury dropped me off at the apartment, and I kept seeing that vision, that horrible vision where I was on the street, alone, nobody, crawled back into a vial of Satin too big to hold the world. Without Swartz, what was the point? Without this job, how in hell would I stay sane?

My street looked dirty all of a sudden, the chipped dirty concrete steps of my old building like a curse. The chipped facade of the building, a building intended to hold office dwellers and stress rather than people. A building I'd lose when Paulsen fired me.

I glanced behind me to see the tailpipe of Bellury's old car turn the corner. Then I went back down the steps and down the street. A streetwalker called to me from the corner, the same one who'd been there for weeks, dirty blond, lewd, and desperate. She called out again, but that was a drug I couldn't take, one that would eat me from the inside, bind us together, and destroy us both. Part of me regretted that intensely; another person, another body, another mind and pleasure sounded like perfection, like the best drug in the world, but . . . I'd stick to what I knew. I'd stick to something that wouldn't destroy anyone but me.

So I walked, and walked, my coat turned up around my face, while my brain played back the vision, alone, alone. Five long city blocks to the bus stop, past the liquor store, the big glaring neon-lit liquor store, the only drug in the world Bellury's test wasn't designed to pick up.

I found myself inside the store, picking out a bottle of bourbon, the expensive kind, the smooth kind that warmed you all the way down. I passed other, desperate customers, one normal-looking couple, and a stocker boy. I got to the register—and realized I didn't have any money, that I'd hamstrung myself or let the department hamstring me for just that reason.

Paulsen was probably going to fire me anyway.

So I stole into the clerk's mind and told his brain I'd already paid.

I was halfway down the sidewalk home, precious bottle in hand, when I realized . . . If the watcher had shown up then . . .

My hands shook, and the terror, the outright terror of what I'd done, of what I'd sunk to, hit me. I threw the bottle as far from me on the street as I possibly could, the glass shattering like my entire life.

I barely made it back to the apartment in one piece, and huddled, shivering, in my bedroom with the Mind-space blocker on so Cherabino couldn't see, couldn't see how low I'd come.

It took me hours to even think about sleeping.

CHAPTER 17

Saturday and Sunday found me either on service projects—I invited myself to the AA project, even—or sitting in the hospital parking lot, as close as I dared go. I talked to Selah twice. I talked to Swartz once, on the phone. He could barely form words.

The medic was supposed to go on Sunday, and from the phone calls I made, he did. No one could give me any more updates, though, and Selah stopped answering the phone.

That afternoon, I invited myself to Bellury's house, where he set me to cleaning out his garage, hours and hours of backbreaking dirty work.

I was grateful.

Monday midday, Cherabino looked up for the third time from her paperwork. "You're brewing again."

"Ummph," I said miserably.

"I'm getting the edge of that, you know."

"Sorry." I tried to shield, and failed. The telepathy was working fine, but I lacked the motivation to do anything right now. I settled deeper in my chair, a dark depression settling in on me.

After a moment, she sighed and turned all the way around. "Fine. Let's go through this again. Is there anything you can do to help him?"

"No."

"And his wife—Selah's her name, correct? Does she need anything?"

"No. Half the NA chapter's there doing errands for her and sitting by his bedside. The medic's already done what he can do. And the hospital . . ."

"You said you can't go back to the hospital. How absolute is that?"

"Pretty damn absolute. It's a hospital. People die in hospitals—it's a nightmare for a telepath, and my brain is as stressed as it can be right now. If he's not actually dying, I have no business being there. And even then, I'm risking everything to go in for ten minutes." I had an appointment to see the medic later. In the meantime, there was nothing I could do; the hospital said he was stable.

"Well, then." She sighed again. Looked at her paperwork, before stuffing it in a file. "Get your raincoat. We're going out."

I stared at the desk in front of me.

"No, seriously, get your raincoat."

I sighed and got my raincoat.

We were halfway there, rain making the world streaky and the anti-grav unstable, before I thought to ask where we were going.

"Gun range," Cherabino said. "The one across the street is down for maintenance, and the outdoor range is useless in this weather. Fortunately this is a firearms-friendly town, and the department got us a group deal."

I looked out the window, too miserable to really care. "You're going to practice, then."

"You are."

That made me look up. "I don't need to use a gun, I'm a telepath." I hit her mind with a prick of instant pain, to prove my point. My head responded with a tiny burst of light and reaction pain; much less than I'd expected.

"Stop that." She built up her walls again. "Guns make loud sounds and great smells. Plus they're a big component of the certification I think you can qualify for without much trouble—maybe a PI license, or a special type-four deputy A. Plus you obviously need to get the stress out. There's nothing like plugging a hole in a target to do that."

"If you say so."

She pulled into the parking lot of the low building labeled INDOOR RANGE, stopping way, way too fast in this weather. I was thrown forward against the seat belt with an "oof."

She stared at me, anger coming from her now. "Stop it with the poor-me act. Seriously. You're not the only one who's dealing with death; half the guys in the department have parents old enough to have serious medical problems. Plus we've had three deaths in the county this year on the job. It's less than last year, but think about it. Three families whose daddy or mommy isn't coming home. It's crappy, and it's not anything anybody wants to deal with, but it's part of life. You need to rage, you need to get drunk, you need to go out and do something stupid, I understand. But this passive thing. You can't do it. You can't afford to give in like this."

"Don't lecture me. Really. That's Swartz's job." I got out, closing the car door behind me hard. It was raining, a steady stream of icky nastiness, the first burst of clouds heavily laden with pollution and worse things; I huddled inside the raincoat and hustled to the sidewalk under the dubious awning.

She put the car in park and followed, cursing steadily under her breath.

The low building looked like any dark beige old store in the area, dirty and faded from years of sun. The sign,

PATTY'S GUNS AND INDOOR RANGE, could barely be read, it was so old and sun-faded, even under the too-thin green awning, which was unraveling in places. I could smell the pollution in the air, or maybe I was smelling my own anger.

Cherabino caught up to me. "I'm—"

"Shut up. If we're going to do this, let's get it over with." I'd never held a gun in my life, but if it would get her off my back I'd do it and gladly. Plus there was a point to distraction—that's something they emphasized in the program. You felt like crap, you wanted to fall off the wagon, you found something useful to do. Something not dangerous. Something that wouldn't get you in trouble and regrets later.

I pushed open the door and walked through. And immediately felt out of my element. Guns, endless racks of big guns, small guns, and even the occasional cross-bow, lined the walls. Things that looked like Cherabino's cop-issue pistol. Things that looked like the rifles taken out by hunters. Things that looked like neither, and both. All lining the walls four high and filling glass cases like you'd find at a fine jewelry store. And judging from the tags, the guns were just as expensive.

The proprietor, a gruff overweight woman with a square jaw and an intricate Celtic tattoo on her arm, nodded at me when I came in. "First time? What are you here for?"

Cherabino pushed by me, and the woman's demeanor changed. "Ah, he's with you. Looking to shoot another rifle? I've got a new Ruger bolt-action tactical model. . . ."

"No, this time we're just using the range," Cherabino said, holding up her pistol wrapped in its holster where the woman could see it. "I'll buy the ammunition and rent a couple of hearing-protector sets." Her sensei emphasized respect in these situations, and she was happy to pay for

ammo she didn't need to show that respect. Besides, she
needed to pay rent on the space she was using; it was only
fair.

The woman nodded and produced two boxes as if by
magic, one smaller, that clunked against the counter
behind the glass display case. The other, a larger one that
opened to reveal two sets of large headphone-looking
things, the kind that covered the entire ear.

Cherabino paid and ushered me to a smaller door in
the back of the shop, something I hadn't even noticed
before she'd pointed it out. We were in . . . sort of an air
lock, a space between two doors. She made me put on
earplugs and the clamshell things, and then we were off
through the door.

It looked like a scene from the movies, only dirtier.
Stalls like horse stalls from a barn were lined up in a row,
guys with guns pointing at the concrete wall thirty feet
away, the paper targets set up.

The first *crack* hit me in the confined space, and it
took everything in me not to hit the deck. That was a bad
sound. A dangerous sound, a sound that crawled into the
back of your head where the survivor lived, and told you
to run. When I'd heard that sound on the streets at a lower
decibel, people had died.

Cherabino pulled me over to the first stall. Three more
cracks hit the space, two higher, mostly dampened by
the ear protection. Those didn't make me do more than
flinch. But the last—another dark, deep *crack* like the
world blowing apart—made me want to run. Hide.

Cherabino said something to me, but the sound was
lost in the space. She repeated herself louder, but I still
couldn't hear; instead I listened in through the Link, the
words behind the words.

She demonstrated how to load and unload the gun, the
cartridge snapping up and in, the upper part of the gun

sliding forward to indicate a bullet in the chamber. She made me repeat the motions, loading, unloading. I handled it gingerly, all the time struggling not to flinch every time I heard that dark, deep gunshot *crack*.

"It's a gun," Cherabino said, me hearing most of it through the Link. "It's not going to bite you. I mean, gun safety is good—watch the end of it—but it's not going to do anything you don't tell it to. You don't have to be so cautious."

She took the gun back and set up a paper target, the mechanism carrying the thing all the way down the range away from us. "Loosen up, enjoy this."

Meanwhile the *whoomp, crack, crack* of the gun range kept burrowing into my brain, telling me to be somewhere, anywhere else.

"Adam." She brought my attention back to her and away from the line of tough-looking men and woman, only some cops; the rest for all I knew about to shoot me dead on the spot. "Adam."

"What?"

"Pay attention." She demonstrated the correct double-handed stance. "Watch your hand; with a semiautomatic like this one, the top of the gun will pop back and it'll get you if you aren't watching. There's a kick." She adjusted her stance, and for the first time I could see the muscle tension behind the movement, like she really was expecting it to hit her hard. Then she squeezed the trigger three times.

When she pulled the target up, there was a tight cluster in the center body. Kill shots.

She reset and handed me the gun. "Your turn."

My hands shook and I tried to brace myself for whatever kick she was talking about.

"Loosen up," her breath came by my ear.

The shot went wide, nearly hitting another guy's target

down the range. The gun had leaped in my hand like a rabbit on speed.

Cherabino was all too close, the warmth of her body tangible as she adjusted my hands on the gun, my arms in front of me. "Now try to hit the target this time, if you can."

Something about the comment hit me like a burr on the butt, and adrenaline was already pouring through my system. Just to see if I could, I stole into her mind in careful degrees, control shaking, and "borrowed" her gun skills, the muscle memory she'd built over years of practice, the skill that was sitting on the forefront of her consciousness. I was rewarded with the headache of the century, pounding pain and brief flashes of light, but I did it. I actually did it. The skills sat in my head like a foreign lump, and, squinting through the pain in concentration, I sank into them.

I shot—and hit the target. To the right of center, but I hit it nonetheless. I squeezed off another round, and another, the shells flying off the gun and onto the floor as the gun made that strangely visceral *crack* in the small space.

I shot a perfect card the next time, almost as good as Cherabino. But the next was all misses, as her memory fought with my reality. I shot another card, and another, inconsistently, and finally stepped back, my head and arms aching. Despite everything, I was smiling like an idiot. I'd done it.

All those exercises and all the pain were finally worth it. The telepathy was coming back.

"Good shooting," Cherabino said, with a satisfied smile, and handed me the broom to clean up my shells from the floor.

As we returned the gear to the gruff lady behind the counter, I realized I hadn't thought about Swartz in an hour. Part of me was suddenly guilty, and the rest oddly relieved.

"Now let's get you some food. Then back to the station. I've got an appointment with the district attorney I have to make."

On the way back in the car, Cherabino let the silence sit while my head pounded dully. Finally I broke it.

"Are you serious about keeping Jacob away from the Guild?"

Her conflicted emotions darted around like a school of fish fleeing a predator. "Is that even possible?"

"If we're careful." I had done my research, and with a tag in my head—I poked around to make sure Stone wasn't there—with a tag in my head and under unnamed debt, I was happy to do anything to keep the Guild from getting what they wanted. "If he's careful. His medical condition will help us at the moment—reasons for people to be coming and going, reasons for him not to mix with the regular kids."

"Won't they catch him on the test?"

"Better than even odds they won't. Teleporters don't always show up on the screenings, especially with another talent to mask the signature. To look at, he's a midrange telepath. He can take a few classes, learn a few skills in a roomful of loud minds and probably no one will notice. Opt out of the Guild when they ask, do just fine. It'll be rough around the time of the screening, but it'll get easier if everyone's careful."

I shifted in my seat, pulling at the seat belt so I could face her. "Cherabino, you've got to understand. He has to be trained. Especially with the teleporting—we can't let that go. He could do damage to himself or someone else. And he needs a solid ethical footing. But there's a friend of Kara's, an independent associated with the Irish here in the city. We're going to contact him, and we're going to pay him to talk to us about details. I have the feeling if he won't train Jacob—quietly—he'll know someone else who will." The thought of this working—of me sticking one to the Guild—was lifting that depressive feeling. That, and the telepathy coming back and, though I wouldn't tell Cherabino, shooting holes in things.

Cherabino shook her head. "You yourself said the Guild has absolute legal jurisdiction."

"If you're Registered, sure. Unless you protest or you apply somewhere else. Over a certain level it's mandatory—but there are loopholes. And hell, Isabella, I'm going to do everything in my power to put him directly in the middle of one."

"My sister says she won't move to the Cayman Islands."

"They aren't recognized by the US Guild anyway. And you have to be born in Russia to join their Guild, most of Europe is hostile, and India has an extradition treaty. But the Irish Guild . . . the Irish Independent Telepathic Corp takes Americans, if you don't have a record and you can convince them you have something to offer them. We get him trained and we apply there. It'll be a fight, but we'll get him through the system, and the Guild won't be able to do a damn thing. He can live right here in Atlanta and the treaties make him untouchable."

A cautious hope was starting to grow in her mind as she pulled to a stop at a stoplight. "All my sister wants is to raise him herself. If this would let her keep him at home . . ."

"It's hell living with an untrained telepath, worse with a teleporter," I said, with strong warning. "And keeping the secret will be worse. It'll take the whole family. The earliest the Corp will take him is fifteen. It's a long time. And he'll need an anyonide shielding installed to block—"

She was suddenly there, her lips landing on mine in a

short, intense kiss that half merged our minds in a beautiful, intense moment. Before I could really get into it, she pulled away; the light had turned green.

I blinked, trying to catch up. "What—?"

"Thank you. Sincerely, from the bottom of my heart. My sister will be thrilled." She looked back up and put her hand on my cheek; I had to block quickly to keep the sexual thoughts from seeping out. "Thank you."

"What does this—?"

She pulled away, and got stiff. "Just let it be, okay?"

"Okay."

The rest of the trip was spent in silence, with me doing my best to hold my fractured thoughts to myself, control my headache—and wonder what the hell that had meant.

CHAPTER 18

"What is it?" Paulsen's voice was annoyed, and I almost turned around and left right then.

"Come in," she said.

If anything, the pile of papers on her desk was higher than I'd ever seen it. A huge pile of folders climbed the side of the desk, and brightly colored sticky notes covered the back wall like shingles. She'd even stuck a few to the cactus—one of the blooms was half-broken in favor of a bright yellow note about payroll.

"I had a question," I said, stalling for time.

She gestured to the chair, which was currently covered in yet more paper. I moved a pile and sat carefully on the edge of what was left.

"What's the question?"

I couldn't shake what Cherabino had said. "Would a PI license work? For the certification requirement?"

"I don't see why not. Assuming you're eligible. Why?"

"The Guild for certain isn't going to renew my license, and you did say I needed a certification to keep my job."

She made a face, looking exhausted. "There's a case to be made for independence, for sure. That's part of how I got you back on board the second time. You're a . . . rare commodity, in that respect. We hire a few PIs occasionally, when we're booked up and need some basic footwork done. It might be easier to get you accepted in under that bracket than otherwise. Assuming you can deal with the Guild. They called twice this week, and it's not a recommendation." She sighed. "Even if you survive, though, your hours are going to get cut back. You won't be able to do as much out in the field; we just can't afford to share with Homicide that much. I'm losing another interrogator for certain."

I nodded, numbly. "Those are personnel files there on the floor, that huge stack."

She nodded. "Somebody's going to have to be cut. Several someones. And the uniformed police force is no exception. We have to do another round."

"Why not fire me? Why give me the chance, then? Especially with the Guild calling you. I don't understand."

She leaned forward, and glanced behind me. "Close the door."

I did as she said. I sat back down with a sinking feeling.

"Look, the truth of the matter is that we don't pay for your health insurance. We don't have to pay any state or federal taxes on you. The Guild handles all of that, and what it doesn't handle, there's a legal loophole to cover it. You have one of the highest confession rates in the department and you get results. Furthermore, I'm a sucker for a hard-luck story. You check a lot of boxes here. You also need a hell of a lot of handholding, kicks in the ass, and enough drug tests that the lab sends me flowers on my birthday. But you're half the cost of a cop in your job, and your results are as good or better."

"That's why you've been lenient."

Paulsen shrugged, looking sad. "I like you, but I like a lot of the guys we're having to put out on the street, and their families are not going to understand. Frankly, it's a numbers game right now. It's hard to say no to half the cost when half the cost is doing twice the work. I'm willing to work with you on the rest of the crap. I've been doing that for years. I'll kick you in the ass every day if I have to, and Lord knows I do enough handholding in this department already for a whole fleet of kindergarten teachers. Even the top brass agree with me on keeping you on, with a simple overtime cut—like I said, it's a numbers game. But this new policy. . . . Well, there's a reason they call it policy. Politics is what it is, pure and simple. It's not about the money. It's about getting votes in next year's election."

She folded her hands. "Have you thought about becoming a private investigator for real?" she asked.

"What do you mean?"

"You should start thinking about options. A backup plan at least."

"You think I need a backup plan?"

"It would be wise. Did I answer the question you came in here for?"

And here was the fork, the decision, the moment. Should I tell her? Swartz would say, Absolutely, take responsibility, and it was high time I did. "I screwed up."

"How?"

I told her about Bob, and the phone call from the federal guy. At the end of it, she looked even more tired. "And he was okay with you having this information?"

"He said he was."

"Then you are a lucky, lucky son of a bitch. That could have gotten us all hip-deep in more crap than you have any concept of. Hell, we might have been swimming in agents and jurisdiction faster than you can say when."

I paused. "Am I in trouble?"

"For getting Bob to raid federal databases to get information you probably could have gotten for a please and a thank-you? Are you in trouble? Yes, you're in trouble. Go out and get me results now. A nice, shiny arrest would be perfect. Or come hell or high water, numbers game or none, there's nothing I can do for you."

The medic met me in the lobby of the medical office building next door to the hospital. It was a place of worn cushions and waiting rather than panic and ghosts, close enough for convenience for him and far enough to protect me. He'd agreed without much fight, but then again, he was Guild.

The cushy waiting area in the lobby was already full of people flipping through magazines and talking in a small, dull roar. The other side, the side with four uncomfortable chairs, a razor-sharp prickly plant, and a small desk with a phone, was empty except for me, with a good fifteen feet of empty space.

Boredom, waiting, and discomfort seemed the trend of the space, and that I could deal with. No one was dying here; no one had died recently, or died again and again in one spot over time. No one's emotions here would try to kill me. No cops were judging me, no suspects trying to outdo each other in mental volume and protests of innocence. Actually, this lobby was quite restful. If it hadn't been for my worry about Swartz, I'd have camped out here for the winter.

When the medic came through the doors, no one noticed. After the Tech Wars, they'd worn robes, big pretentious showy robes with a large Guild purple seal. The idea was to identify anyone with medical training—especially anyone who could do Guild-certified medical miracles—so you could see them at a glance. Starting a few decades after Koshna, though, when the Guild got everything it wanted while the normals dealt with a staggering economy and few options, well, the men in the showy robes got shot. They got shot enough that even the Guild had to change its mind about dress code.

So now, the microkinesis medic dressed in normal blue scrubs, with a tiny lapel pin with the Guild seal sitting right below his chin. You'd almost have to know what it was to recognize it.

I was grateful to see the man was a stranger, and just a little too old to be one of my contemporaries; he wouldn't expect me to know him even if I was active. Mid- to late forties, tall and thin, he said his name was Vega, I believe. He had a presence to him, like most of the good medics did, a humility that said he held lives in his hands every day . . . and never was able to save them all.

Vega came over, nodding to me before taking a seat smoothly. Deep circles under his eyes attested to his recent labor, and his hands—before he clasped them firmly together—were shaking.

It had been a long time since I'd interacted with a medic; even when we were in training, our specialties didn't really overlap. He was concerned with the fine-grade physical world, manipulating cells and nerves and organ sections, forcing a faster rate of cell division for critical nerve healing, breaking up the proteins that let a cancer cell divide. Pulling out toxins from a failing liver or, in this case, forcing the cells in the artery to divide and bind together, the tissue to grow faster and stronger. My work, on the other hand, while just as delicate, had had everything to do with the mind—the physical body, to me, was still a mystery.

"You were the one who wanted me to meet you here," Vega said quietly. "What do you need to know?"

"How is Swartz? The old man you healed as a favor. How bad is the long-term damage? What were you able to fix?" I paused. "Could you use regular language please? Every time I talk to the doctors here, I can't understand them."

"Okay. Let me think how to say this." He took a breath.

"It was good that you called me when you did. The damage in the blood vessels was extensive, and the tissue wasn't going to hold up well on its own. The surgeon, well, I am certain he is qualified in his own specialty, and the patient was alive and stable. But there was damage from the surgery that needed to be repaired—and repaired carefully. A very difficult task, but the results, I believe, were good. How can I say this in plain language . . . ? The immediate area has been cleared of blockages—which I ensured that the body absorbed safely. Plainly, I had to force cell regrowth in an extensive section of the arterial wall. I believe the scarring should heal cleanly, with enough elasticity to improve long-term quality of life."

I knew he would be expensive, but I'd talked to the accountant, and I had money saved up. "What does 'improve' mean, exactly? In plain language—for a heart patient? Swartz won't do well confined to a bed."

The medic sat back in the chair, as if looking for more support for a tired body. "In plain language, then. He should be able to walk around normally, even climb stairs if he takes them slowly. He'll be able to live normally if he'll pay attention to his body and its limits. He may have to sit for part of the day to teach classes, for example. But he will have to build back up to such things, and there are costs involved. I can say the system is unlikely to clog again, at least for several years, decades if he takes care of himself. But it won't be what it was."

I sat back, the import of all of this suddenly too much to bear.

"What do we need to do going forward?" I asked. "I know I went through classes on this, but I can't seem to remember how to push recovery. I'm not sure we ever learned about anything this big."

"No, it's fine. In a telepathy focus, you wouldn't." Vega sighed. "As I told his wife, it's important for him to eat protein, a lot of real animal protein, for a few weeks while his body replaces the protein I stole from the muscle tissue to repair the scarring. He'll be weak for a while, and he'll lose far more weight than looks natural, but that's part of the process. In a few weeks he should be ready to start working on his endurance."

I swallowed. "What do you mean, endurance?"

"It will take time to learn to walk any distance again, to stand and talk for long periods. It may always hurt him to get his heartbeat above a certain level. The scar tissue isn't going away. It will not be the way it was, ever."

"This is the best the Guild can do? You've made him a cripple."

He sat up then. "Your friend nearly died. The best the normals could do was give him another year or two—and that if he survived the next week, which was highly unlikely. I've just given your friend his life back. At considerable cost to myself, I might add. I'll be in pain for days—if not a week—after this, and I'll be lucky if I can keep food down at all for that time. A little gratefulness wouldn't be out of order here."

"I'm sorry," I said. He was right. Every apology still felt like rehab, still felt like my nose in the dirt, swallowing dust and crud. "Thank you. Thank you for saving my friend. I will never forget this."

He sighed and stood up, and I noticed this time how controlled the movement was, like it hurt, like it hurt on a deep level.

"Listen, about payment . . ."

"I was under the impression that this trip would be covered by the Enforcement division."

"I'd like to pay you what I can. In money. The rest we can set up on an installment plan, or work out some other way."

He nodded. "Here's how you reach the correct parties

to work out details." He held out a small circular chip, like a poker chip, with silver edges. Inside was written a phone number. "Sorry about the pretension, but they find they get lost less this way."

I put it in a pocket. "Thank you. Really. He's important to me."

"He must be."

CHAPTER 19

"You're late." Cherabino stood in the lobby of the Peachtree Building, arms crossed, foot tapping. Michael was next to her with one of his notebooks, jotting the occasional item as passersby crossed the lobby.

"I got caught up." I didn't specify what in.

We were standing in one of the largest skyscrapers on earth, with a huge bank of escalators going up three stories from the marbled lobby floor to the main elevators in a towering display of anti-grav technology. Stairs floated, apparently without support, in a long line going up, up, carrying people in a smooth glide on clear floating glass panels.

Each floating stair fed up through a belt, settling into the anti-grav fields individually, like smoked-glass rectangles falling up a waterfall in neat rows. The power required to run the thing had to be as much as (or more than) a full transcontinental floating Mack truck—or three—and the materials were specialized and highly tuned, but the real technology of the place was in the rotating belt below, and the stabilizing panels on either side.

"Is Swartz going to be okay?" Cherabino had read it off my thoughts without any sloppiness on my part.

You're getting better at this, I said. But I didn't really care what she read off me, not right now. Swartz was going to be fine. That was all that mattered in the whole wide world.

Cherabino nodded, responding to the thought thread, and Michael came up on the balls of his feet, his cop's instincts reacting to body language that didn't match the verbal conversation. On the streets, that meant there was another layer, a deeper layer—and frequently violence in the works.

I smiled at him, which settled him slightly—and put the conversation back firmly on verbal ground. "They're on the third floor, right? The most prestigious?"

Cherabino nodded. "Where everyone is forced to come through the escalators here and see how rich they are. Let's get moving."

I stepped onto the next plank carefully; it wobbled before taking my full weight, rising smoothly up the stairs. The handrail next to me was a shiny but conventional belt system—I held on to it firmly.

"Doesn't this bother you?"

I shook my head. "Gravity works on another system, somehow. Doesn't interact with Mindspace at all." Which was good; if the anti-grav systems made the waves in Mindspace that strong electromagnetic and quantum fields did, I'd be in trouble just walking down the street with all the cars overhead. "Don't ask me why it works like that."

"Why would it bother him?" Michael asked.

"Strong electromagnetic fields and Mindspace interact. Pay attention next time we visit the morgue. The coolers give off a . . . Well, it's faint, but it's unpleasant. And in the grand scheme of things, they're not even that strong. If you want to get away with fooling me about something, that's the time."

I found my footing on the regular ground and turned left. There, in a single sheet of artificially grown ruby, the words FLAWLESS ARCHITECTURE appeared, raised and in black. And I'd thought the Guild was pretentious.

"Why are we here again?" I asked Cherabino as we got closer to the smoked-glass wall. "I thought we already interviewed this guy over the phone."

"I'm out of leads and feeling thorough. The Dymani Systems interviews were a bust. Besides, sometimes people will tell you things a few days later they won't tell you at the time. And maybe we have better questions."

Cherabino pushed through the ruby-handled door, Michael behind, and I hustled to keep up.

"DeKalb County Police Department, Detective Cherabino and team," she was saying as I finally entered, as she flashed her badge. "I need to speak with Dan Hamilton's supervisor. I believe his name is Edelman."

The receptionist, a striking woman in her twenties with an expensive dress and hair dyed to mimic the hide of a zebra, looked closely at her badge before picking up the phone.

Edelman was a short man and very wide, bald with white eyebrows, looking like nothing so much as a shaved short Santa. He was even wearing a red shirt under a plain gray suit with white trim. But when I got closer, the impression changed—his nose was red, with the broken-blood-vessel look I associated with heavy drinkers, and the circles under his eyes were deep and dark. He slumped as if the weight of the world was on his shoulders, and even a few feet away, even with him practically mind-deaf, I felt his worry and anxiety hit me like an anvil dropped from a high building. Huh. It was late in the day for me to be picking up even strong emotions without trying. Either he had a nontrivial Ability level or I was better today. A lot better, for no good reason.

Edelman's office was a small space, three metal walls and a smoked-glass front, a large wooden desk sharing space with an architect's table in the background. There was a great deal of dust on the architect's table but none on the desk.

Cherabino shook the man's outstretched hand, settling into the chair he indicated while Michael and I took up standing positions near the door—now closed, at Edelman's request. Introductions were accomplished quickly, and then Edelman spoke.

"I told you over the phone, Detective, Hamilton hasn't shown up for work. He's still gone, and good riddance. After this long without calling, it's mandatory termination anyway, and after that blueprint went missing . . ."

Cherabino said, "There was a blueprint missing?"

"Yeah. We found it a few days after he flew the coop, and I can't prove anything, but I'm sure the bastard took it. He's always doing something sneaky, and I'm—"

"Why is this important enough to mention in your first sentence?" I asked.

Edelman blinked. "I thought you knew about this."

"Obviously we don't. Catch us up, please."

"I called the TCO and everything. You can't possibly say that—"

"We're not here to bust your chops, Mr. Edelman," Cherabino cut in. "We're trying to find out what happened to Emily Hamilton."

The TCO? What in the hell were in those blueprints?

Edelman sat back and took a breath. I could hear him cursing a blue streak, loudly, in his thoughts. "No, no, I guess I deserved this. Giving the whole team unrestricted access to the archives, you'd think I'd know better. But it seemed stupid to tie people's hands from doing their jobs, and there's some good old designs there you can sell like

new with just a little modification. I've always said, recy-
cle, reuse. It's cheaper for everyone."

"The blueprints?" Cherabino prompted.

"They're perfectly legitimate business records. You
can't possibly think we're in violation of the Tech Control
laws. Like I said, I called the TCO. I'll give you the case
number. You can verify it."

This guy was scattered and worried. I took a step forward, putting a hand on Cherabino's chair so she'd let me
run with it.

"Edelman, is it?"

The man nodded hurriedly.

"Edelman, no one's here about the Tech," I said. "Just
tell us what the blueprints are for. An old data center?"

He shook his head. "One of the big computer-driven
hotels. There's a whole series on the proper installation
of the resident supercomputer Tech system in a decorative bank along the spine of the building, you know,
where you could see it from the elevators. It's a gorgeous
piece of architectural history. It's worth studying, just for
the design! But the blueprints—only the Tech pages were
stolen. You have to understand, only the employees ever
get access, and we have the strongest security available
by law. I never thought—"

"Why do you think Dan Hamilton was the one to take
the blueprints?" Cherabino asked. "You said everyone
had access."

Edelman, if even possible, looked more upset. "One of
the receptionists was cleaning out his desk this morning.
She came across—she saw . . . "

"What did she see, Mr. Edelman?"

"A corner, torn off, from where the wood in the desk
drawer had pinched it. It has the correct serial number.
The only serial number. We don't repeat them, you see.
We can't. In three hundred years of business, we've never

repeated the number. That son of a bitch stole from us, and worse, he stole something that could cause us regulatory trouble. If someone hadn't gone to look for that exact file, I shudder to think how long we might not have noticed it missing."

Cherabino sat forward in her chair. "So, when did you notice it exactly? How long had it been gone?"

"Like I told you, a few days after he stopped coming to work. It could have been missing for weeks, I suppose, but the bastard disappeared. Obviously he took it and ran."

I backed up and let her do her thing, squeezing as much information from this round, earnest guy as could possibly be done.

I was starting to think Cherabino's case and the hijackings were related by more than my suspicion.

I called the hospital and got bumped around among four departments until somebody, somewhere bothered to look up the records.

"Jonathon Swartz?" The file clerk made a "hmm" sound.

"That's right." I gave him the birthday. "Where did they put him?" Maybe if I was lucky, they would transfer him to that office building across the street and I could actually visit.

More "hmms" and the sound of rapidly shifting papers, then, reluctantly, a few keystrokes. Finally: "Ah. It says here he's been released after medic therapy, whatever that means."

"Released?"

"As in, on his way home. Probably a relative took him home—they usually make a note of it if someone had to call a cab."

"He's okay?"

"I'm giving you the information I have, sir. If there's a

follow-up scheduled or an ongoing issue not in the chart, I wouldn't know about it." He paused. "Who are you exactly again?"

"A friend," I said, and hung up the phone.

I grabbed my coat from the back of the chair and looked at the clock. Bellury had already left, but it was close to quitting time—maybe I could get Cherabino to drive me over there.

Ten minutes later, I was sitting outside her cubicle impatiently while she finished up her current project. Probably Swartz wouldn't even see me. Probably he was sleeping, and Selah was awfully protective, or had been, the one time I'd actually seen her after . . .

I took a breath, told myself there wasn't time for a cigarette no matter how much I wanted one, and sure as hell I wasn't going to Swartz's with thoughts of my drug echoing in my brain.

The patch in my head was bothering me, bothering me a lot. I poked at it, despite the sharp pain it radiated down my spine. I poked at it—

"Stop that," Cherabino said from the end of the cubicle. She was standing up, pissed. "Whatever that is, stop it. If you ever want us to actually leave, I have to finish this and I can't do that with whatever that is going off like a buzzer. Now, are you going to let me do my job or what?"

I slumped farther down in my chair. "Stopping now."

She glared at me for one final moment. "Fine."

"Fine."

But she was still standing there.

"What?"

She blew out a breath. "It's going to be another twenty minutes, probably. If you're bored you can work on that PI paperwork that I got you."

I straightened in the chair. "When did you get me paperwork?"

"This morning. Bellury keeps them on hand for the disability folks and retirees. If you'd told me you cared sooner . . ."

"I didn't know I cared sooner," I protested.

"Well, if you want them, they're in the front file in the top cabinet drawer. Try not to make a lot of noise, okay?" She paused, and for once I actually saw real concern in her. "Swartz is going to be okay, you know that, right?"

A hundred responses went through my head, some flippant, some real and full of despair and horror and hope.

"He will be. Now do work and we'll go see him so you can see for yourself."

In a voice that cracked, I choked out, "Cherabino?"

"What?"

I took a breath. "I found that Irish teleporter we talked about. He says he'll meet Jacob next week. He doesn't want me there that first time, says I'll throw off his tactics. But you can go, he said."

"Thank you."

"You're welcome."

"I still need to work right now."

"I know."

She pulled out my old chair—now Michael's—and held it out for me.

I found the right papers and sat down.

Two minutes later, Stone was in my head, the intrusion like a clanging dissonant bell.

I heard what you did with the payment, he told me. *You realize that's only a tenth of the value of the service.*

I swallowed, hard, and tried to raise shields—I wanted him out, not that that would happen—but I also wanted Cherabino not to overhear.

Even less than that, Stone continued. *And now you've opened a tab. Unless you have a little over two million ROCs in change sitting around, you need to talk to me about alternatives.*

You said you'd announce yourself, not start up a marching band in my skull, I responded. *And two million is ridiculous. It was three hundred thousand ROCs when I left, tops.*

I'm sorry. He modulated his tone, getting a lot quieter. *That was ten years ago, before the cardiac shortages, and the Guild rate increases across the board. That's still the bill.*

I hope you're proud of yourself for fleecing me. Now get the hell out of my brain.

This isn't over, I heard.

Like an expert file clerk, he fanned through my surface thoughts quickly, pulling out details and emotions I hadn't realized I had. Thirty seconds of unwanted, unnecessary scanning—

You agreed to this.

—and then it was over.

I got my breath. Cherabino was already on her way over, sensing something wrong. *You don't have to be an asshole about it,* I told Stone.

And for a moment, I felt the comment register and his regret in return.

I'm doing my job, he said. *And I'm doing it fairly.*

And then he was gone.

Cherabino sighed. "This had better be a genuine problem and not a return to the distract-Cherabino game."

I ran my hands through my hair and tried to figure out how to explain—without admitting I was working with either the Guild or anyone else in my head. I couldn't figure out anything.

"I'll be downstairs when you're ready."

She took longer than she'd said, of course. Cherabino was a workaholic, and stressed lately. So I called Swartz from the phone near the coffee closet, the hallway empty. It was past quitting time for first shift, and the next seemed oddly deserted. I was wondering if they'd been gutted in the layoffs. It was getting so the other cops wouldn't even look at me.

The phone rang.

"Hello?" a gruff voice answered. Swartz's voice.

Something inside me suddenly relaxed. "Hi, it's me."

Cherabino showed up downstairs maybe forty-five minutes after I hung up, her hair mussed like she'd been fidgeting with it. There were deep circles around her eyes, and her forehead was creased. I could feel her worry, frustration, and anger trickle down the Link along with her exhaustion.

"Are you okay?" I asked as she settled against my borrowed desk, the downstairs eerily deserted, the large panel of windows in front of me dark with night. "What's worrying you?"

She rubbed her head. "Remember the pushy woman from the funeral? The one who had the sexual harassment complaint against her?"

"Yes?"

"Well, the interview didn't give us any more information. Andrew got her financials to check out, and she didn't have the contacts to trade for Sibley's services, as near as we could tell. We ruled her out while you were at the hospital. And the Hamiltons' finances were too messed up to tell anything, Andrew said, while we're talking about financials. Right now we're thinking it's one of the other poker players—we're still tracking him down—or Edelman, if not Hamilton himself."

I waited.

Cherabino sighed. "Anyway, I got a call from a detective out in Chamblee. The woman has been murdered. Dead, in her condo, has been for days. It took the detective this long to trace the connection to our case. Anyways, he says the ME found something weird and he thought I might care to come see it. I told him we'd go in the morning."

"'We'?"

"It's something about the brain. You did pretty well with the brain stuff before, right? And tonight we have to go see Swartz."

"It's too late. Selah said before we had to be there before nine if we were coming."

Cherabino paused. "You should have told me. Work is not as important as—"

"I talked to him. On the phone."

She settled down on the edge of my desk, softening. "How is he?"

"Groggy. But Swartz, if you know what I mean."

"That's good to hear." She waited, but I didn't have anything else left to add. "I'm sorry. I should have asked."

"Yeah."

"Do you—"

"Can we get some dinner?" I asked. "I don't want to be alone right now."

"There's a new pizza place a couple blocks from here."

"That sounds great."

The dinner was greasy and terrible, but Cherabino laughed for the first time in weeks, laughed full and long until her joy cut me to the core. I went home, to my empty bed, and tried very hard not to want what I couldn't have.

I called Swartz in the morning and talked to him for a long, long time.

CHAPTER 20

I met Cherabino at the Chamblee morgue bright and early. It looked a lot like the DeKalb morgue except that everything was new and squeaky-clean. The quantum-stasis refrigerators buzzed louder in Mindspace, the medical examiner was thinner and blond, but other than that it could have been the same place.

Detective Strangely, the guy who called us in, was waiting for us inside, next to a long stainless steel table and the medical examiner.

"I appreciate you calling us," Cherabino said. "The funeral home already have the body?"

The ME shrugged. "There wasn't a reason to hold it. We have plenty of pictures and a few organ cross sections. Strangely tells me you might be interested in the results."

"I would at that," Cherabino said.

The ME fanned out a number of pictures on the steel table, pictures of internal organs and butterflied brain, heart, and lungs, and grisly measurement tools. "Like I told Strangely, she seems to be in good condition for her age. Minor plastic surgery, the usual amount of scarring on the lungs from living in the city, a healed multiple fracture to the right tibia that required surgery and implanted cartilage, an artificial kidney, and extensive dental work. All items that could be found in any forty-five-year-old woman in the world. She was prediabetic. What I can't tell you is exactly what killed her."

Cherabino perked up. "And why is that?"

"Well, her heart stopped. Her tox screen is clear, and there doesn't seem to be any cardiac abnormality or issue that would cause it to stop suddenly, on its own. There's no apparent trauma other than a minor blow to the head around the time of death. Not long enough to bleed into the skull; it might have been a concussion, given more time, but it definitely did not kill her."

Detective Strangely held up a hand. "She was found on her kitchen floor, a spot of which had blood on it. Looks like she fell headfirst."

"Result not the cause, then," Cherabino said. "What did happen? Do you have any clues?"

"Well . . ."

"Well, what?"

The ME shifted. "I've never seen anything like it."

"Like what?"

She shrugged and pulled out another photo, and a petri dish with a small gray sample on it. "You know the hindbrain? The seat of breathing and heartbeat, all the things we never think about? In this case, well, it's so much mush."

"Mush?" I interrupted, stomach sinking. "Are the cell walls intact?"

The ME frowned at me. "It looks like paste. It won't hold up to pressure, and it's definitely not cancer."

"Yes, but are the cell walls intact?"

"Yes, I suppose. I would have noticed if they'd been blown out."

Oh, crap, let it not be . . . "Is there any reason to suspect some kind of extreme pressure, or trauma, that would do this?"

"Not really."

"Any explanation for this at all?"

"Listen, if you've got something to share with the class, share it," Cherabino said. "Neither she nor I have all day here."

"It's a telepath," I said, and a strange sense of déjà vu overtook me. "It's a way you can kill someone as a telepath, and there's no way in hell I can tell you any more than that." Hell, the watcher might turn me into mush himself if I said anything more than that. Assuming that was one of his skills. If not, he could always call in a favor.

"Why in hell would the Guild want to kill this woman?" Detective Strangely asked grumpily. Of course she assumed telepath meant Guild. Mostly it did.

"I don't know. I honestly don't know." But I did know how she died—how she was killed, her brain the focus of so much energy directed at a particular spot through Mindspace . . . "This took training. Training and raw power."

All the threads of my life seemed to be focused on one horrible moment. "Could we have another Guild serial killer?" I asked.

"Sibley?" Cherabino frowned. "I've seen your federal files. There's no affiliation with the Guild, anywhere, not here, not in England."

"The Guild's not the only source of telepathic training. Not like they'd have you believe."

When I would say nothing further, Strangely swapped information with Cherabino and threatened to show up at the department if she didn't share information on her ongoing case.

"What the hell was that?" Cherabino asked me in the car.

"I have to call Kara."

———————

Kara answered the phone on the first ring. "I'm in the middle of something right now."

"It's me."

She took a breath I could hear over the phone. "I only have a minute. Is Swartz okay? Did the deal work?"

"It looks like it. Thus far his prognosis looks really good."

"I'm so glad!"

"Me too. Listen, I'm getting a strange death up in Chamblee that looks like a telepath execution. Do you have any—"

"Damn it."

"What? I didn't—"

Kara made a frustrated sound. "We have a Minder missing, somebody who had a business contact out in Chamblee. This one could be a murder in our jurisdiction. I'll look into it as soon as I get back from the courier office."

"I'd appreciate it," I said. The Minder most likely could do that kill, but that was Guild jurisdiction for certain and nothing I needed to worry about for at least a few days. It occurred to me: "Why the courier office?"

"Oh. Tamika called in sick today and they needed advice on who else to pull in. It's the busy season and that's my old department."

"Is there any way the two are related?"

She laughed. "Don't be silly."

"If you say so," I said. Kara would know better than I would anyway. "I just thought I'd report it."

"I appreciate that. I'll send it through channels—somebody may come out and talk to you in a week or two, if that's okay."

"As long as it's not Stone, that's fine."

"You guys having trouble?"

I paused. "It's more that I just don't like him."

Stone showed up at the station, at quitting time. I was already half out the door; I kept going.

"We'll talk about this away from the station. You're making me look bad. Well, worse than I have to." I hadn't felt him in my head all day and I was getting twitchy. I hustled down the street two blocks, to where the trees grew in deeper and the government parking lot across the street, at this time of day, belched cars in a steady stream.

Then I turned around. "Why are you here?"

"You're a mess of emotion right now," Stone observed.

"So sue me."

"I can come back."

I ignored that. "Why are you here?"

"The Guild has decided what they want in return for your favor."

My hands felt loose, itchy, like I needed a cigarette and I needed one now. "And what is that?"

He shifted, and I got a vague sense of discomfort from him. "You're in a position to know things. You're connected to one of the best homicide detectives in metro Atlanta—and more importantly, the one who knows the most other people of the type. You interview hundreds of suspects a year. Your boss has one layer of administration between her and the DeKalb County—and to some degree Decatur City—politicians. You're in a position to know things. We'd simply like you to share some of those things with us."

We'd been over this, but I had a debt now. "What kinds of things? Anything we're cleared to talk to the press about I'd be happy to send to you first, but I'd have to clear it with Paulsen."

"This is not an official relationship. Anything cleared for the press is probably not something we'd be interested in. My superiors simply . . . well, they want inside information into what the normals know and how it's going to affect the Guild's interests."

So they wanted me to spy for them. To use Cherabino's barely-there trust as the stepping-stone for their stupid power plays. "And how am I supposed to know what the Guild's interests are?" I asked, to buy time.

He glanced down the busy street, body language almost too casual. "You're not a stupid man. I think you can figure out the details."

"Why don't you spell it out for me?"

I got a strong sense of discomfort from him, which was odd. Either he was getting lazy or I was healing a lot faster than expected.

"Power. The Guild wants power over its own people and its own destiny. It wants to develop stronger Abilities, stronger ties within its community, and it wants to protect all of those things from the degradations of normals, no matter how well meaning. If it affects Guild power, Guild profit, or lets the normals get leverage against the Guild in any way, it's not in the Guild's best interests."

"I'm not Guild anymore."

"I know," he said, and suddenly the implacable Face of the Guild had given way to the quiet, competent, powerful cop vibe I'd gotten from him a few days ago. "And I know you want to stay neutral and keep your own counsel. I don't think they're asking you to get involved. There were things you could have done much worse with the Bradley case. If you wanted to torch the Guild and all it stood for, you would have done it then. You were raised at the Guild. You must have some vague remnant of patriotism for your people."

"It's not patriotism if it's not a nation."

"In a lot of ways, the Guild is the only nation that takes up the whole world," he said, a much more radical—and naive—thought than anything I'd encountered before.

"If you say so," I said to cover my ass. "Let me get this straight. You want me to spy on my friends, share confidential police information that may or may not allow bad guys to go free and the Guild to get the jump on the law?"

"You owe the Guild a debt. A debt you agreed to."

"And I still haven't seen Swartz. I've paid what I can afford through your system. It's a lot of cash."

"It's a drop in the bucket compared to the fees you owe."

They had me by the balls. But even so. "I still haven't seen Swartz. I'm not agreeing to anything until I see Swartz with my own eyes."

"It was a bad idea to involve the old man."

I put my hands in my pockets; they were shaking. "Yeah? And why is that?"

"Now they know he's important to you." He let the implied threat sit in the air a long, long moment while my mind flashed to the vision of me, alone, without Swartz, without anyone.

Finally Stone met my eyes and spoke past the threat. "Fairness is something I pride myself on. Fairness and getting to the truth. I'll wait a little longer, if I have to, but I'll get to the truth. If you're planning to take down the Guild—"

"I'm not," I said hurriedly.

"—if you're planning to choose the normals over the Guild—"

What did that even mean?

"—then it's my job to make sure you're not a threat anymore. I can and I will use whatever force is at my disposal to do so."

And then a chill went through my entire system as

this guy, this guy I kind of liked, was the executioner again.

Which is probably the reason I was so surprised by her voice.

"You have *got* to be kidding me!" Cherabino said.

Cherabino crossed her arms. "What the *hell* nerve do you have *coming here*, three blocks from the *police station,* trying to work out a drug deal? I ought to string you up—"

"You must be Detective Cherabino," Stone said, absolutely unmoved. Cherabino was about three feet from him now, and if he didn't start taking her more seriously she would have him on the ground with a kung fu move faster than he could blink. What he did then was another matter, but—

"Cherabino," I interjected.

She ignored me. "Who the hell are you?" she asked Stone. "I thought I knew all the perps in the area, but if you're new you'd better—"

"Cherabino."

"—stay the hell away from my station because—"

Cherabino! I yelled through the Link.

She stopped cold and sent me a glare that would melt lead. "Stay the hell out of my head and I'll deal with you later."

What?

"Edgar Stone." He gave a nod of greeting. "I'm this man's new Guild overseer."

She sputtered. Finally to me: "Is this true?"

"Is what true?"

"Is this true!"

"He's Guild. That much is true, and he's been sent—"

"Guild. And you didn't tell me." She pulled back and hit me—hard. With her full weight behind her. Pain exploded on my jaw like fireworks, and the world tilted as I fell.

The sidewalk hit me with a *thud* I could feel in my bones, and Cherabino fell over too, cursing up a storm at the "damn Link, damn Link, damn Link, I'm getting the hell up!"

Then her shapely rear stalked away from me, wobbly but far too quick.

She'd thought he was a drug dealer, my mind reported numbly. She'd thought I was buying, on her territory, right in the middle of everything where anyone could see me.

But worse, she'd assumed I was working behind her back, I was working for the Guild. And that—that—was a deeper betrayal, to her. She'd believed me earlier, when I'd told her what I'd told Paulsen. She believed me that I wasn't dealing with the Guild more than I had to. But to see me here, with apparently friendly body language, outside the station . . . it was a betrayal, and her distrust had crystallized.

"Does she do that often?" Stone's voice asked urbanely.

"Go away," I said, jaw grinding against the rough concrete.

"I'm not going anywhere until you tell me your answer. I can't. You should know that by now."

I picked my pride and my shame up off the ground and peeled myself away from the sidewalk.

"What's your answer?"

The world crashed in on me and I saw my future, what it could be, and the betrayal I'd seen in Cherabino's eyes. "I can't do that. I can't spy on my friends, on the people who've actually given me a chance and kept me on the damn wagon. I can't. Burn me if you want, find something else, come after me hard for financials or forced labor or lockup or whatever the hell you need to do, okay? But leave Swartz out of it. He's an old man. An old, sick man whose only crime is to try to help people get their worlds back in order."

"That's your answer?"

I nodded.

A silence filled the street as the cars kept pouring, pouring out of that parking garage and taking to the skies and the streets in steady streams.

"I'm sorry to hear that," Stone said.

I ran up the battered stone steps at the front of the building, sucking in air hard, and slowed at the top, right at the door. Sweat pooled on the back of my neck as I opened that front door. . . .

An unmarked police car, Cherabino's car, screeched away down the street with her at the wheel. It burned rubber around a corner, then squealed as she demanded the anti-grav engage too suddenly—it limped into the air, narrowly missing an airbus, and left like all the demons of hell were following.

Part of me, the tiny part that leaked through the Link, followed her, me running too, all my hopes disappearing behind her.

In the front of my head, I felt Stone announce himself. I slammed up every shield I had, tolerated him only for the few seconds it took him to rummage through my mind, and stood, panting, as he pulled away.

I had no secrets. I had no damn secrets anymore. And Swartz . . . and Swartz . . . how the hell was I going to explain all of this at our next morning coffee meeting? Would we even have another morning coffee meeting?

I limped into the cold air-conditioned lobby and walked, like a funeral march, to the coffee closet. There, I locked the door and ate four stale donuts until my brain stopped screaming, until the fight-or-flight thing settled down and I could think, a little.

When I came out, Bellury was standing there waiting for me.

"What's this about you talking to a dealer this afternoon?" Bellury wanted to know. He had a boxy leather case in his hand, the same case—well, I knew what that case was. Another damn drug test.

CHAPTER 21

By the time I called that night, Selah said Swartz was sleeping. Frustrated, I got Bellury to drive me home.

"I didn't do anything," I said as he drove. "Really."

"We'll know for sure when the test comes back tomorrow," Bellury said. He turned left, down a street into the bad part of town that neighbored my apartments from the east. It was out of our way to go this way, but Bellury had been a semiretired cop for a long time, and he was watching the streets carefully, hoping someone would be stupid enough to commit a crime where he could see it and have to do something about it.

"Cherabino's mad at me. I mean, really mad."

"She's been mad before."

She had. This time felt different, though.

"If you're telling the truth, it will come out. She'll calm down."

"She doesn't trust me, though." Bellury didn't trust me either, but the knowledge of that didn't cut at me.

"She's a cop."

"It's personal."

"Is it?" Bellury asked, glancing over at me. "You falling for the detective?"

"That's not what I meant."

"You sure?"

A note of question lay in my own mind. A real, honest question. Had I fallen for her?

After a pause of far too long, with Bellury smirking, I had to say something. "I've proven myself, over and over. What more does she want from me? I've done everything she asks. I've worked hard." Swartz said you couldn't have a relationship if you couldn't keep a plant alive. And I'd killed more plants than I could count; long hours did not a good horticulturalist make. But this was Cherabino, beautiful, cranky Cherabino, and more than anything I wanted . . . well, I wanted her.

I batted the thought away like I'd fight down a craving, but it stuck back up. Bellury had twisted the tiger's tail, and now the thought wouldn't leave me alone. That kiss . . . and her. The way she smelled. The way she laughed. The way she cared, all too much, for the victims. For justice.

She was beautiful, was Cherabino. She was strong, and difficult, and stubborn, and deadly smart.

"She's the only one who doesn't know," Bellury said quietly.

I realized with panic—and then with a pang—that maybe he was right. That everybody else saw. That I— when I wasn't stuffing it in a closet and sitting on it—I saw too. But not her. Not her, and wasn't that ironic? The only one in the whole department I shared headspace with, the only one I was Linked to, and I'd hidden my feelings so well she didn't see me.

"You think I'm going to keep my job?"

"I don't know, Adam. I really don't know."

Linda Powell, Emily's sister, came back on Wednesday morning. Cherabino had asked Mrs. Powell to bring in her niece.

"Children know everything," she'd said yesterday. I

had no reason to disagree; I didn't have a lot of experience with normal kids, but the trainees at the Guild seemed to get in everyone's business. The younger, sometimes, the more details they seemed to know. Of course, the youngest children in the Guild were in the fourth grade or so, but supposedly Laney Hamilton was about that age.

At the moment, Cherabino was sitting in the observation room with a migraine that, despite my best efforts, was leaking behind my eyes. She'd asked the tech if she could turn the lights way, way down, and faced with her misery, he hadn't been able to say no. She had a high pain tolerance, which her sensei liked, but when she came into work sharing this much pain it wasn't pleasant for me. At least it distracted me from going over other things, things I couldn't afford to think about right now.

I was already in the interview room. I'd tried to book the clean one, but Clark had scooped it up for this rich man's robbery case and wouldn't let it go. So here we were. The surroundings were only the second step of hell, much less bad than the worst interview room. And the dirt layer was light; we actually let the cleaners in here occasionally. But it wasn't a palace either, and the mirror-slash-observation-window behind me was smudged and covered in various types of dirt.

Bellury escorted the sister in with a big smile and a sandwich he'd purchased on my credit—I was tired of him stealing my lunch. Mrs. Powell held her niece tighter against her side and stared at me disapprovingly.

I gestured to the two seats I'd set up for them at the end of the table, complete with two cups. Mrs. Powell got a steaming cup of tolerable department coffee, and Laney got our best cup of artificial orange juice. They also spent far too much time getting settled.

I introduced myself to Laney, assuming that the older woman wasn't going to give me the time of day unless I had a good reason. "I heard you just got out of school." This was Emily's little girl, and I would be kind to her no matter what it cost me.

"That's right. It's a half day. The teachers have to be there the whole time, but we get to leave early." Laney was a thin kid, with long limbs, dirty blond hair that fell pin-straight to her shoulders, and a pair of glasses that made her look a lot like an owl. She was too young for corrective procedures, I assumed. She had an air about her of awkwardness, all angles, and, as I'd suspected in the crime scene earlier, she had a low-level Ability—and was controlled for that age. With her father, probably she'd had to be.

"What grade are you in?" I asked.

"Fifth. I'm on a team with some sixth graders, in soccer, though."

"You must be pretty good at soccer, then, huh?"

She frowned at me and pushed up the glasses. "When are you going to ask me about my mom?"

"What?"

"That's why I'm here, right? Because my mom is dead and you want to know if I know anything that might help you catch the guy who did it and find my dad."

"That's right," I said, and looked at Mrs. Powell, who shrugged. I radically revised my strategy for the conversation. Clearly this girl was the more-information, better-information type. "We're trying to figure out why it happened so we can keep this guy from doing it again."

The girl nodded and took a breath. "I've been thinking about it. A lot of people don't like my dad, but my mom has a lot of work friends and people who like her. You want to know about enemies, right?"

"If you think something happened with those enemies recently. Yes, please, but friends too, if they had fights recently."

Laney then proceeded with a surprisingly coherent fifteen-minute rundown of most of her dad's associates and began on her mom's.

"Hold on," I said.

She stopped midsentence and sniffed. I could feel the emotions she was holding back at talking about her parents, sadness like a hurricane on the other side of those owllike glasses. I wished there was something I could do for her.

"We don't have to do this now if you're sad." I glanced at Mrs. Powell for support.

"Yes, honey. You've already done a lot. Nobody would fault you for needing some time, would they?"

I could take a cue. "That's right."

She sniffed again and then lifted her chin. "I need to help. I want to help, okay?"

"Okay." I understood needing something to do. The trouble was getting the useful information out of her rather than the dross. How to phrase it? "I guess what would be most helpful is anything that changed in the last few months. Anything unusual."

"He hit her less," Laney said. Mrs. Powell turned her head in shock.

Laney was being so matter-of-fact about it, I couldn't do any less. "How often?" I asked.

"Hardly once a week. Sometimes even less. The last few months he's been calmer. Mom seems calmer too."

Mrs. Powell looked terribly uncomfortable, as if a terrible secret were being aired in public. I'd met her kind before and had no use for them. The facts were what mattered, and hiding these kinds of secrets only made them worse.

"Anything else that changed in that time?"

"A few months ago Emily was complaining of money

troubles," Mrs. Powell said. "Lately they seem to be doing better."

I gestured at her to settle down. Then to Laney: "Do you know what the money trouble was about?"

She nodded, looking down. "I overheard them talking. I was at the top of the stairs where they couldn't see me. I'm not supposed to listen."

"What did you hear?"

"Dad got a pay cut at work—a big one—and I think it was his fault. He said it wasn't a lot. And he got mad and yelled, and said if Mom was making her commissions they'd be fine. She kept saying something back, but I didn't hear it. She didn't yell so much."

I nodded encouragement. "What else?"

"A while ago, they had this fight. Mom said something about taking care of the money, but he was yelling about needing more money. He lost some, somehow. Probably gambled it," she said, in that too-adult voice. "He loses a lot that way. Then he started hitting her again, a lot. She had a black eye she tried to cover with makeup, but you could still see it. That's when she started leaving me alone."

"She left you alone?" Mrs. Powell said.

I gestured for her to be quiet. "Laney, tell me about that. Anything you can remember."

The girl looked back and forth between us and finally at the table. She pushed up her glasses again. "She told me I had to be good and not to tell Dad she was going. This was poker night," she explained, as if that explained everything. Maybe in her world it did. "She rented me a movie and ordered pizza, and then said not to leave the house and be good. She said I couldn't have Dora over either, which I thought was mean."

"When did she leave? When did she get back?"

"She left about eight, right after the pizza came. I watched the movie and then I went to bed like I was supposed to. It was a school night."

"Did your mom look tired the next morning when she took you to school?"

She nodded. "She had like three cups of coffee. But Dad had a hangover and stayed in bed, so he didn't know."

"I see."

"Once I watched two movies instead of one, and I fell asleep on the couch," Laney added. "When Mom came home, she woke me up and she was really mad."

Mrs. Powell put her hand on her niece's shoulder. "Where did she go, Laney?"

"There was mud on her jeans and she had to clean her shoes, and the floor. I don't think she went to the grocery store or the movies or anything. But when I asked her, she said not to worry about it. Adults are always telling me not to worry, and then bad things happen." The emotion was welling up again in a flood.

"Laney," I said, with just enough punch to distract her. I held up a hand to keep Mrs. Powell from interrupting.

"What?"

"Anything else? Anything new?"

She frowned, and thought, the wheels turning and focusing the emotion into something useful. "Well. It's not important. But Mom had a new friend over. She said they knew each other at the Guild."

I had a sinking feeling. "What was her name? What did she look like?"

Laney frowned. "I don't know her name. She wasn't very nice to me. She was a black lady with long hair and not much makeup and she wore flat shoes with work clothes. Mom says if you don't wear high heels to work, it looks like you don't care. Once there was a bald guy there.

I didn't like him at all. He looked at me funny. I went to my room."

Tamika was there? And now she was missing.

"Do you remember what he looks like?" Mrs. Powell asked when I didn't. "The bald man."

"Could you draw a picture?" I added. Maybe the bald man was the missing telepath or Sibley.

"I can't draw."

"Can you describe him?"

She thought about that, the tears held at bay for a moment anyway. She finally shook her head. "He was bald. I didn't like him, but Mom said he was important to her plan. She said she was almost ready to tell me about it."

"Her plan?" Mrs. Powell asked.

Laney looked up and nodded. "She wouldn't talk about it, but last week she asked me. If she and Dad got a divorce, would I choose her?"

"And what did you say?" Mrs. Powell was almost foaming at the mouth to know.

"She's dead now! What does it matter?" And Laney started tearing up again.

"Laney. Laney, I'm sorry. Just one more thing. It could help."

She sniffed. "And what is that?" Tension was like the blade of a knife in the room.

"Do you know what a telepath is?"

"Yes." She took a breath. A tear ran down her cheek. "They came and tested us. If you can read minds or do stuff, they take you off to live at the Guild. Or they give you lessons. I guess you have to get your parents' permission or something. I kept hoping they'd pick me so I could live at the Guild, but it didn't happen."

Poor girl, when the Guild test was her best chance at another life. On the other hand, my own story wasn't all that different. "I'm a telepath, a Level Eight if you know what that means."

Mrs. Powell grabbed her arm then, but Bellury was abruptly there and Laney pulled away, leaning forward.

"Can you read my mind and stuff?"

"Not without your permission. If you'll let me, though, I'd like to borrow your memory. I'd like to figure out who those two people are."

The girl sat back, thinking.

Bellury kept a tight watch on Mrs. Powell. "It's her decision," he murmured.

"Will it help?" Laney asked.

"It might."

"Okay."

"Really? That's it?"

"Well, you're not going to hurt me, are you?" Now her eyes narrowed.

"I promise I won't."

"Okay, then. But if you do I'll scream and you'll be in trouble."

"I understand," I said gravely. "I promised, though."

Five minutes later, the girl and her aunt were leaving, and I stopped Mrs. Powell at the door.

I handed her a card, my card. "If there's ever anything I can do . . . ," I told her.

She hesitated before tucking it into her purse.

Afterward I sat, trying to recover from the challenging read. Blocking out a migraine via Link while reading a twitchy fifth grader whose mind kept wandering was not a task for sissies. Especially while keeping my promise to her.

My head pounding, right now my nose was full of the smell of kerosene, the heavy-sharp, bright smell I hadn't smelled in ages. But Laney had, all over her mother, the last night she'd described, when her mother had come in late.

A few days before, Tamika—it was indeed Tamika—had visited, with a bald man in tow. A bald man who walked with the controlled power of high-level military training.

Tamika in the memory had seemed nervous, and had kept glancing at him, then back at Emily. She'd tried to get Laney away from the conversation, and quickly. Was Sibley threatening Tamika? Had he used her to scout out the house?

I spent the rest of the day in the interview rooms, interview after interview while I tried to figure out how this had happened. On my break, when I had a minute, I pulled the casebook from Cherabino's empty cubicle. She was in court, or working from home, or something. In the back of my head, she still had the migraine pounding.

I searched through every one of the inventory entries for the house. The blueprints were absent. Either they were hidden well or—I sat down in Cherabino's chair—or Sibley had gone there to steal those blueprints. Those blueprints of Tech. Maybe Fiske was using them to assemble a Tech supercomputer from the blueprints with all the parts that had gone missing.

And he'd used Tamika to do it.

I visited Cherabino's cubicle, the lights in the area turned down, all of the lights directly over her cubicle all the way off. A kind of hush had fallen over the area.

"We have a problem," I said quietly as I entered.

She was facing away from me, her head cradled in her hands, eyes closed. She mumbled, sounds that meant "Could you talk quieter?"

"Migraine?" I asked gently.

"Yes."

"Want me to come back?"

She forced herself up, her eyes narrowed to slits. "What's the problem?"

"I think Sibley forced Tamika to help him find and kill Emily. Maybe for those missing blueprints. The trouble is, the Guild can't find her."

"Who's Tamika?" Cherabino asked cautiously.

I caught her up, and it was like a light went on inside her, the driving force that pushed her on.

"Call Michael back in from the scene I sent him on. We're going to find out about these blueprints, you're finally going to tell me everything you know about Emily Hamilton, and we are going to call every damn hospital and morgue until we find your missing woman. Or we're going to find her some other way."

"Are you good for this?" I asked quietly.

"I'm still here, aren't I? If I'm at work, I need to work."

I paused for a long time, then sat down next to her. "I'm not working for the Guild." And my drug test came back clean. It wasn't a drug dealer, I added silently. Nobody around here would sell me anything anyway. I'd tried.

"I know," she said, still staring at her desk, fighting through the haze of pain. "I called Kara this morning. She told me what was going on."

She winced as Michael walked into the cubicle and knocked on the wall far too loudly.

Michael paused, sack of donuts from the corner deli in hand. "I brought you food," he told Cherabino.

"Whisper," I said, quietly, as another pulse of migraine pain made it through my shields.

Cherabino was already unpacking the donuts.

"I borrowed the chemical file on kerosene from Dotty like you asked," Michael told me, handing me a laminated card.

"Oh, good," I said, eyeing a powdered donut Cherabino was already claiming for herself.

"Tamika first," Cherabino put in, mumbling around the donut.

I opened one of the side drawers on her desk and pulled out a small bottle of migraine pills, handing it to her. "Meds first. Then we figure this out together."

She took the pills, and Michael found a chair.

CHAPTER 22

After a long meeting where we all hit our heads against the metaphorical wall, I snuck away before the next block of interviews and called Kara one more time.

"I can't do anything about Stone," she said. "I'm sorry, Adam, I can't."

"I didn't figure you could. That's not why I'm calling."

"Why are you calling?"

"Have you seen Tamika? Has anyone else?"

"No, no, she hasn't been back to work. We sent somebody to check her apartment, but she wasn't there either. Did you make her mad? Should we be looking for her? With what happened, I feel an obligation to—"

"That's not what this is about." I cleared my throat. "Listen, I believe Tamika has been threatened by a hired killer named Sibley to give up sensitive Guild information about courier routes. We think that's why the hijackings lately. Did she seem off to you lately? Can you find her? She could be in danger. Emily is dead, Kara. This isn't a trivial concern. And Guild courier information—well, I don't need to tell you what a train wreck that could be. We're finding biological Tech, Kara, and I'm pretty sure it belongs to you."

"Wow. Well, officially, the Guild neither owns nor has any interest in any technology forbidden by the Koshna

Accords. Biologicals seem a bit crazy, though, don't you think?"

"They were under the seal," I said, as much as I dared say over the open phone line. "I think she's caught up in all of this, and besides the security implications, I really think she could be in danger. Can you find her, please?

"She works inside the Guild. She lives on Guild property. There's no way anyone got close enough to threaten her without us knowing about it. And seriously, Adam, I would have known about anything like that."

"I'm sure Emily's sister is thinking the same thing about her sister. And now she's dead. I'm asking you as a favor, Kara. This is Tamika, and I feel like I have to do something. And that Tech . . . could you at least look into it?"

Kara sighed. "I'll rearrange my schedule and take care of it this morning."

"I appreciate it."

She called me back two hours later, after lunch, when Cherabino was in court and Michael unavailable. I transferred it to the phone outside the coffee closet so Bellury wouldn't listen in.

"Are you certain Tamika is under duress?" Kara asked me, voice all too serious.

"I'm not certain of anything right now."

"I ask because—well, a number of her things are packed up. Neatly. She's not at the courier office, she's not at her apartment, and a significant percentage of her things are missing, along with her. According to the security guard, she left the campus yesterday under her own power. She even smiled at him. And as near as I could tell, the truck you're referring to—it was her order, Adam. No one else requested it."

"Courier office." Suddenly it all clicked together. "Tamika has been working for the courier office. In logistics. Shipping things."

"I told you that."

I took a breath. "What if she's in this on her own volition? I have a witness linking her to Emily before she was killed. And she works in the courier office. The courier office, Kara! She can order whatever she wants!"

"Where are you going with this?" Her tone was scared more than anything. "Are you saying—"

"We've been looking in the wrong direction. The hijackings, the murder, that's why she was at the funeral."

"Adam—"

"Find me where the next courier load is being delivered. Find me the information so we can intercept these guys. So we can catch them in the act."

A long pause. "You really think Tamika killed Emily?"

"Yeah, I do. Unfortunately I do." I owed Tamika. I had to make restitution. But I had to find Emily's killer, and if they were one and the same . . . Cherabino said we owed the victims justice. That justice was the most important thing we could possibly give them.

"Adam?"

"What?"

"I'll send you the information by courier in the next hour. If . . ." Her voice broke. "If I was wrong and set up that woman to take advantage of the Guild, to kill someone we should have been taking care of . . ."

"Kara, it's not your fault," I said. It was mine. Mine for getting distracted, mine for not putting it together.

And then she was back, her voice matter-of-fact, too matter-of-fact. "I'll get you the time and place by courier in the next hour."

"Thank you."

She took a breath. "You should know. We went through

her work papers. There's a . . . well, a sketch. A highly technical sketch for a, shall we say, box to influence brain waves. Our technical people in the research department say it's sound, and that it's developed enough to work in the real world. They claim they haven't seen it before."

I paused. If the Guild—if Kara—was sharing this, there was reason to be concerned. "Okay. Well, she worked for Dane. She had access to his research just like I did."

"And there's some parts missing from the Guild research labs."

"Great," I said. "Just great." This was turning into the perfect storm.

I found Morris in front of the public coffee table upstairs in the detectives' cubicle area, her standing impatiently while the closet coffeepot spat air and hot water, steam and a sour, almost-coffee-beans smell across the area. Upstairs in the detectives' cubicle area felt deserted, fewer people here than there used to be. I told myself they were just out on cases, but I knew some of them—most, probably—had been laid off.

"There's a stash over the microwave in the food closet. They're real coffee beans."

Morris scowled, her Valkyrie-like features fierce. If I hadn't been so used to Cherabino, I might have stepped back. I should have felt her intentions along with it, but now, midafternoon, I had to concentrate to pick up anything from a normal. "All I could find was the fake stuff. The pot they had on had been sitting all day. It looked like a hockey puck."

"Probably similar."

As the mechanism finished its brew cycle, she darted in to fix a cup of it anyway. She must have needed the caffeine pretty badly; the circles under her eyes were deep and she moved like she'd been up far too many hours. I spent the effort to read her and found her exhaustion was deep and wide. Maybe she hadn't slept at all.

"I need your help," I said. "I have information about where the hijackers are dropping their goods this afternoon. We have a couple of hours before it happens."

She blinked. "The hijackers who took out a high-security silicon chips shipment last night? Those hijackers? Where did you get this information?"

"I only got it a little while ago," I said. "And . . . let's just say it'll be inadmissible in court and you probably don't want me to give you the details." Since Cherabino was gone, I didn't have an easy way to introduce Kara's information unless I went through Paulsen—which seemed bad for my job security. And the clock was ticking. I was hoping Morris would take the information without a lot of questions.

A slow, dangerous smile spread across her face. "Let me finish the coffee and we'll pack up."

I knew the area, or I had known it, years ago and high as a kite. Things looked different now, in full daylight, after the city had started a reclamation project on the old industrial complexes, now apartments for yuppies. Aircar garages on the roofs, the ground-level entrances locked up tighter than the police holding cells, local businesses in the area still sporting heavy iron bars. The only people walking carried small packages and wore jackets just large enough to conceal firearms, even in the middle of summer, and the streets two blocks down from the apartments still never seemed to get clean.

The abandoned school building was still there, though, smaller and shabbier than I remembered it, bricks falling down into the alley. It was surrounded on all sides with dirt and squatters, a veritable haven for shady deals of all types. This used to be Marge's territory, back when I still knew all the players.

We sat on the crumbling top floor of the building across the way, looking down into the now-empty alleyway in back of the school. A tattered awning and piles of dirty boxes were its only decoration. There were unmarked police cars and uniforms on foot sequestered in various hiding places around the area, and plenty more sat waiting and ready to move when the hijackers finally arrived.

The trouble was, they had been due to arrive half an hour ago. Morris, crouching next to me on the gritty floor, shifted. She was getting restless; I could see it in her body language and in occasional flashes of impatience darting through the fog of Mindspace like minnows through a cloudy lake.

"What's the time?" she whispered, maybe the twelfth round of the same question.

I told her.

She shifted again, her legs getting tired, as the radio on her hip sputtered faintly, almost white noise.

"Give it another minute," I said for the dozenth time, but it was falling flat, even to my ears.

Morris glanced back at me, then pulled her radio from her belt and turned up the volume. "Units in Tango Charlie, this is a Ten Fifty-Nine. Repeat, Tango Charlie, this is a false alarm. Let's go home, folks."

Through the broken window in front of us, I could see a couple of uniforms round a corner, rifles held loosely pointed to the ground. Not too far away I could hear the high-pitched humming sound of a fusion engine warming up as a police aircar went from idle and cold to ready to fly.

Morris's hand with the radio was halfway back to her belt when a string of numbers and urgent calls for backup hit the airwaves. "Hijackers!" the broadcaster finally said in the department's preferred plain-language call. "Repeat, multiple fatalities and restricted materials missing from Al's Secure Computer Depot, Clairmont Road, next to the Veterans Hospital. All units available, backup. Back-up immediately. Black industrial flyer heading north through restricted airspace, no tags. All units. All units, pursue."

Adrenaline soaked the air as every cop in the area stopped everything—but we were at least thirty miles out of the way. We'd been caught with our pants down.

Morris stared me directly in the eye. "I swear to you by all that is holy, if you're working for them, if you set this up so that area would be empty—"

"I wouldn't—"

"—I will find out, and I will bury you."

"I didn't—"

But she was already down the stairs, leaving me to catch up as best I could.

CHAPTER 23

By the time I got back to the department, it was almost quitting time. Morris was at the computer store, going through evidence. And I—well, I'd been left on the side of the road like so much baggage.

I looked up from my borrowed desk at the sound of running shoes across the hard tile of the main walkway, maybe fifteen feet away. It was Michael, running. Where was he running to? What was going on?

"Stop running!" the dispatch officer called out.

"Sorry." Michael dropped into a trot.

With the advantage of angles, I headed him off at the front door, arriving out of breath. "Is Cherabino okay?" I panted. I thought I'd probably know through the Link, but I hadn't felt much from her for hours and now he was running. . . .

"She's fine. Murder scene, priority, across the city," Michael said. "I just located Hamilton."

"The husband we couldn't find? Can I come?" If I sat at that desk any longer, I'd probably do something stupid. Like force myself onto the team interrogating the witnesses to the hijacking—not the thing to do if anyone was suspecting me of aiding them. And Kara had forbidden me to call her again for at least another hour.

"You can come, but we need to move. Now."

"You got it." I was tired; it was late. But I wasn't that tired.

He held the door for me. "Cherabino's not in on this one. This is a rough bar."

It took me a second to figure out what he was asking. "I'll be able to handle myself. I have battle training."

A small nod. "We've got a patrol car requisitioned."

A second later he was halfway down the front steps of the building. I had to hustle to catch up, lungs panting in the polluted afternoon air.

Michael parked in the middle of a seedy-looking parking lot in a run-down strip mall south of Decatur. The front of the lot was dominated by the remains of what once had been an air-traffic routing station for computer-controlled aircars, dismantled in the aftermath of the Tech Wars, all the parts yanked out and the empty rusting shell left. It said a lot about the area of town we were in that no one had bothered to take it down; an empty molding mattress took up most of the inside, while the outside was graffiti upon graffiti, but it still stood. Even the red kudzu climbing over the concrete walls looked dull, its color fading as its bioengineered cells began to lose the battle against the pollution it was supposed to be clearing.

Most of the shops in the strip mall were closed for good, another having an Out of Business sale, and a title pawn and the bar anchored the rest of the rotting building. The parking lot was cracked and unpainted, and cars parked at odd angles. More than a few vans left the lot right after the police car pulled in. It was that kind of neighborhood.

Michael put the car in gear and hesitated.

"What?" I asked.

"Well . . ."

I waited, trying to open up enough to understand what

the hesitation was about. Michael wasn't particularly loud in Mindspace, so I didn't get a whole lot from him unless I meant to. I strained, reaching out, and found he was thinking I wasn't a cop. It didn't give me an idea of what the holdup was. I made myself wait him out, and watched one very dim and transient flash of light spark on my right side. For this late in the day, even that was a great sign. I was healing, and steadily.

"Okay," Michael said, seeming to come to a decision. "You don't have a badge, so I can't send you in by yourself. And the whole back of the place seems to butt up against the interstate; I don't think he's going to get anywhere else quickly. So we'll both go in the front door and see what there is to see. If we have to run him down, we'll run him down."

"Do we have to run?" My lungs didn't like anything over a walk.

"Probably. This guy's been hiding. I don't think he's going to come along quietly."

"I'll keep up," I promised, but vowed to myself that I wouldn't be running.

The sign at the bar said PEG LEGS, with a faded drawing of a pirate with a disturbing smile. The windows were too dirty to see into, and there was an extremely large cockroach with mottled blue spots on its blackish carapace working at a bit of rotten food on the sidewalk. It skittered away as we approached. Another bioengineered cleaning creature, maybe. It took a moment for my eyes to adjust to the darkness of the interior of the bar. To the left was a rotting wooden bar, black spots near the floor, metal bar stools spotted with rust, and to the left a small lake of beat-up tables. The place smelled strongly of old sour beer, urine, and dirt. Not the good clean smell of dirt freshly turned in a garden, but the old, nasty, speckled smell of a back alleyway covered in old filth. The patrons, who looked as dirty as the surroundings, stared at us. None of them was Hamilton.

"Nice place," I said to Michael.

"There a private room in the back?" he asked the bartender currently glowering at us. When he got no response, he flashed the badge. We pretended not to notice the large numbers of patrons pulling out money and packing up to leave.

"What's it to you?" The bartender was a short, round guy with the stub of a cigar in his mouth. How he talked with the cigar in place was one of the mysteries of the ages.

Michael moved to the bar, apparently ignoring the patrons, though his body language—and position—showed he was on alert more than usual. "I'm looking for a man by the name of Dan Hamilton. I've been told he's here. And unless you want me to call in a query on your liquor license at the health inspector's office, I'd recommend you help me find him."

The bartender chewed on the end of the cigar for a moment, then pushed a glass aside. He pointed down to the end of the bar. "First door there is the third door on the right in the hallway."

Small, beady eyes watched us as we walked the length of the bar, past suspicious and angry-looking patrons. The mental smell in here was worse than the physical.

Oddly enough, the back hallway was relatively clean, with only the faint smell of cigarette smoke and peanuts to distinguish it. The floor had piled boxes of foodstuffs along one wall, with the first door open to show the mop and paper products of a supply closet. The second door was closed. The third was. . . .

I felt the mind before I saw it, sudden panic shouting loud enough I could feel it dully without even trying. The door flew open and Michael staggered back; it had hit him in the face.

Dan Hamilton, the tall, beefy white guy we'd been searching for, staggered out of the room, his appearance ragged and his fear strong enough to smell. He dug in his heels and made a break for it, getting maybe six steps down the hall toward the sign marked EXIT before I could react.

Michael was running too then, with the solid commitment of someone who was going to catch the suspect or die trying.

I looked at the hallway, Hamilton just now reaching the outside door. I looked at Michael, still too far behind.

I sighed and ran to the end of the hall, lungs gasping.

Hamilton hit the back alleyway, a long horizontal space with nowhere to go other than back around the side of the building to the front parking lot. And he put in a burst of speed, serious speed, outdistancing Michael. Who was this guy, an Olympic runner?

I stopped cold in the alleyway, struggling for air. No way I was going to catch him on foot. It was afternoon—I was tired. But I had to try. I reached out, mind straining, and connected with his. I had him down and disabled before my telepathy gave out, my vision overcome with stars, pain bursting like fireworks. He slowed down, quickly, and slumped, in stages, to the ground.

Michael caught up, breathing hard, and pulled Hamilton's slack arms into alloy strongcuffs. He checked his pulse and seemed satisfied. Only then did he turn around to look back at me.

"That was you?"

I nodded, still breathing hard. The pain was starting to ease as I walked over, but my brain was not happy with me. Suddenly I was having trouble reading the sign across the way, and Mindspace had disappeared. I'd be fine in the morning, probably, but I was done—out—for the day.

Michael frowned, looked down at Hamilton, who was currently sleeping the sleep of the dead, drool and all. "Next time, get him before I have to do the hundred-yard dash, okay?"

I nodded, then tried to figure out how to ask. Oh, hell. "That didn't bother you?" Most normals would be freaking out and asking lots of questions about whether he was going to wake up and whether I was going to do that to them next.

"Not really," Michael said. "Beats the hell out of a stun gun. You reloadable?"

"What?"

"Can you do more than one of these in a chase?"

"I'm not at full capacity right now, but normal circumstances? I don't know, maybe three or four in a row before I need a break. Why?"

He shook his head. "Damn shame. If we had more of you out on patrol—well, it's a damn shame." I stayed with Hamilton as he went to go get the car for transport. Wow. It was the nicest thing anyone had said about me in years.

And he'd done it while I'd panted my lungs out in the middle of the chase in front of him. Huh.

Michael kept surprising me.

"He's finally woken up," Bellury told me quietly the next morning, in the hallway outside the cleanest interview room. I had the door cracked so I could keep an ear out for the suspect I was currently interviewing, a hysterical woman with a flair for dramatics who I was almost certain had been running restricted weapons across state lines for the last six months. As expected, the hysterics went from loud to nonexistent when I left the room. Then, too late, a whimper pitched to come through the partially opened door.

I sighed. "Hamilton? After sleeping all night, he's waking up now?"

He nodded.

"And Cherabino's still out in the field. See if Michael has a minute and see if you can find the man a cup of coffee, please. I need to finish this one up before I can do anything else. She's on the edge of letting the act slip, I think."

Bellury shrugged. "Coffee's not going to do it with Hamilton. He's been begging for a cigarette for the last ten minutes solid. I had to take the things from him twice—apparently he had a holdout stash."

Great. And DeKalb County ordinances wouldn't allow smoking indoors for suspects for any reason up to and including imminent death. "I'll see if I can't take him out back later. Think he's going to run once he's outside?" It could be dangerous to knock him out twice in twenty-four hours with mind tricks, and that didn't look good to a jury. My Abilities had only sparked one police brutality charge, and I'd like to keep it to that one. Plus I felt good this morning and didn't want to waste the mental juju on knocking him out.

"Might do ankle cuffs to be sure," Bellury said thoughtfully.

"That's a good idea."

"I'll get us a pair with the coffee."

"Thanks." I took a minute to compose myself, and went back into the room. The hysterics resumed, grating on my nerves like sandpaper on a skinned knee. She knew she was being recorded, right? Even when I wasn't in the room?

"Mrs. Clamp," I began.

The rest of the interview took twelve minutes—four to catch her in a lie, three to press my advantage and intimidation factor, and five to record her confession.

"Thank you for coming in, Mrs. Clamp," I said, and smiled at her before closing the door.

I could feel Dan Hamilton's anger through the door, a stubborn steady heat like banked coals in a fireplace. I took an extra moment to settle against that anger, to force down my own in return. He'd beat Emily, he'd hurt her, the woman he was supposed to love, a betrayal of everything that was human and decent. He'd proven himself scum by so doing, no true man, and deserved to be drawn and quartered on the streets. But it would do Emily's memory no good to scream at him. It wouldn't bring her death any justice. It wouldn't help me find Tamika or shut down Sibley. And who knows? Tamika could have nothing to do with Emily's death; that part could be coincidence and a stop on the way to the hijackings. Kara still hadn't found her, Morris had found no connections—when she was talking to me—and Cherabino was hopelessly tied up in a higher priority for the moment.

So it was up to me. Hamilton had to know something. I opened the door and made myself smile, made my body language friendly and open, when what I really wanted to do was beat him within an inch of his life.

Hamilton was a large man, scuzzy looking right now, dirty and unshaven. He was leaning forward in the chair, leaning against the table, and his right foot was fidgeting, moving back and forth in a twitchy motion I recognized. He was harder up for a cigarette than expected, hungry and angry, and his head hurt.

Oddly, this didn't give me any sympathy for the son of a bitch.

"Mr. Hamilton," I said. "Thank you for waiting. I assume

we've read you your rights?" I met Bellury's eyes across the room, and he nodded, slightly.

I had a small bag full of files with me, and I made a show of unpacking all over the table, stuff strewn everywhere, most of it far too much in Hamilton's space for comfort.

As expected, after about the third thing he pushed it all, forcefully, away. "You can't hold me like this. I ain't done nothing wrong."

"You ran from a police investigation." That wasn't a crime, or at least not anything major, but it looked bad, and most suspects realized that. Innocent people didn't run—or at least, that's what the cops believed. "You ran from us when we tried to bring you in for questioning." I paused in the middle of my unpacking, making a show of thinking. "Oh yes, and there's the matter of your wife's body being found in your home. Your wife's murdered body." Entirely too long ago—Emily deserved justice faster than this.

"I didn't kill her." Hamilton sat back and glowered. Went back to fidgeting.

"You don't seem surprised to hear she's dead."

"I don't know what happened, okay? I came home late—real late—and there she was. I'd had a little too much to drink. It took me a minute to figure out what had happened."

I took a seat. "And you ran."

He looked tired then, suddenly very tired. "That wasn't somebody breaking into the house. It was just luck I wasn't there for them to kill me."

I leaned forward. "You think they were there to kill you and murdered Emily, say, by mistake?" Even the thought made me angry. "Why the hell would you think that? You owe too much to the bookie?"

Now he was angry too; he leaned forward also, until we were far too close over the table. I didn't back down.

Finally the tension broke and he leaned back and started fidgeting again, his eyes going to the lighter in my front shirt pocket. "You give me a cigarette and I'll tell you all about it."

"You tell me all about it and I'll give you a cigarette."

He frowned, hard, the anger rising.

I waited.

"I'll tell you some, but you give me the cigarette now."

"You can't smoke it indoors."

"Fine."

"Fine." I pulled out one of my blue smokes and passed it over the table. He grabbed it like it was a lifeline, just smelling the thing. I saw a shadow of myself in that moment and hated him all the more. "Who would want to kill you?" I asked, but it came out sarcastic and bitter.

"Other than Emily?" Dan said. He shook his head. "When you've got the kind of talent I've got, you make plenty of enemies."

"Like the bookie?"

He sat up. "I paid the damn bookie off. Did he tell you I didn't? My trade was worth fifty thousand ROCs, easy. If he says otherwise, he's lying."

And suddenly it all came together in my head. "You traded the blueprints—those blueprints you stole from your work—to pay your gambling debts. You realize that's a felony Tech violation."

"And that worm Edelman had the balls to threaten me about it. Never thought he'd actually follow through, though. And for Emily . . ." He trailed off then, like he actually felt something for her, like she was a person and a punching bag both. He played with the cigarette. "Well, it was time to get lost for a while. I assume you caught him and he told you about the prints? Well, I've got him red-handed on the threats. You want to make a deal, I'll testify against him, you get a murderer for free. The prints weren't all that great and you can't prove I took them anyways."

He looked up. "You want to hear about the whole she-bang, you gotta let me smoke."

I had to swallow my anger again as I took him outside, grabbing one of the beat cops with a gun to act as guard. I lit up my own smoke while he did his, to try to seem companionable. To get him to try to trust me. Emily's sister had said he was a braggart, and I was starting to see that.

We were standing behind the main bulk of the Head-quarters building, facing a bedraggled courtyard in between office buildings, a courtyard that never did seem to grow grass, despite the fact that one of the office buildings facing us had a low roof that sparkled in the sun. Sun. With all the rain lately, even with the awning above me I was soaking up as many rays as I could in self-defense. I needed to absorb more vitamin D; we all did, with that much rain going.

Hamilton smoked all the way through a cigarette before he would talk. Finally he reached for a second—and I gave it, with a question.

"Why are you so sure it's Edelman? You guys don't get along, I understand that, but it's a hell of a jump from that to murder."

He took a big, long, obsessive drag on the cigarette, then blew the smoke out of his nose like a belligerent bull. "Edelman never liked me. Was always jealous of my talent. That's why he was always riding me, trying to get me to slip up. You know how it is. It got so bad I had to go blow off steam now and again. So maybe I spent too much with the poker and the picks. Bastard drove me to it."

I'd met this guy—or men just like him—in rehab. I couldn't say I was any more impressed with it in the real world. Swartz said blaming everybody else for your screwups was how you kept screwing up. "How'd you find the blueprints?"

"I'm not saying I took the blueprints," he said, but he was thinking about them, and it was early in the morning on a day I was feeling spry. I got all the details I wanted, clear pictures of strange diagrams that had biologicals on them. Not just computers, but the semisentient computers that had nearly crashed the world. Powerful, forbidden diagrams and he'd had them for two weeks before he even thought to sell them. Having that much power, that forbidden knowledge in his hands, had just gotten him off.

"Did your bookie take a look at them? Is that why he let you off the debt?" I asked. "We're not being recorded here." Then I saw something in his mind—"What was that extra diagram of anyway?"

"I talked to a guy about it. It's a wireless networking setup designed to work with—"

One sudden gunshot cracked over the courtyard. My concentration broke and I was back in my own head.

My eyes searched for where the sound had come from—there, at the top of that office building. That shiny something I'd seen earlier reflected the sun again.

Next to me, Hamilton's mind spat pain—then grew faint.

I turned; he was on the hard concrete slab, collapsed. Blood poured from his throat in heavy spurts, arterial blood.

Crap, he was— I yanked off my long-sleeved shirt, buttons flying in my haste, wrapped it around his throat. The beat cop was already gone, on the way for help.

"EMT!" I screamed, all I could do. "EMT!" My mind echoed the call as loud as I could make it, with all the power of a Level Eight telepath pitched to be heard by even normals. I called again, "EMT! Help!" louder and louder as my hands grew sticky with Hamilton's blood, pouring out all over my hands as I tried to hold pressure to the wound.

The scars on my arms mocked me as I crouched, helpless, while Hamilton died.

A near army of help arrived, but far too late.

CHAPTER 24

Cherabino showed up with the EMTs, her hands full of a nasty rifle.

"Where did he go?" she asked me.

I still had my hands on Hamilton's neck, but they'd gone slack. I'd felt the void when his mind had gone . . . wherever minds went when you died. There was no pretense now, but I hadn't moved from my crouch.

"Hey!" Cherabino said, poking at me mentally. "Where did he go?"

"Where did who go?" The answer leaked through before I even finished the question. "The shooter. He was on the roof across the way, but—"

She was off and running before I had a chance to think. And then—I was after her, my lungs laboring with every painful stride. I couldn't let her go alone. I couldn't. Not her. Not if I had to run a million billion miles.

Cherabino was across the courtyard and in the front door of the building I'd indicated within a few seconds. I got in somewhat later, just in time to see the stair door slam shut in the lobby.

With a sigh, I pushed through—only to be knocked down by her coming the other way.

"Damn illegal floaters," Cherabino spat at me. "He's headed to Decatur Square."

An old lady in the lobby gaped at us as Cherabino

pushed past her, hard. I made it back to my feet, lungs laboring—damn cigarettes—and tried desperately to at least keep her within sight. In the courtyard, my shoes squelched in the mud, feeling a million pounds heavy.

I could see the floater in the sky as Cherabino paused at the street, her gun pointed up. But she didn't take the shot, and the floater got smaller. The hooded figure riding the small, less-than-three-foot anti-gravity platform, wobbled briefly in midair; but he corrected, pulling on the small cords that were all that gave him balance. Floaters were like surfboards for the sky—small, nimble, quick. But instead of surfing over water and sand, you floated over buildings and unforgiving concrete. One misstep and you died. There were reasons these things were illegal.

Cherabino holstered the gun and started running again, a steady stream of curses echoing through my mind.

She ran for over a mile, every stride hitting pavement painfully in department-mandated shoes, sweat dripping down her face, determination and cussed anger driving her on. I fell farther and farther back, finally dropping to a walk as I felt her frustration intensify. Even at a walk, I was getting suspicious glances from passersby—the blood on my hands tipping them off to something. The department would get more than a few calls about this.

I walked, panting, trying to let my heart and lungs catch on to the fact that I wasn't dying, then pushed back to a painful run. By this time other cops had passed me in pursuit, but I still wasn't going to leave.

By the time I caught up to Cherabino, we were on Church Street, near the public transport hub—and Cherabino was standing, panting, in the middle of the street.

Cars honked at her, and she flashed them a badge and a finger and didn't move. One of the other cops, with a sigh, started directing traffic by the library.

Cherabino was standing, frustrated. She was looking

at the entrance to the underground tram, and beyond it, the bus station and taxi circle. All areas without so much as a single camera after the latest Privacy Accords ruling. All very well and good to say the public deserved not to be recorded, but it made a cop's life living hell.

"You got a good look, right?"

"No." She seriously considered punching me out of sheer frustration. "How could you take him to the smoking porch? That's like a kill box at the back there, and he was connected to our murder. Our murder with connections to Them." To the Darkness, she meant, the massive organized crime group to which Fiske was supposed to be connected.

"He needed to smoke." You couldn't smoke at the front of the building or in the parking lot.

"Well, you may have cost us this investigation." She sighed and walked away, knees aching, back in the general direction of the department.

A car honked at me and I got back on the sidewalk, feeling failure crushing down on me like a falling piano.

Bellury opened his car door. "Get in. We're going to drive until you can tell me what you're going to do next."

"Okay," I said numbly.

We drove, around and around, until Bellury finally headed up Clairmont.

I sighed and sat back in the passenger's seat, the same passenger seat I'd been in on the way to the hijacked truck, the same seat that had taken me to the meeting with Swartz's medic.

I was certain now the hijacking case was connected to Emily's murder. Otherwise, why kill Hamilton? Why bother, unless those blueprints, that stolen Tech, and Sibley's order to kill Emily were inextricably connected? Tamika was clearly up to her ears in it all, and as much as it pained me, I couldn't be thinking about her anymore as anything but a suspect. I owed her, yes. But I owed Emily too. And I owed my job, my present life, and Cherabino far more. I had this nagging feeling that all the pieces were on the board now—that if I could just see them clearly, I'd be able to solve this case.

So I turned things over and over in my head, looking at everything from as many angles as I could, waiting for the puzzle pieces on the table to start fitting together.

We passed a nice-looking senior center, an older gentleman in a small, staid floater-assist chair waiting to cross at the light, and I was still thinking.

"If you had a large-scale criminal organization, what would you do with blueprints for Tech and Tech parts?" I asked Bellury. "Not just sell them, right? By the way, where are we going?"

"My house. If you need to think long enough, I want some of the leftover lasagna from last night," Bellury said evenly. "And it depends on how much money the final product will get me versus how much use I have for it myself. Are we talking about Fiske here?"

"I don't think I'm supposed to talk about him, actually. There's apparently a complicated, delicate investigation in the works."

He shrugged. "Paulsen asks me for input. I'm already in the loop."

I turned all the way around in the seat to look at him, seat belt pulling at my shoulder. "What?"

"I worked with the special organized crime force for ten years," Bellury said, still in that flat, no-big-deal tone. "Rachel said we were getting too old for her to deal with the stress. So I found something less dangerous. Paulsen will still call me into meetings sometimes for background."

I stared at him.

He glanced over. "If you don't close your mouth, the flies will fly in. Now, Fiske? I guess we're talking about the hijackings, since you're involved in that case too. First thing you'd need, whatever you did, was someplace to put the stuff together. Atlanta—at least the east side—is too hot right now. Somebody would eventually catch on."

"Oh," I said eloquently.

"But like I said, mostly that's above my pay grade these days. And criminals change tactics over time. That's life."

"I see."

But my mind was going over and over this idea of needing a place, somewhere to take the Tech. Not too close—Bellury was right, that would be too risky for somebody as smart as Fiske was rumored to be—and not too far, because road transportation would be an issue with the increased police presence there.

Well, if you couldn't take it by road—Guild courier routes. I'd take it by Guild courier, obviously, but if you couldn't . . . well, there was always the airport. Emily's father apparently had a stake in the DeKalb-Peachtree Airport. Maybe you could . . .

Airport. Emily's daughter had smelled kerosene on her. Kerosene, according to Michael's handout, was also used as jet fuel. Jet fuel, airport, and then Emily ends up dead. Right after Tamika and Sibley visited her, and the blueprints changed hands.

Everything fell together like a perfect puzzle. It all made sense.

"You're brooding," Bellury said.

"No, I'm thinking. Can I get you to take me on a quick side trip? I need to test a theory."

CHAPTER 25

The airport was a monumentally huge open space, ground covered in wide strips of concrete and grass, and the air smelled crisp, like fall, with the earthy scent of cut grass and dirt thrown in for good measure . . . with the faintest, lightest smell of kerosene wafting in the breeze. The sun beat down on my head as across the length of the field, two boxy hangars, wider than they were tall, anchored the airport. They looked small until I realized that the low shape to the right of them was another building, this one half as tall, with people like ants scurrying at its base.

I folded myself back in the car and put on the seat belt. Bellury, with the windows cracked to enjoy the rare sunny day, drove closer on the ground-level little airport road until he reached an open area beside one of the hangars where other cars were parked. He pulled in and turned off the engine, then looked at me.

"I want to look around," I said in answer to his unspoken question.

He nodded without comment. He was the only one, maybe, the only one in the department not to care how much I read his mind.

He pulled his gun holster from the glove department and strapped it on. There were times Bellury sidelined me with how deep the cop instincts really went. A gun in your glove compartment? And he buckled the fastenings with the unconscious ease of a man who'd done this for years, over and over, until it became another habit, like breathing. Bellury might be old, might be perfectly happy to settle into light duty, but he was still a cop. Sometimes that caught me by surprise.

I closed the car door behind me, and the smell of fuel and oil, sun and grass, metal parts and sun-cooked metal siding was overwhelming. It had been raining for weeks, and this much sunlight was nice, like a strong cheerful slap on the back from the fusion-powered star above us.

I needed to find confirmation here—a clue or two that would crack the case wide open—and get back to either Morris or Paulsen, or both, to finish up the job. If I was right—and I could prove it—we would close two cases. And maybe, just maybe, I would have earned my spot in the department for good.

I walked forward, around the circumference of the huge hangar in front of us. Corrugated metal sheeting made up its sides, relatively new sheeting by the looks of things, and the white paint bent the light oddly, like small oases in the afternoon air. Some kind of supermaterial, maybe. The side soared up maybe three stories above us, straight up, a boxy and hard-cornered shape.

The front of the hangar was a huge, rolling door—probably on hydraulics, by the look of its heaviness—currently closed. A smaller door to the right side was open.

I told Bellury to follow me with a gesture and went through the door, on high alert but not really expecting anything. The telepathy was much more reliable lately, and it was early enough in the day that I was sure I could handle any bad guys long enough for Bellury to bring out the gun.

The inside of the hangar was about what you'd expect; a few high windows cast long dust-filled lines of sunlight down onto the planes. Specifically, four small aerobatic planes in bright colors nearer the door, and farther back, a mammoth thick-necked jet with wide bulges along the side for anti-grav and extra room for cargo—the wing-span took up practically the whole of the hangar. It had a plain gray paint job, which was odd. Even the serial number on the tail was small.

"Hello?" a rough man's voice called out. A high scraping sound came suddenly, like a metal piece scraping hard against concrete. Then a few seconds later, a guy in mechanics' coveralls came out, rubbing his hands with a rag.

"Can I help you?" he asked me.

I paused. Oh, crap. I didn't have either a cover story or a badge. My mind raced . . .

Bellury stepped forward. "The kid here is thinking about buying an airplane and wants to know what the storage fees are in your little operation. How much access will he have to the plane on, say, holidays and week-ends?"

The mechanic named a number for hangar rental, which I had no idea whether it was too high or not. Then he added that all rental folks had their own keys and had to pass a background check. He gave me a sideways look, suspicion in every line of his body.

I straightened a bit, staying absolutely relaxed. If there was one thing you learned by working for the Guild, you could never tell who—or what organization—really had money. The most seemingly simple people in the world had major purse strings. On the other hand, you could tell who didn't have money: the ones who blustered and tried to impress everyone in sight. People with money—real money—didn't really care what you thought of them, if you were the help. They also didn't particularly care about price tags as long as they got what they wanted.

So, with body language absolutely relaxed, I asked,

"You available to do annual flight checks? Or am I going to have to pull the thing out every year and have it shipped to another shop?"

He blinked, and I could see that he bought it. A short conversation later, I'd managed to talk him into letting us wander around, "see the facilities on a spot check. I've found the average day is much better represented if I don't give warning, I'm sure you understand."

The mechanic shrugged. "We do have cameras on the facility. We have permits for them all, and signs posted, but it bothers some people."

Bellury got tense next to me.

"I'll keep that in mind," I said. Odd that they had cameras. Private businesses didn't usually have them, not the least of which because it was hard—and expensive—to get around the privacy laws. It also could cost them significant business, as most normals didn't want to be recorded anymore, not since the data piracy of the Tech Wars had made it all too easy to find out everything about everyone. The only places you saw cameras anymore were multimillion-ROC jewelry stores, larger banks, courthouses, and the interview rooms at the station. Pretty much anything else was hamstrung by the cost, the laws, or the prevailing public opinion.

The mechanic nodded. "Keep out of the back building. That's the owner's office, among other things, and he gets real testy if you interrupt him. He certainly won't approve your rental if you bother him."

"Understood."

After a cursory look around the rest of the airport, we approached the shorter building toward the back, where a small white van was parked.

I tried the door—which was open—and stepped through.

A small air-conditioned office had a hip-high pile of boxes next to the large desk, boxes with labels on the side saying ELECTRONICS COMPONENTS. The permits and bills of sale were attached to each box in brightly colored papers and seals; legitimate, so far as it looked.

And on the other side of the room, coming through a door there, was a middling-height bald man with a military bearing, carrying a small cube-shaped machine covered in wires, with a small blinking light on top.

"You must be Adam," the man said, in a lower-class London accent. "You see, this is why I thought we should cut ties with the airport after the termination decision. All too easy to trace our involvement backwards. But I was overruled. Fortunately, you two look like you're alone."

"Who are you?" I asked, suddenly worried. "What's that thing in your hand?" With the missing Tech, and blueprints, and sketches, unidentified machines seemed ominous. And his words . . .

"That's not important," he said calmly. He seemed to be staring at Bellury intently, and something felt odd. "You can do as I say. Pick up two boxes, exit the building, and climb into my white van parked on the curb."

"Okay." Bellury picked up the boxes.

What the . . . ?

"Hold on." I dropped shallowly into Mindspace to see what I was up against.

I saw a strange bent-light effect around the box, and the traces of waves it had just let out, odd waves. And behind it—the sharp mind whom I'd seen before at the crime scenes. The strangler. Sibley. The bottom fell out of my world. I had just been crazy, monumentally stupid. He was right—we were alone.

I reached out with my mind to disable him—but before I could, he pushed a button and the thing he held lit up with a second light. A strange compulsion hit me, enough to break my concentration. I stared at Sibley. He was fascinating in that moment, like a cobra with its hood spread, his every movement mesmerizing. That square-jawed face, the bald head, the broken nose, the little burn scar near his ear—fascinating.

"And you, my dear Adam. You want desperately to follow my instructions."

"That's right," I heard myself say, unable to take my eyes away. In the back of my mind, I tried to pull away, to figure something . . . this wasn't right, but I couldn't figure out why. I had to follow his instructions.

"You want to follow your friend down to the van, but don't forget an armful of the boxes yourself. We're going to load the van. But don't get too far away from me, now."

"That would be bad," I said as I did what he asked. It was important I stayed close to him.

My training was starting to kick in. I slowly parsed out this weird feeling, this . . . force coming at me through Mindspace. Like clouds hitting my brain obliquely, like another dimension, something was changing the shape of my mind . . . or more accurately, getting me to change it. But knowledge wasn't mastery; I could no more stop walking in the direction he wanted, I could no more fight this mesmerizing fascination than I could fly.

Bellury, ahead of me, slowed down, to look around, and Sibley moved faster to stand in front of him as we made the transition back outside.

"What . . . ?" Bellury mumbled, and shifted the boxes in his hand so he could reach for his gun.

"Give me the gun," Sibley said firmly, and then accepted it. "Open the door and set the boxes in. It's unlocked." Then to me: "You too. Go quickly and carefully and don't fight me."

"You got it," I said, despite myself.

After loading was done, we piled onto the long bench seat in the center of the van, and Sibley put the blinking machine on the floorboards while he put handcuffs on us. All the time that mesmerizing force stayed steady in my brain, and my eyes settled on the grapefruit-sized cube like it was the most fascinating thing I'd ever seen. When Sibley spoke, I obeyed. Was this why none of the victims had struggled? Even Emily . . . had the shape of her mind protected her some?

What would it have been like to sit there while Sibley strangled you to death, unable to lift a finger in your own defense? Was I about to find out?

The seeds of true fear began to grow inside me.

We waited for a long moment; then Sibley turned all the way around to look at us. "Bellury, forget the last few minutes, as much as you can. And fall asleep."

Bellury slumped over.

"What are you doing? What are you . . ." I trailed off.

Sibley's attention turned to me, that sharp, calm attention like a small cruel child staring at a bug. "Quiet now."

I fell silent despite myself. My heart fluttered in my chest like a bird trapped in a tiny cage, frantic, frantic to get out. I tried to talk, but I couldn't. . . .

"Keep your thoughts to yourself. Calm down now."

And despite every bone in my body, despite all my panicked effort, I did. My mind settled into smaller, calmer analytical circles, but my heart . . . my heart kept that frantic movement in my chest.

Sibley turned around, humming to himself, and took the car out of park. Outside, like tears, the sky began to rain.

Ten minutes later, we were turning into an old office park in a wooded area off North Druid Hills Road. About the time I'd recover my will enough to struggle with the handcuffs—maybe once every three or four minutes—Sibley would find me through the rearview mirror and order me back down, back to silence and calm. It should have been terrifying, frustrating, horrifying. But I couldn't feel anything or think anything without an artificial, disturbing calm lying on top of it like a heavy pillow cutting off my air.

Bellury was still sleeping to my right; Sibley had sent him back as soon as he began to stir. I was behind Sibley, on the left of the bench seat, watching the cube's lights turn on and off.

The car pulled into a parking lot and moved to a front door of an office building. A woman stood at the door, an overweight woman huddled under an umbrella that shielded her face.

We stopped, and she opened the passenger door, shaking out the umbrella.

"Hello, Adam," Tamika said, and got in the car. "Thank you, Sibley."

The last piece of the puzzle clicked into place, but it was too late.

The van was being raised by a hydraulic lift, a slow, heavy lift with a square concrete floor currently climbing the floors of the parking garage, like the main arm on a soda machine. As another floor went by, through the open space between them I could see pine trees below, nearly endless pine trees yellowed with pollution.

The lift drew even with a floor perhaps ten stories above ground level, its concrete edge lining up with the edge of the permanent floor. Ahead, through maybe a hundred feet of textured reinforced concrete, a large wide door stood open under a sign that said DYMANI SYSTEMS, BUILDING 4, LOADING.

Tamika twisted around in the passenger seat, and Sibley brought up Bellury's gun. The car doors were locked and the lock next to me was busted off, so that the only way to get out was through one of them. The mesmerizing force from Sibley was starting to wear off, and I could speak again.

"I have one question," I said to Tamika, ignoring Sibley by sheer force of will. "Why Emily? Did you plan her death from the beginning?"

"No," Tamika said. She paused for a moment, like she was considering whether to speak to me. Finally she shrugged. "No, I really did think she hated the Guild and the normals as much as she was pretending. But all she wanted was the money, and then she wanted to *do the right thing*." She laughed, a sound entirely devoid of mirth. "I guess she got that from you, Professor. You'd think she would have learned better."

I sat up, ready to extend my—

"Settle down, don't use your telepathy, and don't fight this," Sibley told me, that hateful blinking cube in his hands. The cube—I realized all at once that this must be Tamika's machine. The machine she built from that sketch. From Dane's teaching.

"You created a brain wave compulsion machine. To make up for your lack of Ability."

"The Ability you stole from me!" her voice snapped.

And then Tamika, the sweet girl I'd taught for years, the quiet, nice, polite woman I'd known, grabbed Sibley's gun. She settled herself against the back of the passenger-side seat and shot one bullet before I could react. I winced, braced for pain—but there was none.

Next to me, Bellury cried out and was suddenly awake and clutching his shoulder. A steady litany of cursing while he went for a gun at his side, a gun that wasn't there, his hands clumsy in the cuffs.

Three more shots, deafening in the small space. *Boom. Boom. Crack.*

The warmth of blood hit my face—warm, sticky blood—and that horrible, horrible calm imploded.

In Mindspace, the world sucked in in a burst, a black hole of death realized. I fought my way away, away, anything to keep from being sucked in . . . and finally succeeded.

In reality, in the car, the strong, acrid smell of urine filled the air, and the side of my leg next to Bellury was wet. His body slumped toward me, his head hitting my shoulder with a thud.

I pushed him away, frantically. Bellury was . . . Bellury was . . .

The van's sliding door on the right side away from me opened, and Tamika's arm pulled Bellury away, down, with gravity, until he slumped on the ground outside the car. Then she shot him again, standing over him.

She turned back to me, meeting my eyes, and suddenly the nice girl I'd known was gone.

"You should have died in the gutter. You should have lost everything—like I did. And since you didn't—I'll take my justice from you."

CHAPTER 26

"Keep your thoughts to yourself and stay put," Sibley told me, and that mesmerizing compulsion spread over me again until I couldn't—I couldn't think about moving. I stared at him, unable to help myself, as he walked around the car to Tamika.

He walked down to the huge doors to our left, box still in hand, and as he walked I realized the doors were much bigger than I'd thought. And the company name—Dynami Systems, the same company that Emily had worked for. My eyes continued to follow Sibley as he walked, this fascination almost—almost but not quite—keeping me from thinking about Emily, who I'd failed. Tamika, who I'd failed just as badly. Bellury, who . . . my mind shied away.

"We need to go," Sibley said as two guys with guns came out of the entrance. He gestured for them to go toward the van. "Unload this thing—fast this time. Watch the electronics—they're delicate. And you, miss, you'll need to check in with the boss." He projected his voice loudly enough to echo off the sides of the specialty material that made up the walls of the garage.

"Why are these two here? And why are you running so late?" Tamika asked. "This is not what we agreed on. Fiske said you'd—"

"I'd do the job and do it well. But you keep hamstringing me with *requests.* I specifically warned you the risks went up if we kept the association with the airport. You knew the smuggling was risky."

Tamika moved toward him. "And you were supposed to kill him last week anyway!"

"It was too early, I told you that." And they degenerated into an argument while I fought the compulsion, slowly, slowly, trying to wiggle out of a too-tight straitjacket.

Bellury lying there, just lying there, only fueled the anger that let me fight.

Finally it occurred to me—I didn't have to move. Not outwardly. I didn't even have to call for help; thinking that thought still hurt, actually hurt. I could no more call for help than I could run a marathon in the next two seconds. But I didn't have to.

As Sibley walked down to talk to one of the guards, I took a breath and poked at the watcher's tracker in my head, poked hard—the one thing Cherabino had forbidden me to do. I poked harder, searing pain washing over me, pain like an ice pick to the brain—but I couldn't move.

Pain. Pain. Pain. Like a beacon, almost, or a nasty lighthouse run by a madman, shooting lasers instead of plain simple light. Pain. Only then did I stop poking at it. Only then . . .

And in the quiet afterward, while I was trying to catch my breath, came the smell and the taste of Cherabino. Beautiful, annoyed, competent, angry Cherabino.

What the hell are you doing? she asked me mind to mind. *I told you to stop it with the moods! And the pain, that's just . . .* She thought of kicking my ass, literally, figuratively, and then flipping me over onto my face on the concrete while her knee went in my back and she gave me a long, detailed lecture about how she *needed to work.*

I stared at the carpeted car floor for a long moment,

trying to catch up. The compulsion didn't apply to this, I told myself. It was a Link, not telepathy. Not telepathy. I made myself believe it. *Cherabino!*

What, asshole?

I found Tamika and Sibley—but he has this thing. It's a compulsion machine. I think she made it—she used to work for Dane. She has the skills. I don't know. They took us to a small office park on North Druid Hills, in a Dymani Systems building. I can see armed men over by the entrance, but I can't move. I need help. Please. Now. Bellury's alarm thing went off, but they shut it down. And then, with panic I couldn't suppress, *They killed him. He's dead. They killed him.*

Shock and anger pushed over the Link like fire; then they were gone, and Cherabino's no-nonsense cop thinking snapped into place. *Where are you? How many are there?*

I replayed my memories of the day in a panicked fast-forward stream—*Stop.* She breathed. *Stop!*

I stopped. *What's wrong?*

I'm not a . . . damn it, you're giving me a migraine. Stick to words, okay? Words. She was struggling not to put up the walls again, struggling to put her own crap aside and deal with the situation. *I'm not a damn telepath. I need words.*

With the compulsion weakening, I looked over at the building entrance and tried to get a view in Mindspace of how many there were. *I don't know, at least ten.*

Damn it, Cherabino said. *Half a dozen police cars with heavy rifles. At minimum. We can't see what's in that building, and odds are that's where you'll be by the time we get there. Damn it, Adam, that takes hours to requisition. Days, worse. I can't just . . . Are you sure he's dead?*

He's gone from Mindspace. The sound of the door lock disengaging made me look up in panic.

Call Kara, I told Cherabino, fear running down the
Link without me helping it.

The door next to me opened, and two men with guns
and a female telepath of considerable strength stared at
me. She was Tamika's age, give or take, pale with freckles and no sense of humor.

After that was . . .

Like a knife to butter, something tore through the connection between me and Cherabino and I was stuck,
alone, in my own head, the watcher's tag hitting me with
pain in response, like an ice pick to the brain.

Someone grabbed my sleeve and I fell, my side hitting
the concrete with bruising force.

I reached back out again, again, past the pain,
gripping—and hit a fog, the frustrating horrible fog of a
local Mindspace telepathic block. The woman scowled
down at me. "We're going to have to move to plan C. This
idiot managed to talk to somebody before I shut him
down. This is going to cost us extra time."

Then she nodded to one of the beefy guards. He hit me
across the head with the butt of his gun, and with a burst
of stars, the world went black.

I woke up with the female telepath standing over me. I
jumped back—and couldn't. I was sitting in an old-style
wooden chair, my hands bound behind my back and to
the chair. I tested the bonds.

"I wouldn't," the telepath told me. She was slight of
build with a heart-shaped face, not very tall, and her dirty-
blond hair and freckles might disarm most of her oppo-
nents enough for her to get in the first strike. Me, on the
other hand—well, I'd had my ass kicked too many times
by Jamie, who looked like a young cookie-baking grandmother. Looks didn't mean anything when it came to the
mind.

I eased back, noting that my legs were free. She was at the wrong angle for me to kick her. Time to try words instead. "So you're a Minder, huh?" My brain kept flashing back to Bellury, and I kept forcing it down. *Get through this first. Get through this, and then you can think about it.* "Wait, are you the missing telepath?"

Her brow wrinkled. "How did you . . . ?"

I nodded to her tailored skirt. "Um, well, that's standard issue for Minders who don't have the cash yet to blend in with the fancy clients. Nobody else wants that gray-brown color. Plus you have a brighter spot on the shirt from where your badge was. Right breast pocket, standard-issue size." Actually the shirt wasn't all that faded, but when her hand went to the spot, I knew I was right. "And a telepath disappeared at the same time Tamika did. It should have been obvious you were working together. Do you have a name?"

"Coleen," she said, and crossed her arms in a stance that was probably supposed to be intimidating. Her cuteness didn't blunt the real threat she posed.

"No last name?"

"None that I'm giving you. You realize I've seen your file. You're not the first Structure guy I've ridden herd on."

I suppressed the urge to make the obvious sexual comment and stuck to something more neutral. "You're counting on me to be out of practice, then?" Hopefully my injury hadn't made it into the file, at least not the version she'd seen. Some advantages to secrets, after all.

Coleen nodded. "You're old, and you haven't had to take recurrents. Plus Structure guys are slow. And you've been working for normals, which is even worse."

And that got me the last bit of information I needed. She didn't know about my injury, and she was definitely a Minder, and a young one at that. If she was relatively fresh from graduation (which the clothes implied, either that or some large expense I didn't know about), well, she'd definitely have a much better reaction time mind to mind than I would, even at full strength and practice. That's what Minders were trained for, after all, protecting high-profile clients from anything mental anyone could throw at them. And from what little I could see of her presence in Mindspace through the blocking shield, she wasn't weak, and she wasn't careless. She'd be a strong mental guard, here to make sure I didn't call for help.

I shifted in the chair a bit, unable to keep myself from pulling at the bonds. "What do you—"

She took a step back and Mindspace suddenly felt charged. "Seriously, don't. I didn't give up my spot in the Guild to go down to an out-of-practice punk. You won't get ten feet before I take you down like I took down that saleslady."

She had killed Emily's boss? Another question answered too late. I'd stay put for now, save my move until she wasn't expecting it.

I finally let myself take a look around. We were in an office, a medium-sized basic office from a hundred movies and even more office buildings, a file cabinet or four to the front of the room, a battered metal desk, plain beige walls, and a bookcase. Nothing exciting. Nothing interesting. Not even a window to climb out of. The phone jack in the wall, not far from the closed heavy door, led to an old-style black boxy phone on the desk. "You don't expect me to try to strangle you with the telephone cord?"

She blinked, and a burst of nervousness floated through Mindspace before she damped it down. Interesting. I'd been bluffing, but if physical confrontation made her nervous, I could work with that.

"Why give up your spot in the Guild anyway?" I asked, to keep the conversation going, trying to get all the information out of her I could. "You're a little young to know Tamika as a classmate, and illegal Tech seems an odd thing for a Minder to get involved in."

"Tamika works in the logistics office," Colleen said, in that tone of voice teenagers take with adults, like I was too stupid to live. She was too old for it to look natural. "She helped me get something through one of the couriers. And then she helped me get a deal with enough money for my brother to—" She shut up then, frowning, like she'd just caught on. "I see what you're doing. You're trying to get me to like you so I won't burn you out later. Well, it's not going to work."

Of course it was going to work; she was practically handing me all her secrets on a platter, shielding in Mindspace or none. I had this down.

And then she hit me with pain—real, honest-to-goodness pain, pain that ripped me open and up, pain down every single nerve fiber I had, the pain of a third-degree burn over every inch of my body. My skin, my fat, my very bone burning away in red-hot fire.

An interminable time later, she let it go. I panted, desperately, my muscles knotted and sore from spasms; the echo of my screams still hung in the air.

That stance—her arms crossed, her too-young eyes weighing me—that stance no longer seemed cute.

She was stronger than me, probably, and her pain tolerance was a hell of a lot stronger than mine. For the first time since I'd awakened, I started to sweat in earnest.

Faintly, faintly, I heard Cherabino's presence poking at me from the inside.

Adam. Adam, pay attention, damn it! Her tone was like she was yelling at me, but the volume was barely above a whisper, like Coleen's interdiction shield couldn't quite block a Link even with its best efforts. *Adam!*

What? I replied, with as much mental volume down the Link as I could manage without leaking into Mindspace. *Tell me you're almost here.* I was starting to get tired, and in this context, that wasn't good for my life expectancy.

You should be able to hear the sirens. Five, ten minutes tops. Traffic is hell on North Druid Hills. Hang in there.

I glanced at Coleen and looked away. I had to keep my body language completely neutral—otherwise she'd suspect I was up to something. For not the first time, I was glad communication over a Link didn't travel through Mindspace; if I was careful, I'd get away with this.

Any new information about the layout? Cherabino asked.

Boxy building with a huge deck with a lift on the side, with a bunch of trucks parked on the lower levels. There's at least one strong telepath and six guards in addition to Sibley and Tamika.

Who's Tamika?

The one I told you about earlier. She's the one who killed Bellury. And Emily. The girl I burned out at the Guild. The one with the box that can make you do what they say. I took a breath, forced myself to think of anything that could help her. *I strongly doubt they're alone here. I got the impression . . . it was only a second. If I had to guess, if my life depended on it . . .*

It might.

I took another breath, slowly, so as not to attract attention. *Maybe fifteen minds, then, maybe twenty, and all of them strong and professional. Be careful, there's at least one building behind this one. Worst case, more reinforcements; best, well, you've got office workers to think about. Either way—these people are good, Cherabino. Coming after them is going to be extremely dangerous.*

If you think I'm leaving you there, you're an idiot. Just give me a better idea of where—

Another intense burning pain stole my breath and made me scream out loud, burning horrible melting pain—

And when I came back to myself, the feeling of Cherabino was gone. Utterly gone. Worse, the door opened, and Sibley, Tamika, and an armed guard walked in.

"Be still," Sibley told me, and that weird mesmerizing thing happened again; I literally could not take my eyes from him.

Beside him, Coleen stood, still wary, and on the other side, Tamika. The guard took a stance next to the door. And Sibley pulled the telephone line from the wall and detached it from the phone.

"Unfortunately, the latest batch of my cords has a regrettable tendency to shatter," he said in a quiet tone, and pulled the telephone cord tight. "I'm afraid we don't have much time now; my employer is expecting us to maintain his schedule tightly. But. We have a few more pallets to load. So. This lady has given my employer a great deal of useful resources and information. In return, she has about ten minutes here where she gets whatever she wants."

I was looking directly at Sibley with my full attention.

"Let me rephrase." Sibley pulled the cord around my neck, settling in behind me, his breath falling on my ear like a lover's. The cord pulled against my neck—not tight, not yet, but all of the slack disappeared in a slow pull. "Pay attention to Ms. Johnson over there. Stay completely still."

My heart sped up, terror engulfing my veins, but I couldn't move so much as my eyelids. I watched her in Mindspace instead, the sodden twisted knot of her mind like a fortress, a fortress my mind wouldn't be able to touch. If she couldn't reach out, neither could anything touch her in turn.

"Did you hear me, Adam?" his voice asked in my ear.

"I'm listening," I murmured, moving my mouth as little as I could and still answer him.

"Good."

Faintly, in the background, came the sound of sirens. But they would be too late—too late. All it would take was one movement from Sibley's hands and I would die, slowly and horribly. Somehow I knew he was too good to snap my neck right away; I knew, with dreadful certainty, that he would draw it out.

"Sirens," Tamika said.

"We can't be sure they're for us," Sibley said. He nodded to one of the guards, who went out of the room. "Make sure we've got plan C in place, please. There's enough ammunition and manpower to hold us to our timetable even if the police do show up for us. The floor is yours, ma'am."

Tamika widened her stance. Gone was the shy, self-assuming girl I'd known once upon a time; in her place was a strong, angry woman with a purpose.

"Now, Professor. Not that you're a professor anymore. I've been thinking about this since the funeral and your insensitive idiotic apology."

"Thinking about what?"

The cord tightened around my neck, and the smile on her face widened. Just when the world was starting to go black, Sibley let up.

I struggled to breathe, struggled with everything in me, panting hard.

"Stay still," his terrible voice said in my ear, and I stopped panting. I barely breathed, the air hissing down my now-sore throat. I couldn't move. I wasn't allowed to—

"We're running out of time," the guard said from the door.

Sibley made an agreeing noise next to my ear. "Let's hurry this up."

The thick blanket in Mindspace, the thick shield the Minder had held, was starting to lighten, and Tamika's twisted mind settled in front of me. I couldn't move to look up. I moaned, unable to move even enough to speak.

"Talk if you want," Sibley said.

"Why did you kill Bellury?" I whispered. "Why him? He didn't do anything to you."

"You ruined my life," she said, quietly, intensely and for the first time I heard an echo of that pain, that real devastation that I'd seen all those years ago when she'd realized what had happened. "You put my mind through the shredder for no reason at all other than your own stupid selfish pride and a drug. A *drug*. A thing. You burned me out, so that I never, *never* will feel another person's mind against mine. I'm alone now. I'll always be alone. And I figured out how to destroy you. How to make you feel alone like me."

Her hand came into my field of vision as she gestured toward the telepath. "Coleen thinks she's figured out what it is you did to me. While Sibley makes you hold your mind still, she'll turn your mind inside out and shred it to careful, painful pieces. Just like you did to me. But she'll make it slow."

Tamika stood back, frowning contemptuously. "Let's get on with this."

Coleen moved forward into my field of vision. "You need to tell him to drop his shields now. This will take a good five minutes or more."

There was one last thing I had to know before I died, or worse, had my gift stripped away. I took a shallow breath and asked it. "Why—Emily . . . ?"

"She had a connection I needed," Tamika said, standing over me. "Coleen, now is the time. It's time for me to have my justice."

"Not—justice. Is . . . revenge," I choked out, my heart beating so fast I was afraid it would burst out of my chest. "Revenge," I repeated, but I didn't believe it. In my heart of hearts, I believed I deserved whatever she did to me.

She shouldn't have killed Bellury, I thought, as the cord tightened, and Sibley said, "Drop your shields." Bellury didn't do anything to her.

But—but my shields didn't drop on their own. That feeling of mesmerizing attention had dissipated and I could move. I could move! I pulled forward—

And got yanked back in the chair. Sibley was suddenly standing over me, pulling the cord with such angry force I knew I was going to die. "With eye contact this time, then. Drop your—"

And the world *wrenched* as someone teleported in, my mind screaming as I was used as an anchor.

Kara?

Stone came up from a crouch, mammoth dart gun in his hand, firepower pointed directly at the guard. And then he opened fire.

I was on the floor before I could think, deafening cracks of gunshots tearing through the room. A trail of fire hit my neck. I put my hand on the spot. It was bleeding like a stuck pig but seemed more or less intact; a graze maybe. Shocking, hard pain, nothing at all like the pain of a telepath.

The guard was down, unconscious, and Stone and Coleen were grappling mentally, the waves of their struggle disturbing Mindspace like the sea during a storm, as they flailed and fought with painful cruelty.

Then Coleen lost it; Stone's mind enveloped hers, and she went down. Her nose ran with blood from what he'd done, and her body went boneless. Her head struck the floor, hard.

Mindspace was fading in and out now, my vision going blurry, so I surfaced out of the shallows.

Tamika was standing behind Stone. Tamika, the one person in the room immune to whatever telepathy could throw at her. She had the heavy telephone in hand, lifted it—

And Stone couldn't get out of the way in time. It hit his skull with a *crunch*. He fell, his mind going spotty and cold before unconsciousness. The guard and Coleen were down on the floor, out cold. Sibley, his nose bleeding from something Stone had done, grabbed me by the arm. He pulled me up, the side of my neck still streaming blood. A lot of blood in this room. A lot.

Sibley said calmly, "If we don't leave now, we may not get away."

My mind wouldn't focus; it was like a display of fireworks, bright shiny fireworks I couldn't look away from. I stared at him, drawn in oddly—and I felt the cord around my neck twist and tighten again.

Tamika said, "If Fiske wants the last few designs, you'll have to get me away from here in one piece. He'll never find them otherwise."

"I promised you we'd get away clean. There's the lift to the back, and we have plenty of firepower. Stop talking and start moving."

"Fine."

I was choking, choking, as Sibley yanked me through the door and down the hall.

As we entered the hallway, I realized the fog that had been blocking my telepathy was gone. Gone! I reached out through the Link to Cherabino.

We're pulling up now, she said clearly, her mind settled on what needed to be done. *Stay out of the line of fire.*

Relief—and guilt—hit me like an anvil while I struggled to keep up with Sibley, my hands around the cord, trying ineffectually to get some slack as he yanked me down the length of the hallway. *You're here?*

With Kara and a couple friends. You did say there was another telepath—

Suddenly the connection was cut off cold as I found myself face-to-face with another man, this one with a Guild patch, a goatee, and some kind of significant weight in Mindspace. How many telepaths had Tamika talked into joining her cause? This was getting ridiculous. Was someone at the Guild involved with this group?

"We have trouble," Sibley said. "A guy Jumped in the middle of things. You said nobody could Jump through the field you set up."

Goatee looked familiar. Had he been another one of Dane's students? His face wrinkled up. "I said, unless there's a Link I don't know about or a tracer. That almost never happens." He grabbed my arm and rifled through my brain, his mind going straight through my thin shield before I could think to increase it. Finally he pulled out and kicked me in the shin so I almost fell. "He's got both. Nothing I would have seen while he was unconscious. We keep him blocked, the Guild can't follow. But really, your best bet is just to kill him."

I was spending too much time among normals, getting sloppy. I built my shields up to battle strength and swore to myself it wouldn't happen again. It couldn't happen again, no matter how tired I was.

"Fine," Sibley said.

"I want my justice," Tamika hissed.

"Pay attention to me, Adam." Sibley shifted me over to his other side, hand still on my back, me still oddly focused on him. "Sorry, we're out of time."

"A few more minutes, okay? I want him to suffer."

We ducked into an elevator. When the doors opened and Sibley increased his speed, she had to stretch her short legs all too fast to keep up. She had a scowl on her face as we dashed through a long, cold hallway.

As we rounded the corner, through the window—finally—I could see the cop cars, lights blazing, pulling into the parking lot. Two large guys with huge automatic weapons started laying out ammunition clips in front of them as another opened the glass window. This was about to get ugly. Really ugly.

There was a door up ahead, at the end of the long hallway. I'd take my chance there, cord or no cord; Sibley had that odd mesmerizing machine, but so what? It wore off, and it could be circumvented. Even odds if I could disable the telepath in front of me, I could take down Sibley too.

And Tamika—well, she might be immune to mind games, but she was a small woman, with maybe one more shot in the gun, without any extra ammo that I could see. I might die—it only took one bullet, and she'd have plenty of time while I was taking down the telepath and Sibley—but I had to try. I had to. For Emily—for Bellury.

I was preparing myself mentally, quietly, behind subtle walls and misdirections I hoped would get this Goatee telepath off my back. He was testing my shields, tap, tap, to check for weaknesses. Tap, tap, to check for vulnerabilities. What would happen would happen; I couldn't warn Cherabino or her fellows, as much as it hurt to admit that, without tipping off my own set of problems. I had no illusions. If it came down to it, Sibley would kill me to save the trouble of transporting me. When the cavalry arrived, my life expectancy dropped. I had to move while I still had the mental strength to do so.

I took a deep breath as Sibley nodded at Goatee to open the door.

On the other side were three more guards, gun muzzles pointed directly at me.

More importantly, behind them was large warehouse space—row after row of shelves two stories high, boxes piled on every available surface, and cranes on tracks far above carrying items in sleds hanging from long hooks. Bright fluorescent lights perched all the way at the top, thirty feet above our heads, banks of windows at the same level adding fresh white sunlight to the mix.

A tangle of machinery and parts was piled to the right. In the center of the far wall, a bright beam of sunlight coming in around an open moving truck on a loading dock, its back end settled against a raised forklift that beeped slowly as it backed up. A small group of guards and workers were loading a truck.

And to the left, a long row of machines, machines with clear glass covering more of the cell-like biologicals I'd found in the wreck earlier. Real biologicals, shimmering blue-vein-covered cellular-looking green bodies with long extensions like dendrites, extensions that melded into tubes and circuit boards, extensions that kept the things alive. Maybe six, currently each running their machines, pulsing slowly, living anathemas. A nest of wires stuck out of one of the machines from an open panel, as if an installation hadn't been finished when we walked in. Here, in this one room, was enough technology to bring the entire country to its knees.

The sound of air moving across the space came from fans in the walls, and the low hum of working machinery settled in the room, a sound that hit the back of your teeth, and a smell like burned ozone and dust permeated the space.

The biologicals weren't networked yet. I could tell because Mindspace shimmered like the haze of an oasis, moving in unexpected jumps and starts around the biologicals like waves. They were on, the fields they produced making the world feel like the deck of an ocean liner jumping beneath me. But they weren't linked, not yet; I could ride out the waves.

"What in the hell are you doing?" I asked Goatee. "This stuff could kill you. Will kill you. Killed half the world and more."

"From the actions of a madman and a security hole, neither of which will happen again," the telepath replied. "The Guild has been experimenting with this stuff for years. Tamika's right. It's time to even the playing field. And if we make millions doing it, well . . ."

"The Guild will come after you. That Enforcement agent was only the first of many."

"Maybe. Maybe not. Either way we're prepared. We have enough backing to ride it out even if they do come."

And the full import of what was going on hit me. The Guild, playing with Tech? Real Tech? Biologicals and machines of every kind? I knew they'd done it a few decades ago, played with powers beyond what they should. I knew they'd flirted with disaster—I'd seen that this summer, when one of those machines threatened everything if the secrets got out. But that was midlevel technology, still illegal but nothing world-class, nothing like the stuff that broke the world from the inside. This—it bowled me over, the sheer gall.

Nobody should have this technology. Nobody should use it, period. No one should want to; a death toll of millions with people still living who'd seen it should be enough to ensure that. I couldn't believe, I literally couldn't believe, that the Guild—or any part of it—was doing this knowingly. What possible advantage did this give them? This stuff burned out telepaths.

Tamika ran her hands over her gun. "We have four minutes while they finish loading. I'm having my say and then you're going to kill him."

"Get moving!" Sibley gestured at a few of the loaders

who were staring. "We leave in five!" Then to Tamika: "Our people in the front won't hold them for long, and for every death, I have to answer to my boss. You have to answer to Fiske, personally, and he'll want more than money to pay the bill. I'd suggest you hurry."

With that, he turned and left, clearly intending to join the forces holding off the people.

He left the cord attached to my neck. The cord, like a choke collar for a dog. I felt cold, strangely cold.

"What could you possibly have to say to me that's worth all this?" I asked Tamika, numb at last.

She stepped back, looked at me with disgust. "You still don't understand, do you? You don't give a shit about anybody but you. It's my life we're talking about."

"And you're killing innocents along the way," I said, suddenly certain I was going to die and unwilling to go down without fighting. I reached out, hard, at her mind— but it was too twisted. I couldn't get a grip. I couldn't do anything.

And she had a gun, currently pointed at the floor, a gun with one more bullet in it. If that wasn't enough, a trained telepath and a guard with a huge automatic gun stood beside her, ready to take me out.

CHAPTER 27

While Sibley hurried the rest of the group, now loading the last few machines, another three men with guns settled in front of the one window in the room, maybe two feet away. I heard the sound of gunfire and screaming from the parking lot past them, only somewhat muffled by the building. They couldn't possibly get away from the back before the cops got them, could they?

Goatee and the guard next to Tamika looked on, impatiently. They kept looking around, kept monitoring radios, and kept waiting for her to finish her goals. *She is in charge here,* I thought. *For the price of horribly dangerous Tech, she's managed to buy her way into real power.* Suddenly, as if from a distance, I heard the crackle of gunfire beginning. I swallowed, and prayed—really, truly prayed—that neither Cherabino nor Kara would get hit.

Tamika laughed, a bitter sound. "You know, this wasn't as much fun as I thought it would be. And turning your head inside out probably isn't possible. Not without Coleen."

"You could let me go. It would be the right thing to do."

"The right thing to do? I'm tired of you and your right thing to do." She frowned. "You know what?" She looked at the guard behind me. "Just kill him."

"We need to talk about this," I responded immediately, then flinched as the guard's gun stopped inches from my head. My hands were out, my back cowering away.

She raised her gun—and I had nothing left to lose. There were five of them, five minds, one a relatively strong telepath. I couldn't take them all out at once with Deconstruction tricks. I couldn't disable or put to sleep or do anything in Mindspace fast enough. And I was exhausted.

But I had one card still in my pocket. One painful, difficult card. I was a Level Eight telepath. Level Eight. And, even exhausted, even lacking all control, I'd healed enough to have my power back—my raw, overwhelming numbers. And I had the truth.

Goatee had forgotten to shield. Amateur.

I had one shot at this—one. I had one chance to make it right.

Tamika opened her mouth, and I tore open every boundary I had. I let it all go, and projected at full strength. The first thing telepaths were taught never, never to do. And I'd pay for it—I'd pay for it.

But for now, for now, I poured literally every ounce of power I had out, like a long scream at the top of my voice, holding nothing back, uncaring of damage.

I pictured Bellury's face as he died, shot to death like a dog. Killed, for my sins. For my guilt. I poured that guilt, that guilt that would never go away, out with every inch of me. I poured it out, with anger, with shame, with guilt, in overwhelming quantities.

The faces around me were ripped open with raw emotion, but it wasn't enough. The telepath was starting to get his bearings, starting to bear up under it.

I opened the last box, the scary box, the box that made me shiver and sweat and scream. I opened the last box and forced it out into the air, into Mindspace with all the strength I'd been born with and all the strength I'd gained in a lifetime of work and sweat and tears.

I opened the lid, and let my deepest fear out of its prison.

The monster—the horrible monster—that lived in the basement of my mind, the nasty guy that whispered I knew I wasn't good enough. I knew I'd ruined it all, I'd fucked it up, I'd pissed it away. And I'd never, never amount to anything but pure stupid, helpless failure. Failure. Junkie. Guilty. Useless. Fuckup.

Tamika called me names then, but the monster liked names. It added names to the mix too, horrible names that spouted out of me like a flood, names and shivering pain and fear of what I'd never be, fear that crawled into everyone's brain, pain that wouldn't let them go.

I fell to my knees, the helpless fury turning inward as the monster roared with its full breath. The only thing I could see, as my vision started to go from the strain, from the horror of holding all of this open and out, from the shame of the monster and everything it said I was—from the horrible belief—the only thing I could see was the others hitting the floor, all the way down.

I heard someone crying like their world had fallen apart. It might have been me. But another voice joined it, and I didn't have two voices. The monster pulled out its claws—

And another voice joined the chorus, this one confused. "What in hell are you doing?" Tamika's voice echoed into the room. And her footsteps went over to one of the guards. "What's going on? I told you to shoot!"

The only woman in the world whose mind was so twisted, so wrenched, even my worst monster didn't touch her.

The sound of a bullet, sharp and hard.

An impact on the floor inches in front of me. A miss. She was out of bullets.

I took a breath, and poured out my last reserve into Mindspace; this was it. This was it.

Something hard scraped along the floor, then the sound of a handgun cocking as Tamika took the guard's gun.

This was it. There was nothing I could do.

Failure. Junkie. Guilty. Useless. Fuckup. This is exactly what you deserve, the monster said, and the room moaned.

The *crack* of a high-caliber bullet echoed through the room.

I opened my eyes, the shock loosening the monster's hold. No pain, no physical pain. I wasn't dead.

Tamika fell over, blood seeping through her shirt.

A bullet went off from the handgun when she hit the floor—and it hit one of the guards, who screamed.

The last thing I saw before the monster dragged me back under was Cherabino, Isabella Cherabino at the door, nose wrinkled like she had a migraine, holding a rifle.

Inside my mind, the world was black with swipes of red, swipes of red that hung in the air to spell out my failures. Every mistake, every choice I'd made on the streets— stealing and worse, cons and worse, the people I'd mind-raped for money, the death of my friend, the death I couldn't stop—tortured me. Bellury getting shot, me unable to do anything. Cherabino calling me a failure and meaning it. Paulsen telling me I'd lose my job. Swartz, holding his chest, almost dying.

The vision, suddenly all too real, the certain knowledge that I'd be alone, completely alone, without even a roof over my head or the right to call myself clean. Without any self-respect. With the certain knowledge that nothing—nothing—I did would ever make it better.

The cold, dark monster who whispered, *Why go on?*

And into the blackness of my mind walked a woman in police-issue heavy body armor, black plates somehow reflecting that light that didn't exist here. Cherabino held a gun, and she took aim at the monster.

The thing, like a huge bat, spread its wings and claws— and she shot. Three times. Directly in its chest.

It laughed. *You can't kill me. You have no power here.*

And for Cherabino, for Cherabino I stood up.

I looked into the face of my biggest fears, at that lying mouth . . . I looked at the monster I'd been running from for years.

"Hand me the gun," I told Cherabino.

She did, the gun surprisingly heavy and real in my hands, and I shot, slowly, carefully, taking aim like she'd taught me to do in the shooting range. It disappeared like smoke, and then reappeared. It laughed and started to get bigger. I shrank back.

Cherabino huffed. She turned and slapped me across the face, hard.

"Ow! What the hell was that for?" I cradled my face, which was going to have the imprint of her hand for sure. The monster had retreated, though; maybe the distraction of the pain was keeping it in its place. It still hurt like a mother.

"I don't know. I'm new at this mind stuff. You're in a coma and I grabbed your arm." *On purpose,* her mind added, here where there were no secrets. She swallowed, and I could feel her fear, the too-close, too-close, too-close litany her mind was squirreling away, and suddenly she couldn't meet my eyes. She was hanging on, controlling it desperately, with her cop mind, but inside she was afraid. At what she might know—of me and her and worse—and never be able to take back.

But there were no secrets, here, in this space; this deep, the Link was as close as she would allow it to be, which in this case—despite the overwhelming fear, despite the panic, despite the issues laid on her like heavy weights—in this case meant she cared, damn it. She trusted me not to hurt her. And maybe—maybe—her mind shied away from any more.

I couldn't take that trust; it hurt.

"I got Bellury killed," I said, my voice heavy, my own secrets flowing out if she had the peace of mind to grab them.

"I know," she said, and sighed. The job sucked sometimes, and cops made mistakes like anybody else. She'd been responsible for a death herself, her rookie year; it never truly left her. "He was a good cop."

Sorrow ran over me like water, and she stepped forward with a sigh, putting her arms around me, her head on my chest. "Get us out of here, okay?"

I looked over at the monster—who felt very small now. He was me, just a part of me. And I held Cherabino in my arms. I breathed in to smell her hair; and there was nothing. We were still outside reality, still in the construct my mind had made to deal with the thing I'd let out.

I nodded at the monster. He nodded back. Then, holding Cherabino gently, her trust like a delicate flower, I brought us back to reality, slowly.

Reality was painfully bright.

I felt it like a blow when her hand left mine.

CHAPTER 28

Paulsen was there outside Bellury's house waiting for me as the sun started its slow slide to sunset. One of the uniforms had dropped me off, and I'd assumed . . .

"No one has talked to her yet," Paulsen said. "You were the one there, so it falls to you." Her face looked odd to me under the shiny brim of the formal uniform cap. The official skirt also looked odd; I realized then I'd never seen her in a skirt. Even on court days she wore pantsuits and jackets built to hide a gun. She was just a little older than Bellury, I realized. I'd never thought of her as old, not like I had Bellury, but she was older. They might have been in some of the same beats, back in that time. They might have worked together.

"You're coming with me?" I asked, in the loudest whisper I could get my bruised voice box to do. The bandage on my neck from the bullet graze pulled as I tried to look at her.

She nodded. I couldn't read her, not really, but the flashes of light had stopped again. I'd set myself back, with that stunt, but it was only a setback. With any luck, a couple of weeks and I'd be back to full strength.

I looked at Bellury's house's door. Then back at Paulsen. "Will you keep me from screwing this up? Please?"

"I'll try," she said, and gave me some advice as to how to break the news.

———————

After roughly the hardest hour of my life, I sat outside, feeling numb, on the bench in Bellury's garden. I'd lit up a cigarette and was smoking it, trying to clear my head of the suffocating sadness and panic—and my bruised and hurting throat. I'd pushed through as best I could with my bruised throat. I'd talked about Bellury to his wife, about all the good things he'd done for me, and said to me. He and Swartz were—well, half of the foundation of my world had gone away, and it was my fault. I owed him enough to sit there, awkwardly, and croak out what words I could, and try. Now it was over. She didn't want to talk anymore. And she didn't want to see me anymore. She knew whose fault it was, and I knew too.

"Can I sit here?" Paulsen asked quietly.

"It's open." I stubbed out the cigarette and waved my arm to dissipate whatever smoke I could.

Her nose wrinkled at the smell, but she sat down.

There was silence between us, but it wasn't a happy silence. It wasn't a comfortable one.

And all I could think about was that vision, that horrible vision. Would that be me by Christmas? Despair hung over my head, despair and the burned desperate taste of uncertainty.

"I guess I've lost my job now," I said, voice raspy. "With Bellury—"

She straightened painfully, as if my choice of timing was just too painful.

"Just tell me."

"Well . . . you realize I haven't had a chance to even think about all of this yet."

I was silent.

She cleared her throat after a moment. "Well, there will be a full independent review of your actions, I can promise you that. But you also closed a major case." She held up a hand to silence my protest. "This isn't my first rodeo, even if it's yours. Cherabino's still arguing for you hard, and has been for weeks. You're not out yet."

"But Bellury—"

She cut me off again, looking stern. "This is the day for us to remember a good cop and a good man. To plan a proper police funeral to honor him as he deserves. To heal. To figure out how not to do this again, if we can. If you can't do that, if you can't see beyond yourself that much, maybe this isn't the job for you."

"But—"

"Have I made myself clear?"

"Yes, ma'am." I cleared my throat, pushing out the painful words: "What do you need me to do?"

She nodded. "That's the right question. For now, I need you to sit here and let me think."

"Yes, ma'am." And I sat there, letting all the horrible results of all the last few days sit in my mind while I tortured myself over and over again.

I wasn't hardly surprised to feel Stone in my head again at that point.

You survived, I said, with a sense of intense relief.

He was gone almost before I finished the thought.

Since nobody told me not to, I went back to work the next morning.

By the time I got there, it was still early, too early for most of the cops to be at work, and much too early for the army of secretaries to have arrived yet. I sat, alone at my borrowed desk in the middle of the empty secretaries' pool, and drank another sip of honeyed tea. This morning the swelling had set in much worse and my voice was too rough to be understood without something to lubricate the pipes.

I settled in on writing my report of the actions of the

day before, Bellury's death and all the rest, in all my idiocy and all its horrible glory. I took especial care to highlight Sibley's actions and the box he'd carried; he'd finally been captured, toward the end of the firefight, and was currently sitting in a high-security holding cell. I'd do everything in my power to make the case against him stick. Everything. He'd killed Emily for no other reason than that Tamika had asked him to. For no other reason than that Emily had decided to do the right thing.

Finally it got too much, the emotions too raw, too present. So I got up, fetched some tea and some peace of mind, and settled back down at the desk. One more uncomfortable duty this morning. Paulsen said the FBI would call me in a few minutes now, and that, in her opinion, it was not going to be good news.

"You solved the case almost by accident," she'd said, and then trailed off. I knew I'd screwed up. She didn't have to say any more.

So here I was, with the tea in hand, waiting for the phone call. At least Kara had gotten the Mindwave influencing machine before anyone else could make off with it, I told myself. Even if the FBI was about to tell me I was a loser, at least that part hadn't gotten screwed-up.

The phone rang with an earsplitting peal. I picked up. "Hello?" I croaked, and took a sip of the tea to lubricate my voice box.

A man's voice came over the line. "Special Agent Jarrod, FBI. We talked last week about an inquiry."

"That's right. My lieutenant says you were thinking about offering me a job." I took another sip of tea. "I take it that's off the table now."

"Not necessarily," Agent Jarrod said. "There aren't many independent telepaths anymore, and even fewer who are interested in the kind of work we do. While we don't think there's a permanent place on our team—we just don't have the funding for the supervision your lieutenant says you need—I would like to offer you an opportunity as an occasional consultant for our more difficult cases."

"What? What would I be doing exactly? Would this be in Washington?"

"Likely not. You'll be working for a new division of the Center for the Analysis of Violent Crime, and we go where the work is. Our unit is based out of the Southeast."

The bandage on my neck pulled as I shifted too fast. "But why?"

"Ahem. Well, your work on the Bradley case was exceptional, and your skill set isn't easy to find without Guild oversight. Our team would rather not have all of our information available there, as I'm sure you understand, but your lieutenant says you're trustworthy with information. Do you disagree?"

"No, absolutely, I don't share information. It's the principle of the thing." Wait, Paulsen said I was trustworthy? It was like the heavens had opened up and light rained down. I'd done something. I'd proven myself at least somewhat.

"I'd be glad to send you more details in the mail. It's not something you need to decide right now." He paused. "I needn't mention this will be at a considerable increase from your current daily rate salary."

"That's good to hear." I hated to mention it, but surprises were never a good thing. I took another sip of tea. My throat was getting worse, and I'd have to stick to short sentences. "You know I have a criminal record?"

"We are well aware of your record. I'm afraid as a result policy says we won't be issuing you a gun, but I'm sure we can find you a stun weapon of some kind if—"

"I don't need a gun, I'm a telepath." A break for more tea. "When do you expect the first case to hit? I'll need to clear this with Paulsen."

"Of course. And I don't know. Like I said, it's as needed and occasional. I'm hoping we won't need you for a while. But cases come up, and you'll need to be ready. I'm afraid I need an answer from you right now," Jarrod said. "I can send you the paperwork later, but I need a yes or a no right now."

I stalled for time while I took another sip. But the answer arose from inside me like a light turning on. "Then yes. If I can help, I will."

CHAPTER 29

Swartz met me at the usual Narcotics Anonymous meeting a little early; Selah had driven him, then left to run errands. He was leaning on a cane, moving slowly, breathing hard, and the lines around his eyes had gotten deeper. He'd also lost weight, too much weight.

"How are you feeling?" I helped support his arm as we waited for the elevator. I was blocking hard, but even through the shields I could feel he was in pain.

"Tired. Very tired. How are you, kid? That doctor guy said . . ."

"Not a big deal, okay? Let's not talk about it."

He poked my foot with the cane to make me look up. "It's still me. Thank you, all right? That's all I wanted to say."

The elevator dinged. He pulled away, to amble in himself and push the button. I ignored how pale he was and how hard he was breathing; he ignored the fact that I hadn't responded to the thank-you.

As the elevator settled on the basement, he got his breath back enough to demand, "Three things. Grateful. Now, please."

I smiled a small, hopeful, surprised smile. "Cherabino's nephew. Chocolate truffle ice cream. And you. Living."

He grunted in a pleased way, and let me support his arm again.

I escorted him into the small room, saying hello to the others, and settled him down at the front; it was his turn to lead the meeting.

"You sure you're up to this?" I asked, after he'd had a chance to settle and some of the paleness had passed.

He shrugged. "In a month or two I'll be strutting around like a spring chicken. Now I'm tired walking around the damn room. Tell you what . . ."

"What?"

"Why don't you lead this time?" He held out the binder with all the meeting notes, all the words you were supposed to say to lead the group.

"I can't—"

"It's just reading, kid. Reading and asking the right questions. You already know how this goes."

Somehow I couldn't say no, not to Swartz. I cautiously took the binder, its weight in my hands sobering. "I'll try."

"You'll do fine." He nodded to one of the regulars, and called out a greeting to a newbie, then engaged him in a conversation. The whole time I was sitting there, my heart was beating nearly out of my chest.

When the clock hit the hour, I opened up the binder and started to read.

It was late by the time I got home, and I picked up my mail from the basement of the building, the usual pile of junk and a heavy vellum envelope that rustled. The second round of my PI application papers, maybe, or a summons to court. Maybe the FBI papers, though it seemed too early for those. I climbed the stairs with a heavy heart, tired to the bone.

Somehow I wasn't surprised to see my door open, Stone sitting on my couch, with his feet on my coffee table and his arms crossed in a carefully studied ease.

I stopped in the doorway, mail in hand. I was going to

have to move if it was this easy to get in my apartment. "What do you want?"

"You have a wave cancellation device in your bedroom," Stone began. "It's illegal in forty-nine states and most of the Western European block."

"So is Satin," I said, and dropped the mail on the coffee table next to his hip. "And everything the Guild does now, apparently. I'm glad to see you're okay."

Stone nodded. He dropped his legs from the table onto the floor and stood up. "I'm here to remove my tag and tell you my decisions."

I relaxed, all at once. "You decided I'm not a threat," I croaked, my voice rough. "Finally."

"That's not what I said."

I tensed right back up again. "Let's do the tag and we'll worry about the rest in a minute," I whispered, my voice on its way out. Since my shields didn't matter with the tag in place anyway, I let them go. In my present state they were hard to maintain anyway.

Two seconds later the tag was gone, him keeping his mental hands to himself, which I appreciated. I rebuilt my protection slowly, having to work at it. No one but Cherabino would be getting into my head any time soon.

Then I waited, my gut knotting. Stone still had absolute jurisdiction, and for all he'd saved me in that room with Sibley, he wasn't an ally. Not quite. He could still kill me, if he wanted to, and right now I couldn't stop him.

I waited for my fate.

"You're a dangerous man," Stone said. "But, I think, chiefly to yourself. I've recommended you be given a very long leash and otherwise left alone. For now. If you and I hadn't made the deal for the medic, this is the part where I would give you my card, tell you to report any other suspicious Guild-type behavior on time, and walk away. With a stern warning so you know I'm serious."

The beginnings of relief began to stir—and stopped. No tea in sight. *If we hadn't made the deal,* I leaked painfully into Mindspace.

"But we did make that deal, and despite all your shenanigans, you've managed to pay off less than half of the debt. And I'm being generous."

What about the telepaths with Tamika? I asked. *They were up to no good. Don't I get any credit for reporting them? Your damn secrets still haven't gotten out.*

"I know." He paused, and nodded. "That's why you're still alive."

I suppose I should thank you for that. I swallowed. *Did you include credit for the bounties on those rogues?*

"My tally includes those bounties. Like I said, generous. And my superiors expect me to get the full value out of you in a reasonable time frame."

I don't have any more money, I said. Better or worse, I'd had the accountants empty my accounts. *And nothing I own is worth anything in trade. And I won't share any department secrets. I told you that.*

"We'll be working it out of you in labor. Our choice of what kind."

The thought was like a black hole, an uncontrollable descent into something that would rip me apart. *I get veto power,* I insisted. But it could be so much worse.

"You get *one* veto. And lest you think about skipping town on me—"

Would I do that? It wasn't a bad idea actually.

"—or publicizing our deal, or anything that will be embarrassing for the Guild, keep in mind we know about a certain ten-year-old with medical issues and a strong Ability. A ten-year-old you're aiding the parents to hide him from the Guild."

He's medically fragile!

That was out of bounds. *He's just a kid,* I said desperately.

"He's not your concern. And honestly, for the moment, he's not mine. But if you do *anything,* and I mean anything, to make my life difficult, I can and I will use that knowledge against you."

You'll take him to the Guild.

"He's medically fragile," the Watcher said coldly. "There's no telling what will happen to him."

The implied threat hung in the air, cold and merciless.

"Am I clear?"

Crystal. Now get the hell out of my apartment. You have no call involving the kid.

He shrugged. "I'll be seeing you." Then he sauntered out, down the hall, and through the door to the stairs. I watched him go in Mindspace, anger eating at my gut, until he got into some kind of vehicle and drove away.

I sat down on the coffee table, the heavy envelope crackling under my butt. I pulled it out—

The handwriting on the front said Adam Ward. No address.

I opened the envelope. Inside, pictures, pictures that fell from my numb fingers to slide all over the floor. Pictures of me at the station, at my apartment, at the meeting with Swartz. Close-ups.

And floating down to land squarely on top of them, another handwritten note: *I know who you are.—Fiske.*

ABOUT THE AUTHOR

Alex has written since early childhood, and loves great stories in any form including sci-fi, fantasy, and mystery. Over the years, Alex has lived in many neighborhoods of the sprawling metro Atlanta area. Decatur, the neighborhood on which Sharp is centered, was Alex's college home.

THE DRESDEN FILES

The #1 *New York Times* bestselling series

by Jim Butcher

"Think *Buffy the Vampire Slayer* starring Philip Marlowe." —*Entertainment Weekly*

STORM FRONT
FOOL MOON
GRAVE PERIL
SUMMER KNIGHT
DEATH MASKS
BLOOD RITES
DEAD BEAT
PROVEN GUILTY
WHITE NIGHT
SMALL FAVOR
TURN COAT
CHANGES
SIDE JOBS
GHOST STORY
COLD DAYS

SIMON R. GREEN

LIVE AND LET DROOD

The newest book in the Secret Histories series following *For Heaven's Eyes Only*.

Eddie Drood's family has been keeping the forces of evil contained in the shadows for as long as Droods have walked the earth. But now Eddie's entire family has been banished to an alternate dimension. And when he finds out who—or what—attacked his clan, there will be hell to pay...

Praise for the Secret Histories novels:

"Another action-packed melding of spy story and fantasy, featuring suave sleuthing, magical powers, and a generous dash of dry wit."
—*Kirkus Reviews*

Available wherever books are sold or at penguin.com

facebook.com/AceRocBooks

R0108